AIRCRAFT CARRIER

John Winton

SAPERE
BOOKS

AIRCRAFT CARRIER

Published by Sapere Books.

24 Trafalgar Road, Ilkley, LS29 8HH

saperebooks.com

ISBN: 978-1-80055-899-1

The author wishes to acknowledge the award of a bursary from the Welsh Arts Council for the purpose of writing this book.

CHAPTER ONE

This was the best time of the day, actually, just before dawn. The Pacific stars were still shining, the flight deck still wet with overnight dew, or perhaps a little spray misting up from the bows. The island was a large shadow against the stars, all shapes and angles — curious how it was all dark but you could still see the island. It was there all right, with one pale light from a scuttle. Somebody careless with their blackout. There was the sound of waves brushing the ship's side, steadily, on and on, with their own sort of rhythm. No heat yet, no action, no gunfire, no adrenalin, no shouting or tumult.

The pilots had all mounted and settled in their seats. Time to test the radio, try the oxygen. They were all alone in their cockpits, but corporate parts of the squadron. That same smell of oxygen. The aircraft handlers were down there; you could only see their ghostly Lucite wands. Over to port, old *Dainty Delilah* was flying off her Seafires for the dawn CAP. Lovely aircraft, beautiful and delicate, like a rapier, but no good for this Pacific war. Out here they needed something with a sock in it, the good old F4U Corsair, like a long-range meat-axe. One hundred and twenty switches and gauges, no less. Like a cinema-theatre Wurlitzer. A far cry from the old Fairey Fulmar's air speed indicator, fuel gauge and compass. As they used to say, one to get there, one to get back and one for luck. This one was a hydraulic marvel. Spread and folded the wings, lowered and raised the undercarriage and arrester hook, it even cocked the guns for you, did everything but cheer when you hit a zero.

Check the binoculars on their cord, rest them comfortably on the chest. 'Start up Corsairs!' Waiting for the loudspeaker, it still came as a shock that sent a trembling down to the fingernails. Snap switches on, while the handler takes hold of the prop. He is not even a face yet, not even any geometric figure, but the movement is recognizable. Away goes the engine and down goes the handler, flat on the deck, sensible fellow, as he has been drilled to do. There was precious little clearance for a man's head between the tip of the prop and the flight deck. Out chocks, with a gesture, release brakes, take up revs, and roll forward. The wands beckon onwards. Lights waved in front, there goes the tail-light of the next ahead. Now this one, now us. Roll forward, fine pitch on the propeller, hear the engine note changing as the propeller feathers. Rolling now, the island a blur to starboard, that pressure on the back and buttocks, up comes the tail and go, across the bows with a zip like a physical sound. Out and across the sea, skimming over an ebony table with tiny purple cups chiselled into it, then changing to pink, and up into the sunlight. Just like that. Brilliant, splintered light flooding the cockpit, making everybody blink and scrabble with one hand for the sunglasses in the top pocket.

A shape glided into the corner of one eye, up and to the right. It was Ronnie, the starboard wingman.

'Orange Two, this is Orange Leader, closer and lower.' That was their call-sign, Orange. Was it a fruit or was it a colour? Yesterday it was admirals, last week it was carpets and cabbages. Tomorrow it would be dances or animals or party games.

'Orange Two, roger, Skipper.'

A steady roaring in the ears, the fighter direction officer was on the fighter net. 'Orange Leader, this is *Miss Britannia*,

Orange Leader, this is *Miss Britannia*…' Stanley audibly had not had his breakfast yet. 'Course to steer to target, confirm two-nine-one. Time to target seventy-nine minutes, seven and nine, seventy-nine.'

'This is Orange Leader, roger.' He sounded like a bloody tombola caller.

Turning to port and looking down … *there* was a sight to take the breath away. Sunlight was just touching the masts and funnels of the task force, and throwing the shadows of the ships over the shining sea. That almost rhymed. Twenty-five clear-cut geometrical designs emerging from a dark sea. They were steaming into wind and Corsairs were peeling off one by one from *Madame Fifi*, *Miss Britannia*'s chummy ship. That was probably Robert Weston and his merry men.

'Dodgers nine o'clock!'

That would be the CAP. Seafires they were, four of them, in what the war correspondents, in their own inimitable way, called a 'cap of steel'. These were high above the task force and there were two more at sea level, flying to and fro. That was the 'Jack' patrol. That was where you put the new boys, or the old boys who had lost their bottle. Back and forward, back and forward, at sea level; it was enough to drive you round the bend.

The four carriers, with their Avenger TBRs still ranged aft, were like pale autumn leaves from this height, oblong shapes, tablets of grey steel on the water, with dots moving off their surfaces. That one, second in from the west, was *Miss Britannia*. That was home. There was the briefing room, the wardroom, the bar, the cabin, the bunk, down there.

'Orange Leader, this is *Miss Britannia*. Hot Line says nobody at the party.'

'This is Orange Leader, roger.' That was the report from the two early-morning reconnaissance Hellcats. Nobody at the party. No Japanese aircraft on the runways. But nobody at the party did not mean nobody at home.

'Orange Section, this is Orange Leader, down now and flat arse!'

Down they went, lower and lower, a hundred feet, fifty, twenty, lower and lower until you could feel your sphincter squeezing up, well below the radar beams, three hundred knots flat-arsing over the sea. One hesitation, a slip of the finger, at this height and this speed, and goodbye Dolly we must leave you. But you could trim the elevator tabs, and fly to keep the nose down. Lift your hand and the Corsair would lift upwards.

'Orange Two, this is Orange Leader. Lower.' Ronnie hated low flying. He always tried to cheat.

The sea skimming towards you had a mesmeric effect, it took all the feeling out of your legs, so that only the part of you showing in the cockpit really existed.

Twenty-five minutes to target time. Very interesting people, the Japanese. They were dirty fighters and one dreaded to be shot down. There were already grim rumours in the fleet about what had happened to the boys chopped down over the oil refineries in Sumatra in January. No hard fact, but the air intelligence staff buzz was that they had been taken to Singapore and executed. Johnnie was one of them, almost the best wingman Skipper had ever had. He made one pass too many over one of those jungle airstrips. Skipper could see it now: a raw scar of red mud in a brilliant green, with a muddy river just beside it. Hard to think of Johnnie ending up in a Japanese execution cell. Yet the Japanese had more than forty different words for different kinds of winds, gales, breeze, zephyrs, call them what you like. *Hatakaze:* wind that causes the flapping of a flag. *Siokaze:* wind that springs up at the turning of the tide. *Nadakaze:* wind over the open sea. They called their destroyers after them. *Tatikaze:* wind caused by the stroke of a sword. *That* was more like it. *Kamikaze:* divine wind. They had used those over the Philippines and were using them now over Okinawa.

The sea was still flashing along below.

'Orange Section, this is Orange Leader, *feet up!*' It was time to go up and take a look.

At ten thousand feet the islands came up at first, as no more than darker patches of the blue ocean, already in sunlight. *As we in dreams behold the Hebrides.* Theirs was the middle one, Ishigaki, the one shaped like a boot, or a saucepan, or a bloodstain. They had dozens of different words for islands, too. Out binoculars, already focused and adjusted correctly, to save seconds. Hold it — there *was* something on that runway. It was difficult to tell in the haze, but it looked like a bomber. Probably wheeled out of a cave into the sunlight after Hot Line had pushed off.

The best way in to the airstrip was from the south. But they did that yesterday. Today they would come in from the east, with the rising sun, and how very appropriate. There was a bright-red corrugated iron roof in the middle of the town. They called it the Bus Station. They would go down to sea level again, feet above the water, and flat-arse it into town. Go from specks out at sea to shapes overhead in seconds.

'Orange Section, this is Orange Leader. Down now, and flat out, *break!*'

They wheeled and dropped, down through successive coloured layers of the sky. It was a different world down here, a different existence, with the eardrums constantly swelling and popping.

The island was a low wrinkle on the horizon, and there was something, or somebody, missing.

'Orange Two, this is Orange Leader, get lower. And closer. Ronnie, you *must* fly lower.'

Ronnie was scared. But low in this game meant low, but *low*. No Hendon Air Display tactics here. 'High, wide and handsome' meant 'high, wide and dead before dusk'.

'Orange Two, still not low enough.' He would have to get rid of Ronnie. 'For Christ's *sake, Ronnie.*'

There were gun pits between the town and airstrip, and the laddies in them were normally quite good. They would have had their breakfasts by now, and they would be waiting. There was the red roof of the Bus Station, and what looked like a baby's pram in the street, and a bang like a distant shotgun. Faces in the gun pits looking upwards, and barrels like shiny circles, and some smoke. Now level for the runway. It was made of crushed coral, flushed pink in the sun, with some pustules in it where the Avengers had bombed it and the Japanese had filled in the holes overnight. And so it went on.

And there she was — a fine, fat juicy Betty, perched on the end of the strip. Some figures stood beside it. Some senior Japanese officer on his way from Formosa to Okinawa, or possibly even to Japan. They should have got off at first light. Too late now, *mate.*

They started firing a long way off, the three of them fleeing across the coral. Skipper had harmonised his guns at the butts so that the bullet streams from each wing converged at four hundred yards' range. He armed all the squadron with his own special ammunition cocktail of six ball to one tracer and one armour-piercing. He was satisfied to see, at four hundred yards, the Betty seeming to change shape, as though looked at through a heatwave. The wings fluttered and tore, score marks showed on the fuselage, the figures disappeared from the runway. There were more gun pits at the end, ugly holes like blackheads in an old man's cheek. They lifted up, so close that they almost carried away the Betty's radio aerial, lifted away and up, with that tremendous pressure on the backside, and heads lolling, looking to starboard. There was a whiff of smoke back by the Bus Station.

'Orange Two, this is Orange Leader, come in.' There *had* only been three of them on that strafing run. That stupid bugger Ronnie had got himself lost. 'Come in, Orange Two.'

'He's gone, Skipper, he's gone!' A thread of hysteria in Geoffrey's voice.

'Orange Section, form on me.' *Must keep the voice calm.* 'This is Orange Leader, what happened? Steady now, just tell me.'

'Over the town, Skipper. Gun got him. Straight through the windscreen. Blew his head off, must have done.'

'This is Orange Leader, roger. Angels thirty, full boost. *Go.* Course to steer…' A look down at the pad on the knee. 'Zero-nine-zero, magnetic. Nine-oh, as far as we go.'

So, a few feet had made all the difference. A cautionary tale. If it had not been Ronnie, whom one knew, it would have been as funny, in a sick sort of way, as *Struwwelpeter. This is the tale of Ronnie Bell, who tried very hard, but not very well.* No more singing in the showers.

As he climbed, Skipper could see and hear Green and Purple Sections making their runs. The gunners were really alert. Smoke was rolling all over the airstrip. One Corsair went the wrong way, and the other three, like clumsy mallards tumbling in the sky, separated slightly, by what could be a crucial amount. They always were a messy lot. Now that those gunners were in such good practice, something would have to be done about them. Perhaps a simultaneous strafe from ninety degrees to port or starboard, to keep their heads down, while the runway party passed overhead. *Something* would have to be done, anyway.

'Orange Leader, this is *Miss Britannia*. Make your cockerel cro-o-o-ow!' Stanley always accentuated that word, drawing it out realistically.

'This is Orange Leader, roger. Orange Section, check IFF.'

The fleet was always in a highly nervous state and anybody, but *anybody,* flying in from the direction of the islands was suspect. All those itchy trigger fingers fired first and asked later. The fleet's aircraft identification was generally shocking. The Seafire boys, who operated nearer the fleet, had already lost two, chopped down by the fleet's gunfire, dropped by their own mates. With IFF switched on, your special blip, you hoped, would literally clear you on the radar screens.

At 30,000 feet, propellers in coarse pitch, water injection in those long-striding engines, they passed over the Avengers, with fighter cover above and below them, on their way to bomb the runways. Below them, a smudge, just a trace on the sea, was the American air-sea rescue submarine.

Halfway back, they met the cruiser with its destroyer escort. Every aircraft returning from the islands had to be vetted by flying once round and close to the cruiser picket, called the veterinary station. It was uncomfortable, and hair-prickling, to fly low and slow and steady round a warship and see all her guns trained and following.

'Orange Leader, this is Salem Witch…' It was the Vet calling. 'Why only three?'

'Salem Witch, this is Orange Leader, Orange Two, George Baker Yoke.' It made him sound like a bandleader.

George Baker Yoke. GBY. Short for Great Blue Yonder. A somewhat macabre joke, but effective. The initials meant missing, believed killed. The Fleet Air Arm was a mass of initials. They had initials the way other people had complexes and neuroses. CAP: Combat Air Patrol. TBR: Torpedo Bomber Reconnaissance. IFF: Interrogatory — Friend or Foe? RAS: Replenishment at Sea. RPC: Request the Pleasure of your Company. WMP: With Much Pleasure. MRU: Much Regret Unable. US: Unserviceable. LMF: Lack of Moral Fibre…

'Orange Leader, this is Salem Witch, you're clear.' Passed, with flying colours. 'Course to steer, zero-six-six.'

'This is Orange Leader, roger.' Sixty-six. Clickety-click.

As they flew, Skipper kept on missing Ronnie from the corner of his eye. It was like having a limb amputated, like a great gap with a draught pouring in from the cold. Young Geoffrey could move over and take his place. But even when he had swung over to starboard and ranged up alongside, so that Skipper could see his wingtip rising and falling, feet from his own, he still felt uneasy.

Nearer the fleet, there were more identification screens, invisible veils dropped down to protect the ships from intruders. There were high CAP staring down from above, and low CAP craning their heads to look up, and Jack patrols at three levels, and there were all those radar screens turning and peering and noticing. If your face didn't fit, there were the gunners. Every ship had extra 20mm and 40mm guns in every available clear space.

But there was something reassuring about it all. The bees were returning to a friendly hive. The stings were sheathed, the guards were turning their backs.

'Orange Leader, this is *Miss Britannia*, have you now visual. Check fuel.'

The returning RAMRODS were stringing into line astern and forming up on their own carriers. Skipper flew down *Miss*

Britannia's port side, working over his checklist. Back hood. Full flaps. Down undercarriage, down hook, fine pitch ... There should be a mnemonic for it. *Flaps ... Under ... Carriage* — FUC. Perhaps not.

With a fully worked-up squadron, as they were, they should be able to land on at 22-second intervals. *So here we go.* He could see Tiny the batsman and the glowing yellow bats he was holding out. Tiny was a big man, and he had needed two burly naval airmen to hold him upright when he batted on a returning strike in a rising gale off the Norwegian coast nine months before. The bats looked like undersized oranges in Tiny's enormous fists.

Corsairs had such long engine cowlings that one had to bank to port, turning fairly sharply all the way, to look over the side, and straighten up at the last moment. It should be good. Skipper saw Tiny nodding and knew it was good. White and grey wake from the ship, a smear of brown funnel haze floating away to starboard, the grey-green deck just coming into sight.

Cut, and Tiny whipped away his bats and jack-knifed as though somebody had just punched him in the stomach. Each deck landing was the same as all the others, and all the others were totally different from each other. Skipper cut the throttle, and there was a thump and a drawing back. Open the throttle again, hook clear, signals from ahead, roll forward, select wing hydraulic folding lever, down comes the safety barrier, the great bulk of the island shuts out the sun to starboard. Skipper was aware of seeing the next astern land on, in his mirror. Rolling forward, wings almost meet overhead with a heavy vibration. The marshaller cuts his own throat with an expressive gesture, shut throttles, almost silence. One more RAMROD and one less.

Chief Air Rigger Petre was standing beside the starboard wing trailing edge. Normally he would have come up on the step with some comment, but not this time. He already knew about Ronnie. The flight-deck grapevine was working. For most of the ship the news about Ronnie Bell would not be noticed any more than the slap and bump of a wave against the bows. But in his squadron, for those who had known Ronnie, his death was a space, a hole which had not yet even begun to harden and seal around the edges. Ronnie was dead, so long live everybody else. Besides, it had happened so many times before.

Before he did anything else, Skipper went up to the bridge to see the Captain. It was the first step demanded in a ritual for the dead, the first rung in a kind of hierarchy of commiseration. The Captain was sitting in his huge, high bridge chair, smoking the inevitable dark cheroot, wearing khaki tunic and shorts and a rather comic baseball cap, with a long green peak, which somebody had given him on a visit to an American carrier in Ulithi lagoon. Skipper had never quite fathomed the Captain's real feelings when a member of the aircrew was lost. So much depended upon circumstances. In training, he was critical, concerned, even censorious. In action, he was sympathetic — but that was too uncomplicated a word. The Captain held an unusual emotional balance, taking the loss personally, but looking beyond at its effect upon the whole ship's company.

The Captain's war, like that of all his contemporaries, went back to September 1939, and he had been at sea almost the whole time. In a sense his war had begun even earlier; he had been First Lieutenant of a destroyer in the Mediterranean during the Spanish Civil War, and he had once been a junior officer in an aircraft carrier on the China Station in the early

Thirties — an era of junks, pirates, gun-runners and drug smugglers. The Captain was regular, straight-stripe Navy, all Dartmouth, Greenwich and Whale Island. He was, of course, not a flyer, and Skipper sometimes suspected he still secretly looked upon flying as vaguely ungentlemanly, unseemly. It was unsporting to hit a man beyond normal gun range. Yet Skipper knew that the Captain recognised his aircrew were now his main armament and that his Squadron COs controlled that armament. The Captain would quickly ask his COs' advice, in a way which constantly flattered them. Skipper had come to admire and respect the man increasingly as their months of service together had lengthened, and he sometimes felt the Captain's reciprocal interest in himself.

The Captain turned his head at the sound of Skipper's footsteps and, hoisting himself round in his chair, he offered his hand in a curiously formal handshake.

'I'm sorry to hear it, Skipper.' He used the nickname unselfconsciously, as though unaware it could have been his own. 'The same thing?' The Captain knew of the problems they had had with Ronnie.

'Yes, sir. Low but not low enough. If you get right down, you're safer. It is always hard to hit a pheasant going right for your hat. Same principle, sir.'

The Captain nodded at the example, drawn for his benefit.

'He was basically a good pilot, sir, but he would not be taught beyond a certain point.' Skipper shrugged his shoulders. What more was there to say? He had not liked Ronnie much, but then, it was not his business to like or dislike people. His job was to make people fly against the Japanese.

'What exactly happened?'

'I'm not sure, sir, exactly. He was behind me. Geoffrey Tilling, the port wingman, had a better view.'

'Fetch him.'

Geoffrey, when he arrived on the bridge — anxious at the summons, somewhat overawed and awkward with his words — had not much more to contribute than his first description over the R/T as they climbed away from Ishigaki. Ronnie Bell had lifted up for a fatal half-second and the gunners had got him through his windscreen. As he listened to Geoffrey tell his story, Skipper saw what an impossible task the boy had been set: to describe how a colleague had died beside you. The finest poets in the language had faltered at that, and Geoffrey was just a grown-up schoolboy. His father was a water board official and they lived in south London — Croydon or Penge or somewhere. And here he was, explaining to professional naval officers how one of their number had been chopped down in the course of their profession. Because Ronnie had been RN, the only RN officer in the squadron. The rest, including Skipper himself, were all RNVRs. And now there were none. It could be — Skipper hesitated before formulating the thought, even to himself — that Ronnie had died *because* he was RN. He had just that shade, Skipper thought, of unbendingness, that tinge of superiority. Off the Sakishima Gunto only the flexible man who was right on top of his reflexes, the real nervous learning reacting man, ever survived.

After the Captain, Skipper went to see Commander (Air) and his assistant, Lieutenant Commander (Flying), continuing his round of commiseration in order of decreasing seniority. Wings and Little F, as they were always known, were in Flyco, the small open space with a parapet overlooking the flight deck, where the eternal wind burnished the cheeks and tugged everlastingly at clothing and hair, and would, sooner or later, whisk anything loose away into space. In hurried phrases, whilst the other two craned over to look at the flight deck, answered telephone calls and broadcast messages, he told them what had happened. He minced no words: it was all Ronnie's own fault. *De mortuis nil nisi bonum* was all very well, but here, while the struggle for Okinawa was going on to the north, the living outweighed the dead a million times over. Post-mortems might save more lives. So, always the question to be answered was, was it anything wrong in our routine? Was it just Ronnie's own ham-fistedness, or is there anything we should be doing to safeguard the rest?

After Flyco, it was Stanley the Fighter Direction Officer, sitting naked to the waist with the sweat running down his chest, in his hot, dark little hell-hole full of radar screens in the centre of the island. Forced draught fans were roaring full bore, and two portable desk fans were trained on Stanley's face, but his office was still as airless and oppressive as an oven. Again the questions: was it the direction, was anything not clear, did we run you into a pig's ear, could he not *hear*? No, said Skipper, no and no and no. It was like visiting and reassuring the relatives of the deceased, in a left-handed sort of way. No, he died a good death. Nothing in his life became him like the leaving of it.

Skipper was always careful about debriefing. It was important not to let it become perfunctory. It was important to listen with attention while the pilots described their experience. One could learn a great deal, about the target, the sortie and the man, from a phrase, from a word, even from a tone of voice. Ops marked the position of Skipper's Betty on his chart of Ishigaki runway, and put a cross for Ronnie on the perimeter where they had flown in. There were, Skipper could see, one or two crosses now beginning to accumulate around that airstrip.

After debriefing, Skipper could have gone to his cabin aft, but the ship was still at Action Stations, State Two — a relaxed state, but the watertight doors were shut, as they would be all day, and it would take him a quarter of an hour to get aft. The effort would exhaust him, in the heat. There was a row of cabins in the island, and Skipper was once again amazed to see officers washing and shaving. Was it *really* only a quarter to seven in the morning? For the aircrew, time was disjointed. There was operational time, Japanese gunners' time, and there was ship's time, breakfast time, and there was a personal time, no time for thought. There was a galley in the island and Skipper had breakfast, scrambled powdered egg and fried potatoes which were not potatoes but something called Pom, and tea which tasted of bird-seed. So, it had to be the ready room, where the chairs were deeper and more comfortable than any others on board. People were going to and fro, brushing irritatingly past Skipper's feet. He wanted to roar at them. *Don't you* understand? he wanted to bellow at them. *Can't you* see?

There were a thousand things, as Squadron CO, that he could and should be doing — seeing the Chief Air Tiff about mods to the aircraft and the state of serviceability in general, seeing Michael the Senior P about a replacement in the short term for Ronnie, seeing the squadron chief about the sailors going up for the next Captain's requestmen and defaulters, seeing Geoffrey about switching to starboard wingman for the rest of today; all these people to see, things to be doing. But Skipper was too tired to do any of them, and dozed off in his chair until Ops shook him for briefing.

Skipper got to his feet. This was a Fleet Air Arm pilot's life — sleep until somebody shook you awake and told you it was time to fly again. Sleep, shake, wake, fly, then sleep, shake, wake and fly...

It was 8.30 and this time it was high CAP for an Avenger bomber strike on Ishigaki. The strike was to be accompanied by another Corsair fighter RAMROD offensive sweep, and the Hellcats from the flagship would beat up Miyako. Skipper was relieved to see that A-Able, his regular Corsair, was available again. He abhorred superstition and strenuously discouraged it in his squadron. A boy could mentally work himself into a physical spin, literally, merely because he flew without his lucky pyjamas on, or his girlfriend's teddy bear, or his lucky Australian shilling in his pocket, or his lucky sunglasses, or his lucky scarf. Ronnie had had a lucky Ovaltiney badge, which he always pinned to his shirt on a strike, and a fat lot of good it had done him. All the same, Skipper could not repress a sense of pleasure and relief in climbing into the familiar cockpit with its hundred familiar scrapes and scuffs and scratch marks.

High CAP, at an average of 30,000 feet, was an eye-swivelling, neck-wrenching, head-craning business, never flying at the same height or on the same course for more than half a minute, snaking and switchbacking and weaving from side to side and up and down, watching and turning, turning and watching, over the tubby Avengers below. The strike was like a battle far off and long ago, minute bomb bursts on the runways, several separate dust hazes; it was like watching somebody bomb Mars, although Skipper fancied he could actually hear the detonations.

On the way back, Stanley vectored them out to a bogey to the north and Skipper peeled his flight off the top to look. It turned out to be a Liberator not transmitting her IFF properly. It was probably one of MacArthur's, so nobody in the Navy would have been told anything about it. MacArthur and Nimitz were supposed not to get on too well together. They broke off at a mile, but the Liberator had her guns trained on them, so they had not been asleep in that ship.

When they got back they found that the Avengers had lost one, and *Dainty Delilah*, next in line to port, had lost a Seafire from the CAP. *Madame Fifi* had a Corsair down from the RAMROD. With Ronnie from the dawn sorties, this was the worst morning so far for the task force off the Sakishima Gunto. This was how it was going to be, not a sudden dramatic rush of losses, as at the Sumatran oil refineries, but a slow bleeding away of the squadrons, day by day. A war of attrition. This was trench warfare in the air, a steady, relentless chipping away at the enemy's strength.

Somebody said that the Corsair pilot was seen to get out, and somebody else said the US lifeguard submarine had got him. But the Avenger was a certain goner. It had been seen to plunge into the middle of the main runway on Ishigaki and nobody ever got out. It was the turn of Henry Darling, the Avenger Squadron CO, to make the rounds of the Captain, Flyco, the air direction office, and so on. Skipper had barely known the pilot and the observer. Odd that one could serve in the same ship with someone for nearly a year, ever since the strikes off Norway, and hardly know him. In fact, Skipper had known the observer since the days of the big Malta convoy of 1942, but knew nothing about him. But the telegraphist-air gunner, Petty Officer Bennett, had been one of the ship's characters. He was a brilliant deck-hockey player, and much in demand with his accordion 'squeeze-box' at ship's concert parties. So 'Wiggy' Bennett was gone. It was best to forget him, shut him out of your mind.

Later they heard the flagship had lost a Hellcat, ditched into the sea. Somebody saw the pilot get into his dinghy. At the next briefing, Ops mentioned the ditching drill. He had not done that for days, but now it was news again. Otherwise, it was the mixture as before, interpreted in the figures and letters chalked on the ready-room board: weather, call-signs, target photographs, map of gun positions. Skipper felt he could have drawn that from memory.

'What about strays?' he asked. 'Last time, we closed a Liberator all ready to go.'

'We're looking into that.' Ops' brow wrinkled at the implied criticism.

'That's all very well, looked at from *here*.' Skipper had not meant the remark to be funny, but everybody else laughed nervously. Ops' brow creased even deeper. He, too, was RN. Score two this morning.

'As I said, Skipper, we're looking into it.'

Skipper sensed the relief on the faces behind him when they heard the target was Miyako, generally supposed to be the less deadly of the two major islands, although Skipper himself could not understand how this opinion had ever grown up. It was six of one and half a dozen whangers on the other. There were already as many crosses on Miyako, perhaps because aircrews eased up slightly there, believing it was a less dangerous target. They should bear down all the harder instead.

Skipper made that point with some force at the squadron 'huddle' — so called after they had all seen that movie about American footballers, and indeed Skipper sometimes felt like a football coach, giving his team a pep talk before they went out on to the field. This was to be an all-out strike, with all the squadron aircraft that were serviceable, eleven of them that morning. Michael, the Senior Pilot, was to take his flight to Karimata, in the northern tip of the island, where the Japanese had a seaplane base, rarely used.

Although Skipper knew what Michael was, and how potentially dangerous such a man could be, he still almost loved him. He probably loved him more for his weakness. Michael appealed to that five per cent aberration that *Esquire* magazine said lurked in every man, but was normally no more important or significant than his nipples. But Michael's sympathy, his intuition, his courage, made up for everything. He had a DSC, won over the *Tirpitz* a year before, and the squadron vowed it should have been a VC. Michael was so good a pilot that Skipper told new hands to the squadron to stand up in the goofers and watch him land on. They were lucky to have him. He should by rights have got a squadron of his own by now. Perhaps he would, when this squadron stood down from operations — whenever that would be. Doctors and psychologists who would have wet themselves if they ever went near Ishigaki gave solemn lectures about fear and wounds and resolution in combat and recovery rates and time after operations and nightmares, when the proper solution was staring them in the face: give all air crews a set time on board and have them relieved promptly when their time was up, as the Americans had learned to do, the hard way. As it was, the air group joined and served on, and on, and on, and on, until they dropped — literally.

Miyako was certainly a more pleasant-looking island, greener, flatter and somehow friendlier. It had the same pan-handle shape from the air, a blob and a spit, and it was supposed to have more people on it than Ishigaki. Skipper had once tried to find out about the people of the Ryukyus. The islands had been under Japanese control and closed to all outsiders for years before the war, so the information in the great pile of books and documents from US military intelligence that the Schoolie produced was many years out of date, as their authors admitted. Skipper had started to read them, but their dry pedagogic tone had defeated him. Those were people down there, not insects or rock plants. They had babies, they ran from aircraft, they were not even Japanese.

There was one old man who knelt in a little walled garden at the edge of the Nobara airstrip, just by the coast. Skipper had passed only ten feet above him on two previous strikes and he had never even looked up. God knows what grew in his little garden — worms, probably. Miyako Shima was in the Miyako Retto, which was part of the Sakishima Gunto, which in turn formed part of Ryukyu Retto, an important chain in the Nansei Shoto. The Japanese had as many names for collections of islands as the Eskimos had for snow. But in the meantime, they were all targets.

There was nothing at Nobara, not even the old man in his garden. It was as bare as a baby's bottom. The runway was swept clean and clear, as though they had come to inspect it. Not a gun spoke, not a funeral note. They turned across the island and headed for Hirara, flying across a neat, delicate and somehow fragile landscape of tiny fields and thin white tracks, spidery links threading between patches of green, with dots of huts. It was a miniature landscape, seen through a diminishing glass.

There was a bit of a harbour on the western coast, nothing much, just a jetty and a couple of wooden fishing vessels. Some Fireflies from *Dainty Delilah* were busy above it, working it over with rockets and cannon fire. That squadron was full of Royal Marines, all as daft as a blind Chinaman's brush. Their aircraft were rising and falling over the target like starlings. They had probably got hold of a small coaster, not more than fifty tons, carrying fish, or rice, or a bit of coal or some firewood — something very basic, bound to be.

There were some suspicious-looking lumps at the end of Hirara strip.

'Domino, Domino, this is Domino Leader, one run only. Get close. *Break*!' Ronnie's place had been taken by Edward, the squadron spare prick, because Skipper had not wanted to break up any of the other flights. He must be good enough, because Skipper had barely noticed him.

The landscape leaped up to meet them and rocked several degrees before they straightened up on their strafing run. Still no gunfire. And there she was! A great big shiny new Betty bomber again, painted bright blue, large as life and twice as natural. It must be Tojo's birthday!

'Domino, Domino, this is Domino Leader, blood for supper!' It was uncannily like Ishigaki a few hours before, although the light was better, the picture harder and sharper. They fled down the runway on their single pass, firing from a long way off. The Betty was sagging on one wing as they streaked over it.

The guns began as they reached the perimeter and started to climb. With mild surprise, Skipper decided they must have moved the batteries. The angle was new. Somebody once said that gunfire had a smell, especially when it hit you. Skipper smelt it now, it was that close. Very much closer than usual. The Corsair shook and began to vibrate as though it wanted to shake itself out of the sky. After near-misses the whole frame seemed to go on trembling for minutes afterwards, as though the cab was as scared as you were. Skipper could feel the unhealthy vibrations through his fingertips.

'Domino Leader...' Geoffrey and Edward were both trying to speak at once. Edward fell silent, as the new boy. 'Skipper, I think you're hit, Skipper!'

'Where?'

'Tailplane.'

'Anything else?'

'Negative.'

'No smoke?'

'Negative.'

'What's it look like?'

'Fairly bad, Skipper. Like somebody bit a big chunk out.'

'*Big* chunk?'

'Well … maybe … *fairly* big…'

'Roger. This is Domino Leader, we'll go straight back. Course one-one-five magnetic.'

When Skipper tried to steepen his climb, the Corsair gave an ominous lurch and the vibration nearly wrenched the joystick out of his hands. Skipper's mouth flooded with saliva and his stomach knotted until he gasped with pain. With horror he realised that his bowels had almost betrayed him. He knew now what the Americans meant when they said 'keep a tight arsehole'. He remembered the lad in the early days at Quonset Point who had demonstrated conclusively that a Corsair would not pull out of a spin. The boy had obviously known what was going to happen to him before he hit, and had lost control of his bowels. That cockpit afterwards, as somebody said, was like an abattoir with the blood and shit.

Skipper's fingers and palms were slippery with sweat and he could feel the goosepimples all over his legs. He had a fleeting sensation of disgust, as though he were sitting in a bath of slime. He swallowed the saliva and tried to relax his forehead muscles, which had contracted the skin in a fierce scowl. At least the gauges were all steady and reading correctly. It was just this vibration which went and then came again, as though the Corsair had suddenly remembered it was hurt.

Stanley, who never missed a trick, passed the bearing and distance of the American lifeguard submarine, in case Skipper needed her, and reassured Skipper that the air-sea rescue Walrus amphibian was being spotted on deck for use. He had also cleared Skipper's flight with the veterinary cruiser, which passed them without comment. *Why*, thought Skipper, *if they can do that in an emergency, why can't they do it all the time, without all this tedious spotting and delays?*

Miss Britannia, when they reached her, was already steaming into wind as hard as she could go. Skipper could see that from her broad, boiling, creamy wake. He also caught the green light, meaning they were ready. On his final circuit, Skipper made his checks. Everything in order... Flaps, undercarriage, hook ... Hook ... That was it ... No hook. Obviously shot away. As he turned on his finals and approached the deck, Skipper gritted his teeth and winced. It *was* going to be all right. He would *not* follow Ronnie Bell so soon.

The vibration was much more serious, so that it seemed that only Skipper's grip was preventing the Corsair falling apart. Skipper made up his mind, he would *not* follow Ronnie Bell. There was Tiny, there was the deck, and there was an almighty bang as he crossed the round-down. After the cut, the aircraft seemed to stop flying and literally fall out of the sky. The undercarriage held and the aircraft began to roll, seeming to accelerate rather than slow down. One by one, the impotent arrester wires slipped underneath and the big barrier was rushing up at appalling speed. In a dreamy moment Skipper remembered that old song: *And loud in my ears, the sweet angel choir sang ... 'Floating in, floating in, float, float, float, barrier prang!'*

The grinding and rending of the wires, biting into the Corsair's wings and engine cowling, seemed to go on for a surprising time. When it stopped, Skipper stayed in his cockpit, still resting his weight against his straps. *Cracking show, I'm alive! But I've still got to render my A25!* He could tell by the unnatural angle of the aircraft that something was very wrong back aft. Chief Air Rigger Petre's face appeared to starboard, with one of the helmeted crash-men in the whitish-grey fearnaught suits. Skipper undid his straps and stood up, turning round to look aft.

The tailplane was gone, completely. Two aircraft handlers, far aft on the flight deck, were manhandling its distorted shape towards the ship's side. The end of Skipper's Corsair was just a jagged-edged hollow tube. Skipper felt his mouth swimming with saliva again and, remembering just in time to turn to port away from Chief Air Rigger Petre, he bent over and vomited down the side of his aircraft. When that stopped, Skipper found to his shame and dismay that he was crying.

CHAPTER TWO

Skipper was surprised by the number of people who came to the memorial service for Ronnie and the Avenger crew in the ship's chapel that evening. The Captain was there, of course, while the Commander took his place and looked after the shop on the bridge, and Wings, and Little F, and some of the ship's heads of departments. There were many from Ronnie's squadron and the Avenger squadron, as one would expect. But there were also some ship's officers whom Skipper would not have expected. In the ships and shore establishments Skipper had served in, the non-flying officers kept themselves very much to themselves. The flyers and those concerned with flying lived in a world of their own, and a carrier tended to be two ships in one.

Skipper himself hardly knew the name of a single ship's officer in *Miss Britannia*. He was aware that there seemed to be dozens of engineer officers of various kinds, but who they were and what their mysterious duties were down below in the ship, Skipper had no idea, nor had he much inclination to find out. Such officers could not be expected at an aircrew memorial service. However, here were several, including the Gunnery Officer, who had hardly ever before been known even to acknowledge a pilot's existence. But Skipper remembered sometime hearing that Ronnie had been at Dartmouth with Guns' younger brother. Blood and Darts stuck together thicker than sea water.

There were very few ratings. Skipper was not surprised at that. The chapel was amidships, so designed as to be easily reachable from forward and from aft, but the sailors still looked upon it as 'officer country', as the Americans said. Besides, it had been a long day and a hard day and it was time for sleep. The sailors always took a realistic, unromantic view of life and death. Time was that *when the brains were out the man would die, And there an end,* and so it was for the ship's company. Memorial services were a waste of good kip time.

One of the few ratings there was Chief Air Rigger Petre, in the back row. He always turned up, like a fat commemorative crow. Everybody in the squadron, even Skipper, was to a greater or lesser extent afraid of Petre. Everybody felt that no matter what happened, Chief Air Rigger Petre's eyes had seen it all before. He was a pre-war Fleet Air Arm rating, whose service went back two decades to a time long before the Navy had regained control of its own air arm from the RAF. He would have been on pension now, after twenty-two years' service, but for the war. He had been a survivor of *Courageous* in 1939 and had spent two days in a boat after *Glorious* went down in 1940. He lost two toes to frostbite but his fat, he said, had saved his life. He walked off *Ark Royal* in 1941 without getting any of his remaining toes wet.

Skipper meant to ask Petre some day about his war experiences. Petre had watched them fly off against *Bismarck* and *Tirpitz* and in innumerable shipping strikes in the Channel and along the Norwegian coast. Many of those he had followed off the deck with his eyes had never come back, and Skipper had heard from the squadron's chief's mess that Petre had some scary tales to tell of the darker side of aircrew life, just beyond the line of madness, where no briefing on earth could ever help a man. That was the side of their life they never talked about. It was not mentioned in the glossy little soft-covered books His Majesty's Stationery Office produced for sale on railway bookstalls and for uncles to give small boys for their birthdays. *Fleet Air Arm*, one of them was actually called. *We will go up and fight,* it said, somewhere in it. From Deuteronomy. It sounded fine, but they never went on to complete the reference. That particular passage described how the Israelites defied God's advice and got beaten by the Amorites. So it was a classical text for a pilot, though not in the way it was meant. *Never carry out a RAMROD against the best intelligence from On High,* was the message.

Skipper got up to read the lesson. It was from Ecclesiastes. *'Remember now thy creator in the days of thy youth, while the evil days come not, nor the years draw nigh, when thou shalt say, I have no pleasure in them...'* Skipper looked across at Chief Air Rigger Petre's expressionless eyes. He could probably recite this by heart. *Then shall the dust return to the earth as it was; and the spirit shall return unto God who gave it.'* There is one corner of Ishigaki Bus Station that is for ever Dartmouth, Whale Island and England.

Skipper waited while the files of men moved out of the chapel. He himself was in no hurry; he liked the cool and somehow civilised little compartment. With its wood panelling and its faint smell of polish, it struck a note of luxury when everything else in the ship was bare and oily and functional, stripped of most of the things that made life more comfortable.

This was the time of day for relaxation. The last CAPs had landed on half an hour earlier and flying was over for the day. The task force had withdrawn from the striking area and was steaming south, through a moderate swell from the south-east, to join the Fleet Train and begin fuelling the next day. Skipper himself was still recovering from his crash. He had soon collected himself after his exhibition of weakness on the flight deck. Now, he felt sore round his shoulders and his back ached a little, but the doctor had seen him and passed him fit, and he was alive. He was in what Michael called a 'post-prangial' state of exhilaration. It would pass, and give way to fresh apprehensions, but in the meantime he was alive and still on his feet. Not so poor old Able Annie. Full fathom five hundred and fifty-five she lay. She was judged written off, and everything valuable and attractive and easily movable — guns, radio, clock, instruments and gauges — had been taken out of her — 'cannibalised' was the word. Then she had been trundled down to the round-down aft and tipped over the side. Skipper had watched her go, slightly surprised at his own lack of reaction. It was like the news that a neighbour's dog had been put down — one felt sorry, but there it was.

As Skipper walked forward along the passageway he could see men still at work in some of the ship's offices on either side, but in the messes they were just getting ready for supper. The daily rum issue, postponed in deference to the flying programme from the traditional noon time, had just been made. The hangar was hot and empty except for the sentry, and Skipper felt the sweat springing out under his shirt at once. There were two men working on a Corsair on the port side. The panels over the engine had been removed. The two of them wore only a pair of oil shorts and both had long oily sweat-marks, like ragged dark sashes, across their backs. They both wore stout shoes and socks. Light sandals and flimsy plimsolls were all right for the Home Fleet in the summertime, but out here you could fry an egg on the flight deck quite early in the morning. Men who slept on the flight deck in harbour often had to wait until half-past eleven at night before the metal deck had cooled enough for them to put out their camp-beds.

Skipper heard the footsteps behind him and knew that Wings was catching him up.

'You OK after your episodes and excitements today, Skipper?' It was a ritual question, a formal way of opening the conversation. Wings knew very well that Skipper was fit.

'Fine, sir. No flying tomorrow, so in any case I've got a day or two in hand.'

'Yes.' Wings paused for so long that Skipper wondered what was coming next. 'Tell me ... I gather you feel that Ronnie Bell rather brought things on his own head today?'

Skipper frowned and pressed the thumb and forefinger of his right hands against his shut eyelids. This was not the time or place to discuss that. Why the bloody hell couldn't Wings go and browbeat Henry about his Avengers? Skipper opened his eyes.

'The fact is, Ronnie Bell didn't fly low enough to be in a low-flying squadron, sir, and that's the long and short of it. I told him until I was blue in the face, I gave him extra coaching, I talked to him like a Dutch uncle, I threatened him, once I even dropped him from the flight and made him do Jack patrols. I was just pissing against the wind. He just hadn't got the balls for it.'

'I see. Well, OK. We just have to watch out for these things.'

With a shock, Skipper realised that this was not the first time Wings had subtly and indirectly questioned his leadership of his squadron. Wings had been a fighter pilot, still was, and a very good one. He had started off the war in Skuas and in those strange and fabulous birds, the Rocs, the ball-turreted fighters that could not fire ahead. He was up there in Flyco strictly on merit. But it occurred to Skipper that maybe Wings was still mentally down there on the flight deck, flying along with the squadrons.

'You going to write to his old man?'

'Of course, sir.'

'Fine. We've sent off the signal.'

That was all one had to do after the loss of a pilot. Lose a half-inch spanner or a pair of flying overalls and one had to spend the next six months filling out reams of forms. Lose a pilot and there was one brief signal, always in a standard format: *A. Name. B. Date. C. Squadron. D. Type of aircraft. E. Reason. F. Remarks. No remarks.* There were never any remarks.

Ronnie's name and address of next of kin were perfect, just as Skipper would have expected. Lieutenant Commander Ronald Rowland Bell RN (Retired) and Mrs Rowland Bell, The Old Rectory, King's Pontreville, near Newton Ferrers, South Devon, Telephone No. 9. Skipper wondered who the other eight were. He could see it all: family house, dogs in the garden, Virginia creeper on the wall, sun hats and strawberries and cream, fruit blossom and bees, jam and Jerusalem. Commander Rowland Bell would be something in Plymouth: maintaining boom defences, or morale, or mail, or keeping the Commander-in-Chief's operational diary up to date. At home he would be a pillar of the local Home Guard, just as Mrs Bell would be a tower of strength in the WVS. They would, in fact, be just like Skipper's own parents.

The next-of-kin signal was part of another small squadron ritual of bereavement. Next in the sequence was the collection of his belongings. If it was a sailor, his effects would be auctioned on the fo'c'sle one day in the dog watches, with everybody bidding over each other, and winning, and putting up the same item for auction again, to swell the proceeds to their messmate's widow or mother. But an officer's gear was packed away, to be returned one day: his uniform, almost always with one single wavy stripe and wings on the sleeve, his framed picture of his parents, his letters, his studio portrait of his girlfriend, his paperback books, his underpants, spare pair of flying goggles, his sunglasses, his sunbathing sandals, his snapshots of flying training in America, his own deck landings taken by the ship's photographer, the string of dubious cultured pearls he bought for his girlfriend in Colombo, his shirts, towels, toothpaste and hairbrush, and some dirty pictures he bought somewhere or other — how would *they* go down in The Old Rectory, King's Pontreville, Newton Ferrers, South Devon, Tel. No. 9? Putting them in his pocket, Skipper stared at the rest of Ronnie's gear. This was the man. This was all there was. No more. All mutely said, *Don't judge me too harshly, please.*

Ronnie had had no particular friend in the squadron, nobody Skipper knew of that he could ask for some inside information, some local colour, to put in the letter to his family. Geoffrey probably knew him as well as anybody, but only because he flew port to Ronnie's starboard. Rodney Pritchard, the fourth in the flight, might know him better, but Skipper could not be bothered to go and ask him. They had been a lucky squadron and Skipper had had very few such letters to write in the last eighteen months. Not like the ship's Avenger squadron, after the holocaust caused by the fighters, gun barrage and balloons over the Sumatran oil refineries. The Squadron CO and the Senior P and both their entire crews had gone, and three other crews, for good measure. Skipper had no idea who wrote the letters for them on that occasion. Perhaps Michael might have done it. He was better at it than anybody. It was part of his personality: Michael always knew what to say.

Skipper got out his pad of best writing paper, the blue-cream with the ship's crest heavily embossed on it at the top. This was the best pre-war quality stuff, the canteen manager said.

Heaven knows how he still got it, but it was a reminder of piping peace in war. Even the feel of the paper was hopeful that better times would come again.

Dear Commander and Mrs Rowland Bell. Skipper stopped and stared at the paper. Michael would do this so much better. *I have the sad duty ... I am very sorry to have to write to you on the subject of your son's death ... I am writing this sitting in my cabin after a very long and hectic day's flying in which your son ... I have to admit I never liked your son very much, but now that he is almost certainly dead ... Dear Commander and Mrs Bell ... If I told Ronnie once I must have told him a thousand times, he must keep his head down ...* 'Must' underlined. Start again. *Dear Commander and Mrs Rowland Bell ... I am writing to you now, hoping that something I say will help to offer you some consolation after the news that your son was missing, believed killed, in action today. I have to tell you that I think it very unlikely that ...* No, start again. *I, as your son's Squadron CO, can assure you that your son conducted himself in all his duties according to the very best traditions of the Service in which you and he both served, just as you would have hoped and believed he would have done...*

New paragraph. *He was the only regular RN officer in our squadron of eighteen officers (the rest of us are all Wavy types) ...* Wavy types? Was that too flippant? *The rest of us are all RNVRs. As such, your son always brought a touch of the old Navy tradition into our squadron life. The younger pilots looked up to him as an example of how to fly. He will be a great loss to us all. But, as I said, I hope this letter will come as some consolation to you.*

Once started, it came surprisingly easily. Skipper signed his name at the bottom of the page. That was that. That was Ronnie Bell. Ronnie Bell was now a matter for the *London Gazette,* for the obituary columns of *The Times,* a note in the back of the Navy List, and — in due course, if this war ever ended and if anybody ever survived to see the day — they would put his name up on a great slab of granite somewhere on Southsea Common, or on the windy plains of Yeovilton, or even in the church which must be near The Old Rectory, King's Pontreville, near Newton Ferrers, South Devon, Tel. No. 9.

Before going to bed, Skipper went for a shower in the officers' bathroom in the next flat. The passageway was quiet and hot. The ship was rolling quietly and easily. There was nothing in the air, nothing on the radar screens. Even the last flashes and glowings of the American task forces to the north had long since sunk beneath the horizon. Skipper arrived at the bathroom door with his towel and his soap, and he fancied he heard singing and then whistling, and somebody scrubbing themselves. Skipper stopped dead at the door.

'Ronnie?'

The hair prickled on the back of Skipper's neck. The singing and the water rushing stopped. Skipper walked along the short row of shower stalls. One of them was freshly wet, with steam rising from the pool of water on the deck. But there was nobody there.

'Skipper?' Michael was at the bathroom door, also with towel and soap. 'What's the matter, Skipper?'

'Nothing.'

'You're as white as a sheet, Skipper. Have you seen a ghost?'

'Oh, for God's sake don't say that!'

'What's the matter?'

'Nothing really … nothing…' Skipper was not sure himself what he had heard. 'It sounds daft, but I really thought I heard Ronnie Bell singing in here, just as he used to do.'

'Singing? Ronnie?' Michael held up his hand. 'Skipper, just watch it. Don't you go getting the twitch now. That's all we need. Ronnie Bell wasn't much of a loss, whichever way you skin it. But *you* would be, Skipper. You're our best hope of getting out of all this alive. So watch it.'

Skipper looked again at the wet shower stall. It was fresh, no doubt about it. But it must have been somebody who had just slipped out without being seen. As for the singing and whistling, it was a big ship and full of acoustic tricks, with the incessant noise of fans and other machinery; one dry bearing could make a screeching noise. The lower hangar was only one deck above and a steel wheel on a steel deck could set up peculiar resonances some distance away.

Nevertheless, Skipper felt his mouth swimming with saliva again, and the same exhausted sickness overcame him as when he had climbed out of his cockpit that morning. Once again his stomach heaved, and he vomited over the floor of the shower stall. He leaned his forehead against the partition, hoping this would pass over soon. That was twice today, once in front of his Chief Air Rigger and now in front of his Senior Pilot, and he was their Squadron CO, supposed to set them an example.

'Skipper…' He felt Michael's hand supporting his elbow. 'It'll pass. It will.'

'Yes.' Skipper wiped his mouth with the back of his hand. 'I know.'

'It was that prang today. It looked bad, and you never really get out and walk away. You may think you do … until the first time you try to get to sleep after it.'

'I know.' Skipper straightened up and turned on the water, full pelt, to wash the mess away. 'Thank God there seems to be plenty of water tonight.' The fresh water was turned off always at action stations, and even when supplies were supposed to be restored, there were often shortages and stoppages. The engineers below had a constant struggle to distil enough fresh water for all, so Skipper had heard. Baths were banned in the officers' bathrooms, and even showers were supposed to be used sparingly. But Skipper took a long-handled mop from the bathroom cleaner's locker and swashed and swished it around the deck, using water profligately, until the shower stall was clean.

'Have you *ever* had a prang, Mike?'

Michael flushed slightly. His flying, Skipper knew, was impeccable, pure, like a work of art. 'No, actually I haven't. But I can see from looking at you what it must be like.'

Once again, Skipper felt himself warming to Michael's sympathy. 'Well, all I can say is, don't.' Skipper looked around him. 'Somehow I don't feel like a shower now. I'm off. Goodnight, Mike.'

'Goodnight, Skipper. And remember, we're relying on you to pull us all out alive.'

In the event, Skipper went to sleep at once and slept soundly, sleeping through dawn action stations. When Skipper awoke guiltily and went on deck, the air was clean and bright and salty, and the sea for miles around was full of ships. The fleet, like a bride, had a train of tankers, repair ships and supply ships, and an escort carrier to provide CAPs over the replenishment area, and another carrier with spare aircraft and replacement aircrews which, as Michael said, 'was like having your own ambulance and hearse following you around'. It was called literally the Fleet Train, and it was, Skipper had been told, by far the most motley collection of shipping the Royal Navy had ever assembled. He could well believe it. The Americans, who had started the idea of a fleet train, operated with fast, modern ships manned with regular officers and ratings under US Navy regulations and discipline. But the British Fleet Train had some warships flying the White Ensign, some Royal Fleet Auxiliaries flying the Blue Ensign, and a number of merchantmen under Admiralty charter still flying the Red Ensign. Some of the tankers and store ships were almost brand new but others were more than thirty years old and looked it. One wondered how they had ever survived the 12,000-mile passage out from home. There was a Dutch hospital ship, a Danish tanker and Belgian and Norwegian ammunition ships and, back in Manus, there was a Panama collier. Some ships had RN crews, others had merchant seamen who had signed special article forms, some even had plain civilians. Skipper himself had seen ships come alongside with men of many different nationalities on board. What the problems must be of organising such a fleet, Skipper could not imagine. Many of the crews did not even have the same diet.

The smallest ship, a dot on the horizon, was a salvage tug, which was supposed to tow damaged ships out of danger. But Skipper had heard, and could see from the Signal log, that she was always breaking down and having to be towed herself. So there was always a trace of humour and of companionship about the Fleet Train. All together, they made a cheery sight. It was good to see so many different ships, faces and ensigns. It was a truly United Nations fleet. All these different elements had come together to fight the Japanese, and in more optimistic moments one felt that the Japanese could not possibly win with all this against them.

Replenishment periods were often as noisy as a strike against the Japanese. Far off to starboard, two of the six-inch cruisers and one division of destroyers were firing at drogue targets. They were miles off, but the sound of their gunfire came and went, ebbing and flowing, as the towing aircraft changed course. The fleet's gunners did not get nearly enough practice against aircraft, and the day might very well come soon when they had to prove themselves in earnest. From the earliest days in the Pacific the Americans had packed their ship's upper decks with anti-aircraft guns and warmly recommended the British to do the same, for surface targets were almost non-existent now. Lieutenant Commander Gus Dempsey USN, *Miss Britannia*'s US Navy Liaison Officer, said frankly he did not think she was able, 'like all you Limey carriers', to look after herself, just as he was critical of the armoured flight deck, which he said made the ship 'hotter and heavier' and able to carry less aircraft. 'You Limeys,' said Gus, 'are still fighting the battle of Jutland all over again. There's a whole new war going on out here in the East and you guys ain't got used to the idea yet.'

There were always strangers at the bar at lunchtime in replenishment periods. They were nearly all staff officers, from the Task Force Admiral over in the battle wagon or from the Carrier Admiral over in the flagship. They flew over, or they transferred by light jackstay, or occasionally the ships slowed to put down a motorboat, or perhaps, as Michael said, 'they came out of the woodwork'. This constant coming and going, with equally rapid changes in ship's and squadron personnel, with extra passengers, intelligence officers, civilians with special information and other mysterious people who just came and went in wartime, created a feverish, transient atmosphere in a wardroom which, Skipper was told, was quite unlike anything in the peacetime Navy.

Skipper was always fascinated by tales of life in the regular Royal Navy of the Thirties. It was like hearing folk tales and troubadours' ballads of some remote period of life of unimaginable stability; of long three-year commissions on the China Station or in the Med; the round of port visits to show the flag, when the fleet moved round a circuit like a Tudor monarch's progress; the regattas and the concert parties; the travelling wives; the cut-throat competition for promotion; the poor pay. But, it seemed, or so they told Skipper, the weather was fine (except for the occasional storm much rougher than *he* had ever seen), the gin flowed and the sun shone on the British Empire, on which indeed, it never set. From those days, the Navy still derived a residual confidence that encouraged and infuriated and amazed Skipper. The officers and ship's company of this ship were serenely aware that they could not be beaten. In spite of everything that had happened, in spite of the shocks and scares and tragedies, the ships that had been lost, the men burned and drowned, in spite of all the mistakes and stupidities, everybody was still quite confident that all would be well in the end. It was marvellous, really, when one thought about it. It was a strength money could never buy. And, judging by the news from Europe, their confidence was not misplaced.

Whether the same would be true of the war against the Japanese, Skipper was doubtful. Those gunners on Ishigaki had no rational chance of winning. They were hopelessly cut off, and were being mown down every day be ceaseless air attacks. Yet they were as keen and ferocious and as accurate as ever. Skipper had heard rumours of the landing planned for Japan in the coming autumn. From the way the Japanese had resisted in the Pacific atolls and were even now resisting on Okinawa, the staff were already talking about the awesome number of a million Allied casualties. And that was just to take the southernmost island of Kyushu. It seemed the war was going to go on for ever. The story was that from one insignificant speck of a coral atoll, the US Marines had taken one survivor, a Japanese private who had tried and failed to commit suicide. The other 4,000 of that garrison had all died. If that was what the Japanese did there, what would they do when they were fighting on the sacred soil of metropolitan Japan? It hardly bore thinking about.

Fuelling had begun at eight o'clock. The captains of the big ships in the task force still shuddered at the memories of their early attempts at fuelling, with faulty, untried gear and inexperienced crews, both in the tankers and in their own ships. They remembered steaming for hours at a time astern of a slow tanker, fishing over the bows with a grappling iron for the floating coir line with the buoy on the end of it and hauling the hose line inboard, in a welter of parted lines, split hoses and frayed tempers. Now, admittedly, it was much better, with the ships fuelling alongside the tanker at a much higher speed. But even though fuelling went better than usual it was late afternoon before the last lines were cast off and *Miss Britannia* could draw away from the tanker, haul out of the fuelling area, work up speed, and turn into wind to land on replacement aircraft.

Skipper and Michael went up to the island to watch. They had professional reasons for going. They had two replacement pilots coming on board and first impressions were always revealing. As they expected, the island galleries — 'the goofing positions', as they were called — were packed with spectators. The goofers came to watch the flying and for some fresh air, so they said, and so they did. But they also came for some excitement. Like the spectators at the bullfight, or in the Roman amphitheatre, they always had an unexpressed and hotly denied yearning for blood.

The gallery was so crowded that Skipper and Michael could not get near the front. They could have gone elsewhere but, perversely, Skipper decided to pull his rank. He grasped the shoulder of an officer in front. It was one of the ship's officers, an engineer Skipper did not know. The man objected. Skipper yanked him backwards and took his place.

'Look,' he said, grimly, 'do you *mind*? This may be *fun* for you, mate. It's a *business* for us. Understand? Right.'

Another officer, somewhat shamefacedly, made way for Michael. 'Two for us today, Skipper. Richard Fenton and Richard Trumble. Don't say it, don't say it...'

'*Un embarras de Richards...*'

'You *said* it...'

They both watched the Corsairs flying round and coming down the port side. As always, the ships guns were manned, and were training to and fro. There was a twin-barrelled 40mm Bofors mounting a few yards away from the goofing gallery, grinding around and back, back and around, like great searching metal antennae. The fleet was always wary of stray Japanese aircraft. At dawn, at twilight, at mealtimes, whenever the guard was dropped for a moment, a solitary Japanese aircraft could drop out of cloud and attack. Normal operational ranges meant nothing. Many of them had no intention of flying back.

The first new boy, like a new boy at school expecting to be critically examined, took a wave-off the first time round. This was normal. Tiny often waved off the first time, to let the fellow have a good look at an operational deck before getting down to business.

'These two look as if they know what they're doing. I hope they're ours.'

'They are, Skipper. They're coming on first.'

The two Corsairs made neat, unspectacular landings and were followed on by three Avengers for Henry. The last aircraft of the day was another Corsair, which approached in a fast, tight, confident swinging turn. Tiny, for some reason, did not like it and. waved off. The Corsair lifted sharply upwards, jauntily pulled up its undercarriage and, while doing so, dipped its wings. There were many ways of dipping — in salute, in warning, in admonishment. This was admonishment. To Skipper and Michael and Wings and all the air group looking on — it said, *How dare you wave me off!*

'Ho, ho,' said Michael, 'who have we here?'

The Corsair went round again, approached in an equally fast turn which Tiny could not cavil at, landed and took the middle wire in its middle, and came to rest in the middle of the flight deck, just like the demonstration landing in the training film.

As the Corsair taxied past the island, wings folding upwards as it went, the pilot smiled up but shook his fist, and the watchers on the platforms and in Flyco were left to decide for themselves which, the smile or the fist-shake, was meant to have the greatest importance. When he had climbed out of his cockpit and began to walk jauntily aft towards the island, the pilot swept off his leather helmet and shook out a shock of brilliant blond hair.

'Stap me, quite a character,' said Michael, without enthusiasm. 'I wonder who it can be?'

It was, as they discovered, a relief for Herman, the CO of the other Corsair squadron. Quite unexpectedly, out of a clear blue sky, a relief for Herman had arrived, to everybody's surprise and delight, and especially Herman's. It was not before time, as everybody knew. Herman — so called, inevitably, because his surname was Goring — had, in the phrase, lost his bottle. He had flown fighters for so long and had survived so much that he had grown very cautious. He was so cautious that, as his own squadron said, he had grown a beard in case he cut himself shaving. Herman was one of the very last survivors of the naval pilots who flew with the RAF in the Battle of Britain.

In that long glorious summer of 1940, Skipper himself had just come down after his first year at Oxford and was helping out with the harvest on the Park Farm, which used to be called the Home Farm, when the battles reached their height. From their Wiltshire fields, they had been too far away to see the dog-fights, but they had seen the highest contrails in the sky to the south and the east, and an occasional aircraft had flown overhead, making for Bristol. One day, above the Cotswold foothills to the north they saw a barrage balloon adrift, with a Spitfire in pursuit of it. The Spitfire dived and made one firing pass. The balloon collapsed in a fierce, brief flame which had flared out before it reached the ground. That Spitfire might have been flown by Herman. Skipper had often meant to ask him. If so, he owed his presence here to him. For something in that short episode of violence had so affected Skipper that he never went back to Oxford. By the time the next term started, he had already joined the Navy and started his part one training for aircrew at Gosport.

Skipper always enjoyed and looked forward to an evening drink when the wardroom bar opened at six o'clock. Even at sea, in wartime, even in the roughest weather, on all occasions except when actually in the striking area, a small group always gathered by the bar, as the grille rattled upwards and the bar steward stood looking expectantly at his most faithful customers. A few wore whites, most khakis, with some flying overalls. It was a pleasant time to relax and chat, to sum up the day. It was, as Skipper knew, a custom dating from the spacious, civilised days of the pre-war Navy.

The first thing Skipper saw when he entered the anteroom was the grin which split Herman's bearded and normally gloomy visage from ear to ear. Skipper had never seen him grin like that before, indeed he could not remember ever seeing

Herman grin before. Skipper could not help noticing the contrast between Herman's tatty khakis and his tired face, his eyes staring cagily from under his great bushy brows, like a large, timid circus animal terrified of having to learn any more new tricks, and this smooth, blond newcomer with his sharply pressed white shirt and shorts which, by some miracle, he must have brought with him somewhere in his Corsair.

Skipper was going to sign a chit for his drink, but the bar steward shook his head and nodded at Herman. 'Lieutenant Commander Goring's RPC, sir,' he said.

'My RPC,' said Herman. 'My only chance. I'm off first thing in the morning, God willing. Come and meet my relief, Skipper.' At the very word 'relief', that broad smile spread over Herman's face again.

'*Salaam*, Skipper,' said Herman's relief, shaking hands. His name was Gordon, and Skipper at once mentally dubbed him Flash, and certainly the name suited him. Skipper had never heard of him before and knew nothing about him, but he had seen from the joining signal in the log that the man had a DSC, so he must have been somewhere. Skipper was all prepared to welcome the new man with conversation, to talk to him, as from one Corsair Squadron CO to another, when he saw to his astonishment that Flash Gordon had already turned away and was looking elsewhere. Skipper was utterly taken aback. He and this man would be working together in the future. Surely the newcomer wanted some advance knowledge of what to do and what to avoid? Skipper's tips could be, literally, life-savers. But even when Herman, never noted for his outgoingness, tried to give his relief some cautious and hard-won advice on leading a squadron over the Sakishima Gunto, Skipper noticed that Flash Gordon laughed him away, as though determined not to listen to anything unpleasant. Skipper could see the pilots of Herman's squadron, when a few of them came in and were introduced, looking covertly at each other in dismay. Had they, he imagined them wondering, exchanged King Log for another kind of King Log?

Skipper had new members of his own to meet, the two replacement pilots who had flown on that afternoon. They were, Skipper could see, extremely young; they could neither of them be much more than twenty, fresh out of Operational Training Unit, brilliant fighter pilots already in their own estimation, itching to show the rest of the squadron how to kick the tyre, light the fire and smash off, as the saying went. They were almost stereotypes of what new aircrews should be: one of them was tall, the other short; one dark, the other fair; one shy and rather diffident, the other cocky and self-assured. This was their first operational wardroom, their first operational squadron. Like everybody else, they were anxious to do well, scared of doing badly, just like Skipper himself in 1942. They might do well. They might not be here tomorrow. Aircrew in wartime had the most transitory existence of all. Like mayflies, they came and vanished. *Youth's a stuff will not endure*, and youthful pilots sometimes did not endure long enough even to be given a mess number. This was the main reason why aircrew took so little part in the organisation of wardroom life. The ship's officers said it was because all aircrew were too thick or too ignorant or too lazy to lend a hand. But Skipper knew this was largely unjust. The trouble was that a pilot probably would not be still on board when the event, or the audit, or whatever it was, took place.

'You both up to date in everything?' Skipper asked them. He did not mean inoculations or vaccinations, or even news from home, as they both realised. He meant, were they in full flying practice?

'Yes, sir,' said the cocky one, who was Richard Fenton. 'We did CAPs over the tankers and the rest of them most days. And we did a weapon training course at Nowra before we set off. So we're pretty well up to date, sir.'

Richard Trumble had hardly said a word. Something familiar in his face stirred in Skipper's memory.

'I remember a Trumble when I was at Harrow...'

'My elder bro, sir.'

'How is he? I used to know him quite well.'

'He's in Burma, sir, with the Tank Corps. He's a major now.'

'Have you seen him recently?'

'Not for years, sir. Not since he joined up, in 1940.'

'Ah well, it won't be long now,' Skipper said, without believing it himself. *'Forty years, forty years on,'* everybody used to sing, as though they believed it. That was just about how long the war was going to last, at this rate.

'Yes, sir, I hope so, sir,' said Trumble.

'Were you at Harrow when I was there?'

'Oh, yes, sir. I was there your last year, sir, when you were Captain of the Eleven.'

'I'm afraid I don't remember you.'

'Oh, no, sir, of course you wouldn't.'

'But I recognised you vaguely just now, because you look a little like your brother.'

'Thank you, sir.'

They ate supper, of some kind of soup with bits in it, thin toast, omelettes made of powdered egg with mashed powdered potato, and a pudding of stewed prunes and orange segments from a tin. Nobody dressed formally at sea, and the Commander, as President of the Mess, only insisted on one rule: no bare torsos in the mess at any time. The warning was really necessary, as Skipper well knew. Some of the wilder aircrew loved to be deliberately eccentric in their dress at every chance they got, hoping thereby to shock and outrage their older, staider, straight-striped messmates. They were quite capable of coming into the wardroom in swimming trunks.

With Flash Gordon's astonishing jocularity and Herman's equally uncharacteristic good humour it was an eerie meal, and Skipper was glad when he had finished. It was strange to think of Herman going home now. Home for Herman. Homes for Hermans. Homes fit for Hermans to live in. Were there such things?

Climbing the ladder towards the Air Operations Room after supper, Skipper found himself humming that song again. *'Forty years on, when afar and asunder ...'* Here they had a different song, to the tune of 'Lili Marlene' — all songs these days were to the tune of 'Lili Marlene' — which went something like *'Back to Ishigaki, Back to Ishigoo, Back to Ishigaki, those sods will wait for you.'* It was a daft song, and dafter words. The squadron ratings sometimes made up more words, but mostly it was *Ishigaki, Ishigoo...*

In the AOR, Skipper settled down to look at the latest photographs, read the latest signals and intelligence summaries and study the squadron's combat reports. Skipper always insisted that every man of his squadron write out a report after every operational sortie. The boys hated it, and tried to avoid or skimp it, but Skipper kept them up to the mark. Other people's reports could be vitally informative. A point here, a comment there, a hint hidden between the sparse and laconic lines, might be the difference between flak and no flak. It was from studying lots of such reports that Skipper himself had deduced the presence of an extra gun battery on the northern perimeter of Ishigaki which nobody had picked up from the photographs, or traced back from its shell bursts. Out here, a detail like that could mean living or dying.

Skipper had expected to see Flash Gordon there. The man, after all, would probably be leading one of the first RAMRODS tomorrow morning. But somebody in his squadron said Flash Gordon was still in the wardroom. The pilots standing around looked at each other.

Skipper hoped it might be something different for his boys, but it was not. It was Ishigaki again. He could feel the tension in Geoffrey and one or two others standing beside the noticeboard. There was no doubt about it. His squadron most emphatically did not like Ishigaki and, if he did not watch out, they would be getting a phobia about it.

Wings came in and saw Skipper. 'Ready for Ishigaki again, Skipper?'

What a question. Supposing one said, *No, not ready*? Skipper knew Wings was watching him very closely. 'Quite ready, sir, although I hoped … I hoped we might ease off that this time sir, with two new boys…'

It was not the thing to say, or the way to say it, and Wings made the obvious and crushing reply. 'The other lot have a new CO. Can't get much newer than that, can they?'

'No, sir.'

'Anybody *seen* Lieutenant Commander Gordon?'

'I think he's still down in the wardroom, sir.'

'Well…' Wings looked perplexed. 'I suppose he'll be up here later, will he?'

Nobody could answer that, and Wings walked somewhat uncertainly out of the office. Skipper meanwhile sat down to complete the form required after every aircraft crash, and necessary now after his barrier entry that day. Admiralty official form number A25, it was called. It was not a complicated form, but it was tedious, and Skipper wished he had a pound for every one he had filled in for himself and had assisted others to fill in. Chief Air Rigger Petre was the expert on them. He was the only man who really knew how to fill in Admiralty forms. How many had he completed, and then got the officers concerned to sign? And how many of those — forms, aircraft and men — were all at the bottom of the sea by now?

Before turning in, Skipper called at a few of his squadron's cabins. It was a pre-strike ritual he had fallen into the habit of doing. The boys liked it. It gave them reassurance, and it gave Skipper himself the chance to gauge their feelings. Most of them were reading, or writing letters, or just lying on their bunks staring at the deckhead. They were in general a grave lot. Aircrew had this reputation for boisterousness, and certainly they could celebrate when they put their minds to it. But for most of the time they were a sober, quiet, hard-working and conscientious crowd of young men.

Skipper called on Michael last. He was lying on his bunk, with all the lights out except the dim police light in the corner. There was a smell of tobacco, although Michael himself did not smoke. He did not even turn his head when Skipper knocked and stepped in.

Skipper remembered that this would be Michael's bad time. Michael was as brave as a lion, the bravest man he had ever met. But that meant that he was more afraid than anyone else.

'Is it bad this time, Mike?'

'It gets worse every time, Skipper. I don't mind it while I'm doing it, but it's lying here thinking about it while we're steaming up closer and closer to it. I sometimes imagine myself flying off the front end of the flight deck and falling straight down into a damn great pit.'

Skipper nodded. That was when a pilot's life began, past the end of the flight deck. Once past that edge, you had to be a pilot. Cross that line and you were on your own.

'Do you think we're going to survive, Skipper?'

'Now, look, Mike, you know that's not the kind of talk that...'

'I don't. I've written myself off. I never expected to get this far. Seeing Herman in the mess today, all fat, dumb and happy, it came back to me. He's home. He's made it.'

'Do you want me to put you on Jack patrols?'

'Don't joke, Skipper. For one thing, Wings would never let you.'

'Why not?'

'He hates my guts. He hates your guts. He hates *all* our guts.'

'I don't believe it!'

'I won't argue with you, Skipper. What do you make of Herman's relief?'

'I don't know. What do *you* think?'

'I think he's solid with fright. He's so scared he can't think or say anything straight. He's laughing to stop himself screaming. Coming, here to a strange ship, strange squadron, to a war he knows is a killer, he's shitting himself with fright. He doesn't want Herman or you to tell him anything about it because he knows if you tell him what's in wait for him he'll never make it to his aircraft tomorrow. And I know just how he feels.'

'Perhaps that's a good thing, Mike. Perhaps it would be a bad sign if you weren't nervous before strike days.'

'Nervous? Skipper, you *are* in a droll mood tonight. *Nervous?* I'm scared sick, and I don't mind admitting it to you. Sometimes I feel that everything I am most afraid of in life is waiting out there for me the moment I get off that front edge.

By the way, did Geoff tell you he found Ronnie Bell's Ovaltiney badge? It had slipped down behind his bunk.'

'No, he didn't. So?'

'So, he didn't have his lucky charm with him when he got chopped.'

'Ah, I see what you mean.'

'Omens, omens, Skipper.'

At dawn, it was what Michael called 'Monday morning weather', raining slightly, with the ships of the task force mostly hidden from each other in mist and drizzle. There was still some way to go to the striking area, and when the weather cleared Skipper took the chance to try out the new boys. It was an exhilarating occasion. It was always exhilarating to find new talent, and there was no question the two new Richards were good. Richard Fenton, the cocky one, was especially good. Skipper threw his Corsair around the sky and was pleased to see them both keeping station on him. After the tightest turn, Fenton was still there to starboard, close, horrifyingly close. There was no need to tell *him* to go low. When Skipper got down low on the sea, lower and lower until that familiar tingling, took over like a hot enema, he found Trumble inches above him and Fenton inches below, flying straight as a level edge.

Back on board, Skipper waited beside the island door for the two of them to catch up. Their landings had been as competent as anyone's in the squadron. Fenton was sweating with excitement and exertion, his hair plastered down as though he had been swimming.

'Was that all right, Skipper? Were we OK?'

'You know it was damned good, so don't fish for compliments. Yes, it was, it was bloody good. You'll survive the war, lad.'

That, as all the squadron knew, was Skipper's highest compliment. *You'll survive the war, lad.* Skipper had no greater praise.

CHAPTER THREE

Herman was actually sitting in the back seat of an Avenger, still grinning, waiting to be flown off, when the news about Flash Gordon was received on board. Herman would be flown off to the fleet train, thence to Leyte, or maybe even straight on to Manus. From there the RAAF would fly him to Australia and then he would take a ship home to the United Kingdom. The trip was not fixed, of course. No trip ever was in wartime. It would depend upon the contingencies of the war and the exigencies of the Service and it would certainly take weeks, perhaps even months. But Herman was quite content to leave it to chance. His smile lit up the whole back cockpit. They could see it from the island.

It was a measure of the ship's concern to get Herman away as quickly as he wanted that he was sitting in the Avenger at all, for it was *Miss Britannia*'s turn to mount the task force's major RAMROD strafing effort against the airfields and it was going to be a heavy day's flying. Skipper had already led one RAMROD over Ishigaki and was standing on the bridge, reporting to the Captain, when Wings came through from Flyco with the news.

Quite suddenly, one of Flash Gordon's flight of four Corsairs had come up on the R/T to report a disaster. It was difficult to get the details from the shocked pilot, but it seemed that Flash and his starboard wingman had gone down over Miyako, and a third Corsair, badly damaged, had ditched offshore. The only survivor, a lad called Godfrey Burns, was still orbiting over the ditching spot, calling for help, and ignoring all rules of R/T procedure. He was repeating over and over again that he had not seen anybody get out of the Corsair. Stanley had refrained from pressing too hard for information because everybody for miles around with ears to hear could tell from the voice that the boy was almost hysterical. The ship wanted him at least back alive. But, from hearing Burns' disjointed commentary, and reports from the other RAMRODS over the islands, it was clear that Herman's squadron had suffered a catastrophe.

Wings jerked a thumb over his shoulder at the flight deck. 'All right to get Goring back, sir?'

'Oh, *no!*' Skipper's protest burst from him before he could stop himself. Instinctively, without time to think, or remember that the Captain was sitting just beside him, Skipper knew that he must intervene to stop an act of gross cruelty. 'You couldn't do that!'

'Why not?' Wings turned, angry and puzzled, to stare at him.

Skipper stared back, trying, *willing* the man to see the truth, without having to have it put into bald words. *Herman's over the hill, can't you see that? He's finished, he's had it, he's a goner. He's a dead man, he's no use to us.*

'Why ever not? All we've got to do is make a broadcast. The Avenger's still there, spotted aft...'

All we've got to do is make a broadcast? All you've got to do is kill a man...

'Yes, I know *that,* sir...' Skipper was sorry he had emphasised the word in such a way the moment he did it, but he plunged on. 'But you can't bring Herman back, sir. He's finished his tour.' *How can one actually say it? Herman is all washed up.* 'It's only fair, sir.'

'*Fair!*' Wings snorted scornfully. 'I'm not interested in being *fair.* All I know is he's a Corsair Squadron CO and he's on board, and it's on board we need a Corsair Squadron CO right now.' Wings looked past Skipper, at the Captain. 'Shall I get him back, sir?'

The Captain nodded at Skipper. 'I'm interested to hear what you have to say. You think we should let Herman go?'

'I *do,* sir, I really do. I don't mean to be insubordinate or question anybody's judgment, but really, sir, Herman's had his time. He's been relieved, he's on his way, and if you bring him back now and make him fly again, over Ishigaki…' Skipper could not find any words to describe what he meant and perhaps it was better for his argument that he could not, for his silence was more eloquent than anything he could have said.

'All right,' said the Captain. 'Let the Avenger go. Who's the Senior P of that squadron?'

'Douglas Mayhew, sir.'

'He's all right, isn't he?'

'He's very good, sir.'

'Well, he can take over until we whistle up another relief.' The Captain looked at Wings. 'OK with you, Brian?'

Wings grimaced and let out a resigned sigh. 'Yes, sir, quite OK with me.'

'Well then. Well done, Skipper, you've convinced us.'

'Thank you, sir.'

But, as Wings went past him on his way back to Flyco, Skipper knew from his face that this might be a Pyrrhic victory.

The Captain got off his chair and went, with everybody else, to the bridge windows to watch Herman fly off. The Avenger trundled past and into the air, with Herman still grinning and waving.

'Never seen Herman quite so happy,' said the Captain. He looked at Skipper. 'Thank you for your advice. I am quite sure we did the right thing.'

'Thank you, sir, I'm sure we did.'

Michael and his flight had found Godfrey Burns still orbiting, taken charge of him, and led him back to the fleet. When the Corsair came on, the story of the action was imprinted upon it. News of the disaster had already spread through the island and the sight of the Corsair confirmed everybody's worst fears. There was a very large hole in the starboard side of the fuselage, behind the engine. The starboard wingtip was a jagged edge, as though somebody had roughly amputated the last two feet. The tail-fin and both elevators had several ominous pockmarks punched in them. The lad had done extremely well to bring it back at all and make such a decent landing. The Corsair taxied forward, without folding its wings, and stopped in the deck park. There was a pause but the pilot did not get out. The doctor and the flight deck first-aid party had already gathered round and the rumour came back that Burns had fainted. Oil or hydraulic fluid, or petrol, or something, dripped from Burns' Corsair, lying on the flight deck like symbolic blood pools. When they reached him and pulled him out, the word was that he had a bullet or a piece of shrapnel in his thigh. Each additional snippet of news, added to what was already known or suspected or rumoured caused fresh ripples of consternation in the island, all mounting on top of the general dread that Herman's squadron (everybody still thought of it as Herman's squadron) had received a stunning blow.

Willpower had kept Godfrey Burns flying back to the ship. Now, safely back, he was suffering from the reaction, sliding into shock and obviously in great pain. Nevertheless, he had to be properly debriefed. It was essential, for the survivors to go on surviving, to know what had happened over Miyako that morning. All those flying on later RAMRODS had to know what hit Flash Gordon's flight. So they brought the stretcher into the briefing room, laid it on the table and propped Burns up with lifebelts and cushions so that everybody could see him. The briefing room was packed, with more men pressing in from the passageway and some standing outside, on tiptoe to see and straining to hear. While the rest of the returning RAMROD flew on outside, and the island shook and rattled with the sound of engines passing, Ops slowly, gently, but relentlessly, extracted the story of Burns' flight.

It had been, from all aspects, a complete balls-up from the very start. Flash Gordon had taken off first, as flight leader, and at once set off for the target as though he could not wait to immolate himself upon the guns, so precipitately indeed that the rest of flight who took off after him had difficulty in catching him up. Skipper himself had been airborne at the time and had heard Stanley admonishing Flash Gordon in that curious half-jargon, half-code of the fighter direction officer. 'Mandarin Leader, this is *Miss Britannia*, you're high-stepping,' Skipper heard Stanley say. 'Slow, slow, quick-quick-slow, swing it and swing it...' It meant that Gordon should slow down and weave from side to side, to let his section catch up. In the mist and overcast of that early morning, when it was harder than usual to form up correctly, the flight had had to look for their leader and when they eventually found him they had the psychological disadvantage of having formed up in haste, breathless and dishevelled, like runners who had lost their way and had to catch up. Instead of a compact welded weapon system, Flash Gordon's flight were just four aircraft flying somewhere near each other. And they had been flying together for the first time. Flash Gordon had not taken the chance that morning, as Skipper had done, and as Henry Darling had done, to try out his new flying colleagues alongside him.

They had flown in towards the target low, but not nearly low enough, at about fifteen hundred feet, which was high enough for them to be detected but too low for them to see anything. Then Flash Gordon had taken them up to 4,000 feet and had actually made one slow, leisurely circuit of the airstrip whilst he had a look at it. The Japanese gunners, evidently recognising a greenhorn when they saw one, held their fire, and Flash Gordon had decided the airfield was virtually undefended. In short, they had done everything wrong they could have done wrong. Burns' listeners were outraged as well as appalled.

'Didn't you *say* anything? You've been over Miyako several times.'

'Yes, I have.' Burns' voice was weak, more from the accusation than from his injuries. 'But I couldn't say anything.'

'Why ever not?'

'Well sir, I *couldn't*. He was the CO, sir, the *CO…*'

So, thought Skipper listening, naval discipline had led up into the valley of death — and, for this man, only just out of it.

'Go on. What did the CO do then?'

There was a subsidiary runway which crossed the main runway at an acute angle, and led directly like a pointing arrow to the hangars, buildings and other likely targets. At the end of this runway were two low hills, not much more than grassy knolls, one on either side of the entrance to the runway, like the pillars of a gate. It was an obvious approach to the airfield, so obvious indeed that the Japanese had stacked guns to defend it. Herman, Skipper and the other Squadron COs had abandoned this way in very early on, as being so dangerous as to be suicidal. But Flash Gordon had seen the hills and the runway and the target buildings, on a promising approach line, and taken his flight straight down the throats of the gunners.

'Didn't you *say* anything, even *then*?'

'*Drop it.* Go on, Godfrey.'

They had not even got down low on the deck, but had flown in at what Flash Gordon had thought quite low enough, about seventy-five feet. The gunners began to get hits an astonishingly long way out and Godfrey thought that even Flash had had second thoughts as they were in the middle of their approach, because he thought he began to say something, but he never completed it. The port inner wingman had not even reached the runway perimeter before he went down. Flash Gordon himself crossed the main runway, grazed the top of one building and his Corsair cartwheeled in flames into the field behind. The starboard wingman had reached the sea and ditched. Only Godfrey, on the outside of the port flank, returned. So, in one sortie, Herman's old squadron had lost two pilots missing, almost certainly killed, a third pilot missing believed dead or drowned, and a fourth seriously injured. Four pilots and their aircraft — a quarter of the squadron's fighting strength. It had been an unmitigated disaster.

There was time for coffee before the next sortie. As he drank his, Skipper reflected on the story of Flash Gordon's first, last and only RAMROD. Talk about *Struwwelpeter*. This one was more like Elizabethan tragedy. Yet, curiously, there were few lessons to be learned from it. Only a madman would have chosen that approach.

Flash Gordon's whole behaviour had been very strange, from the moment he came on board. Skipper wondered whether they had, in fact, been told all they should have been told about Gordon's operational background. There had been something feverishly neurotic about him. It would be ironic if it turned out that Herman had been relieved by another CO who had lost his bottle even more comprehensively than Herman himself. In the meantime, there was another sortie to be flown.

Miss Britannia had a large intelligence department, with several officers, radio operators and coders, who provided general intelligence of enemy intentions and dispositions. The sources for most of it were obvious, from photographs, debriefings, and studies of strike statistics, but some of it was too often accurate to be coincidence or intelligent guesswork and Skipper suspected a deeper source, possibly even a break-in on Japanese codes. But it was not his business to enquire. That morning, there was fresher and hotter intelligence from another source on board, the 'Y' Party. They were a pale-faced but devoted band who inhabited a stuffy little hutch of an office at the end of the corridor behind the Air Direction Office, full of radio receivers and tape recorders, where they lived an unhealthy, bespectacled, owlish existence. They had all passed a joint services course in spoken Japanese and kept watches twenty-four hours about on their radios, listening out for the faintest whisper on the Japanese networks. The Japanese seemed unconcerned or unaware of this eavesdropping and were remarkably indiscreet, often speaking in plain language and giving valuable information of intentions in clear. Now, the 'Y' Party were reporting very much increased radio traffic, much of it from Formosa. It was all in code, which was itself a pointer of its importance, but the patterns and transmission times of the broadcasts suggested, almost certainly, another batch of aircraft reinforcements staging through the Sakishima Gunto.

After briefing, Skipper found Richard Fenton in the passageway outside the Aircraft Control Room leading out into the flight deck. He was jogging up and down on his toes, like a runner before a race. It was strange how these athletic images kept on repeating themselves. This would be Richard Fenton's first sortie over Japanese territory. The other Richard was also making his debut, in Michael's flight.

'Nervous?'

The boy was obviously reluctant to admit such a thing. 'Well, yes, sir.'

'Good show. If you weren't nervous there would be something wrong. You want lots of nerves, bags of adrenalin. You've got to be absolutely on top line. You saw this morning what happens when you make mistakes.'

'Yes, sir.'

'Remember, keep close in, wingtip to wingtip. Whither thou goest, I goest, and vice versa.'

'Yes, sir.'

'OK, let's go.'

Skipper took off in thick mist and a low overcast down to about five hundred feet. He climbed, blind, through the cloud until it thinned at above five thousand. The high sky overhead was bright and blue. Skipper half-rolled, looked downwards and saw the blur of Richard Fenton's Corsair in the murk. Its plan silhouette rapidly solidified and in a moment the boy was tight in beside him. Geoffrey and Rodney soon fell in on their stations on the port side. Richard Fenton being a new boy, Skipper kept close to him on the starboard wing.

It was no weather for flat-arsing, so Skipper decided on the high approach, at 35,000 on oxygen. From that height, Ishigaki came up again like a black stain on the indigo rim of the horizon. But this time their target was Iriomote Shima, a large-ish island some miles to the west of Ishigaki. It had a little-used airstrip in the southern, flatter half of the island. Skipper had never visited it before, but from the intelligence maps and briefing he expected it to be by the coast, with its guns pointing out to sea. For this reason, Skipper would have liked to have attacked from the north, but Iriomote was comparatively hilly for the Sakishimas, and it was always risky and unwise to attack downhill. Hills tended to push an aircraft upwards just when they should be getting down low. That was why Skipper never attacked the Ishigaki airfields from the north. This one would have to be a single run, fast and low, right up out of the sea, and up and out over the hills.

Visibility below was never very good from a Corsair, a fact of life the air direction officers had to bear in mind when they gave a Corsair pilot a vector to fly towards a bandit. A Corsair had to be vectored in from below, for the best chance of the pilot seeing his target. Put him in above, and he might well overfly without seeing it.

Skipper had not actually located the Iriomote airstrip through his binoculars when he saw the tiny, sparkling flashes, like spurts of sunlight reflecting off two or three hand-held mirrors and, now that he knew where to look, he caught the faintest suspicion of a dust haze behind them. He knew what those meant. He had seen them before in Sumatra. They were fighters, taking off and climbing.

They must have slipped in from Formosa in the last two hours — just as the 'Y' Party had suspected — refuelled, and were now ready to go again. An American task force had only stopped pounding this airstrip the night before, yet here were the Japanese operating fighters from it already. It truly was an endless war. It would have been far better to have caught those fighters still on the ground, but Skipper's RAMROD was just too late. Only minutes too late, but in this trade minutes were traded for lives.

Now that they had taken off, there were still a few moments left to decide what to do. The first thing, at any rate, was obvious.

'*Miss Britannia, Miss Britannia*, this is Mongoose Leader … Bandits three off, Juggins Island, gaining.' They were probably still too low to be picked up by the ship's radar sets, and this would give Stanley a minute or two of extra warning.

Far below, Skipper could actually see them now, three pale green moths in very good formation, moving out over the dark blue and white wrinkled sea. They looked as though they were flying very slowly, but this was a trick of the sight angle from this height. It meant they were climbing steeply, as their foreshortened silhouettes showed. The colour of their wings changed and deepened as they altered course. Skipper fancied he could even pick out the red 'meatballs' on their wings. It was astounding from how far away the colour red could be seen. On their way out east, they had been ordered to paint out everything red on their aircraft, even simple warning notices such as HANDLE: PULL HERE. Out here, anything red meant enemy.

'Mongoose Leader, this is *Miss Britannia*…' In the crackling static, there was just the slightest trace of excitement in Stanley's voice. 'Roger your bandits. Tracking now … Bearing from you two-nine-fife, I say again *two-nine-fifer*… Angels five…'

Stanley now had his enemy on his screens and Skipper heard him begin to summon up his forces, calling in Michael's flight from the east and two more flights from *Madame Fifi*. Skipper heard Roger Weston acknowledging and then sighted the glint of wings a few hundred feet below him. There, below and some miles to the east, were eight more Corsairs. The Japanese were still climbing, springing up like partridges into a poacher's net spread out for them above.

Although he could see his quarry plainly now, with no mistake about the red meatballs, Skipper was reluctant to lose any of his precious height until he had a firm attacking vector from Stanley. He knew he would probably get only one firing pass. In nearly five years of war and over three years of operational flying, these were only the second airborne enemy Skipper had ever seen. He had missed the first ones over Sumatra. He was not going to make the same errors this time.

The Japanese were flying eastwards now, in a tight vic of three, and the range had come down to six miles.

'Versailles Leader, your vector is three-two-fife, I say again three-two-*fifer*, angels twenty, two zero…'

'Baffin Leader, your vector…'

'Snapdragon Leader, your vector…'

The clipped radio messages gave a vivid mental picture of Stanley mustering his men, allocating them heights and courses, stacking them in layers above their enemy, ready to smother them.

Now was the moment. 'Mongoose, Mongoose, this is Mongoose Leader, Tally-ho!'

In silent thought, he had often tried to assess his emotions when he was doing this. But now, as before, his only feeling was determination to kill them. Making the gun switches as the cockpit tipped over and they began to drop through the sky, it was all as easy as rubbing silk.

The Corsairs lost height so rapidly that the Japanese aircraft bounced up into close view with disconcerting suddenness. They were all three Oscars, Nakajima army fighters, actually painted blue, not green, with the great blobs of red shining as though in luminous paint. They were much more graceful than the identification pictures, so fragile, thin-winged, like the balsa-wood models schoolboys made. They each had perky little tailplanes, and teardrop cockpit canopies, with one solid round head inside them.

The notches were sliding by on the gunsight. It was a stern attack, quarter deflection shot, the range closing very quickly. The port-hand Oscar flicked upwards and vanished, but before the other two could do the same the Corsairs were upon them. The delicious drumming, through his thumb on the button, seemed to last for hours but it could only have been for a few seconds. Skipper could see no tracer, but there was no doubt about the hits. There was an explosion, similar to flak, and both Oscars disappeared. Skipper thought he saw small pieces of debris flying past him out of the corner of his right eye.

It was just as they had imagined it, just as they had practised it so many times. This was the ultimate. There was nothing else like it in the world. They had smashed those two Oscars out of the sky. Skipper added his own howl of joy to the great roaring already dinning into his ears.

His flight were still formatting tightly on him. Fenton was so close a man could have stepped over from one wingtip to the other. That, of course, was why the Oscars had disintegrated. Four Corsairs, three point-five Browning machine guns in each wing, meant twenty-four guns driving a pulsing steel shaft through the Oscars. They always said that Japanese aircraft were made up out of kits anyway.

A plume of thin smoke was going down some miles to the west. That must be the third Oscar. Skipper opened his mouth to comment and became aware of the bedlam on the radio. Everybody was shouting, yelling, jabbering. It was like the bad old days over Sumatra, when any incident was the signal for complete radio chaos, which could have been dangerous.

Several times the strike and escort leaders were unable to make themselves heard. Since then, everybody had made an effort over R/T discipline. But now they were like a lot of new boys again. Still, with three out of three Oscars splashed, perhaps it was excusable. These were the task force's first kills over the Sakishima Gunto.

As the uproar ebbed away, Skipper could hear Stanley asking for reports.

'*Miss Britannia*, *Miss Britannia*, this is Mongoose Leader. Claim two Oboe Oscars splashed…'

'This is *Miss Britannia* … radar confirms … Congratulations … *Big* splash!'

'This is Mongoose Leader. Intend resume RAMROD on Juggins Island.' This was risky, as Skipper knew, because the activity in the sky would have alerted every Japanese between here and Formosa, but combat exhilaration made him feel immortal. Besides, he was curious to see Iriomote from a sightseer's point of view.

Once more they came in, flat out, across the sea. Once more Skipper noticed how comforting it was, like an extra layer of protection, to have a wingman who kept close in, without having to be urged all the time. Fenton was a lucky lad. His first operational sortie, and he'd shot down an Oscar with his Squadron CO. *There* was a lucky little lad indeed.

It was a makeshift airstrip with fewer facilities than any of the others on the islands: one runway, some buildings at the seaward end, and some trenches dug in the ground across the front. There were some guns, because a few puffs of smoke appeared as the Corsairs hurtled over the beach.

Halfway down the runway, there was what looked like a farm wagon, but the hoses gave it away. There was actually a donkey or a small mule in the shafts. A horse-drawn Japanese petrol bowser! Fenton opened fire first, killing the donkey, before firing at the bowser which blew up in a pall of flame. *Bye bye, Dobbin.* It was a bloody shame, but anything that helped the Japanese, or had any connection with them, had to be destroyed.

Not many Japanese aircrew got away alive after being shot down. There were no official instructions, no official approval or disapproval, it was never mentioned at briefings, nobody ever discussed it, but everybody knew, and everybody was ready. Skipper, like all the others, would not hesitate to machine-gun a Japanese pilot — in a dinghy, on the ground, or dangling on the end of a parachute. The Marquess of Queensberry might not have approved, but the Marquess of Queensberry had never had to fight the Japanese.

Skipper would have liked another run, but those Oscars and the first strafing run must have used much of their ammunition, and the Iriomote gunners had been so bad they could only improve. There was always a line to be drawn between valour and discretion.

'Mongoose, Mongoose, this is Mongoose Leader ... Home, James, and don't spare the 'orses.'

Chief Air Rigger Petre was ready on deck with a great smile and a hard handshake. Skipper had never known him so jovial. It was rather like seeing the oracle at Delphi grinning. Clearly dead Japanese tickled him. Only deaths, disasters and ditchings amused Chief Air Rigger Petre.

'Of course, they're not confirmed yet, you know, Chief.'

'From what I hear, sir, those Japs are drawing their tots with their ancestors now, sir.'

It was marvellous how Petre heard all about these things, even out here on the flight deck. Skipper had no doubt that

Chief Air Rigger Petre could now write up the combat report as accurately as if he had been there.

He stood on the flight deck and took a deep breath. The thick overcast had completely disappeared. It was now a fine, inevitable Pacific day of bright sunshine, with a row of small woolly white clouds to the east, and a brisk flight-deck wind that pushed Skipper along as he began to walk aft to the island. It really was holiday weather. People paid for this in peacetime.

Richard Fenton was just climbing down out of the next Corsair aft. He, too, was beaming, his eyes shining.

'Enjoy yourself?'

'Oh, yes, sir!'

'Proper little killer, aren't you?'

'I suppose so, sir.' The boy looked slightly abashed. 'It was the greatest feeling in the world, sir.'

'Bar one. Look, you've been on an operational sortie with me. You've been shot at alongside me. There's no need to call me sir. Skipper.'

'Aye, aye, Skipper.' Fenton did not hesitate. As to the manner born. 'I was going to ask you about it anyway, Skipper.'

'Were you indeed?' Skipper turned away to welcome Geoffrey and Rodney. They walked aft, as a happy knot, as a small band, one flight of Corsair pilots together, towards the island where they found the atmosphere was like a dressing room after the team have won the Cup. Men were passing to and fro, grinning and shaking hands and slapping each other on the back, in a hubbub of conversation which was like the R/T over Iriomote all over again. Part of the joy was pure, part relief. It was good to have something to shout about, after Flash Gordon.

Skipper saw Michael standing in the ACR doorway. He went up and hugged him. 'Was it you who got that other Oscar?'

'Yep. We sure dropped that ornery son of a gun.' The Wild West accent reminded Skipper, as it was meant to do, of a run ashore in Durban when they had seen *Destry Rides Again.*

Skipper laughed delightedly. 'And how did your new boy go?'

'Richard Trumble? Ah, so-so.'

Skipper's smile faded. 'So-so? No better than that?'

'Put it this way. I never really noticed him. He was always there or thereabouts. But how about your little ... *assassin?*'

'You get that feeling about him too, do you?'

'I'll say. It's written all over his shining new Sunday-school face. That boy's a natural born killer. A proper little Billy the Kid. That sort would murder his grandmother for the thrill of it. Sometimes I wonder if the Japs really know the sort of thing they're up against, with characters like that. In the long run, they're far more deadly than these suicide laddies. Incidentally, there is a rumour that our Oscars were suiciders, or intended suiciders.'

'How could they be?'

'For a start, they all had what looked to me like 500-pound bombs slung underneath them, and at that height and that course they were heading east looking for trouble. Loaded for bear, as they say.'

'Did ours have bombs underneath them?'

'Yes, saw them myself. Didn't you notice? That's why they blew up like that, right in your faces.'

Skipper did not comment, but mentally he cursed himself for his carelessness. He had not noticed their bombs. That sort of omission could be fatal. Admittedly, they had come down from above and the bombs had been slung below. All the same, that was a serious lapse. Skipper had believed that the sheer weight of fire power had destroyed those Oscars, whereas it was far more likely that a lucky round had touched off one of the bombs and the detonation had blown both aircraft to pieces. However, the lesson had been learned now. Skipper would not overestimate the hitting powers of his machine guns again.

'Talking of which, Skipper, Ops wants to see us all right now. Apparently there's been another of those semi-religious pep talks over Japanese radio from Tokyo, calling on all the Sons of Heaven to do their bit wherever they may be. And there's some signals about a Japanese battlewagon coming south.'

'Oh, Lord.' Michael was as good as Chief Air Rigger Petre at getting information. It was astounding how close they had their ears to the deck. 'This looks as if it's going to be a long, long, day.'

'Oh, there's something else. Herman's mob have lost another one, over Ishigaki.'

'Who was it?'

'Nosmo King.'

'The squadron funny man? God, they're really going through a bad patch.'

'Wings has taken them off RAMRODS and put them all on CAPs until they calm down a bit.'

Skipper ate a stand-up lunch in the ready room, of foul coffee from a kettle, and corned-dog sandwiches, and — a civilised touch — a glass of port from the bottle which Michael surprisingly produced from the squadron locker in the passageway outside the ready room. *Miss Britannia* had stopped flying for the time being and had turned to run downwind. With no cooling flow of air along the flight deck the island soon became stiflingly hot, and its compartments seemed to Skipper to be unusually full of bodies, rushing to and fro, in an overheated atmosphere of unceasing activity. This surely was like the view of hell in medieval literature: immense heat and noise, and unwearying and unnecessary activity, with everybody rushing round and round, for ever and ever. Skipper felt his midday headache coming on. He had flown two sorties already that day and would have at least two more before he could get to bed.

He had a few words with the other pilots of his squadron as they came and went in the ready room. He was reassured to find them in good heart. They all seemed to have done well. Perhaps the squadron needed a diet of blood. A little bit of bloody success bucked everybody up; they thrived on blood for supper. It might also be partly due to Fenton. The word had gone out that the squadron had a new boy who was all for it, a really good killing ground-strafer. At least it made a change from Herman's squadron's alarms and excursions. But it also served to put everybody, whether they liked it or not, on their mettle. Skipper decided he did not much like Fenton, and he was liking him less and less on further acquaintance. But, as he himself had said over and over again, he was not in the business of liking people or of having them like him. His business was to fly them against the Japanese, and at that Fenton was turning out to be something of a discovery.

As the minutes passed, Skipper became aware that the mood in the island was changing again. That first back-slapping exhilaration had gone as quickly as it had come, and the old familiar apprehension was back again. From the top priority 'flash' aircraft warning signal in the log, from snatches of conversation from the sets in the corner tuned to the fighter network, it was clear that some kind of climax was approaching. Not only the remnants of Herman's squadron, but everybody, was doing CAPs. For the first time, the task force was being thrown on the defensive. There was now no doubt that the Japanese were launching that great aerial offensive which intelligence had been hinting at in vague terms for over a week.

'It's called Kikusui,' Ops told a packed, sombre-mooded briefing room before the next sorties. 'We've established that that's what the Japanese code word for this offensive is. It means "floating chrysanthemum".'

Skipper moulded his lips in a silent whistle. Once again he marvelled at the Japanese capacity for finding beautiful and romantic names for deadly matters. Unlike the Germans, who gave their undertakings hard-bitten Teutonic names, or the British, who were quite likely to call a major offensive Operation Much-Binding-in-the-Marsh, the Japanese always used words for flowers, or winds, or sea states or mountains.

'But, as you can imagine, these aircraft may float down like chrysanthemums but they do *not* spread sweetness and light. It seems that the Japanese have several hundred, perhaps even near a thousand, serviceable front-line aircraft on Okinawa, and several thousand more in airfields in southern Kyushu. That is far more than we ever believed likely. We thought that Halsey's Third Fleet strikes earlier this year had washed out most of them. But we were wrong. They seem to be able to produce them out of caves and every nook and cranny. Since dawn this morning they have been making an effort to completely swamp the American CAPs and for a time they actually succeeded. We've just heard from the nearest American task group that at one point just after breakfast they had over two hundred Hellcats airborne and they weren't enough to cover all the bogeys they had on their screens. Their most westerly radar picket destroyer said that at the same time he had over sixty bogeys on his screen within twenty miles. That destroyer was later sunk, and they've lost two more since, and two of their carriers have been near-missed. They also report one suicider hit on an ammunition ship in their fleet repair anchorage in the Kerema Retto, south-west of Okinawa. When that one went up it took the two ships adjacent to it with it and the noise of the explosion was heard by ships thirty miles out to sea. One Marine unit in the north of Okinawa, that's over a hundred miles away, reported they could see the pall of smoke from their gun positions. So you can see, gentlemen, that something pretty big is brewing up, and the intelligence word is that we're next in line. We're going to cancel all RAMRODS and Avenger sorties for the rest of today and put the maximum muscle into CAPs.'

Ops turned towards his blackboard with its assortment of chalked symbols and letters. 'As you can see, we're going to put the emphasis in high CAPs, because they seem to be coming in at about 10,000 feet, some a bit higher, a few a bit lower, but 10,000 is about the mark. The standard of flying is not very high and, of course, we can expect it to get even lower. As the Yanks say, there is no such thing as an experienced kamikaze pilot…'

Ops waited for the buzz of laughter to run round the room and die away. 'The thing to watch for is what the Yanks call the Gestapo plane. These are normally two-engined fighters — Tonys or Nicks, or perhaps even a bomber, with a Jap version of a fighter direction officer sitting inside them. He looks out for likely targets and then directs his merry men on to them by radio. He's the man to get.'

As Skipper climbed back up into his Corsair he noticed at once the two brand-new bright-red 'Rising Sun' insignia pasted on the side below the cockpit, to denote his two fresh kills. Chief Air Rigger Petre had wasted no time. It was premature, but it was good for morale. Heaven knows what the sight of two flashes like that would do to Richard Fenton. After that, there would be no holding him.

They were high CAP at 35,000, which was in itself something of a compliment. For fighter CAPs, the higher the better. High CAP was better placed for interceptions and, statistically, always saw more action. They reached altitude in a steady haul up from the deck and at once began to roll and weave, roll and weave, looking out and looking round and looking down, and rolling and weaving. Up here, it was a high, almost stratospheric world of deep blue and purple air, far above the thin layer of white cloud at least 10,000 feet below. Up here, it was extraordinarily calm and beautiful. It was God-like at these heights, waiting high above the earth, waiting for some unwary transgressor to trespass into the forbidden space below. Fenton, close in to starboard, looked like a demon from a medieval manuscript, with his eyebrows arched above the black snout of his oxygen mask, and the earphones like the beginnings of horns.

Skipper had hardly settled his flight at altitude when Stanley came up on the air.

'Chinatown Leader, Chinatown Leader, this is *Miss Britannia*, bandit, one off, seven-five, seventy-five miles, closing, angels two-seven. Your vector, two-eight-seven, I say again two-eight-seven, get on with it, Skipper!'

'This is Chinatown Leader, roger … Going to call the cattle home…'

The four Corsairs swung round on the new course of two-eight-seven and opened up the taps towards their target, slowly losing height as they went. Stanley was nothing less than a genius. They saw their bandit, almost dead ahead and slightly above them, dead on the estimated time. It was a Big Betty bomber, painted a dun olive-green. As they swam up towards her on her starboard bow, ready for a beam attack, there was that brilliant red ball shining out from her side. She had a broad-based tailplane, like a shark's dorsal fin, and one thin fang of a front gun projecting ahead. She also had a tail gun, trailing back like a ready sting. As they closed in towards her, the dorsal turret above the fuselage trained in their direction.

'Tally-ho!' This would be one of those Gestapo planes.

The words had hardly left Skipper's lips when a great section of the Betty's fat underbelly seemed to fall away, as though she had suddenly dropped a huge silver bomb. The jettisoned portion slipped down and towards the approaching Corsairs, seeming to pass underneath them, so close that Skipper involuntarily flinched. As it flashed beneath him, Skipper realised that *this* was the weapon. The Betty was now harmless. It was actually a tiny aircraft, shaped like a stubby pencil, with a double tailplane and a surprisingly large central canopy. It was, in fact, a flying piloted bomb.

'Chinatown … Break starboard … *Go!*'

They wheeled and dropped away after their new target. It seemed oblivious of them, cruising serenely down ahead of them. When they finally settled in behind it, they seemed to be gaining. The range came down steadily and just as Skipper was about to fire, three intensely bright points of light glowed on their target's tailplane, and at once it seemed to leave them behind. The range opened rapidly. The four Corsairs were diving at full throttle, at near four hundred knots, but the little silver ship outpaced them. They could go no faster, whilst their target steadily drew away.

'Jesus Christ, what have we here?'

Skipper tried a long burst of machine-gun fire, putting tracers across the fugitive's wing. It was a long way out of killing range, but just occasionally the sight of tracer frightened or persuaded an inexperienced pilot to do something stupid. But their opponent's tail fire burned steadily, and still it left them behind. No piston-engined fighter in the world could catch that. It was clearer than ever that this was some form of piloted bomb, almost certainly rocket-powered. Fenton, too, tried a hopeful burst and Skipper fancied he might actually have caught the target with a few rounds, but the little aircraft diminished in size until it was no more than a black smudge, plunging downwards at tremendous speed towards the fleet.

The first duty now was to warn the ship. 'Bandit type unknown, possible course one-one-zero, estimated speed of approach six-zero-zero knots, I say again, *six-zero-zero* knots…'

'Chinatown Leader, this is *Miss Britannia*, roger your bandit. Six-zero-zero knots, roger…' Stanley's voice betrayed no disbelief, nor did he ask for a repeat of the message. Skipper might just as well have reported seven-tenths cloud at 10,000 feet, for all the reaction Stanley revealed. Skipper felt mildly disappointed.

When Skipper's flight had attained patrolling CAP height again, the Betty had long since gone. Obviously she had turned tail the moment she had dispatched her cargo. Half an hour later, Chinatown Flight were vectored out to another bandit, but it too had disappeared when they reached interception point. After five minutes, there was a suspicion of another radar contact but, once again, it vanished before any action could be taken. This sequence of false alarms, which had certainly started as solid contacts, with a constant stream of radio traffic, comments and instructions and interception data, gave a running picture of the Japanese probing against the fleet's defences, with every now and again a sudden purposeful dart, like that flying bomb which had escaped Skipper's flight.

As Skipper led his flight on to the deck, he noticed the flight deck and island unusually bare of goofers. A plague had swept the multitudes off the goofing positions, and when Skipper went in for debriefing he found out why. The flying bomb which had eluded his flight had also eluded all the other CAps, both high and low. Sheer speed had carried it past, making plots out of date before they could be established on it, outdistancing fighters before they could intercept it. Its extraordinary speed, which had added a new dimension to that form of attack, and the pilot's single-minded plunge towards the earth, had brought it through all the screens and on a direct hitting course for *Miss Britannia*. The Captain had put the ship through the most violent manoeuvres, throwing her vast bulk from side to side in a furious zigzag, but it had seemed that nothing could save the ship. But perhaps one of Fenton's hopeful rounds had found its mark, wounding the pilot or damaging his controls, or perhaps the pilot himself was raw and nervous. Whatever the reason, he had missed. But the terrifying living bomb had plunged into the sea and detonated, throwing a column of water hundreds of feet into the air in the ship's wake, only about a cable and a half astern. It was, as somebody said, a sight to put any goofer off his food for a week.

As usual, Ops had a word for it. 'Ohka,' he said. 'OHKA. It's the Japanese word for cherry blossom.'

Once again, Skipper raised his eyebrows. Yet *another* picturesque word for a deadly weapon.

'We've just heard,' Ops went on, 'that the Yanks have been near-missed by these things eleven times today...' Through the whistles and gasps, Ops said, 'But this is the only encouraging thing about it. They were *all* near-misses. Not one hit. It suggests that the things are too fast for their pilots to control them properly. They obviously have to aim them and once aimed there's very little the pilot seems to be able to do if the target shifts. From our own experience and from what we can gather from the Yanks, all these Ohkas seemed to line up on their targets from a long way out and once they are lined up they never shift targets. With what we have now, there does not seem to be much we can do about it once the Ohka is on its way. What we must try and do, therefore, is to nail the carriers — the mother aircraft, if you like — before they can launch their offspring. This means interceptions at further and further ranges, and CAPs will just have to get in fast, once they've been given the vector. Just to make the mother aircraft turn back is as good as shooting it down.'

Skipper and the rest left the briefing sceptical about their chances. Skipper was one of the very few who had actually seen one of the new weapons, and he did not hold out much chance of an interception once the living bomb took wing. Skipper could have glossed over it, been more optimistic and painted a less bleak picture. But he believed that only realists survived over the Sakishima Gunto. Like the Victorian schoolmaster, he had to be cruel to be kind.

Skipper hoped for another sight of an Ohka, but as it happened the last two CAPs of the day were uneventful. The Japanese, it seemed, had shot their bolts until the next morning. Nevertheless, when Skipper landed on after the last CAP, he was aware of the new, sombre mood of the ship. That bomb had been a shaker. Dozens of men had seen that tower of water rise up astern and everybody on board had felt the reverberations through the soles of their feet. One direct hit by one of those might sink the ship, despite the four inches of armour plate on the flight deck. In spite of all the Japanese successes early in the war and since — at sea, in the air and in the jungle — in spite of the aircrew losses over Sumatra and the sporadic Japanese air attacks then and afterwards, everybody had still subconsciously regarded the Japanese as inferiors. All, but especially the aircrew, had a kind of residual combat arrogance towards the Japanese. But that flying bomb had concentrated everybody's minds wonderfully. If the Japanese could get *that* close with *that* much explosive, then this war they had just joined out here in the east took on another perspective entirely.

At the end of the day, Skipper pushed through the blackout folds around the island door and stepped out on to the flight deck. It was his custom, whenever he could, to take the air, walk back aft to the starboard accessway and then down by the starboard side ladders to cabin and bed. It was all over for the day, the last flight, the last query, the last photographs and signals, the last argument with the ACR over aircraft availability, the last forms filled in, the last fuel returns studied, the last decisions made. Now for a glass of whisky in the wardroom and then bunk.

It was a pitch-dark night, no stars, no moon, no lights, but the sea was still consciously there all around, invisible but still in some curious way perceptible, darkling and shifting, as though a thousand million tiny lights were glowing deep in its depths. There were the shadows of other ships, in their night-cruising passage stations, clustered all around the four carriers who were the fighting core of the fleet. Skipper had to pick his way carefully in the dark. The flight deck was covered with obstructions, with arrester wires and the metal cowls which housed their sheaves, with uneven deck plates and all manner of miscellaneous gear and fittings, eyebolts, hooks and deck rings, obstacles of all kinds. He was concentrating so hard on where he was going that he almost bumped into somebody standing by himself looking out over the starboard side at the nearest carrier abeam. It was Douglas Mayhew, Herman's Senior P — and now, *faute de mieux,* Squadron CO.

'How is it, Douglas?'

'Oh, all right.' Douglas, Skipper knew, had acquitted himself very creditably that day. Nosmo King's death had been just one of those things, which might have happened to anybody on any day, and was in no way Douglas's fault. All the same, Douglas would have to take a very firm hold very quickly on that squadron or he would very soon have no pilots left fit to fly at all. It was in Skipper's squadron's interest, as well as Herman's, to stop the rot as quickly and completely as possible. Skipper sensed that this, in the dark, and after such a day, was one of the rare times when sympathy was right and proper.

'Look, Douglas, I'm very sorry indeed about today. I can guess what you must be feeling like.'

'Skipper, can you give me some advice?'

'I doubt it. What about?'

'About being a CO. I've just been landed with this and I'm all at sixes and sevens about it. What should I do?'

Skipper could not help being flattered. After all, although he was a Squadron COmmander of some experience, he was still only RNVR, and here he was being asked to comment upon leadership, one of the great mysteries of the straight RN.

'You want me to tell you. Well, you can't do anything much today or tomorrow, or even this week. It's going to take a little time.'

'If I last that long.'

'If you last that long.' Skipper remembered that Douglas was taking over in almost impossible circumstances. To go straight from Senior Pilot to CO in the same squadron was always difficult, so difficult that new COs were always appointed to fresh squadrons. But to do so after all the turmoil caused by Flash Gordon, and with everybody aware that the appointment was probably only temporary anyway, was almost a hopeless task. Perhaps, Skipper thought, it would have been better to have hauled Herman back. But then Skipper recalled Herman's face, and knew he had done the right thing.

'Well, what I suggest is that you pay special attention to giving every man his due. If somebody makes a cock of something, then jump up and down on him, *whoever* he is, in your largest hob-nailed boots and let everybody see that you're jumping up and down on him in your largest hob-nailed boots. Similarly, if somebody does something good, well then, you give him a red recommend and you let everybody know who's getting a red recommend, and what for. Don't rely on noticeboards. *Tell* everybody. There are one or two other things I have learned. Study your blokes as closely as you can, especially your pilots. Learn as much as you possibly can about them, and always measure what they're doing against your own standards of what you think they *ought* to be doing. Humour them. If a bloke wants to fly with another particular bloke, or share a cabin with him or go ashore with him, then try and oblige. It doesn't do any harm and may do a lot of good. If he wants a particular aircraft, or wants to fly off in a particular place in the range, then try and oblige him if you can. It's like those footballers who always want to run on the field first or last or next to the goalkeeper. I don't encourage superstition, but you have to admit it's very strong in the squadrons, and anything that makes blokes fly better against the Japanese is all right with me. Always turn up whenever one of your sailors is coming up before the Commander or the Captain for requestmen or defaulters. And I should try and visit your squadron mess deck a couple of times a month at least if you can manage it. Be approachable. Don't take anything for granted. But if you get a good man who's shown that he is reliable, then I should let him get on with it. He'll do it better knowing you trust him and, of course, that's one more thing you won't have to worry about yourself. This is a hell of a mouthful, Douglas, and I have a nasty feeling I am being wiser in talking to you than I have succeeded in being myself in actual practice. Like godparents, promising all sorts of things they've never ever been able to do themselves. Remember, it's all a game of blood in the end.'

'Well, I'm very grateful to you, Skipper. I do feel better about it now.'

'Good show.'

They had been so absorbed in their conversation that they had walked up the flight deck, subconsciously navigating the obstacles, and back to the island door again. Skipper pushed through the blackout folds again.

'Ah, there you are, Skipper!' Wings was standing in the ACR doorway, with a signal log in his hand. 'Here.'

Skipper read the pink priority signal. 'Where's Dinagat?'

'Oh, one of the American airfields on Leyte.'

'No survivors.' The USAAF Liberator which had been giving Herman and other passengers a lift to Espiritu Santo had crashed on take-off, killing everybody on board. It was all a game of blood in the end.

'I thought you would be interested in that,' Wings said, walking away. 'Oh, by the way,' he said, over his shoulder, 'the Captain would like to see you.'

CHAPTER FOUR

Climbing the ladders up to the bridge, Skipper noticed again how brightly lit, how hot, how crowded and noisy the island superstructure always was. Even in these so-called silent hours, after pipedown and the majority of the ship's company had turned in, the island never slept and was never quiet. There was a constant background of noise: typewriters and fan motors, voices over loudspeakers, a door grinding across on its runner as somebody came out of an office, another voice demanding something — a signal perhaps, or a time or a figure.

Through the open doorway as he passed, Skipper saw a man with headphones sitting back in a chair and looking up at a light in the corner, his lips moving soundlessly. Another man crouched before a bank of valves and wires and condensers, one of many he had drawn out from a mass of them which stretched from deck to deckhead. Next door, two men watched a row of glowing radar screens. In one of a row of cabins, Skipper saw a figure stretched out naked on the bunk. He had put three portable fans on the deck and trained them to blow upwards over his body, but Skipper knew how useless they were. Idly Skipper wondered how whoever it was — it looked like Ops himself — had managed to scrounge three of those portable fans when the normal allocation was one per cabin.

The bridge, by contrast, was always dark and cool. The large armoured-glass windows forward and on both sides had all been opened wide and a breeze blew through the whole wide, dark space of the compass platform. The only lighting was from the dimmest red of the instruments. The only sounds were tiny and only noticeable because of the surrounding silence: the slow ticking of the gyro compass strip repeaters, as they clicked across from one half-degree of course to another and clicked back as the helmsman put his wheel over. From one of the radio sets fixed to the after bulkhead, a low voice, barely audible, was reading out strings of figures in a just-discernible American accent; it was probably the data for the latest meteorological forecasts. As Skipper passed, the bridge messenger switched the receiver off.

Skipper was always interested in what happened on the bridge. Here was the secret of the ship. Here all the various strands of the ship's life, about which Skipper himself knew very little, all came together. He would have liked to have known more, and when he first joined he had tried to arrange for himself and his squadron officers to take a greater part in ship's affairs and, to some extent at least, answer the criticism of the ship's officers that aircrew took no notice of anything that happened below the hangar except their beds, booze and breakfast. But the sheer pressure of flying operations had soon scuppered all Skipper's good intentions. It was all Skipper could demand of his pilots that they simply stay alive and go on flying against the Japanese, without worrying about when both watches of seamen fell in, or how many pounds of spuds they ate in a week. And besides, he had had very little response from the ship's officers. Most of them showed little interest in the aircraft, except after a particularly gory prang. Aircraft were those bothersome things that made a lot of unwelcome noise and disrupted the ship's routine. As the Gunnery Officer was once heard to say, *This ship would be quite all right if it weren't for the aircraft.*

But the Captain was different, and Skipper went to see him, as always, with anticipation. He was, as Skipper expected, sitting in his great high chair, looking out ahead. Skipper sniffed the whiff of his cheroot as he came up.

'Permission to come on the bridge, sir, please?' It was a custom which was not strictly necessary, and many people did not observe it. But Skipper liked to do so. It smacked of the old Navy, of touching one's hat to the quarterdeck.

The Officer of the Watch, who happened to be the Gunnery Officer, withdrew his head from the hood around the nearest radar screen and nodded at Skipper.

'Yes, sir, please.'

The Captain had turned his head and shifted his weight around in his chair at the sound of Skipper's voice. 'Skipper?'

'Sir.'

The Captain settled back in his chair again. 'You've...'

'Commander (Air) showed it to me, sir.'

'Good. I wanted you to see that.'

'Sir...'

'And I also wanted to tell you, so that there can be absolutely no doubt or question about it, that I think your advice this morning was sound. Looking back, it would have been preposterous to have kept Herman on board and made him fly again.'

Preposterous was not at all the word Skipper would have chosen himself, but he was grateful for the Captain's support.

'Thank you very much indeed, sir.'

'This business, now —' the Captain waved the signal in his hand — 'is beside the point. Quite something else. It could have happened to anybody at any time. I wanted to make sure you knew that. I also wanted to ask your advice about something else.'

The Captain had a trick of looking past Skipper, at the horizon, constantly on the lookout, even though he was addressing somebody standing immediately beside him. It was a discomforting habit but effective. Skipper had seen the Captain sight and report aircraft before anybody else on board, while actually signing the forms his secretary had brought up for him. Now, whilst still looking at the horizon ahead, the Captain peeled another signal from the sheaf in his hand and passed it to Skipper. It was a long signal, on pink paper, which in the bridge's dim red light was impossible to decipher.

'There's a light in my sea-cabin aft there.'

The Captain's sea-cabin was a spartan little compartment, a bleak place to spend so much time in at sea. There was a bunk and an overhead light, a strip of carpet, a washbasin and a mirror, some more signal logs and books in a rack, a photograph of the Captain's wife in a frame, and one fan, whirring on a stand in a corner. The fan was training round and up and down and round again, automatically worked by some kind of crank mechanism set in its hub at the back, so that it spun automatically, like an angular neck craning and staring, and craning and staring, endlessly. It merely stirred the hot still air in the cabin, which had all its deadlights battened down. A chink of light up here in the island could be seen for miles around.

There was a light above the head of the bunk. Skipper switched it on and sat down to read. He had already almost guessed, half-suspected what it was, and by the tingling of his fingers as he read he felt he was only confirming what he had always known. This was the Supreme Allied Commander South-East Asia's Headquarters Intelligence summary, sent from Kandy in Ceylon, of the fate of the aircrew survivors lost over Sumatra three months before. Skipper read the names.

There were nine of them, four of them from this ship alone: J. V. Carey — Johnnie Carey, his own wingman — and R. L. G. Rhodes, Dusty Rhodes of the Avengers, and his entire crew. They had all nine been captured by the Japanese in or near the oil refineries or in the jungle outside. They had been taken to the Japanese area army headquarters in Palembang where they had been starved, abused and ill-treated. After four weeks' apparently fruitless questioning, they had been taken by ship to Singapore, to the gaol in Outram Road for interrogation by the experts, the sinister *Kenpeitai*, the Japanese secret police. There they had been subjected to a daily routine of systematic torture, of beatings and questionings, more beatings, kickings and more questionings. Skipper wiped away the saliva on his lips. This bloody bloody endless *bloody* war.

After another four weeks they had all been broken down, or perhaps the Japanese tired of them. The Japanese had a well-known contempt for prisoners. A man captured was not a man at all, but a body without honour. One day, in the middle of the afternoon, they had all nine been loaded, blindfolded and bound, into a truck and taken to the beach north of the great POW gaol at Changi. The Japanese often made Allied POWs who were to be executed dig their own graves, but these prisoners were not to need graves. They were all beheaded by strokes of a Japanese ceremonial sword wielded by an army officer. Two of them were not swiftly killed and had their bodies badly hacked about before they died.

Skipper marvelled at the circumstantial detail in the report. It was either from a secret eye-witness, or the Japanese had had a traitor present. The nine heads were collected into a silk bag, embroidered with the rising sun. The nine bodies and the silk bag were all weighted with rocks and taken out to sea, about half a mile offshore, in the Captain of Singapore dockyard's own personal barge, where they were dropped overboard. The report gave the time of day, three o'clock, the date, the names and ranks of the murderers, and even noted an unconfirmed rumour that one of the bodies had surfaced again further round the coast and a Japanese minesweeper had been sent to find it, but without success.

Skipper took the signal back to the bridge. 'It was very kind of you to let me see this, sir.'

'Was it? Kindness wasn't in my mind at all. I want your advice. You and I and the coding officer of the day are the only ones who've seen that. What should I do? Should I make it public? Should I tell the ship's company? Should I put that, just as it is, on every noticeboard in the ship?'

Skipper sensed that there was a great deal more behind this questioning than first appeared. Nevertheless, he plumped for his first impulse. 'I should give it the very widest publicity, sir.'

'You would? Why?'

'Well, sir, it's something everybody should know. Something they should never be allowed to forget. This is what happens, this is the sort of enemy we have, this is the other side if we don't win.'

'I think we all know that.'

'Do we, sir?'

'Well, I have to admit that report shook me, Skipper. I've never been so shocked in all my life. Those men were genuine prisoners of war, and were entitled to the status and treatment of prisoners of war. To suffer something like that … That is what I wanted to ask you. Might this not have an adverse effect on the aircrew, if they knew about it? Make them hold back, with the knowledge that this might happen to them if they were shot down?'

'Oh, no, sir.' This time Skipper was certain. 'If you'll excuse me, sir, it isn't as simple as all that…'

The Captain's smile was broadly visible even in the dimness. 'I didn't think it was going to be *simple*.'

'But no, sir, it doesn't work like that. We're past all that. That sort of thing just doesn't come into your head at all. Besides, sir, it's been pretty common rumour in the squadrons for some time now, what the Japs do to aircrew who are hacked down. I would give this the very widest circulation, sir. I would make certain that everybody on board knew it by heart. In any case, there are aircrew from two other ships in this signal and even if *we* agreed to keep it dark, they might not, and it would be bound to leak out. Even in this ship, it would be impossible to keep it quiet. Johnnie Carey was my wingman and quite a well-known character in the ship. So was Dusty Rhodes. I think a clear, full accurate account, for everybody to see, is far, *far* better than rumour, sir. Because there's bound to be rumour.'

'That's right. Well, I just wanted to know what the aircrew thought.'

'And there's the press over in the flagship, sir. They're bound to get wind of it and I hear they're pretty stroppy. They give the Admiral a hard time every now and then.'

'Do they? I didn't know that. I'm only glad we don't have any in this ship. Good. That's it, then. I wanted to get a view from the aircrew. Thank you, Skipper, I am most grateful to you. Tell me…'

'Sir?'

'Tell me, did you ever consider turning over to the regular Navy and taking a permanent commission?'

Again, Skipper felt that he had seen this question looming up from a long way away. 'Not really, sir. I can't say I've ever given it much thought. I mean … I don't mean to be…'

'No, no, that's all right. It was just a notion. Anyway, goodnight, Skipper, and thank you for your advice.'

'Goodnight, sir.'

Back in his own cabin Skipper blessed for the thousandth time the policy which gave Squadron COs single cabins, as though they had the status of ship's heads of departments, almost as though they were captains of their own little ships. This Captain and this Commander insisted on the policy rigorously, as they insisted upon all the aircrew's privileges and perquisites, but Skipper had heard of other carriers in which the ship's officers tried constantly to erode the aircrews' position. The question of cabin allocations, always a sensitive subject, was where they generally began their offensive.

Skipper needed space and solitude to think, because he knew, and he guessed that the Captain knew, that he had not quite told the whole truth on the bridge. He had, in fact, thought of a permanent RN commission, many times. Not to leave the Navy, not to go back to Oxford, to stay, as it were, still at war, was an uncomfortable prospect but not a novel one. It would, of course, cause dismay in the family. Not going back to manage Daughton — that would set all the tongues in the village and the county going. Not many from their part of Wiltshire ever joined the Navy. Mother had a remote relation, so remote Skipper could not recall his name, who was a Captain RN; all Skipper knew of him was that he was supposed to have been at Jutland. Years before, a boy from the village had got a girl into trouble, as they still said, and run away to sea. Father had served with the yeomanry in the other great war, when grandfather was alive, but it was always expected of him, as it was expected of Skipper, that he would come back and work the land. It was traditional to take up arms in a time of danger. But when the need was over, one put the arms down again and went back to one's real life. They put the quaint, quilted suits of armour from the Mahdi's war up on the wall by the great staircase, as they had done at Daughton, with the knobkerries and the little round shields. They put the curious mementoes and the medals in the glass-topped display table by the morning-room window, and the photographs of Father in the field — in his khaki and his puttees and with his Kitchener moustache, grinning out at the camera over the canvas bucket and washbasin, somewhere in France, like one of those Bairnsfather drawings — they put those on the wall in the back passage to the laundry room. Would Skipper's great-great-grandsons one day stare at him, sitting in the cockpit of his Corsair, with his leather helmet and his two Rising Sun 'kill' flashes, as at a caveman displayed with his primitive weapons? Maybe they would. But this war had an extra, personal edge. The treatment of those prisoners …

Skipper was struck by a pang of thought. Would this mean another letter to Johnnie's wife? She was a nice little girl. Skipper had once met her. She lived with her mother now, in a little house at Whitby in Yorkshire, beside the sea. Probably it would. That was a duty they had never talked about when one joined the Navy.

Like many RNVRs, Skipper had joined the Navy in a mixture of patriotism, concern for the way the country was going, excitement at the thought of a new life, apprehension at what shape that new existence might take, and a degree of unadmitted condescension. They were joining, they told themselves, for the duration, just to help out, because the Navy and the other professionals at the game were clearly not going to be able to cope on their own. In the meantime, there was no need for any of them to get totally involved, as the regular Dartmouth full-timers obviously must. But before long

Skipper, perhaps more than most, had been drawn in by the Navy, intrigued and captivated. He could not help admiring the unemotional way in which the Navy received him and the other entries, trained them, admonished them and praised them. He was respectful of the superb confidence of the officers, in themselves and their Service. They really were different, in minute ways which only someone like Skipper, who looked for such differences, would notice: they wore their uniforms in a certain way, they drank gin and bitters where an RNVR would prefer beer or, without ever admitting it, even a soft drink; they sang pre-war songs like 'Muddy Water in my Glass' instead of such interminable Fleet Air Arm tribal chants as the one about 'I've still got to render my A25'. Many of Skipper's preconceptions about the Navy had not survived his initial training and almost none the pressure of operational flying. But still … always Skipper had to concede. They did have something.

Skipper came awake at the light knock on his cabin door. That certainly was the knack of a professional naval officer — to be able to get up at once at dead of night. Perhaps he would make a professional, after all.

'Three o'clock, sir.'

Skipper looked at his watch. Three o'clock in the morning.

'Good God. Why so early?' He could not recognise the man in the doorway.

The man's manner was defensive. It was never an easy job for a sailor to go around shaking officers unexpectedly in the middle of the night. 'Commander (Air) would like to see all Squadron COs, senior pilots and senior observers as soon as possible, sir.'

'Whatever for? We're not flying until five o'clock.'

'It's all been changed, sir.'

Skipper groaned. That could be the motto of the Fleet Air Arm. 'Ain't you 'eard, it's all been changed!' Skipper could tell by the throbbing of the deck that the ship was at a faster speed than usual. These cabins down aft were very sensitive to the ship's vibrations.

'OK, I've got the word.' Skipper swung his legs off the bunk and switched on the cabin light. The ship's daily orders were on the carpet by the door. They were normally distributed throughout the ship last thing at night. Squadron COs rated their own personal copy, delivered to their cabins. With the sheet of paper was another, the signal about the fate of Johnnie Carey and the others. The Captain had evidently wasted no time in giving it the maximum publicity. Or perhaps he had already decided before he asked Skipper's opinion and that conversation had really been concerned with something else. It was difficult to tell with that man. If this report did not fire everybody up, nothing would. Skipper read through it again, and again felt a trembling of indignation. It was, in the end, senseless violence. Whatever information the Japanese had beaten and kicked out of their prisoners had been of little use to them. Whatever knowledge they had gained of the task force's methods and tactics had clearly never penetrated to their garrisons in the Sakishima Gunto.

Skipper caught Michael up on one of the ladders leading to the island.

'You read it, Skipper?'

'Of course.'

'I'll tell you this, I'll have one of them for every one of ours. For each one of ours I'll get one of them. Starting today.'

Skipper was taken aback by such a violent reaction from Michael, who was always the cool, collected one. He meant to tell him to calm down, that such a frame of mind was dangerous over the Sakishima Gunto. But it was too complicated, too early in the morning, too much altogether, and Skipper let it pass.

This briefing was a full muster. The Captain himself was sitting in the front row. Wings was there, and Stanley and all the Squadron COs, senior pilots and observers. Some of them were wan and yawning from lack of sleep, but they were all there. Skipper, indeed, was one of the last to arrive, to a sharp glance from Wings. Skipper resented the implication. It was hardly his fault if his cabin lay at the end of the rounds of the man shaking the aircrew.

Ops had new figures chalked on his little board, and a new map beside them. Skipper recognised it as Formosa, a long island lying off the coast of China. It was the shape of a sausage or, as somebody said, making Wings turn round and frown, 'like a turd'.

'OK, men,' Ops said briskly. 'This, as you can see, is Formosa. It's where a lot of these suiciders start off from and the Americans have asked us to have a go at them where they live. They asked MacArthur, too, but apparently he has not been active enough and, as we are the nearest, it's our turn now. We've all heard about chrysanthemums and cherry blossom and all that. This, men, is the orchard.'

Ops pointed to the map. 'As you can see, there is a big mountain range down the centre of the island and when I say mountains I mean real ones — ten, twelve, thirteen-thousand footers. There's nothing much to interest us on the eastern side, because the mountains come right down to the sea, except the river estuary and the town of Giran, which will be one of our targets. Our main interest is in the north and round to the west of the island where there is quite a bit of coastal plain and some quite large towns — Kiirun here on the northern coast and Taipei just inland, which is one of the main towns in the island. It has a big airfield, here in the suburbs at Matsuyama.'

'Suburbs?' said somebody. 'It sounds almost civilised.'

'It is. In the sense that it is a densely populated area, quite different from the Sakishimas and it will be comparatively heavily defended, of course. Right, sir?'

Wings got up, to carry on the detailed briefing. 'We've been asked to knock out the main airfield at Matsuyama, which is a training field for suicide pilots. And it is particularly well guarded with gun batteries. So this is going to be a maximum effort, all-out show, with everybody up.'

Skipper grimaced, but was careful to turn his face away from Wings. Wasn't every day a maximum effort, all-out show, 'with everybody up'?

'Matsuyama is also an assembly factory for the Ohkas. They are brought up the west coast by rail in crates and assembled in sheds on the north side of the airfield.' Wings produced with a flourish a large print from a folder and pinned it to the board. 'There'll be a chance to look more closely at this later. This is about ten days old, this photograph, and here are the sheds … here, along the northern perimeter of the field. I'm told they used to be old tea warehouses before the war. Our main effort will be against the airfield proper, but somebody...' Wings turned and his eye swivelled round to fix upon Skipper. Was it fancy, Skipper wondered, or did he detect a gleam of malice in that glance? 'You, and your squadron, Skipper, will beat up the railway which runs into Taipei from the west and south. Here...'

With an equal flourish, Wings took out another large glossy print, of a steam locomotive with a rather charming trail of smoke from its funnel. It was pulling a line of about thirty,

Skipper counted them, *thirty-one* low cars, each with a pale-coloured crate upon it.

'Goodness,' said somebody from the back, 'that looks like a new LMS engine, one of the four-six-ohs. Wonder how they got that?'

There was bound to be a trainspotter somewhere in the room, but Wings ignored him and the buzz of amusement he had aroused. Skipper was more interested in the train than the engine. This picture, too, must be quite recently taken, by somebody who must have got up close.

'The Japanese, being a methodical people, run to a strict timetable and we are informed that they get one Ohka train a day arriving at Matsuyama first thing in the morning having travelled up overnight. But the Japanese trains are not as efficient as all that and we don't know exactly when the midnight choo-choo will actually get in. We are told it's been very erratic recently. So you, Skipper, will pick up the line outside Taipei station and follow it out to the coast, here —' Wings traced the line with his forefinger on the map — 'and then take it on south until you meet the train.'

'Do we have bombs for this?'

'Negative. Ground-strafing as usual.'

'How far do we go down for the train?'

'As far as necessary, until you find it.' There was no doubt now of the bleak note in Wings' voice. 'Bearing in mind your fuel state, of course, and the fact that the further south you go the higher the mountains rise and the harder your trip back. We're told there are also some tunnels on the way and the choo-choo-train has a trick of hiding in one of them until the air raid is over. So you'll have to watch out for that.'

Once again, Skipper marvelled at the intelligence effort the Allies seemed to be able to call upon. They seemed to know everything except the engine driver's name.

Wings held up the pink signal, about Johnnie and the others. 'You've all seen this by now? Then I need say no more. Let's have a good day of it.'

It was, in the end, a very good day, although it began unpromisingly. The strike involved over a hundred aircraft, from all four carriers. It had been hastily mounted overnight, the COs had had no chance to talk together beforehand, as they had before the Sumatran strikes, and the squadrons in any case were rusty at forming up in large numbers. As Skipper circled, waiting for his squadron to catch up and form upon him, he could hear old Baggy Burns, the Air Coordinator from the flagship, grumbling and swearing at all and sundry at what he clearly thought was the sinful delay in forming up. Baggy had been in a squadron of Skuas which had shot down the very first German aircraft to fall to British arms in the war, an unwary Dornier flying boat splashed into the North Sea in September 1939, and he had been flying operationally off and on, but mostly on, ever since. Statistically he should have been dead long ago. But Baggy had flown on and on, into a region where statistics failed to register. He was immortal, and insatiable. What would Baggy do, after the war, when there were no more aircraft to fly? It was a ridiculous question. There *was* no end to the war. It was never going to end, and Baggy and everybody else were going to go on for ever.

Eventually, as always on these occasions, Baggy just set off with his own flight around him and bellowed at everybody else to follow him. Ragged as the formation was, and hard though Baggy continued to swear at stragglers, Skipper thought they made a fine sight. It really was like an armada, like a fleet at sea, the aircraft rising and falling as they kept station on each other. Far below, the Avengers clustered in knots, and beyond them to starboard were the Fireflies. This really was a maximum effort which gave everybody a sense of 'going over the top' together, a feeling of brotherhood, of being part of an irresistible force. This was what the Fleet Air Arm could do! If all their critics could just see this! There were over a hundred aircraft here, and the same number over the task force for CAPs.

Forty miles from the coastline the strike broke up into ship components, *Madame Fifi*'s Avengers and fighter escort going for Giran, *Dainty Delilah*'s Avengers and escort peeling off later for Kiirun. The flagship and *Miss Britannia*'s aircraft carried on around the northern tip of the island to approach the main target of Matsuyama from the north.

It was, as somebody had said, quite civilised. Compared to the arid bare stretches of the Sakishimas, this was a blue-and-green paradise. Small towns and hamlets stretched up the foothills, and wreaths of early morning mist slid away, uncovering rows and rows of tiny houses, a mineshaft winding wheel and several very tall chimneys. It was like bombing Bradford or Bingley.

The first flak came up as they approached the outskirts of Taipei, a rapid row of black dots across the skyline as though inscribed by a giant's pencil. But Skipper could see that the flak bursts were badly out for range and height. They were simply sprayed across the sky as though the Japanese battery commander had just woken up and pressed his thumb down on the button, more to arouse the rest of his battery personnel from sleep than anything else. They would have to do much better than that but, as Skipper watched, the flak became even less accurate. These gunners were not in constant Ishigaki practice.

'Santa Fé, Santa Fé, this is Santa Fé Leader. Anybody see St Pancras?'

'Santa Fé Leader, this is Santa Fé Four...' Inevitably, it was Richard Fenton. 'Affirmative. Green three zero, looks like it just beside that very tall, black chimney, beside the river. Green three zero...'

'Santa Fé roger. Got him.'

There was a bandit alarm from the flagship's Hellcats. Skipper could see them wheeling over the mountains to the east, but he had no further time to watch. He tipped over and led his squadron down and across the town, using the tall chimney Fenton had pointed out as a turning beacon. Astoundingly unmolested by flak, they picked up the rails leading towards the coast and formed up in three flights of four, spread out in a shape like a broad spade-headed snake.

The line was double track for some distance out of the town and in surprisingly good condition: gleaming rails, clean track, painted huts and curious pagoda-like signal gantries, which were obviously oriental. No British signalling equipment looked like that. There were few bridges, mostly level crossings, all empty. At that early hour of the morning there was no traffic on the roads, no rolling stock, nobody in sight. In any case the air-raid alarms would have sounded, and everybody would have taken cover.

Levelling out along one straight of at least two miles, Skipper reflected that this line was probably British. Britain seemed to lay down railways everywhere in the world; Skipper's grandfather even had shares in some of them. Skipper was only a few feet above engine-driver level, with his squadron behind and slightly above him. At three hundred knots it was an odd sensation, like seeing a film of a train trip speeded up many times. They had the mountains on their left, flying south, with the sea on their right. The mountains looked down on Marathon, and Marathon looked on the sea. At that quiet time of day, the thunder of their engines would roll across the foothills and reverberate back. So all day long the sound of battle rolled, beside the winter sea. They flashed over a tidy landscape of yellow tracks, green fields and hundreds of waterways — here a river, there a large ditch, but mostly tiny channels patiently dug through the soil, like a great shining spider's web of silver liquid spread over the countryside. The sun was still behind the dark mountains and the whole landscape was still asleep.

There was a suspicious flash of metal far over to starboard. Michael had seen it and with his flight, lifted up and soared over towards the sea. There was a fighter aerodrome at Schinchiku, the next sizable town on their way down to the south. Skipper caught a movement out of the corner of his right eye and saw them, two black silhouettes, probably Tojos or Oscars, framed against the washy blue-and-white sea.

Just beyond a small, sleeping village a long ridge ran out towards the sea and a black hole in its base showed where the line vanished into a tunnel. Skipper pulled back and rose above it, clearing the trees along the ridge by some fifty feet, and dipped down the other side. There was the line again, and another black hole where it came out again. The tunnel was probably half a mile long, possibly a little less, and there, Skipper was sure, their target was lurking.

They flew on for a few more miles, but with every second that elapsed Skipper became more convinced that their quarry was back there in that tunnel. He even thought he had seen a wisp of steam from the northern entrance. They turned back and looked closely at each end of the tunnel. It was just a black hole, with no movement, no sign of life. Skipper's steam was probably imaginary. And yet he was sure the train was there. If he were that engine driver that was where he would be, and that was where he would stay, until the all-clear sounded. The problem was how to flush their snake out of its hole.

They went away, far out to sea, hoping the quiet would lure the train into the open. They hovered above both ends of the tunnel in turn, coming down one by one to strafe the entrance, hoping the noise and ricocheting bullets would force the train out at the other end. With bombs or rockets they might have done more, but machine guns were not enough. The engine driver, whatever his name was, had enough sense to stay where he was. After one pass by Fenton, where Skipper honestly believed he had cut it too fine and was going to fly into the tunnel, Skipper decided to call off the attack. It was a disappointment, and more than a disappointment. It might be giving hostages to Wings, who would be looking for lapses, especially as Michael and his flight rejoined empty-handed, admitting that they had winged a Tojo but it had got away.

In the event, it was worse than Skipper had feared, because everybody else had done exceptionally well. The Avengers had all done well, found their targets and bombed accurately, the Fireflies had done well, the CAPs had done well, with three bandits splashed for certain and six more probables. Nobody had been lost, from strikes or CAPs, and only one Seafire had crashed on deck. The pilot had broken his back. But apart from him it had been a memorable day to show the Americans, who, it was feared, still needed convincing of the task force's combat efficiency. Only Skipper's squadron had let the side's batting average down.

'Are you sure that train was there?' Wings' voice was as accusing as Skipper had feared it would be.

'Well, of course, sir, I can't be *absolutely* sure, but we covered about a hundred miles of track and that tunnel was the only place that train could be. That is, if they did send a train up last night at all.'

'Our information is every night.'

'In that case, sir, it must have been there. If I'd been that engine driver that was where I'd be, during an air raid.' Skipper refrained from pointing out that they might have done more with bombs, as he had suggested. He was growing restive under the implied criticisms. Wings was coming very close to casting aspersions on his courage. Several times, in summing up the day, Wings pointedly referred to the train, 'barring Skipper's train, of course,' and 'with the sole exception of Skipper's midnight choo-choo, which is *still* on its way to Alabam'.'

Others noticed it.

'What's biting Wings?' asked Henry Darling. His Avengers had done very well, and he still had the glow of their achievement on him. 'Why was he getting at you?'

'Oh, I don't know.'

'Even a half-cut baboon could see you had no chance of getting at that train.'

'It's just a difference of opinion. We agree to differ. He differs and I agree.'

'Yes,' said Henry ruminatively. 'I remember the CO of my first squadron had the same kind of problem when I first joined a carrier. He and Wings fell out…'

'It's nothing as definite as that. We haven't fallen out.'

'No, of course not.'

'Well … go on. What did your CO do about it?'

'I don't know.' Henry stroked his chin. 'He got killed soon afterwards.'

In spite of himself, Skipper burst out laughing at Henry's droll delivery. 'Well, thank *you* for that bit of sage advice!'

'Well, it's all a game of blood, isn't it?'

'That's it, Henry.'

'Maybe you'll get another shot at your midnight choo-choo.'

'Hope so.'

CHAPTER FIVE

Skipper hoped and expected to have another pass at the train, and so did everybody else. But the chance never came. The task force's air groups had done well over Formosa that morning. They had established temporary air mastery over most of the northern part of the island. The opposition had been smothered, and targets lay open to more attacks. The first strikes might have been repeated, to win an important, an almost strategic, victory comparable to the destruction of the Sumatran oil refineries. But, because of an unaccountable decision which baffled and enraged the aircrews, no more strikes were flown. Wings was so angry he went to protest to the Captain. But the decision was not the Captain's. It was one of the quirks of war, of which they were all familiar, when ships put to sea, returned to harbour, rendezvoused with other ships, increased or decreased speed, steered one course or another, all according to some haphazard destiny. Skipper had a hint of a possible reason for their withdrawal later in the day when he saw a signal from the South-West Pacific Area's Intelligence Centre, assessing the results of the morning strikes. The wording suggested, in the faintest but most unmistakable manner, that their intervention had not been entirely welcomed. The task force was in the Central Pacific Area Command and Formosa was too near to the South-West Pacific Command. Their flights over Formosa had put too many and too senior noses out of joint. It was yet another example of the traditional edginess between the US Army and the US Navy. As Gus Dempsey would often say in his cups,

'This man's navy got three targets in this war. General MacArthur. The US Army. The Japs. In that order. You Limeys come fourth.'

By noon that day the task force was steering south through squally weather towards the Philippines. Sharp storms of rain swept across empty flight decks, with all aircraft struck down below. It was the beginning of the typhoon season and the fleet passed through the outer fringe of a mighty convulsion gathering its strength far to the west in the South China Sea. Two days later, early in the morning, the fleet entered the great United States Navy's anchorage at Leyte, on the east coast of the Philippines.

Skipper went up as usual to the Admiral's bridge to watch the ceremonies and rituals of entering harbour. It was an experience, an entertainment, he always loved and looked forward to and he was always joined there by a miscellaneous group of officers, ships and aircrew, including the Padre, the Paymaster Commander, the Met Officer, and aircrew such as Michael and Henry Darling. It was the only occasion and the only place that such a varied selection of officers ever came together.

The Admiral's bridge was immediately above the compass platform, and as they were at that time a private ship, with no flag officer, it was empty except for goofers. It was so placed and equipped, with instrument repeaters and broadcast speakers, that the Admiral could see and hear everything, and thus was a superb position for goofing. Michael always enjoyed the sensation of eavesdropping upon the ship at a critical moment. All reports came to the bridge from all over the ship, confirming that the anchors were both ready for letting go, that a certain party of men was now closed up at its station, that certain machinery was available and running correctly, that the

Chief Quartermaster was on the Wheel, God was in his Heaven and all was right with the world.

Other pilots tended to dismiss this activity as 'fishhead flummery' but Skipper found it enthralling. The reports came from so many places, and in so many different accents — Devonian, Cockney, Scottish and North of England — that Skipper was able to appreciate, in a startlingly clear way, how complicated the ship was and how many different skills and personalities went to make her perform properly. Skipper used to wonder, what must it be like to be a permanent part of this extraordinary world, where so many men knew each other from pre-war commissions? What must it be like to be captain of a ship like this, to govern her ways, control and care for those who served in her, be wholly responsible for a period of her history? A ship's captain was immortal. His reputation was secure. His name would be for ever inscribed upon the tablets of stone kept in the Admiralty. For as long as records lasted, his name would remain. It would be remembered at reunions years ahead. To be a ship's captain was to have a reputation, amongst men of reputation. It was not like the life of a pilot in wartime: nasty, brutish and short.

Surely we must win the war with this? The same prayer recurred to Skipper as it had on earlier entries to other American fleet anchorages at Manus and at Ulithi lagoon, when he saw the number and variety of the ships present, the sheer profligacy of American naval strength, and remembered that this was only a fragment of the total force. Skipper rapidly counted up to sixty ships before he gave it up and there were many others hull down to the south in that huge waterway. They passed two battleships anchored in line ahead and beyond them four light escort carriers. 'Woolworth carriers' they were called, but they were still fully fledged warships in their own right, with several

Avenger aircraft ranged carelessly on their flight decks. Beyond them again were lines of cruisers and destroyers, with accompanying tankers, storeships and landing craft. In the clear, rather bleak early light, the whole anchorage had an appearance of cheerful and purposeful activity. A brisk wind was blowing down the roadstead and small waves were banging and slapping against ships' gangways and boats' sides. The water between the ships was criss-crossed with the wakes of myriad motor boats, barges and smaller landing craft. The Americans all seemed to have a boat for every purpose and ten of each on board every ship, in strong contrast to *Miss Britannia*'s tiny flotilla of aged, overweight and mechanically vulnerable ship's boats. As the Paymaster Commander always said when he saw American boats, 'I've been twenty years in the Navy, ten of them waiting for boats.'

Surely we must win the war with all this? Skipper thought. The flagship just ahead had a Royal Marine band drawn up in front of her after flagstaff on the flight deck, an unexpected touch of ceremony in wartime. The responding American bugle calls floated across the water, and every man on their decks — and in the hundreds of boats alongside — lifted his head and stood to attention.

Everybody always chuckled at the Americans' affluence. But everybody also had had enough experience of the war to know that he who had the most tended to live the longest. It was true the Americans had buckets of ice cream, nightly film shows, piping hot water in their ships' laundries, cafeteria-served food and all the luxuries the Royal Navy affected to despise. But they also had a 'can-do' spirit which was unbeatable, and they were as generous as they were industrious. They were fascinated by Limeys and Limey ships and grateful for Limey assistance, however peripheral it might be, in this Pacific War.

At Ulithi, and at Manus, and no doubt here at Leyte, nothing was too much trouble for the American logistics force. For a visit on board a Limey ship, and a few glasses of Limey hard liquor, American officers opened up all the treasures of Solomon, so that the overawed Limey recipients could only say, with the Queen of Sheba, 'Behold, the half was not told me.'

A favourite story went round the ship at Manus that the Captain had just gone ashore to see the American admiral in charge of aircraft replacements. The ship was short of one Avenger and the Captain meant to ask politely, could they possibly have one? As he spoke he could see, through the window of the Admiral's office, lines of Avengers on the airstrip, ranged closely wingtip to wingtip. But, unaccountably, the Admiral had demurred. 'I guess I can't give you one Avenger, Captain,' he said. When he saw the Captain's face fall, he went on, 'You see, Captain, we only issue them a dozen at a time. You can have a dozen.'

Surely we must win the war with all this?

They were just passing a huge floating dock, with a ragged hole and a blackened patch of steel on its after starboard side. 'Somebody's had a go at that.'

'Suicider,' said an Admiral's Bridge-type of voice, which always knew everything. 'Just dropped out of the sky one morning last month when everybody was just getting up. "Man," one of the Yanks told me … "Why, we was just gittin' up and spittin' and scratchin' our balls…"' Whoever it was had a very good imitation American accent, and Skipper turned round to see that it was a bespectacled Paymaster Sub-Lieutenant he had always ignored before. '"…and sayin' Goddamn and what a Godawful war we got here when *zap* …

this thing hit us, *zap!* Shit, man, I thought it wuz the end of this world.'"

'Well, they seem to have got it all in hand now. God, they're swarming all over it like ants.'

'Look at that ship. She's got *medal ribbons* on her bridge!'

Beneath the dull grey bridge superstructure of the nearest American store ship was a bright splash of colour. As they came nearer, the watchers on the Admiral's bridge could see that it was formed by two long planks of wood, painted in blocks of different colours, to represent campaign medal ribbons. They were indeed like giant medal ribbons, six feet long by six inches wide, taken from a Brobdingnagian general's chest.

'Typical Yank swank.'

'I don't know about that,' said Skipper. 'When you think about it, they're no more showing off than our ship's honours board, all polished teak with past battle honours in gold. I think they're rather gay and rather splendid. If you knew your American medal ribbons you could tell how old a ship was, where she's been, what campaigns, and if she's ever been in combat. I suppose you could even tell whether she's been damaged in action. Sort of ship's Purple Heart.'

'Purple Rivet, more likely.'

'That one's certainly got the Guadalcanal medal,' said the Paymaster Sub-Lieutenant.

The Chief Quartermaster had been acknowledging helm orders in a steady monotone almost hypnotic in its consistency. Suddenly the timbre of his voice changed, becoming more urgent.

'Ship's not answering helm, sir!'

They were just passing under the stern of the ship whose medal ribbons they had been discussing. The flagship was only two cables ahead and *Dainty Delilah* was coming up astern, two cables away. Skipper could see the ship's head already swinging in almost imperceptibly towards the American store ship.

'Change to emergency steering.' The Captain's voice was admirably controlled and level. 'Hoist not-under-command signals.'

'Gangway, sir, please!' The watchers on the Admiral's bridge scattered as a signalman tore amongst them, half-grinning at this genuine excuse to make officers jump out of his way, and out on to the wing of the Admiral's bridge. From a locker he took two grotesque canvas shapes, like great black collapsed opera hats, and bent them on to a halliard. As he hoisted them, the black shapes expanded, for all the world like giant sooty ornaments for some incredible Christmas tree.

'Two black balls,' said the know-it-all Paymaster Sub. 'Means we're not under command.'

'Steering ready in emergency, sir.'

'Very good, steer in emergency. Report ship's head.' The Captain's voice was still at conversational level.

'Report ship's head, sir. Ship's head, one-eight-two, sir.'

'Very good. Starboard ten, steer one-eight-five.'

'Starboard ten, sir … Ten of starboard wheel on, sir … Steer one-eight-five, sir.'

'Nothing to port.'

'Nothing to port, sir, aye aye, sir.'

Nothing to port? Skipper looked out in amazement. There was a great solid American store ship only 300 yards off the port bow.

'It means the quartermaster mustn't steer anything to port of his course of one-eight-five,' said the Paymaster Sub. 'If he wavers at all it must be to starboard.'

Skipper was both irritated by and grateful to the youth. In a way, he disliked and envied him. His pimply face, his disrespectful manner towards senior aircrew officers and his confident voice all grated. But this youth had grown up with knowledge, a whole naval lore, in his very bones, which Skipper would have to learn. He was a supply and secretariat branch officer, a pen-pusher, whose part of ship was stores and official forms and paperwork, but he seemed to have more seaman's expertise than all the aircrew put together. It must be something they put into them at Dartmouth.

Outside the bridge window, Skipper could see the signalman hauling down the two black shapes again. The flap was over. The ship's head in fact had only veered off by some four or five degrees during the commotion. It might have been more serious. *Miss Britannia*'s steering gear was always liable to be temperamental, and always when the Captain had least room to manoeuvre. The ship had had a long war and a hard war, and the steering-gear trouble was a relic of underwater bomb damage suffered by near-misses in the Mediterranean years before.

Skipper was very conscious that what he had just seen and heard was a small demonstration of a lifetime's professional experience. Steering-gear breakdowns were one of the least remarkable, almost routine, emergencies a naval officer had to face. It came very early in the book of words of contingencies an officer of the watch had to deal with, after what to do on sighting a light at sea, but before procedure for man overboard. It was elementary. But could he himself have remained so calm and collected in command of a ship of over 20,000 tons with nearly 2,000 souls on board, apparently about to run amok in a congested roadstead crowded with the ships of another nation?

They could hear the Navigating Officer calling out bearings, and Skipper could see Pilot in his mind's eye, skipping from side to side on the bridge, taking bearings on both compass rings. One of His Majesty's Ships did not just anchor anywhere, dropping her hook where the fancy pleased. Every ship was given an anchor berth and approached it along a planned and considered path, monitored by bearings taken on suitable landmarks ashore, so that the Navigating Officer could advise the Captain whether they were still correctly on their anchoring course, and how far they had to go.

Ahead, smoke was billowing from the flagship's funnel and the water was boiling under her counter as she went astern. Faintly Skipper heard the tinny, indistinct sound which he knew was the flagship's anchor cable running out. Soon he felt the deck vibrating gently under his feet. The distant shoreline was still. Then there was a much louder but still curiously muted sound, of *Miss Britannia*'s cable running out. In a minute or two, the ship began to swing slowly to some current in the bay. She had taken her anchor and, for the moment, was safely home.

With the running of the cable, the ship underwent yet another transformation, from a seagoing to a harbour-staying existence. Once more, Skipper could hear the relevant reports coming into the bridge, of seagoing watchkeepers being relieved by their harbour counterparts, seagoing machinery being stopped, harbour-state equipment being started. Ahead, the flagship's Royal Marine band had turned forward and marched on to the after aircraft lift which rapidly lowered them, still playing, out of sight into the hangar below. As though at that signal, the lights on the Admiral's bridge went out, the instrument indicators slid back to zero, and the broadcast repeaters from the steering and conning positions went dead. The main broadcast, switched throughout the whole ship, was still on, however, for the announcement the Captain normally made whenever the ship put to sea, or returned to harbour.

'D'ye hear there?' The pipe of the bosun's mate's voice made everybody look up. 'This is the Captain speaking. We have now anchored at Leyte, the American base in the Philippines. We shall stay here, or at least this is the plan, to stay here for four days, to refuel, re-arm, re-store and generally get ourselves ready for another operating period. We have just received a signal from the Flag Officer Aircraft Carriers, addressed to us personally. I shall now read it to you: "From Flag to *Miss Britannia*. Congratulations on a magnificent showing up the Gunto. May your trident never grow less." I thought you would all like to hear that. Copies of that will be posted up on the ship's noticeboards.

'We have just returned to harbour after spending thirty-three days continuously at sea. That is longer than any other British fleet has done since Nelson's day, in the days of sail. During that period the task force's aircraft flew nearly 2,500 sorties on strike days. This ship's aircraft flew over a quarter of those sorties. The Avengers dropped over 400 tons of bombs on the Sakishima Gunto. Our Avengers dropped well over a quarter of that total. We have been credited with shooting down thirty-three Japanese aircraft in the air and another twelve destroyed on the ground. That is not including probables. This ship has been credited with nearly half the total. Fourteen Japanese aircraft shot down in the air and five destroyed on the ground. I know you will agree with me that this is a tremendous effort and reflects the greatest credit on our air group, and that includes especially their maintenance ratings. We have had a very high rate of availability of our aircraft, a hundred per cent on more than one day. This is solely due to the men in the hangars and the flight deck. I thank you all.

'Now for some bad news, about Leyte, where we are now. I am afraid there are no facilities at all for shore leave. I am told there simply is nowhere to go, so there will be no liberty boats and no shore leave. I am sorry about that. We shall try to make it up to everybody when we get back eventually to Sydney.

'Now for the good news. There is mail waiting for us, quite a lot of it, that has been going round the houses trying to catch us up. I'm told it looks like about four weeks' mail, all at once. So that's good.

'More good news. Because there is no shore leave I am trying to arrange for an issue of beer, two cans per day per man, while we are here. It will be Australian beer...' Skipper heard some sailors in the flat outside the Admiral's bridge giving an ironic cheer. 'We shall set up a kind of beer garden on the flight deck. I must tell you that the beer must be drunk on the flight deck. It is not, repeat *not*, to be taken down to the mess decks. Then we shall have sports on the flight deck and a concert in the upper hangar on Thursday evening, our last day here. That will be something to look forward to after what I am afraid is going to be a rather hectic period of work while we are here. That is all I have to say just now, except once more to thank you all for your magnificent effort in the last operating period. Thank you.'

That, Skipper reflected, had been a remarkably skilful speech: not too short, not too long, lots of information, lots of praise, a bit of stick and a bit of carrot, apologies for the hard work that had to be done, promises of recreation after the hard work done. Skipper had no doubt in his own mind that a great part of the credit for the ship's good performance was due to the Captain himself. He seemed to be able to play on his ship's company's feelings as on a massive and complicated instrument. He never left the bridge area at sea but he always seemed to know what they were all thinking. Perhaps he chatted to the signalmen. Morale was all in the mind. That was a truism. But it took rare qualities to lead a very large ship's company into action. Skipper acknowledged that they were all in the hands of a master, and it was always a pleasure to watch a true professional at work. But, as always when he considered the Captain's job, Skipper fell prey to self-doubts. Could he, if he really went for a permanent commission, match up to this?

Skipper had his own ideas for his squadron's recreation and morale, but to carry them out he had to have the Commander's permission. Skipper liked the Commander, a big, broad, bearded man, the ship's second-in-command, who — Skipper could see — had all the worries in the ship and none of the credit. But, as Skipper knew, it was all to an end. Who would fardels bear, to grunt and sweat under a Commander's life, but for the hope, eventually, of a command of one's own?

Skipper was afraid that his idea would be thought outlandish or ridiculous, but to his surprise the Commander knew exactly what he wanted. 'You mean a banyan!'

'If that's the word, sir.'

'Lord, yes, you mean a banyan. We used to have them before the war. Lord, Lord, nostalgia, nostalgia. I remember the China station, good old Weihaiwei. We used to take the cutter and go duck-shooting. Yes, of course you can have a squadron banyan. You can take the whaler. Good idea. Don't forget to tell the quarterdeck where you're going.'

Skipper caught the unspoken implication in the Commander's voice: he was clearly surprised that an RNVR, and a flyboy at that, should have such a civilised idea as a banyan.

In peacetime a ship of *Miss Britannia*'s size would have had a dozen sailing boats of various types and sizes, but in wartime the boats had all been landed as a fire risk, except one. It was a 27-foot whaler, with fore, main and mizzen sails, of a type which Skipper was very relieved to see was the same as they had used in their very brief sail training when they first joined the Navy. While the Chief Bosun's Mate, the leading hand and several seamen of the duty part of the watch — all loudly and vocally amazed at flyboys taking a whaler away — prepared the boat for lowering, Skipper went to see the Officer of the Watch.

'Banyan!' The Officer of the Watch, too, had pre-war memories. 'God, that's a word from the past. Wish I was coming with you.' Skipper felt that he had inadvertently invoked some traditional naval ritual in going on a banyan. Everybody seemed to approve of it.

'Where do you want to go?'

'Well, that's what I've come to discuss. Where's that, down there?' Skipper pointed to a long, low, green stretch of land, some miles astern.

'Dinagat.'

Dinagat. That was where Herman had been killed. 'No, we don't want to go there.'

'Well, you'd never get there and back in a day in this wind.'

There was another, very much smaller island, out to starboard, to the east. It had a green hump of hill, small bright green trees and undergrowth, and a streak of silver-white beach with waves breaking on it.

'That looks inviting. What's that?'

'Yes, it does.' The Officer of the Watch looked at the chart on the desk. 'It's called Gun Island on this chart.' He looked through another list beside the chart. 'And it's not on the prohibited list. Supposed to be clear of mines and obstructions. How about that one?'

'Gun Island it is, then.'

'Should be dead easy. In this, a nice beat up there on the wind and then an easy trip back with the wind behind you. Piece of cake.'

Again, Skipper took the unspoken point: even a *pilot* should be able to get to Gun Island and back without coming to any harm.

'Keep an eye on the ship while you're away; in fact I recommend you don't go out of sight if you can avoid it. This is your recall signal. Those two flags. Flag Uncle, Flag Yoke. If you see those two, beetle back as quick as you can.'

The whaler was brought round to the port after gangway where two sailors of the watch rigged the sails and sheets. It was all ready when Skipper and Michael and Fenton and Geoffrey and the rest of them, everybody except the duty body, clattered down the steps and into the boat. They all wore football shirts, shorts or old grey flannel bags, straw hats or woolly caps, and they all had towels and bathing trunks. Gus Dempsey was also there, under a straw sombrero, so it was a full muster on board the whaler as they let go the painter and set off, under the curious gaze of a large crowd of bystanders on the quarterdeck. Skipper felt a momentary twinge of conscience at taking his officers away on a pleasure sail when the rest of the ship's company were working. *Miss Britannia* had a tanker secured on one side and a store ship on the other. Forward, level with the forward end of the island, a water-lighter was preparing to come alongside. But, after all, Skipper thought, he and his boys had to fly often when everybody else was safe on board.

Skipper took the tiller, because he felt it was up to him to steer, and because he knew nobody else would. The boat hung a bit, in the lee of the ship's giant overhang, but once clear a wind took the sails, the boat swooped and they were away.

A sudden holiday mood possessed everybody on board. The sheer novelty of it, the excitement and freedom of getting away from the ship, the odd sight of the great aircraft carrier from this unaccustomed distance and angle, the fine day, the wind, the prospect of a swim on a tropical island ... it was all too much, and made them suddenly light-headed with anticipation. Somebody began to sing 'Ishigaki Ishigoo', but somebody else shouted him down and they all began to sing 'Ten Green Bottles Hanging on the Wall'. Skipper, at the tiller, was steering with a modicum of success and was delighted with his new-found expertise.

'Nine green bottles hanging on the wall...'

'What should we do but sing his praise, that led us through the watery maze ... Eight green bottles ... *Thus sung they in the English boat, an holy and a cheerful note* ... Seven green bottles...'

But as they neared Gun Island and Skipper began to study the shore, to decide how he would take the boat in, their singing died away.

The island was not much more than half a mile long, but it commanded the approaches to the great anchorage. A gun battery mounted on that small hump there would overlook the troop transports as they made their last runs into the assault beach. Before a successful landing could ever be made at Leyte, Gun Island would have to be taken and held. And that, from the look of the beach, was exactly what had happened.

The sand and shingle of the beach were torn and furrowed as though by a gigantic rake. Rocks had been hurled aside into heaps, holes had been blown in the strand, so that the eye looked down on several different coloured layers of earth. A wrecked landing craft was drawn up several yards from the water's edge and an amphibious tractor lay half submerged in the short surf. The nearest trees to the beach had been shattered and their trunks lay at all angles. Whole tops of trees had been blown away leaving jagged-edged stumps sticking up to the sky. There were the marks of tracks on the sand, and humps of abandoned equipment against which the sand had formed small one-sided drifts. Above all, as Skipper steered in and the bows of the whaler ground upon the shingle, the atmosphere was oppressive. There was no wind, no sound, no movement. It was though some stupendous blow had struck this island and left it permanently numbed.

'Opposed landing, I guess,' said Gus Dempsey.

Michael was crouched in the bows, about to leap into the water with a line.

'Hold on, Mike!' The boat was already beginning to slew round, and Skipper knew he would have to decide soon. 'Gus, do you think it's safe to go on this beach? Obviously there's been all hell let loose on it.'

Gus Dempsey shrugged. 'Must have been last October, though. Months ago. It should have been cleared long ago and it's not on the prohibited area list. I guess it's OK.'

'OK, Mike, on we go!' The boat had slewed around broadside on to the beach and they all scrambled out, pulling the boat sideways up on the sand. Skipper took the stern line ashore and weighted it with a rock. Then he looked around him.

The pattern of the attack was burned into the island. It was a pattern which had taken Allied arms from the Gilbert Islands to Okinawa and would, it was sincerely hoped, take them on to Tokyo early next year: air strike and sea bombardments, followed by more and heavier air strikes and bombardments, saturation bombardment up to the moment the landing force reached the beach, and then a methodical, steady advance, flushing the Japanese out of their holes with flame-throwers and satchel charges. The Marines had taken the island yard by yard, hole by hole, tree by tree and, towards the end, corpse by corpse. The fiery marks of their passage were scorched through the undergrowth, where fresh green shoots were springing up again. The forces of nature, in covering the wounds of the battle, had left their own scars.

Skipper and his banyan party stood on the beach, chilled by what they saw. There were trenches dug at the top near the trees, choked with some nameless debris. Skipper looked over the edge of the landing-craft deck. The inside had been gutted, stripped of everything, and was just a mass of bare wire-ends, empty bulkheads and broken glass. It had a sticky, sour smell, as though blood had only just been wiped away from it. Skipper felt the sweat springing out on his brow and neck hairs tingling. The beach was haunted. He knew that many men had died here, for this useless, damnable God-forsaken strip of sand and shingle. All pleasure in the banyan had gone. Skipper only wanted to get away.

'Look here, Skipper.' Michael was pointing inside the lines of trees. There was some rotting webbing equipment, rusty tins, pieces of wood from packing cases and a couple of dented petrol jerricans. Somebody had made a lean-to shack of branches and fronds. Skipper was almost afraid to look inside, but there was nothing there and the bare ground was soaking wet. Beyond the campsite was a gun pit with its roof torn upwards and backwards, and beside it a row of posts. They would be Japanese graves; the Marines would take their dead away with them.

'God, what a bloody awful place. It's creepy. Can't you feel it?' Michael nodded. 'There's not even a breath of wind. I get the strongest feeling people died a terrible death here.'

'You feel that? So do I. Let's get back and get out of here.'

On the beach, Fenton was running up and down, high-stepping and short-sprinting, and generally acting as though he were showing off in front of a girl on a beach at home. He certainly did not want to go.

'Oh, come on, Skipper.' Fenton had picked up a rock and was balancing it, hugging it into the side of his chin, in the posture of a shot-putter. 'Now we've gone to so much trouble to get here, let's give it a try. We don't want to go back to the ship just yet.'

Some of the others agreed with Fenton, and Skipper wondered at their lack of sensitivity to atmosphere. How could they possibly enjoy themselves on this fatal beach, where the very air still trembled with remembered agony? But perhaps, Skipper reflected, he should not complain. After all, he was always trying to cultivate just this kind of dispassionate detachment in his pilots. He wanted them not to feel too much. He should not complain now that he had partly succeeded.

Fenton crouched down, paused, and then released the rock with a jerk, achieving a very creditable throw of several yards towards the trees. The rock pitched. There was a shattering detonation, and a tall column of sand and debris towered twenty feet into the air. As it began to settle the dust swirled around the faces of the banyan party as they stood, each one stock still, pinned where he was. Before the sound of the explosion had died away, each man in the party had already measured his own distance from his neighbours and from the boat. Each man tried to recollect where he had trodden on that beach.

'Stand where you are, everybody. Everybody keep still.' Even in that moment, seeing their shocked faces and frozen postures, Skipper had a memory of the children's game of Grandmother's Footsteps, played at parties on the lawn at home. Except for the faces, they might all have been playing that game, hoping nobody would catch them moving a muscle when the watcher turned round.

Skipper looked at the shallow depression caused by the explosion. It was probably not a mine, on second thoughts. Fenton's rock had very likely struck a hand grenade abandoned in the sand, or the nose-cone of a small calibre shell. It might, just conceivably, be a properly laid booby trap which had escaped the mine detectors. There could be others, lurking out of sight, waiting to explode.

'Keep still.' Everybody, as he realised, already was keeping still. Fenton must have covered much of the beach already in his antics. It was a miracle he had not touched something off earlier. Skipper remembered that he and Michael had walked directly from the boat to the trees, and halfway back again. They were on the direct line now, which was almost certainly safe.

'Everybody come slowly towards me. Try to remember where you've stepped before and come the same way. We'll all take the straight line back to the boat.'

Slowly, step by step, as though fighting a rearguard action, the banyan party shuffled back to the whaler, their toes tingling with anticipation at every tread. Everybody got in except Fenton and Geoffrey, who carried on shoving the boat out to sea until they were each waist deep. There, they gripped the gunwale, hoisted themselves dripping on board and flopped into the bilges.

'Well done. Up foresail, set mainsail. Let's get out of this.' Skipper hauled in on the mizzen sail sheet from behind him and put the tiller hard to port to steer the boat out to sea. But the light wind was now blowing directly on shore. Before the mainsail could draw properly and the boat could gather way, the wind had nudged them back inside again. The boat seemed to hang helplessly, neither going out nor drifting in, for a whole minute before the banyan party felt the ominous grinding on the keel. None of them looked at each other but Skipper knew what they were all thinking. He was thinking the same himself: *Any moment now this bloody boat is going to detonate something underwater.*

'Try again, give us a really good shove off this time, and then carry on swimming and we'll pick you up out there.'

Again they pushed the whaler out, until they were neck deep, and then they began to swim. But it was soon plain that the swimmers were moving out to sea while the whaler was slowly edging back inshore again. Soon it had grounded again, this time it seemed a little more firmly.

'Jesus Christ,' said Fenton.

'Don't swear, please. We'll try the other way around. Push the boat around and we'll try it on the port tack.' Skipper had the dimmest of memories from his early seamanship classes that this type of whaler had five oars, three on one side and two on the other, which meant a very slightly asymmetrical hull. It might just sail better with the wind over the other gunwale, just well enough to give themselves some sea room and get out. But for the third time they pushed, and swam, and clambered in, while the boat swung calmly and maddeningly back to shore, as though determined not to leave.

'What about the oars? Get the oars out, why the *hell* didn't I think of that before?'

They looked and searched under the thwarts. 'There aren't any oars, Skipper. We forgot them.'

'We thought we were going for a sail, Skipper, didn't need oars.'

They had started out that afternoon for a pleasant sail, to get away from the ship and enjoy themselves for a bit. Now they were in real danger. This bloody, *bloody* fucking war that always spoiled everything. Skipper managed to control a spasm of rage which almost rose to panic. He could see the growing dismay on the faces of his crew. Thank goodness they were out of clear sight of the ship, though perhaps they might be able to signal. But at least there would be no loud guffaws from the watchers on the quarterdeck and the superstructure galleries. Just look at that shower of flyboys messing about in that boat, they would be saying. All the same, sail or not, they should have had the oars on board. That was a bad slip. It would be no use complaining that the Chief Bosun's Mate should have put them in. Skipper was in charge of the boat and should have checked for himself. Now that he had looked, he knew there was no barricoe of water in the boat either, and he had no doubt that if he counted them there would be some lifejackets short, with not enough for one each. They had sailed off into the wild blue yonder like a bunch of raw, careless amateurs and it was Skipper's fault.

'OK, we'll try again, and this time everybody on board will have to paddle with his hands and with the bailer and anything else we can find. I'll give you the word and when I say so, you all paddle like hell...'

'Say, you there, what the hell are you guys doing on that beach?'

The loudhailer sound came on them as startlingly as a thunder clap. The explosion on the beach had attracted the attention of one of the American inshore flotillas which ceaselessly patrolled the islands and inlets on the fringe of the great anchorage. Many of the nearby hills, paddy fields and rough country hid parties of surviving Japanese soldiers, some of them still armed and organised, who might attempt some form of attack, by swimmers or by gunfire, on the fleet.

The landing craft was full of helmeted men, armed with carbines, and there was a machine gun mounted forward, trained upon the banyan party. The man with the loudhailer stood in the stern, beside the Coxswain. With his grey painted helmet, his padded khaki flak jacket, the pistol at his hip and the binoculars round his neck, he looked an efficient, competent figure, an apparition from another war.

Skipper cupped his hands to shout. 'We're on a banyan.' He was conscious that what he was saying sounded absurd. 'We're having a bit of difficulty getting off the beach.'

He could see the comical reaction on the man's face at the English accent. They had come round the point expecting to find a band of marauding Japanese. Instead they had found a bunch of Limeys all dressed up like something out of Charlie Chaplin, in a boat which belonged to Captain Bligh.

'Don't you guys know that beach is dangerous?'

'We thought this beach was safe.'

'Listen, buster, every beach around here is dangerous, you hear me?'

'Yes, we know that. *Now*. We're trying to get away.'

'What's the trouble?'

It was too difficult to explain. 'Can you give us a tow off the beach?'

'You bet. That surely is jist what I aim to do, tow you away.'

The landing craft drove in towards the beach and went astern. A grinning black sailor stood up on its ramp. A rope whirled and spun and dropped, impeccably in place, across the whaler's forward thwart. Michael picked the end up and secured it round the thwart.

'OK, fellows, here we go…'

The noise of the landing craft's engine rose, the craft backed away, the line tightened and, smoothly, the whaler glided off the beach.

Two hundred yards out to sea, when Skipper could feel a good wind on his cheek, he shouted and waved to attract attention. The landing craft's engine slowed and the line went slack.

'Thank you very much for your help. We can make it on our own now.'

'Negative. We don't know you guys, or what you were doing on that beach. We're gonna take you back where you belong and find out. Now, where're you from, Captain?'

Michael shrugged his shoulders. 'This man was obviously a sheriff in civilian life.'

The landing craft came deftly alongside and the whaler was secured bow and stern. The banyan party and the American sailors studied each other, as though each were inhabitants of another world. The Americans looked down over the side of their landing craft, grinning and chewing gum, just as they did in American films. The Sheriff, a stocky, moustachioed man with the bars of a lieutenant (jg) on his lapels, evidently still hardly believed in his capture.

'Say, do you guys always dress like that?'

Skipper conceded that his banyan party must look strange to alien eyes. 'We're on a sailing party, out for the day. We're out on an afternoon's sail.'

'An afternoon's sail.' The Sheriff raised his eyes disbelievingly to the sky. 'In *Leyte*? Say, don't you Limeys know there's a war on round here?'

'We had heard.'

The Sheriff's expression rapidly changed to a scowl. 'Now don't you get fresh with me, Captain.'

Gus Dempsey spoke up for the first time. 'Lieutenant, watch that lip. This officer here is a Lieutenant Commander and a Squadron COmmander.'

Once more the Sheriff's face registered amazement at finding a fellow countryman dwelling in the tents of the Philistines. 'OK, sorry, Commander. So, hold on to your hats, we'll take you back.'

So, ignominiously, lashed alongside an American landing craft, the squadron banyan party returned to the ship. The Sheriff made his approach in the most ostentatious manner possible, his interrogative loudhailer blaring, making Skipper and his crew cringe with embarrassment. The Sheriff's bawled questions, *'Do you recognise this boat?'*, the figures hurrying to and fro on *Miss Britannia*'s quarterdeck, the faces gathering at the guard rails, the sight of the Commander himself standing on the top platform of the starboard after gangway and nodding vigorously, all made Skipper wish he could sink down on the bottom-boards of the whaler and vanish from sight.

The Sheriff compounded their embarrassment by bringing the whaler alongside the starboard after gangway, which was normally reserved for the Captain himself and for flag officers. Looking up, Skipper could see the Captain's face above the guard rail.

The Sheriff was hailing the gangway. 'Sir, do you know these men?'

'Yes, we do, they belong to this ship.'

'That's OK, then.' The Sheriff looked down at Skipper. 'Home and dry, Captain.'

'Thank you for the lift.'

'That's OK, Captain, any time. Glad to be of service. An afternoon sail.' The Sheriff shook his head slowly from side to side. 'Well, I'll be *horn-swaggled*.' Roaring with laughter, he drove off.

CHAPTER SIX

Waiting above, at the top of the gangway, were the Captain, the Commander, the First Lieutenant, the Mate of the Upper Deck, the Gunnery Officer, the Chief Quartermaster, the Chief Bosun's Mate, the seaman petty officer in charge of boats, two leading hands from his working party, and some sailors from the duty part of the watch. They were, in their way, a representative body of the executive department of the ship, and Skipper wondered where they had all suddenly sprung from. Perhaps a threat to one of their precious wooden boats touched off some hidden upper-deck alarm system, causing them all to muster at the threatened spot. They all had one question, and it was the Commander who asked it.

'What was all that about, Skipper?'

Conscious of his squadron officers coming up the steps behind him one by one, towels and bathing things in hand, grinning sheepishly and standing about, anxious to avoid meeting anybody else's eye, Skipper tried to tell the tale. It was impossible to tell without making oneself appear such a fool. They had indeed erred and strayed from the way like lost sheep. They should have taken more care, but it was difficult to say exactly what extra precautions they should have taken.

But to Skipper's surprise, it was not so embarrassing after all. They were all on his side, because everybody in the Navy shared a common fund of stories about hair-raising adventures ashore, of the shark that came perilously close, of the man nearly drowned under the capsized boat, of the feet lacerated by sea-urchins' needles, of the food-poisoning from eating shellfish, of angry beach-owners, and hornets' nests, and broken ankles. Skipper's landmine was now added to that great store of naval mythology.

Even the story of the Sheriff's part became easier to tell. Skipper had felt himself humiliated by the man's overbearing manner, dominated by his bruising self-confidence. The memory of that scornful accent was still raw. But his audience were curious rather than condemnatory. 'Cheeky Yank,' was all somebody said.

There were practical steps to be taken. Everybody in Leyte must now be warned that the beach was no longer safe. Skipper himself was more than ever convinced that Fenton had touched off a single unlucky relic. But, nevertheless, the beach would be closed and the mine detectors would go over it once again, and the officer in charge of the first mine-detecting detail would have some explaining to do.

As the others dispersed, the Captain nodded to Skipper to join him in his walk up and down the quarterdeck. 'Must have been rather embarrassing, that?'

'Very embarrassing indeed, sir. I felt such a bloody fool telling it all. Then and now. Quite apart from the fact that somebody might have been hurt or even killed. If Richard Fenton had *trodden* on that instead of pitching a rock on to it, it would have been "Goodbye Dolly we must leave you".'

'"Goodbye Dolly we must leave you."' The Captain lifted his head and gave a short laugh. 'I must say, that says it. Made you feel you could never get away from the damned war, didn't it?'

Once again, Skipper was taken aback by the Captain's insight. He had been on board the whole time, had not seen what happened, but he had still divined Skipper's reactions precisely.

'That was it exactly, sir.'

'It's what I would have thought myself. But never mind, the banyan was still basically a very good idea. I wish I'd been able to arrange something similar for everybody. Everybody on board needs a bit of a break.'

Once again, Skipper could see the Captain exercising his magnificent panoramic vision in any affair which affected the ship. He was always able to argue from the particular to the general, to take a lesson from a part and apply it to the whole, to see in one man's predicament his relevance to everyone on board. No man was an island in this ship. The Captain made sure they were all involved.

'I say that because all the signs are that the next operating period is going to be tougher than ever and I want everybody to get as much relaxation as they possibly can, especially the aircrew. It seems the Americans are doing Okinawa the hard way.

They've got more than enough fire power to take any ground they want from the Japanese, but I sometimes wish they would use a bit more subtlety. They've got this new general now, I've never heard of him and nor has anybody else. It seems he's spent the war up to now organising the defences of Alaska. And now he's pitched in right at the deep end in a place like Okinawa. It's going to get a lot worse. The nearer we get to Japan the more desperately the Japanese are going to fight. They think Japan is sacred soil, did you know that?'

'Yes, I know a little about it, sir.'

'For us to invade Japan would be like them coming and jumping up and down on the altar at Westminster Abbey. They've got no fleet left worth the name, but they do have some aircraft, and they're going to use these suicide aircraft instead of a fleet and compensate for the lack of skilled aircrew. They haven't trained enough up after that shebang last year. So we can expect these suiciders to get worse, more intense, as time goes on. Are you going across to exchange notes with your opposite numbers, as usual?'

'Oh, yes, sir. I hope to go across to *Fifi* tomorrow lunchtime or the evening. All depends if there are any boats.'

'Oh, there will be boats. I'll have a word with the Commander. I'm very anxious that all the Squadron COs get together as often as possible. Your turn to be mine host?'

'No, sir, it's Robert Weston this time.'

'What do you talk about? I've often wondered.'

'It's all shop, sir. Aircrew shop. We shoot lines at each other. Try and get people to believe our line-shoots, hoot at everybody else's. Generally, we gossip about the state of the art, sir. Effect of any mods. Any new dodges and wheezes. Is the air-sea rescue side all it should be? Because that is very important for a pilot's well-being. Makes a big difference if you know there's a ninety per cent chance of being picked up. Is there anything more we should be adding to the briefing? How's the met. situation? Any odd thing, sir. Unintelligible call-signs. One of the main things, just coming to a head, is ship-air identification. There's quite a lot of feeling about that in the squadrons, sir.'

'What's that?'

'Mistakes in identification, sir. Our own being shot down by us. It affects the Seafires more than us, because they're always in and out, close CAP, skirting round the fleet gun barrage. But in the end it affects us all. The Seafires have lost two or three already. We think it's bad enough having to deal with the bloody little Nips without having to come home to a mouthful of steel and shit from our own side.'

'I see the point. Now that you mention it, I'll bear down harder on that. Thank you for mentioning it. I'll get Guns to do a special blitz on it. What else do you talk about?'

'Well, sir, as I said, just the general state of the art.' Skipper was conscious of being pumped. The Captain had a tireless capacity for listening. Ship's and aircrew officers often came away from seeing him saying they were quite exhausted from being listened to. 'If somebody's lost some pilots, we try and find out what went wrong and try and put it right. If we've got a new chum, we try and put him in the picture.' Skipper knew they were both thinking of Flash Gordon.

'It didn't work with him.' The Captain reached the end of his quarterdeck beat once more, swung round and stepped smartly off again. Skipper automatically turned and kept in step with the Captain. 'But that wasn't your fault, or the ship's fault. That was a shocking, a really criminal mistake on the part of the appointers. The PMO and I have been making some enquiries and putting some pieces together. I can tell you this in confidence —'

'Of course, sir...'

'— but that man should never have been allowed anywhere near a carrier again, let alone put in charge of a front-line squadron. He was a sick man when he came here. I should have noticed it. But how could you ground a man just on a suspicion?'

'You could never have done that, sir.' Skipper was aware that the Captain, uncharacteristically, was looking for reassurance. So even this Olympian man occasionally had doubts and misgivings, too. It was cheering to know that.

'He'd had two bad crashes in the last nine months, and several near misses. This was no secret. They knew all about it. And they still sent him here. He had reached a state of such neurosis that he simply didn't know what was dangerous and what was not.'

Skipper remembered that Michael had said that Gordon was in a state of such fright he had believed everything was dangerous. It was interesting that Michael and the Captain should have arrived at such diametrically opposite conclusions on the same evidence.

'If you notice anything in any of your pilots — I know I said this to you when you first embarked as a squadron but it's much more important now — if you notice anything don't try and hide it, or let him try and hide it. They'll plead with you, the best ones, to be allowed to go on…'

Skipper himself was not so sure on that point, but he let it pass.

'You're the only one who really knows, even better than the doctor.'

Again, Skipper was not so certain. The line between fitness and unfitness was not a firm frontier which everybody knew when they were crossing. Rather was it a wide grey area of the spirit, into which all pilots strayed at some time in their operational lives. There were those who came out again and those who stayed inside, wandering about for ever.

'If you let them go on when they're not fit, that'll be one more grave on the way. It's a game of blood, as we all know, but it does have its ground rules. Tell me about that Singapore business. Those nine murders. What effect has that had on how the aircrew are feeling?'

'Funnily enough, sir, it doesn't seem to have had all that much of a lasting effect. It hit everybody for a time, of course, and made them mad, but they've all shrugged it off by now. OK, it's a bloody awful war, everybody is saying, but we all knew that long ago. The message clearly is, *don't* get chopped down. Most people have shrugged it off and got on with it. The only person who really reacted to it, I suppose, was Michael.'

'Your Senior Pilot?'

'Yes, sir. He seemed to take it very badly to heart at first. But even he seems to have shucked it off now.'

'What sort of bloke is he, now?'

'Excellent pilot, sir. I couldn't ask for a better or more loyal Senior Pilot.'

'I didn't actually mean as a pilot. As a man. As an officer.'

The last word was only gently, in the faintest possible way, accented. Skipper turned round. The Captain's eyes gave nothing away. Nothing happened on board without the Captain knowing about it. It was quite probable that he knew of Michael's idiosyncrasies.

'As a man, sir, first class.'

'Have you thought any more about becoming one of us, as they say?'

'I wasn't strictly honest with you the other night, sir. I have thought about a regular commission more than once.'

'I knew you had.'

'Can I leave it for just now, sir? Somehow I feel there is a lot going on just now and I won't have a chance to think about it properly.'

'Of course. My question arose from what we were talking about a few minutes ago. If a man's not fit, he's not doing the war effort any good. I've always thought it wrong to expect air groups to go on and on until the end of a commission or they drop down dead, whichever is the later. They ought to be relieved in a proper way at a proper time. The Navy's been very ignorant about air power, you know, Skipper. We've made lots of mistakes. We're a little better now, but we've still got a long way to go. I'm afraid that there are still carriers in the fleet where the RN regular officers treat the aircrew rather as lesser breeds without the law, as though they were in some way not quite respectable. Not people one would take home and introduce to one's family. That's why we're going to need people like you after the war…'

'*After* the war, sir?' The Captain might as well have been talking about the coming of the millennium.

'Maybe. But sooner or later we're going to need men who know about aircraft. A transfusion of fresh blood. Men who *know* about flying, what aircraft can do, and we're going to need them in the top ranks of the Navy. Not like me, a silly old fish-head, stuck up in the island all day … How does it go? *With his thumb in his bum and his mind in neutral…* What's the Fleet Air Arm saying?'

'That expression applies to a fairly restricted class of people, sir.'

'Well said, Skipper! Is it this evening you're going across?' The Captain's loud laughter made everybody on the quarterdeck turn and stare.

'Hope to, sir.'

'Right.'

A word from the Captain worked like a charm. This time when Skipper asked for a boat for the Squadron COs, the Mate of the Upper Deck, who had a tendency to superciliousness toward the squadrons, hurried to oblige and had the Captain's own barge lowered.

The barge was not maintained at the pitch of peacetime, but its gilt dolphins on the cabin roof, its brass rails, its wood-panelled engine covers, its enamel paint and ship's crest medallions on either bow, all retained an aura of peacetime splendour. The Captain's Coxswain himself was at the wheel, the best boat stoker in the ship was in charge of the engines, and the bowman and stern-sheets men went through their boat-hook drill in the approved manner as the boat drew away from the gangway.

Stanley, who always took every chance of exchanging views with other fighter direction officers, had come with them. 'This is almost like peacetime,' he said. 'Clean white uniforms, boat-hook drill, Captain's barge called away, White Ensign at the stern — this is like paying official calls before the war.'

'Is this how it was done?' Skipper asked.

'Oh, yes. Everybody in full fig. And then the governor or the mayor or whoever it was would return the call. Guard and band, pipes and bugle calls, gun salute sometimes, even. You always knew when one of His Majesty's ships was there, all right.'

As the boat skimmed out across the water, throwing a wide foaming wake to either side, Skipper too caught some of the spirit of the moment. It was a fine, open, glorious evening. *Miss Britannia* was a black shape against the streaked sky, with every radar aerial, every line of her superstructure, every curve and point of the aircraft on deck silhouetted. She looked powerful, brooding, magnificent. Skipper realised for the first time and with some slight surprise how proud he was of her, how proud he was to be one of her company.

Madame Fifi, the next ship down the line of aircraft carriers, was the same class but the two ships were by no means identical. There were differences in the patterns and shapes of the camouflage paint on her side and different shipbuilding yards had left indefinable differences, all discernible to a seaman's eye. Their gangway guard rail, Skipper noticed, was not quite the same height and it was a plain white rope, without the smart red-and-white twist in it of *Miss Britannia*'s.

Nor, Skipper also noticed, was it as clean, or the woodwork of the gangway itself so well scrubbed.

The welcome at the top of the gangway also differed from their own ship. There was nobody from the squadrons to meet them and the Officer of the Watch, a Sub-Lieutenant RN, turned away with the words, only just but intentionally audible, 'God, more flyboys.' There was a long delay while a messenger was sent down to the wardroom. While he waited, Skipper studied the quarterdeck, which was almost eerily familiar. The firemain valves, the bollards and the ventilation trunkings were all in the same place as in *Miss Britannia*, although the Officer of the Watch's table, the deck log and the lifebuoy were on the opposite side.

'Skipper, I'm terribly sorry not to have been there to meet you,' Robert Weston was frowning as he shook hands, and he glared at the Officer of the Watch's back. 'I did ask to be informed when your boat was coming alongside.'

'Never mind, we're all here now.'

'How are you, mate?'

'Still surviving.'

'Still surviving! Let's all go and have a drink.'

Skipper followed Robert Weston down through a ship which, again, was oddly familiar. She had the same flats and passageways, the same doors, the same openings. One or two of the bulkheads were painted a little differently, one or two fittings were in different places, and yet otherwise it was uncannily like walking through their own ship, but in a dream, where slight shifts had been made in familiar surroundings.

Skipper had the same sensation of being not-quite-home when he entered the wardroom anteroom. The door, the bar, the magazine tables, the noticeboards were all in the same place, the photographs of the King and Queen on the bulkheads, the armchairs of the same Admiralty pattern, all was the same but there was a difference and the guests felt it at once. This was not the companionable mess of *Miss Britannia*. There was a gay green 'gin' pennant with a white wineglass embroidered on it, but there was no real welcome. Skipper could see that this wardroom was a house divided against itself. Aircrew were aircrew, evidently, and ship's officers were ship's officers, and never the twain should meet.

'What'll you have, Skipper?' The other Avenger CO had taken Henry Darling under his wing.

'Whisky, please.'

'Fag?'

'No, thanks. Don't use them.'

'Of course not. Forgot.'

Robert Weston had lost some hair since Skipper had last seen him. His face looked lined and tired. Skipper noticed his weariness and clumsiness as Robert Weston lit a cigarette, drew deeply on it and suffered a fit of sudden coughing. The thought flashed through Skipper's mind that possibly his old friend might be coming perilously close to the stage of being unfit for operational flying. Yet his losses had been no greater than anybody else's. Robert Weston himself had the reputation of being as safe as the Bank of England. He had never lost a wingman. Flying with Robert Weston was considered to be a passport to survival, a blue-chip investment in the future.

Robert Weston was having some difficulty in attracting the attention of the bar steward, who was at the other end of the bar with his back kept studiedly towards them, busying himself with the drinks of some ship's officers. Robert Weston had eventually to rap on the counter several times with a half-crown. The bar steward was, as Skipper saw when the

Commander came into the anteroom, only taking his attitude from his superiors.

Their Commander was a very tall man, with a beaked nose, purple cheeks with broken red veins, and one of the loudest voices Skipper had ever heard. Skipper had an inconsequential memory of Mrs Fleetwood, the housekeeper at Daughton, and her canary, which sang at times so loudly it actually loosened the wax in a listener's ears. To Skipper's surprise, this Commander obviously noticed the strangers at the bar but made no effort to be introduced or to speak to them. In *Miss Britannia* the Commander, as President of the Mess, would have wished to know who the guests were, whose guests they were, and what their business was on board, as much from politeness and a wish to be helpful as from a proper professional curiosity. But this man merely looked Skipper coolly up and down as he reached the bar.

'Flyboys cluttering up the bar Again,' he said. It need not have been offensive, and with some men would never have been intended so. It was all in the tone of voice. 'Gin, please, Smithers.'

Smithers, Skipper saw, already had the Commander's gin and bitters ready. No dilly-dallying or coin-rapping *there*.

As the Commander moved away with his gin, Robert Weston caught Skipper's eye and nodded. 'I know what you're thinking, Skipper, and you're bloody well right.' He kept his voice so low Skipper could barely hear him. 'It's this bloody ship. The aircrew are treated like shit here. Like absolute bloody shit. It's odd when you think about it. In most ships they bloody well ignore you, except when one of you gets killed.'

This profanity was new for Robert Weston. A Wykehamist, the son of a clergyman who was also a Wykehamist, he had always taken his old school's motto to heart. *Manners makyth man* had always been his family's watchword. Skipper had been at Oxford with him and they had both joined the Navy on the same day, and during their training, when everybody else swore as a matter almost of naval tradition, Robert Weston had refrained. Things must be bad to have reduced Robert to this scowling, swearing, balding version of himself.

'Anyway, cheers, Robert. Here's to the end of the war.'

'Oh, dear God, yes. Roll on.'

'So. What's new?'

'Nothing much. You've got all the news. What about this Gordon fellow? Something distinctly fishy about that, I felt it in my water. What happened to him?'

'Ah, yes. *Well...*'

Robert Weston listened to the story of Flash Gordon's first and final sortie with the detached curiosity of a connoisseur. 'Sounds to me as if there was a screw loose somewhere. I shared a cabin for a few days with a chap called Gordon at Yeovilton. Flash Gordon, they called him.'

'Bound to be the same man.'

'Used to have the most terrible nightmares. Used to wake up in the middle of the night howling like a thousand banshees. We were all very glad when he got drafted away after a few days. Good pilot, mind you. Or was.'

Robert Weston's profanity returned when he returned to the subject of the ship. 'It's bloody disloyal, I know, but the main trouble with this ship is the Captain himself. He's one of the old school, as they pompously call it. Never heard of aircraft, and doesn't want to hear. Guns were the thing, boy, *guns*. He doesn't like aircrew. He doesn't like RNVR officers either. So RNVR aircrew officers are like shit underfoot, and as there are more of us on board than any other kind of officer you can imagine there's a lot of shit underfoot. He doesn't talk to any of us direct…'

'Not even the Squadron COs?'

'Not even the Squadron COs.'

'But you're his main armament, so to speak!'

'Don't tell *me*. I'm well aware of that. He sends us messages through Wings. His Coxswain once told somebody on board here that the Captain started off the war in a destroyer and he used to take his shotgun up to the bridge with him and every time he saw an aircraft, *any* aircraft, ours or theirs, *especially* ours, he used to shoot at it with his bloody shotgun, cackling with unholy glee the while. The view here is that this bloody ship would be a damned sight better off if it weren't for the aeroplanes. Take those off and fit her with rows of sixteen-inch gun turrets all along the flight deck, go back to coal-burning instead of all this new-fangled oil while you're about it, and this lot would be as happy as bloody sandboys. The guns wouldn't need to work, of course. They wouldn't need to *fire*. In fact it would be a bloody sight better if they didn't. All they want to do is maintain them and polish their insides and they're quite happy. Makes a mess when they go off. D'you know, I discovered the other day, somebody was telling me, that in the Mediterranean Fleet before the war, nobody in harbour ever covered their guns until the flagship did, even though it was sheeting down with rain. Imagine that. They had to wait until the flagship signalled them "Cover guns". Incredible. Imagine us striking down and ranging up aircraft all in time with the bloody flagship!'

This bitterness, like the profanity, was new. Robert Weston had been the most pleasant and amiable of men. Skipper was more and more concerned that his old friend might be approaching the point of breakdown.

As usual, Douglas Mayhew had said nothing but had just stood by the bar, smiling and obviously enjoying himself, without contributing. Robert Weston was evidently struck with remorse at having neglected one of his guests. 'I know how bloody hard it is for you, mate, having to take over a squadron just like that.'

'Oh, it's not too bad.'

'I hear you did very well over Formosa and you haven't lost a man yet —' Robert Weston's stricken face showed that he regretted the words as soon as he had said them. All three of them, even Skipper with his distaste for superstitions, turned and wetted their fingers and rubbed them on the bar. 'Touch wood, of course. That's a bloody good squadron you've got there, mate. Old Herman might have got a bit of a twitch towards the end but he was still a very fine squadron man. Shall I give you some advice?'

Douglas Mayhew grimaced. 'No, thank you.'

'That's *right*!' It was the first time that evening they had seen Robert Weston laugh, or even smile. 'That's the right answer, mate. Well, I'll tell you all the same. Look after your wingmen. Make sure *they're* OK and that confidence will spread right through the lot. You've got to make every pilot with you feel he's immortal. We're not, of course. We're all going to get the chop before we get through this bloody game, but in the meantime we've all got to go on acting as though we shall all see our grandchildren one day.'

Skipper wondered whether Robert really meant what he said, whether he truly and honestly believed that none of them had any future. His advice to Douglas Mayhew now seemed to Skipper to be eccentric. It was true that confidence, like fear, could be contagious, but there were many more men on a Squadron CO's conscience than just his own wingmen. Of course one should look after one's own flight, but to argue that taking care of them would have the effect of taking care of the whole squadron was as absurd as expecting to make a whole body healthy merely by looking after one arm. Selfishness was always one of the first signs of oncoming unfitness. A pilot on the way out became more and more obsessed with his own personal safety, a caution which paradoxically often led to more accidents. That Robert Weston should be thinking of operations in terms only of his own flight suggested that his horizon of awareness, too, was contracting. For the first time Skipper felt a growing fear, for his friend and for the future.

Robert Weston was looking around him. 'I must say, it's good to hear us all talking at the bar like this for a change. Not often this happens.'

More aircrew officers were arriving in the anteroom and for a time they heavily outnumbered the ship's officers. The whole room began to take on the appearance of a squadron benefit. The Commander had gone, and the squadron voices were raised in relief and in a roar of conversation. These faces, Skipper thought, could be his own air group. In any gathering of operational aircrew, there was always an undercurrent of apprehension under the gaiety, and even here Skipper caught the unguarded glances he expected to see, the quick looks at the wardroom clock on the bulkhead, as though the exact time, now, was of tremendous importance.

'Your bar open at sea, Skipper?'

'Yes. Well, sometimes. Not up in the operating area. But on passage, or in the replenishment area, it normally is. But I never drink before a flying day and neither do I allow any of my boys to drink. Normally we do all our serious drinking in harbour. Like now.' Skipper held up his empty glass. 'This is a very long ship, Robert?'

'I'm sorry, Skipper, I didn't notice.' Smithers, this time, could hardly ignore them. Squadron officers lined the bar from end to end.

'Long ship. That's a pukka RN expression, Skipper. You're beginning to talk like one of them, aren't you?'

'Like one of *us*, surely? We're all in the same boat, surely?'

'Not in *this* bloody boat we're not, mate. There's first and second class on this liner.'

Skipper did not want to start Robert Weston off on that hobbyhorse again. They were for the moment separated from the rest, and Skipper would have liked to have taken the chance to talk privately. Robert was surely the best man to listen. In the old days Skipper would never have hesitated, but he had seen enough of his old friend that day to make him unaccustomedly apprehensive of Robert's reaction when he mentioned his thoughts of turning over to the regular RN.

'As a matter of fact, you're not far from the truth, actually. I was thinking about … Well, have you ever thought of turning over to a regular commission if they offered you one?'

Skipper had expected surprise, even astonishment, but he was quite taken aback by the virulence of Robert Weston's contempt.

'You must be pulling my leg, Skipper! Turn over to the RN after the war … if there is such a thing? Turn over to the straight RN? You must be *joking*…'

'No, honestly, I'm telling you —'

'Hitch yourself permanently to *this* lot? I wouldn't do that, not for a thousand a year! Not for *three* thousand a year!'

'It could be you're influenced by this particular ship…'

'It could be. It could just be. I'll *say* it bloody well could be. You're dead right it could be, I'm influenced by this bloody ship. I've had a bellyful of it, I can tell you. It's me for civvy street by the very first boat. Not that there's any chance of that...'

Skipper no longer had any doubts that Robert Weston believed there was no future. The plain misery on his face showed it.

'We're never going to get away. We're going to go on and on and on. You know what it's like, screwing blokes up to the right pitch to fly again every time we go to sea. D'you know, the other day I overheard our gallant Commander telling somebody about relieving officers because of the strain they were under, up there in the striking area. He wasn't talking about aircrew, he was talking about ship's officers. *Fishheads! Strain?* They don't know what strain is. The only straining fishheads do is when they go to the heads. Half of them do bugger all all day except sit on their arses in offices below. Half of them never see the fresh air at all. *Strain*, ye Gods. Nobody ever thinks of the strain on *aircrew*...'

'That's true, I'm afraid.' Skipper did not wish to encourage Robert Weston in another outburst. His voice was getting louder and louder, and sooner or later he would say something that ought not to be said and be heard by somebody who ought not to hear it. But still, it was true that nobody really considered the strain of prolonged operational flying.

'D'you know, Skipper, I've just had the devil's own job getting one of my pilots sent out of the ship. I had to, because the way he was going he was going to kill himself and possibly other people too. Because he was all shot to hell. Nerves in little pink ribbons. He was past it. Had it, simply had it. He was just a shell, just going through the motions. You couldn't even bear to be in the same room as him for any length of time because he was so screwed up and nervous. He infected everybody else. There was always something wrong with his cab, always some reason why he couldn't fly. Half the time when he did get up on a sortie he turned back before he reached the target. And this is bad for all the rest who are trying their best, as you know. I think he even affected his aircraft. Like a horse with a shit-scared rider. There are some pilots, their aircraft never give trouble. Start first touch, first time, every day and every time, and bound off the deck as though they couldn't wait. Others, just their touch on anything makes everything turn to shit.'

Skipper nodded. It was a phenomenon he had noticed himself too often for it to be dismissed as chance or coincidence.

'And d'you know, the only suggestion they could come up with for that chap in this ship, the only thing they could think of to do with him was to court-martial him! I ask you!'

'I know, I know the problem. But Robert, don't *shout...*'

'Was I shouting? I'll shout a good bit more before I'm through.' Robert Weston's face was badly flushed and his hands were trembling. He had spilled some of his glass and soaked his cigarette into a disintegrating stump. *'Oh, fuck.'*

'I know I said it before, Robert, but it *is* true. There *are* other ships. There must be more to it than that. Don't you ever, don't you feel at all, that basically it is a great service with some very fine blokes in it? Doesn't the sailors' sense of humour make you curl up and cry with laughter every so often? I know whenever I'm worried or troubled, I go down the mess deck and somebody says something which absolutely creases me. They've got a kind of bounciness. Their repartee ... their sort of ... *serenity*, I think, is the only word. They're not bothered. They know they're the best and that's all there is to it. They can beat the best in the world. They're the best, the rest are the rest, as they say.'

'God, you *must* have got it bad, Skipper! You're talking like Noel Coward on pep pills. There's a place somewhere for you, I'm sure…'

'But surely, Robert, don't you remember when we first joined up, you remember how impressed we all were, even though none of us would ever admit it?'

'Ah yes, dear God, but that was about a hundred years ago. That's all ancient history now and I'm not an ancient historian. I'm just a poor bloody squaddie who's trying to keep himself and his boys alive so they can fly against the Japs again, and again, and *again*…

Was there, Skipper wondered, just the trace of maudlin self-consciousness in Robert's voice? Was he really as depressed and as furious as he represented himself?

Skipper had been aware of the steadily rising noise level in the anteroom, and had attributed it to the racket of a successful party getting under way. But now, in a conversation right at his elbow, he saw that there was an ugly note in the uproar. It was one of the Seafire pilots, whom Skipper vaguely remembered from some other party in the past; he was a short, dark little man, 'Seafire-sized' as they said, with smooth black hair brushed straight back on his head. He looked a dapper little man, as polite as a gentleman s gentleman. But now he was talking to, or rather shouting at, a burly fair-haired lieutenant with straight stripes on the shoulders of his khakis. From the exchanges Skipper guessed that he was concerned with the ship's gunnery department.

'All I know is that poor old Freddie is dead and gone and buried now, and all because your dopey gunnery Joes were too *thick* to know a Seafire when they saw it…'

The ship's officer was very red in the face. 'That's not fair, to say that,' he muttered.

'*Fair?*' The Seafire pilot pounced on the word as though in triumph. 'Who said anything about being *fair?* It's not *fair* any of us are here at all. *Fairness* has got bugger all to do with it. You're supposed to be a straight-up-and-down gunnery officer. You're supposed to know what a Seafire looks like. This is one of the things you are expected to know. Next time one of *your* bods gets killed I suppose you'll all turn towards Whale Island and kneel down and pray and say, "Please God, it's not *fair!*" It wasn't *fair* that Freddie was chopped down by one of *your* stupid, asinine, cretinous Bofors crews —'

'Hey, Tich.' Robert Weston put a restraining hand on the Seafire man's shoulder. He had seemingly already forgotten his own fury. 'Hey, Tich, watch it. You are a guest here, and we've got lots of other guests. I'm sorry to say this —'

'OK, OK, OK, I'm sorry. All right, all right, all right.' The Seafire pilot waved both hands in front of him as though to dispel an imaginary cloud and then, brutally and abruptly, turned on his heel, in a movement which was in its way as rude and conclusive as anything he had said.

There had been a vicious, bitter undertone to the quarrel which had quite shocked Skipper. He had never known that feelings of such passionate intensity could come to the surface in any wardroom, where, he had always been taught and believed, everybody should at least try to follow Nelson's expressed example to become a band of brothers. But the Seafire pilot had right on his side. There was a rising feeling of outrage amongst the aircrews at the numbers of aircraft shot down by 'friendly' gunfire. Sooner or later, the matter would arise in *Miss Britannia*, too, and Skipper decided, with this example in front of him, to treat the whole affair with the greatest circumspection. He had seen how high feelings could run and he would never wish such a scene on his own wardroom. It could so easily happen.

Somebody was at Robert Weston's side with a message. 'Sir, there's a call for you to go up to the Ops Room at once, sir.'

Skipper suddenly became aware that the crowd at the bar was rapidly thinning. People seemed to be scattering even as he watched, disappearing one by one through the anteroom doorway.

Robert Weston came back with an apologetic air. 'I'm terribly sorry, Skipper, but apparently we're going to sea. They want us up in the Ops Room right away. God knows what it's all about but there seems to be a terrible flap going on.'

The Seafire pilot's antagonist was still at the bar, finishing his drink. 'Didn't you get the buzz? We came to reduced notice for steam an hour and a half ago. But of course, *you* wouldn't have noticed, you flyboys. Too busy brushing up your *aircraft identification*, here at the *bar*.'

Once again, Robert Weston held out a placatory hand. 'Oh, come on, Dick, don't be like that. You know feelings are running high about that.'

'*Well.* Bloody hell, do you think we *wanted* to shoot down that boy? Do you really think we feel pleased with ourselves about that? Your Seafire friend there obviously knows nothing about the deadly atmosphere in our department there's been ever since that day. That gun's crew were ready to chuck themselves over the side, for the sheer shame and grief of it all. *We've* got our troubles, too, you know.'

That, also, Skipper decided, was a point of view to be noted and respected.

'I'm sure you have, Dick, all God's chillun got troubles.' Robert Weston's voice was still soothing. He seemed to have entirely shaken off his own malaise of a few minutes before.

'But Tich and Freddie were very close cobbers, you know. And Freddie isn't the only one. There've been three others shot down, two more from that same squadron. They were all picked up, but sooner or later ... But this isn't the time to discuss it. Skipper, look...'

'If you've gotta go, Robert, you gotta go. Don't worry about us, we can find our way to the quarterdeck easily enough. It's just like our old crate, so we'll just follow our noses back to the quarterdeck. We know the way. You push off now, up to Ops.'

'Can you really?' Robert Weston looked relieved. 'I really do feel bad leaving you. But there we are ... It's a bloody game, as we all know.'

They shook hands outside the anteroom door. 'Goodbye, Robert. And you take it easy.'

Their eyes met. 'Yes, I know what you mean. I suppose I must have appeared a little tetchy and sorry for myself. You take it easy, too.'

'You'll survive the war, lad.'

Robert Weston went forward towards the island and the operations room. Skipper turned aft for the quarterdeck, followed by some of the other guests.

As Skipper led the way, they could all see around them the signs that the ship was getting ready for sea. Bulkhead doors were already shut, lighting switched off, fans turned down low. Telephone communications numbers and damage-control parties were closing up for sea. The guests' progress towards the quarterdeck was getting slower and more difficult every moment. Skipper, with a feeling of sharp unreasoning alarm, began to quicken his pace. For no reason, he had a dread of being caught and taken to sea in this ship. He wanted desperately to get back to his own.

The quarterdeck was in darkness and deserted except for one man, whom Skipper guessed was probably the lifebuoy sentry.

'Boats?' The man sounded incredulous, half-derisive. 'No boats now. They've all been hoisted. Half an hour ago, I should think.'

'Oh, God. Where is the Officer of the Watch?'

'Officer of the Watch? Gone up the bridge, I should think. Sea watchkeeping routine now, sir.' The man had realised he was talking to an officer.

'You mean there's no boats to take us back to our own ship? What a —' As he said the words, Skipper knew it was unfair to browbeat a mere sentry like this. 'Well, thank you for your help, anyway.'

'You could try the waist, sir. They might still have a Jacob's ladder or something still down, sir.'

'Good idea, thank you.'

They doubled forward as best they could through the dark spaces and obstacles of the upper deck. In the blackness they barked their shins on the sills of bulkhead combings and stubbed their toes on unseen projections. Once Skipper ran full tilt into an upper deck winch with an impact which half-winded him and brought tears to his eyes. But the fear of being stranded in this ship drove them all on.

In the starboard fuelling pocket two sailors were hauling up a Jacob's ladder. Down below, Skipper heard water slapping against the bows of a boat as it approached the ship's side. With a great surge of joy he made out the shape of the Captain's barge and recognised the Coxswain's voice.

'*Here.* Don't haul up that ladder yet, we've got to get down into that boat there.'

They scrambled joyfully down the ladder, oblivious of the oil stains it left on their white uniforms. In the darkness they

157

missed their footing, and landed in a happy heap on the deck of the barge amidships.

'You think we'd forgotten you, sir?' Skipper could tell by the Coxswain's voice that he was grinning.

'*Never*, Coxswain. But what's all the flap about, do you know?'

'No idea, sir. But I do know the whole fleet's putting to sea.'

The long anchorage was in pitch blackness, with not a light showing anywhere. Skipper could see the Coxswain's head against the dim red light from his compass. He could well understand now how Coxswains who lost their way in this vast harbour sometimes took hours to grope their way back to their ships. But the Captain's Coxswain took them directly back, and it was a measure of the ship's haste that he drove the barge directly under the crane, where it was hoisted almost before it had stopped moving.

As the barge settled in its crutches and the wire-lifting strops slackened as the boat's weight came off them, Skipper looked over the side, where the boat's shipwright was inspecting the lie of the boat in the crutches by the light of a shaded torch. There were other faces, all grinning.

'Thank God,' said Skipper. 'It's like coming home.'

'*Well,*' said the Mate of the Upper Deck, 'it's nice to be appreciated.'

CHAPTER SEVEN

Skipper overheard the Captain beginning his talk to the ship's company as he made his way up to the island from the boat-deck. The voice was coming from a speaker in a small armourers' mess on one of the starboard side gallery decks, and Skipper stopped to listen. The mess deck was new to him, one of the warren of tiny compartments, small messes, storerooms, Bofors ready-use ammunition magazines and flight-deck equipment stowages where aircrew rarely penetrated. Skipper was always finding such unknown territory: the ship was a constant source of fresh wonders and instruction to him, with compartments he knew nothing of and men with skills he had never realised.

'We are now going to sea much earlier than planned, because the Americans have asked us to…' The Captain's voice was level, and pitched slightly higher than his usual conversational tone. He had to allow for the fact that many men would be trying to listen to him above the sound of machinery or the distractions of other noise. 'As you probably know, the business on Okinawa is not going smoothly. I wouldn't be being honest with you if I didn't admit that. So more effort is going to be needed in the next few weeks. Nobody had any doubts that Okinawa was going to be a long and a hard struggle, but everybody now knows that it is going to be even longer and harder than anybody supposed. The further inland and the further south the American 10th Army get, the more fiercely the Japanese are resisting. Furthermore, the Japanese themselves are believed to be mounting some form of counter-attack which will almost certainly be more of the kind of suicide bomber attacks which we already know about.

'I should tell you that there is absolutely no need to be unduly worried by these suicide bombers. They are an unusual kind of attack for us, but we are perfectly capable of looking after ourselves. This means, though, that we have to take extra precautions. From tomorrow, we will be manning a much higher number of our upper deck anti-aircraft guns, from dawn to dusk. This will require special watchkeeping routines which the gunnery department are working out now. It also means that from tomorrow nobody, and I say again *nobody*, will be allowed on the flight deck or in any of the goofing positions in the island except as required for duty, or on watch. The flight deck and island are out of bounds from tomorrow except for certain periods of the day which will be piped. Nobody, repeat nobody, is to go on deck without a specific duty to be there. These suicide bombers are particularly dangerous to personnel on deck so we must cut down the risk. From tomorrow it will be an offence, and I will come down very heavily on anyone who commits it, it will be an offence to go on deck without wearing full anti-flash clothing.

'I am very sorry indeed that the concert party and the flight-deck sports had to be cancelled. I know that you have all been working very hard indeed since we got into harbour and none of you have had any real chance for rest or relaxation at all. As it is, we are sailing now short of some kinds of ammunition and NAAFI stores. All I can say to you all is thank you for all your hard effort and work. Again, I shall try to make it up to you all when we do get back to Sydney. Now, we shall be cracking on as hard as we can, bearing in mind the fuel situation, and we are due to start operating again at dawn the day after tomorrow. We shall go to flying stations tomorrow for exercises and flying practice, on passage, and then first thing on Tuesday morning we shall be back on our old stand off the Sakishima Gunto. That's all, and the best of luck to us all.'

Thoughtfully, Skipper went on up to the Operations Room. He felt that for the very first time this ship was beginning to take the full weight of this war out in the Far East. He now began to understand the undercurrent of tight strain in the American pilots' combat reports he had been allowed to read in Colombo. Some of the more spectacular breakdowns in morale, which the doctor secreted away in his files, now began to make sense. The nearest thing to this grinding war, he supposed, was the battle in the Atlantic, now coming to its end. But even there they at least had a rational enemy and they did return sometimes to their homes and their own women, who were close to the battle. Skipper had an odd thought of that piece in Tacitus: *Close beside them, also, are their nearest and dearest, so that the warriors can actually hear the shrieks of their women and the cries of their children. Those are the witnesses each man values most,* theirs *is the praise worth most to him.* But here there was nothing but thousands and thousands of miles of empty ocean, and to the north thousands of miles of impenetrable, hostile China. Even to the south there was only Australia, which Michael had once said was thousands and thousands of miles of sweet Fanny Adams, with a light fringe of beaches and blondes.

With the air of urgency in the ship, this hurried putting to sea, Skipper had half-hoped for something different this time, perhaps an expedition to the north, maybe even a try at the mainland of Okinawa. If the battle was not going well, then surely the most force should be applied to the main target? He was disappointed and dismayed to see the familiar map of

Ishigaki and Miyako up on the board. However, if the target was the same, Wings was at least propounding a novel and totally unexpected method of attacking it.

'This time, the Admiral proposes to carry out a bombardment of the airfields on Miyako with guns.'

Guns. *Guns?* Nobody spoke, but the aircrew's shock and disbelief were almost audible. Skipper, sitting in the front row, remembered Robert Weston's contemptuous gibes about lining the flight decks with gun turrets. Ye gods and little fishes, it was unbelievable, but they were going to fight the battle of Jutland all over again.

Wings sensed his audience's hostile reaction, and his tone became much more defensive. 'Admiral Spruance's staff have been evaluating our efforts so far and to be candid with you, not to beat about the bush at all, it seems they don't much like what they see. They don't think the peck-marks we're making on the airstrips are much good.' Wings looked down at the paper in his hand. 'Or perhaps it's pock-marks. I can't read somebody's writing. But I think it's pock-marks. Pocks is better than pecks, but anyway the opinion is that neither of them are enough and we must try something heavier. So our Admiral's staff have decided to try a battleship and cruiser bombardment of Miyako on Wednesday, after the first air strikes have gone in…'

Bombardment, thought Skipper. *If this wasn't so serious it would be bloody comic.* If bombardment with heavy guns really was so much more effective, then why were they not bombarding every day? Why indeed had they not been bombarding since the very beginning? If guns were better, then why bother with Avenger bombing and Corsair ground-strafing? If bombardment was better, then what the *hell* had Herman and he and all the rest of them been doing flinging themselves down the flak barrels of Ishigaki and Miyako all these weeks? Never mind the effect on the aircrew. Nobody bothers about *them*. But would it not have been more *efficient* simply to lie off the place at ten miles' range and pound it with large chunks of fourteen-inch metal? *Fire, Master Gunner, when you can see the whites of their airstrips.*

'You're looking a bit doubtful, Skipper. Can we have your views?'

'Well, there's one purely practical point about it. None of us have … I imagine we'll be called upon to spot for fall of shot, and none of us have exercised it or tried it out for … well, I can't remember when … way back, when we first joined the ship and began working up. Bombardment techniques haven't exactly been our forte in these last few months.'

Wings' sharp glance showed he had felt the point. 'We've already thought of that, and we shall be exercising all the communications side of it on passage tomorrow.'

'That's as may be, but it takes time and practice and experience to spot accurately. And bad spotting from the air is worse than no spotting from the air at all.'

Wings frowned. 'I agree, but we can't object to a bombardment merely because we don't think we've exercised it enough recently.'

Can't we? thought Skipper. *We certainly could. Not only could but should.*

'The Captain and the Admiral both think there is a morale effect in a bombardment. Only the aircrew ever see the enemy in a carrier. In fact, we often *complain* that we are the only ones who are taking the weight, while the rest of the ship does nothing…'

That was certainly true, Skipper conceded.

'A bombardment will involve everybody.'

'All that sound and fury, you mean.' *Signifying nothing,* Skipper added to himself.

'Precisely that,' said Wings gratefully. 'It will give everybody a chance to contribute. Besides, it has been proved that ship bombardment has a much greater effect on the morale of people ashore than air bombing…'

Proved? By whom? On what evidence? Once again the Operations Room silently reverberated with unspoken questions.

'Everybody knows the aircraft have to go away sometime. But the ships can lie off and pound away for hours and hours.' That might be, but there were many more questions unasked and unanswered. Why bombard Miyako, when the most dangerous island was Ishigaki? If this new secret weapon was so devastating, then why not hit the harder island with it? There was another point, so important Skipper felt he had to raise it. He was well aware by now that this briefing, like others in the past, was moving towards a state of personal confrontation between Wings and himself. He realised that nobody else had contributed anything. That might be because he was making all the points they wanted to make, and making them well, but it might also be that they were keeping their heads down whilst all this professional naval flak was flying about.

'There is one other thing.'

'Yes?'

'What will the carriers be doing while the bombardment is going on?'

Wings looked quickly away and then back, exasperated, as though Skipper was being wilfully obstructive and his question was tediously unnecessary.

'We shall provide spotting aircraft. CAPs over the bombardment force and over ourselves in the normal way.'

'Yes, but supposing ... supposing these suiciders come after us while the bombarding force is away? We shall be short of most of our anti-aircraft gun barrage?'

'Oh, we don't think that'll be anything of a problem.'

There was obviously no more to be said. The powers that be were determined upon a bombardment, and a bombardment it was going to be. Nothing could argue them out of it.

'So, there it is,' said Wings, with obvious relief. 'We're going to start off on Wednesday morning, at dawn, with a maximum effort. I want the maximum availability. All the Avengers will be up, and we're going to hit those airfields with absolutely everything we've got. With bombing, ground-strafing and heavy gun bombardment, who knows, we might even take the Sakishima Gunto out of the war for good and all.'

In spite of his scepticism, Skipper felt himself warming to those words. 'Take the Sakishima Gunto out of the war for good and all.' They had a brave and heroic ring about them. They might even be true.

Down in the briefing room, Skipper made his usual evening study of the noticeboards. There were noticeboards all over the ship, always covered with notices relating to the ship, the progress of the war, new regulations and Admiralty instructions, lost property, daily orders. Sometimes, Skipper thought, there were too many notices. The day's newssheets were already up, page after page of closely typed and then mimeographed information. *Some of these*, Skipper thought, *are historic.* The image they gave was of a whole world crumbling. There was good news for the Allies in the west, every day, almost every hour. Familiar Axis fortresses were tumbling down, familiar Axis names in defeat and captivity.

Great Britain, United States and Russia are awaiting Himmler's reply to the Allied refusal to accept his offer of unconditional surrender made to Great Britain and the United States. Himmler was no fool. He would do anything rather than surrender to the Russians. *1st Commando Brigade and the 15th Scottish Division across the Elbe in assault boats near Lauenburg, south-east of Hamburg. US 7th Army entered Munich. 8th Army in Venice. US 5th Army in Milan. Mussolini and twelve members of his Cabinet executed by Italian partisans.*

Here at last was some news from the Far East: *14th Army reported at Pegu in Burma.* Then it was back to the west again: *Russian troops fighting street battles in Berlin. Reichstag building captured and 200 other blocks in the city. New Zealand troops crossed the Piave. Patton's 3rd Army reached the river Isov.*

Only in the Pacific were there some hesitations, were the news items couched in the careful paraphrases of the early years of the war: *Nimitz reported that Japanese aircraft attacked US shipping off the Okinawa beaches, causing some damage and sinking one auxiliary surface unit. US naval hospital ship Comfort attacked and heavily damaged by a Japanese aircraft. Series of attacks made on US forces in the Okinawa area had caused some damage to light units of the fleet.*

Some damage to *light* units of the fleet. Nowhere, on any sheet, was there anything at all about *this* fleet, in which we serve. As far as anybody at home knew, there was nobody here. They were still very circumspect about announcing losses to suicide bombers, and for good reason. There was no percentage in letting the Japanese know how very effective they were being. But still, surely *someone, somewhere,* wanted to know about the British fleet in the Pacific?

The Captain's reference to the cancelled sports and concert party reminded Skipper that he had not visited the squadron mess deck for some time. Although it was late in the day and he had not given the sailors advance warning, after supper Skipper took his cap and walked forward along the starboard main gangway. There was no doubt that the air was hotter, and the humidity higher, the further forward he went. As he climbed down one staircase he saw a water cooler, with a little notice strung round its tap like a halter: OUT OF ORDER. That was the nearest drinking-water cooler to his mess deck, and he made a mental note to ask the engineers about it.

Their squadron mess deck was simply part of a passageway leading to one of the midships bomb rooms, with almost no sense of enclosed identity or personal privacy, marked off from the main thoroughfare by a line of kit lockers. There was some sort of storeroom on one side, and a small compartment with electrical machinery in it on the other. The midships bomb-lift trunking ran through the centre of the space, and the men said it gave off strange, hair-raising, groaning and screaming noises whenever the bomb-lift was working. The deckhead was the usual jumble of pipes and light fittings and ventilation trunkings and rod gearing. The bulkheads were cluttered with mysterious junction boxes, fan starters, machinery-starting cabinets and sound-powered telephones. It was not really a homely compartment, but simply a living space for thirty or forty men improvised out of the ship's entrails.

Skipper paused at the doorway, which was merely the opening between the two rows of kit lockers. Some of the hammocks were already slung and there were men in them. Part of the mess deck furthest from the door was already in darkness, where watchkeepers were asleep. Some mess decks in the ship. Skipper knew, were wholly for watchkeepers and were in darkness, with hammocks slung, for most hours of the day and night. The ship was grossly overcrowded, with a full complement of squadron ratings, extra guns crews, and intelligence and coding parties, and there were not enough slinging billets for everybody. Many men had to sleep on the deck, on mess deck bench cushions, or wherever they could find a space to lie down. In harbour many men took camp-beds up to the flight deck and slept there, but at sea everybody had to make do as best they could.

From the doorway, Skipper could see the light shining on the central mess table. One man was writing a letter, two or three were playing cards. Another man was asleep, his head resting on the table, his face to one side, and his tongue protruding as he breathed in and out. Overhead hung a large shining metal fanny for the rum issue. There was a locker at the end of the table where the mess kept their tea, sugar and butter, when they had any, and a large open wooden drawer for their cutlery, as long as it survived the dangers of being tipped overboard with the washing-up water and the depredations of raiders from other messes. In another wooden locker, with bars like a cage, hung several thick china mugs, each with a blue pusser's stripe round its rim. It was a domestic-looking and somehow rather comforting mess deck scene which, Skipper reflected, probably had not changed in essentials for a hundred years.

Skipper took off his cap and knocked on the side of the nearest locker. The tinny surface gave off a far louder, more peremptory sound than he had intended.

'May I come in, please?'

The nearest sailor to the door was Leading Airman Handley, the 'killick' and ruler of the mess. His vast bulk, barrel chest and broad bottom, and his beaming smile under his coloured skullcap, were familiar sights on the flight deck, where he was the Senior Pilots' mate. He was an amiable, imperturbable man, seemingly impervious to rain, wind or sun, and on the flight deck his personality was like a familiar beacon. Skipper knew that they called him Tommy sometimes, after the radio comedian, but most often they called him 'Kittens' because of his size which, they said, always made him look imminently pregnant.

'Sorry I gave you no warning...'

'That's all right, sir, that's all right.' With imperious toecap and irresistibly prodding forefinger, Kittens swiftly reorganised his mess into a posture of welcome, waking the sleeper, clearing off the card-players, rearranging the seating, instructing one hand to go off and brew tea. In what seemed to Skipper, as usual on his visits to the mess deck, no time at all, he was sitting at the head of the mess table with a mug of tea in his hand and an attentive audience.

'Well.' Skipper raised the mug. 'Cheers. Here's to the end of the war.'

An ironic groan went round the mess.

'That'll be the day, sir.'

'Sorry we can't give you anything stronger in that, sir.'

Skipper guessed that somewhere in the mess there was a 'medicinal' supply of grog from the daily issue. Rum diluted with water did not keep well (which was the reason for diluting it) but Skipper knew that they probably still had an illicit bottle, which they would never get out with an officer present.

'What's the food like? Got any better since I last came down here?'

It was a cue subject, like talking about the weather would be at home, and it led easily to others: the chances of getting home, the defective water-cooler, the ship's programme, the cancelled sports, the rumours of a return early to Sydney, the possibility of borrowing better films from the American ships. Skipper was pleased to find how effortlessly he could remember all their names and something about them. That was a professional naval officer's knack. These were the ordinary sailors of the squadron, the pushers of aircraft and the fasteners of buckles, the hewers of wood and the drawers of water. Petty officers lived in the air petty officers' mess, Chief Air Rigger Petre, pavilioned in splendour, in the Air Chiefs' Mess, next to the chapel. Skipper had read and studied all their service documents, and he knew that they really were, as the propaganda and the newsreels claimed, a true citizens' navy. The great majority of them at this stage of the war were HOs, 'Hostilities Only' ratings, who had nothing to do with ships and the sea before the war. They came from all over the country, as clerks, chauffeurs, market gardeners, house painters, garage mechanics, farmhands; one had been a conjurer for children's parties, another had been a professional boxer. They really had left their office desks, their tractors, their shop counters, their factory benches, their workshops and their municipal parks, to go to sea and serve King and Country.

Some of them, as Skipper well knew, were not enjoying their service. He was well aware of their family troubles at home, the minority amongst them who resented service in the Pacific when 'our war' at home was nearly over and everybody else was nearly 'home and dry'. Able Seaman Trebilcock, a Cornishman sitting in the corner, glowering at the world from under a cloud of suspicion was, Skipper knew, getting occasional letters from his mother about the behaviour of his wife. Hardy, the naval airman sitting next to him, came from Rotherham and had landlord trouble. They all worried about rationing at home, and the fate of their families while they were away, and they all felt that nobody knew about their problems.

Sailors pretended indifference and scoffed at what they called *Daily Mirror* ships, whose doings were always being reported in the newspapers, but Skipper knew that they loved to see themselves and their own ship mentioned. But there was hardly ever any reference to them. When the Russians were in Berlin and British troops were across the Elbe, when Mussolini was dead and Himmler suing for peace, nobody wanted to know about 'some damage to light units' of the fleet, far away, off islands nobody before the war had ever heard of.

Skipper was surprised to find how disturbed the ship's company were by the rocket-powered suicider which had come so close to the ship. They wanted to know what were the chances of another coming as close. Skipper could not reassure them. Like the sailors themselves, he felt overwhelmed by the sheer size of the Pacific war. It had a huge shapelessness about it. A sailor needed to identify himself with his ship, his flotilla, his squadron. But the Pacific task forces, stretching literally from horizon to horizon, went beyond the mental horizons of the men serving in them. When there had been only one aircraft carrier in the whole of the Mediterranean, the men in her had felt themselves a vital, focal point in the war. But the men in this ship could see three other carriers in company, and knew there were twelve more American carriers in action to the north, and six more escort carriers of their own back in the replenishment area with the fleet train. Perhaps, Skipper began to concede the point, a bombardment might be the answer and would hearten all hands.

These men were better educated than most of the pre-war regular Royal Navy sailors and, with their varied backgrounds, had infinitely more experience of life outside the Navy. But they had not raised the level of mess deck debate or appreciation of events. Rather, the mess deck had pulled them down to its own status, of deference to officers, parochial preoccupations with immediate affairs and ignorance of most things outside their own work on board.

Skipper was astounded by the sailors' ignorance. Few of them knew the Captain or the Commander's surnames. That was excusable, perhaps, because those officers were always known on board as 'the Captain' and 'the Commander', and a sailor would have to make a special effort to find out their names. But Skipper discovered that almost none of them knew the names of Ishigaki or Miyako. To them, they were just 'those bloody islands' over the horizon. Only Kittens knew that the last series of strikes had been against Formosa and not the Sakishima Gunto. Perhaps, Skipper thought, the serenity he had often noticed and acclaimed amongst the sailors was not the confidence born of a mature philosophy of life but merely the bliss of ignorance. He wondered how he himself would react if he had to live in these conditions in this heat, in this ignorance; with no daylight and no fresh air; going hither and thither as piped; watching aircraft take off and land on again, with no real comprehension of the purpose behind it all.

One of the sailors' most bitter complaints was about the mail. Skipper himself thought the mail deliveries, in the circumstances, were excellent. Mail arrived frequently in less than a fortnight from home, having travelled over 12,000 miles, by way of India and Australia, before being brought up to the replenishment area and then flown up or brought by destroyer to the fleet. Mail in the Home Fleet, earlier in the war, had often taken as long or longer.

There was mail for Skipper in his pigeonhole in the wardroom, one letter each from his mother and father. They both wrote to him regularly, just as they had done ever since he was at Harrow. They wrote, because they thought it their duty and because they both enjoyed it, of home life in wartime which now seemed to Skipper several planets away, in time and space and experience, of Warship Weeks, and National Saving stamp drives, and rationing, and the neighbours.

Mama was always fiercely loyal. Like most mothers, she thought that the whole war effort rested upon her son's shoulders.

It was a very funny thing and rather annoying. I was talking to Bates the chemist and I mentioned again that you were out in the Pacific and he said Oh, do we still have ships out there?

I said Of course we still have them out there, we have more ships there than ever before, because that is what you have told us. He said Oh, just said Oh. I really do think they ought to do more to let people know what you are doing.

You know we had two 'land girls' from the Women's Land Army? Well, they both got pregnant and had to leave. We got two more and they have become pregnant, too! Mrs Fleetwood was very shocked about it and said they were no better than they should be. But your father just said it was like running a stud farm here. We haven't been able to find out who the man involved is...

Mama was very broad-minded indeed, for someone of her age and background. She always took an earthy, very realistic view of life and human affairs. She was very popular locally for that reason, especially with the womenfolk, because they knew Mama would give them good advice, free of all hypocrisy and false puritanism.

Even the writing paper itself was reassuring. It even felt like home, with its thick blue texture, Daughton in that old broad black-embossed lettering, like the best ship's writing paper. Mama always wrote at a small Davenport in her sewing room, where she sat by the window. Father had his desk in his study, where he kept all his scrapbooks of the last war, and the estate accounts, and his fishing flies and hundreds and hundreds of tobacco tins filled with buttons and coins and curiously shaped stones, and odd cufflinks, and a heron's skull, and silver threepenny bits.

The Daltons have sold Dalton Park. You know Philip was killed in Tunisia and they both rather took fright and sold. I advised them against it, but there it is. They got thirty pounds an acre, which was not at all bad, I thought, provided there are no snags with any of the Ministries. We are not our own bosses any more. We haven't met the new owners yet. I hear they come from London, having been in the United States for most of the war. The army have still got Westbrook. I was over there two weeks ago, and I must say I was horrified by what they've done to it. They have made a terrible mess. We're lucky Daughton is not really a big house, so we've escaped all that. It would break your heart to see the damage to the trees and the walls. They've got huts in the park and they're using it as a convalescent hospital. Your mother goes to visit every week. Colonel Wyllie's little railway, the rails all went for salvage three years ago, you probably remember. I still remember us all having rides on it every year on Colonel Wyllie's birthday. I am still having one or two problems myself about salvage, which I will tell you about when you get home.

The advantage of both mother and father writing was that they both gave their own idiosyncratic view of the same events, as from two different angles, presenting a strikingly lifelike picture as though in three dimensions.

The great saga of our gates still goes on. Mr Privett is still not speaking to us. Your father told him that you cannot make Spitfires out of eighteenth-century wrought ironwork, and anyway it is so that we can have gates like Daughton's that we are fighting this war anyway.

We had a very high wind last week which flattened all the daffodils. They are recovering now but they'll never be quite what they were. The snowdrops were better than ever, they're about the only things that will grow under beech trees. The crocuses came up but the blackbirds ate them all again. We cannot get any more bulbs these days. Although I did go to a WVS sale and there were six of the most lovely hyacinths in a bowl, absolutely pre-war; they are past now but they will be all right for next Christmas. So I bought them. They have shifted the Food Office so that it is even further from the bus stop and there is the most unhelpful woman you could ever imagine there now. One doesn't like to say anything but your father is going to have a word with Mr Jenkins…

I sit on the bench twice a week now. We seem to get more and more business to do. So many new regulations. This war has been a godsend for little men in offices; you know, it has been a bureaucrat's benefit and it will never be the same again, even when it's all over. Had a case of profiteering the other day. Selling petrol illegally. A chap from Bristol. He actually got a barrister down from London to represent him. Obviously I can't tell you the details, but this little man in his black coat and his striped trousers, pulling on his lapels and rocking to and fro on his heels, he made old George and I feel very very important and judicial. But we dished his client all the same.

We try to follow where you are but the maps in The Times are so small and fuzzy, and these islands you talk about sound very mysterious and almost romantic. You can hardly see them on the map. I don't think The Times knows where they are either.

There are a number of things I want to tell you about Daughton when you come back. There are advantages for tax and death duties in making it all over to you. But it can all wait until you get back. I always said it was rough on you, being the only son.

Father had this fierce pride in his family and his home. Daughton was his life and soul and, in the end, all his thoughts and all his actions had to bear the intense scrutiny of whether or not they were good for Daughton. He would expect the same of his only son. Skipper avoided thinking about what his father would say if he ever discovered there was a possibility his son might stay in the Navy.

There was a pile of paper several inches thick in the metal tray on Skipper's cabin deck, but he had not the heart to look at it. Paperwork always seemed so difficult and irrelevant at sea. The problems always appeared more biddable, the solutions more feasible, when they got back to harbour. Instead Skipper decided to go on his rounds of his pilots. It was, after all, the day before flying again, the eve of battle once more.

Over the last year, Skipper had noticed from squadron lists, postings, names on signals and meetings in other wardrooms that the Fleet Air Arm was growing more and more cosmopolitan. The straight RN pilot had almost completely dropped out and even the RNVRs were being joined by increasing numbers of Canadians, New Zealanders, South Africans and Dutchmen. Skipper's squadron had had four New Zealanders from the day of its formation. They had been recruited through a bureaucratic quirk: it seemed that New Zealanders who wanted to fly with the RAF had to go to the United Kingdom to join, but they could enlist in the Fleet Air Arm at home in New Zealand. Some Kiwis, Skipper knew, were flamboyant characters, but Skipper's four were very sober citizens. Unlike Australians, their accents and their manners were hardly noticeable. They were all quiet, introverted men, and excellent pilots. As the Captain had once said, all New Zealanders were first-class officer material, every single one of them. Skipper was always on the lookout for cliques in his squadron, always ready to crush any sign of a squadron within the squadron. But the Kiwis flew in one flight, and had done so from the beginning. Now, they made up a perfectly drilled team who understood each other's flying. They shared two adjacent cabins, the two from North Island together and the other couple from South Island. They were all four in the North Island cabin, playing bridge.

'How is it, men?'

'Fine, Skipper.' They all looked up, momentarily presenting a picture of mutual harmony and understanding which Skipper admired and envied.

'Did you get your mail while we were in Leyte?' The Kiwis' mail worked differently from the United Kingdom mail and there had been difficulties and delays.

'Yep. Everything OK, Skipper.'

'Right.' So *that* was all right. No problems there. At the end of the same passageway was Michael's cabin and Skipper felt himself involuntarily tensing as he approached it. Michael's pre-flying black periods were wearing on the nerves. It was the other side of the coin to the superb flying skills he possessed. There was a price to be paid for such talent. Virtuoso pianists and violinists, Skipper supposed, suffered from the same fits of black depression.

But, to Skipper's surprise, young Richard Trumble was there, sitting in Michael's cabin chair, while Michael lay on his bunk.

'Got company?'

'Oh, come in, Skipper.' Michael seemed very much more cheerful than usual. Nevertheless there was a faint but uncomfortable atmosphere in the cabin which made Skipper feel vaguely prickly and uneasy. It was hard to put a finger on it, but it was almost as though the two of them had been discussing Skipper himself and had hurriedly broken off when he came in.

'Skipper, do you think anybody's ever going to remember us?'

'I very much doubt it. Why, do you want to be immortal?'

'No, seriously, Skipper, I've just had a letter from my old mum and she says nobody in our little neck of the woods has ever *heard* of the British Pacific Fleet.'

'She's right. My mama says the same. But there you are. Ours not to reason why. Tell me, what do you think of this bombardment idea?'

Michael grimaced, succeeding in looking contemptuous, long-suffering and much abused all at the same time. 'Well, I was with you at that briefing. It's bloody silly. One of the bloodiest and silliest ideas I've ever heard of. At least, I *hope* it's not going to be one of the bloodiest. I mean, if bombardments are so good for the figure, then why don't we do it every hour on the hour? Save *us* a lot of trouble wouldn't it? I'd far sooner stooge around up top and spot for *our* gunnery boys than have to go down to zero feet and try conclusions with *their* gunnery boys, eyeball to eyeball, as we have to do. I don't mind spotting for a change, but I fear it's only going to stir things up without doing any positive good. Let's just hope it's all such a complete shambles tomorrow that they'll call the whole thing off.'

In the event, to the air group's surprise and slight disappointment, the spotting exercises went moderately well. Without actual physical shell bursts, the practice was not much more than a refresher on communications and terminology. As Michael said, 'You have to talk in a special way when they're all wearing their gunnery hats. You can't just say you've missed, you silly bastards, you're short, you have to give ranges and bearings and corrections to show why, and then because they're too thick to understand it the first time you have to say it all again in gunnery gobbledygook.' But, after some days on passage and in harbour, it was exhilarating to be flying again. Douglas Mayhew had two new pilots to try out, and they all had guns and radios to test, aircraft for flights after routine inspections and modifications, manoeuvres to correct, and loops and rolls to fly, for the fun of it; Skipper's squadron came in to land behind him and Michael, rapidly and correctly, one after the other, taking their wires and taxiing forward, just as the book said. When Skipper went up last thing that night to look at the latest intelligence and the most recent photo-reconnaissance pictures, he felt unusually optimistic.

'First of May tomorrow,' he said to the Leading Photographer, who was sticking the still-wet prints on a display board. 'May Day. *Springtime, the only pretty ringtime...*'

'Mayday. Isn't that what they say on the R/T when they're going to ditch, sir?'

Skipper's euphoria vanished, with his smile. 'God rot you,' he muttered under his breath.

CHAPTER EIGHT

The long day began a few minutes after dawn with a bogey detected by the flagship, range eighty-five miles, to the northwest, probable height 20,000 feet. *Madame Fifi*'s first Corsair CAPs were only just up and had a long way to climb. Skipper listened to Robert Weston's interception on the fighter net in the Direction Room. The CAP had to do the interception on the climb the whole way up. For a time it seemed hopeful, but the radar vector given was not quite accurate enough and although Robert Weston's starboard wingman had a fleeting visual contact the bogey, probably a twin-engined Nick fighter, put its nose down and escaped. It seemed to Skipper, listening, that such an aircraft on such a bearing at such a height at that time of day must be a reconnaissance flight and it seemed very likely that the task force had been detected and reported. The Japanese local air command in Formosa must by now have a fair idea of the fleet's position off the Sakishima Gunto. If they were launching suiciders, they would all know where to go now. It seemed obvious to Skipper that the bombardments should now be cancelled. But the minutes passed and no change of programme was announced.

Skipper went up to Flyco. 'I hear we're still going ahead?' Wings seemed to flinch before the expression on Skipper's face. 'Yes, we are.'

'But for God's *sake*, that bogey spotted us, as sure as eggs is eggs!'

The uncertainty on Wings' face vanished as he seemed to make up his mind to impose his will on Skipper. 'Look, I did put that point. But the flagship came up and said we'd been spotted before and nothing has happened before.'

'Maybe, but we've never taken away both battleships, four of the cruisers and a dozen destroyers from the screen before, *have* we?'

Wings bit his lip and shook his fist, in an odd gesture, as though he could not find the proper words to make his point. 'Look, Skipper, I *know* your views on this and to a certain extent I *do* agree with you, although I don't necessarily agree with your way of making your views known...'

'But —'

'I *do* see your point, Skipper, believe me. But the fact is, bombardments are what they are determined to have and bombardments are what they are bloody well going to get. All we can do now is make sure they go off as well as possible. That's all, believe me.'

At the last moment, Fenton's Corsair engine stopped and would not start again. So Skipper took off with Geoffrey and Edward to fly CAP for him while he did the spotting runs. Fenton's Corsair was wheeled aside, for the engineers to examine.

When he actually came to fly it, Skipper had to admit that a bombardment-spotting sortie was a great deal more civilised and less dangerous than ground-strafing. The navigation had to be more accurate and he spent much time pulling and pushing the retractable chart table in and out of its slot in the instrument board in front of the joystick. It was all a matter of bearings, and times by stop-watch, and graticules, and dead reckoning corrections for wind and height corrections ordered from the ship. It was rather like surveying an estate from the air.

Far below, the two battlewagons lay like great fat grey slugs on the water. The smoke bursts were perceptible as yellow-brown smudges floating across the dark purple sea. With binoculars fixed on the airstrip, Skipper conceded that the fourteen-inch shells had a more definite, *satisfying* impact than the muzzy little smoke pillars of the Avenger bombs. The four cruisers were closer inshore, firing at another airstrip. As the battleships fired to starboard, turned at the end of their bombardment run and fired to port, the watching pilots above had a thrilling view of a great tide of metal weight being poured on to the coral runways. It was fascinating to watch the clusters of salvoes pitch over, creep back, fall short, creep up, pitch on, guided as though by some massive intelligence from over the horizon.

After the battleships had fired, Skipper estimated, nearly 200 rounds of fourteen-inch, and the cruisers must have expended some hundreds of 6-inch and 5.25-inch ammunition, Skipper was surprised to see the bombarding force apparently break off and form up to steer south-east. He had expected at least two more bombardment runs. But, at the same time, he heard Stanley giving out a succession of tight, closely linked radar vectors to the CAPs above *Miss Britannia*. Slowly, it became clear that the carriers were under some form of heavy attack. Stanley's voice was still crisp and clear but, knowing him so well, Skipper could detect the strain beneath those calmly phrased syllables. In the middle of one order, Stanley's voice went silent, as though the ship's radio was dead. Skipper's ears were filled at once with that familiar radio bedlam, which he had hoped was a thing of the past, with a gaggle of pilots asking all at the same time for instructions and reporting bandits, while other fighter direction officers from other ships tried to break in to report bogeys from their own screens and guide their CAPs on to them.

Skipper saw the great column of smoke in the yellow haze to the south, at a range of over a hundred miles. As he stared through the windscreen another gout of black smoke with a small, hot, hard centre leaped up, to starboard of the first. Through the headphones, Skipper heard *Madame Fifi*'s fighter direction officer telling one returning strike to keep clear because the flight deck was obstructed.

Suddenly, as coolly as though he had never been away, Stanley's voice came back on the air.

'Conway Leader, Conway Leader, this is *Miss Britannia*, do you read me, do you read me?'

'This is Conway Leader, read you loud and clear, strength six.'

'Sorry about that, Conway Leader, a slight … contretemps on deck. Cannot, repeat *cannot*, land you on now. Report fuel.'

Skipper's flight had fuel enough left for two hours, two and a half if they were very careful. A Corsair had fuel for five hours in the air, and as they had indulged in no highspeed, low-level runs over the airstrips, they might stretch it further. Skipper had a cold premonition that this time they might need all the fuel endurance they had.

At ten miles' range, Skipper could see the great black mass like an ugly wart growing out of the middle of *Miss Britannia*'s grey-green flight deck. At seven miles he could make out the wide spread of the twisted black metal, stained at its edges with fire-fighting foam. The wreckage of several aircraft lay around its fringes. The suicider had plunged into the flight deck just forward of the foremost arrester wire, where some aircraft had been ranged to fly off the next CAP. He could see figures around the mass and white specks which were possibly stretchers, with dots of men clustering round and eddying to and fro, like a film of children in a playground he had once seen, speeded up to many times the normal.

They orbited for nearly an hour in high CAP, with engines throttled back on the leanest mixture, propellers in coarse pitch, saving fuel by turning and handling their Corsairs as though they were made of cobwebs and cotton wool. Stanley's voice at last broke what had become an almost hypnotic silence.

'Conway Leader, *bandits*, three-zero-niner, angels one niner, range one seven. Your vector three-two-fife ... Acknowledge...'

'This is Conway Leader, your bandit roger ... Calling the cattle home now...'

They swung round to the north-west, all considerations of fuel economy forgotten, engines at full revolutions, propellers in fine pitch, riding their aircraft as though they were made of cast iron and concrete.

There were two of them, two Zekes, seemingly painted brilliant yellow, flying in slightly staggered formation, one of them two hundred feet above and behind the other. They must be tyros to fly like that, close enough to make a larger radar echo but too far apart to help each other, and the leader would be quite unable to see his second man.

'Tally-hooooo...' Skipper let his voice trail off in triumph.

One wing came away at once, almost as though it had not been fixed on properly, and the first Zeke went into a vertical spinning dive. The second also dived to evade, but they wheeled and came back and took him with one long firing pass. There was no smoke, no debris, not a cry, not a bang, not a whimper. The second Zeke just stopped flying and fell out of the sky.

'*Miss Britannia*, this is Conway Leader, two bandits splashed…'

'Have your bandits, Conway Leader. Nicely, nicely…'

The sudden lunge across the miles of sky and the violent combat had dipped deeply into their remaining fuel. Skipper could see that they could take it for another thirty minutes; after that, it was all up to the accuracy of individual fuel gauges, and the vagaries of the aircraft's skin configuration in the bottoms of the tanks; one large dent might give another thirty seconds' more flying, or thirty seconds less.

'*Miss Britannia*, this is Conway Leader. Fuel state red, three zero minutes max.'

'This is *Miss Britannia*, roger. Wait one…'

No matter how he switched the tanks across one another, from port to starboard and back again, from reserve to main and back, no matter how hopefully he read the gauges, with optimistic parallax errors, Skipper could see that even thirty minutes' estimate was now generous.

Minutes passed, while Skipper's flight went back to lean mixture and kid-glove handling. While the fuel gauges sank lower and lower, Skipper considered the other possibilities. He had never had to ditch or bale out and he had an unreasoning fear of either. His mind simply refused to decide for him which he would prefer: to launch himself out of the aircraft into space, or to take his chance down on the sea level.

With less than a quarter of an hour to go, Skipper decided to suggest another alternative.

'*Miss Britannia*, this is Conway Leader, suggest diverting to *Madame Fifi* or alternative deck.'

'This is *Miss Britannia*...' Stanley came back swiftly, as though he had been waiting to squash that very suggestion. *'Negative.'*

Possibly, Skipper thought, the other decks were just as preoccupied. *We're poor little lambs who have lost our way ... baaa ... baaaa ... baaaa.*

Ten minutes' fuel left, at the very most. The others might have even less. Skipper decided he would not even ask them. They had already shown admirable forbearance by not burdening him with their troubles.

'Conway Leader, Conway Leader, this is *Miss Britannia* ... Ready now...'

In the midst of his joy and relief, Skipper still had time to appreciate that they were now being invited to land on a flight deck barely two hours — 120 minutes — after a kamikaze strike. That was brilliant damage control. Thank God for the Corps of Naval Constructors and the armoured flight deck.

'Conway Leader ... special message. We have two only, repeat two only, arrester wires. The after wires, numbers one and two. I say again, *two* only arrester wires. The forward crash barrier will be up to protect the forward deck park. Acknowledge.'

'This is Conway Leader, two only arrester wires, I read you, roger.'

Ideally, with only the two after arrester wires serviceable, Skipper would have liked to have made one dummy pass at the deck to look at the general position. But his critical fuel state precluded that. If he went round again he might never come back. It also meant that his first landing pass had to be absolutely correct. He had to take the first or second wire, or crash into the barrier. If he were waved off, he might not even have enough fuel to gain sufficient height to bale out. This, in fact, would have to be one of the best deck landings he had ever made. Skipper blew out his cheeks and took several deep breaths as though about to plunge into a long swim. He felt the straps of his parachute with one thumb and then jerked back the cockpit canopy. He would not need that, either way.

'Conway Conway, this is Conway Leader, you both ready?'

'This is Conway Two, all ready, Skipper.'

'This is Conway Three, also ready, Skipper.'

As Skipper led his flight from the ship's stern and began to fly up the starboard side, the two Bofors guns on the starboard quarter opened fire on them. Skipper heard a muffled sound but could not decide what it was. Something had happened to somebody, but he could not see what. Before he could investigate, he was fully absorbed in the technical problems of his own landing.

In the end, it was one of the best he had ever made. He held the turn more tightly than usual, picked up Tiny's great grinning face further out, pinched a little on all his signals, shaved the round-down more closely than usual, anticipated the 'cut' by a fraction of a second, and took the first wire precisely. It was technically a nice piece of flying, and Skipper hoped it would cheer everyone up. In fact, it was almost too good. He had, if anything, rather overdone the caution and hit the flight deck very far aft of the first wire. A little more and he might actually have bounced clear over both wires.

Skipper noted the signal that his hook was clear, and began to taxi forward, over a huge spreading multi-coloured stain in the flight deck amidships, with violently inscribed black scorch marks around its periphery and a pale central patch of quick-drying cement. On either side were severed arrester wires, looped and piled like cut sinews, and the wreckage of trolleys and aircraft, heaped aside like smashed children's toys. He rolled over the now-lowered barrier and stopped behind the aftermost aircraft in the deck park. It was an Avenger, with only one wing folded: probably blast damage to the other. Automatically, Skipper completed the routine after landing: wings folded and locked, brakes on, guns safe, radio off, engine cut to the expressive 'cut-throat' gesture of the deck marshaller, harness released. Skipper stood up awkwardly in his cockpit and turned round to watch the rest of his flight come on.

One Corsair was just taking the second wire. He looked aft but there was no sign of a third. There was only one more. The other Corsair came up the flight deck, its wings folding as it came, and stopped next to Skipper. He could see by the fuselage letters, and by the face in the cockpit, that it was Edward. So Geoffrey had gone. Those starboard after Bofors guns had shot Geoffrey down while he was in the landing circuit.

Deliberately, Skipper climbed down from his cockpit and then, almost as though his legs were obeying somebody else, he began to run aft as fast as he could. The hard flight-deck wind helped him on his way, getting behind him and boosting him into the air, so that he soared and hurdled over all obstacles. The exhilaration of the free physical movement even began to temper that first hot surge of his anger. The huge rosy face of Kittens loomed up, with a questioning look, but Skipper brushed past him, running so hard that when he reached the Bofors mounting, the wind and the slippery deck made it difficult for him to stop, and he came to an undignified and scrambling halt. But when he saw the apologetic look on the officer of the quarters' face, all his anger returned.

Though his face was shadowed by his steel helmet and closely framed by the white cloth of his anti-flash gear hood, Skipper recognised the know-all Sub-Lieutenant who had been on the flag-bridge entering Leyte. He, too, had recognised Skipper, knew what he had come for, and what he was going to say. He held up his hands in a gesture which was meant to be defensive and placatory but which only inflamed Skipper more.

'You *silly* fucking *bloody* ridiculous...' Skipper felt as though he were choking on his own spittle, and his throat was gobbling so that he could not get enough words out quickly enough to vent his fury. He could hardly prevent himself leaping up on to the gun mounting and attacking that face. 'Can't you tell *the fucking* difference between *a fucking Corsair* and a fucking *Jap*, you bloody little murderer?'

Skipper's yelling was drowned in the roar of an aircraft which had flown in behind him, from the port quarter, roughly in the landing circuit approach. It flew out to the starboard side, level with and only a cable away from the island superstructure, before beginning to climb up and out on the starboard bow. It was a radial-engined fighter, with a large bomb visibly slung underneath. That, Skipper thought, might cause problems when he came to land on. But he was a silly twat, whoever it was, buzzing the ship like that. He was simply asking to be shot down, coming in like that, and he was damned lucky not a gun had opened fire on him. He must have been gliding in towards the ship behind Skipper's back and eventually he had passed not fifty feet above him. With everybody as edgy as they were, that was asking for trouble.

As Skipper watched, the fighter banked and rolled to starboard, still climbing. For a moment it was in full-plan view, like one of the pages of the aircraft identification manuals, and Skipper saw the red balls on its wings. It was a Japanese Oscar, about to make a second pass at the ship. For some reason, the Japanese pilot had decided his first dive was not accurate enough, and he was going round again. In a few seconds from now, he would make another diving attack.

Fascinated, rooted to the spot where he stood, Skipper watched the Oscar flatten out, fly astern to the starboard quarter, turn, and begin its approach. Its wings were straight as a razor, with two circular blobs in the centre, like a top-heavy figure of eight, formed by the engine cowling and the bomb beneath. It was growing perceptibly larger already, and it was unmistakably aimed at Skipper himself.

As the guns in front and behind him opened fire, with the terrifying jangling of the aircraft alarm and the flight-deck broadcast speaker bellowing, 'Alarm aircraft starboard, take cover, take cover, take cover...' Skipper started into motion, as in a dream, and ran for his life towards the nearest starboard walkway. He sensed Kittens panting beside and slightly behind him and there were others too, dim figures, on the edges of his peripheral vision, all running for their lives. The ship was turning sharply to starboard and the flight deck heeling to port, so that Skipper felt himself running uphill, as in a nightmare. In spite of that, he was in fact moving so fast that when he reached the flight-deck edge he almost missed the walkway rail and for one horrified moment thought he was going to fall over the side. Somebody actually did fall, and Skipper saw his spread-eagled figure hit the sea.

Skipper lay prone on the metal walkway and wrapped his arms round his head. As he did so, Kittens landed on top of him with a crushing impact that drove the breath out of Skipper's lungs.

Skipper shut his eyes tight and tried to draw breath. Above the sound of his straining lungs he heard one long shrilling whistle, a shuddering jolt which seemed to depress the ship's whole hull several feet deeper into the sea and then a detonation which was so loud that paradoxically Skipper felt he could hardly hear it at all. It was so great, and went on for so long, that Skipper felt that he himself was part of the explosion, as though his own body were expanding like the hot gases of the bomb and his own disjected members flying apart like the shrapnel of its case. Above him, Skipper could feel Kittens' body shaking and twitching and jerking, as under a tremendous electric shock, prolonged beyond the point of human endurance. A towering column of water crashed inboard, filling the walkway to its sill and pouring down the ladders, drenching Skipper where he lay, filling his mouth and nostrils, until he was sure he was going to drown. Pinned by the weight of Kittens' body, Skipper could not move his face to free his breathing, and he lay under the cataract of water which went on crashing down, unabated, until Skipper was convinced the ship had been sunk, they were all fifty feet underwater and would never see the sun again.

When the noise and the water had stopped, Skipper was still caught under Kittens' body. The man simply would not move his great weight. Skipper struggled to get up.

'Get off me. Get *off* me, you silly bugger…'

As Skipper thrashed from side to side and fought to get up, Kittens still lay immobile. Eventually, Skipper was able to raise his chest from the deck, manoeuvre his elbows under his body and press upwards. Kittens rolled half sideways, until his body struck the guard rail stanchion and could turn no further. Skipper wriggled from underneath him, turned over and sat up.

The whole cast of Kittens' face had been pushed to one side, as though he had sustained an enormously powerful boxer's punch on the jaw. One eyeball protruded and the other had actually come out of its socket and was dangling by its optic nerve on Kittens' pounded cheek. Kittens' bright cap, flight-deck jacket and trousers were soaked with blood. The man had been riddled with splinters seemingly from head to toe. He had almost certainly saved Skipper's life. Kittens' great bulk had absorbed the whole of the shrapnel shower which must have raked this little walkway from end to end. There was a jagged piece of black metal beside Kittens' head. Skipper picked it up. It was still warm to the touch. Beyond it, Skipper could now see that the walkway was littered with debris: more shrapnel, shards of steel, flakes of grey and green paint, a long strip of cloth like a piece torn from a shroud or a winding sheet, with what looked like Japanese characters on it. Skipper could smell the lingering acrid whiff of the explosive and beneath it a more elusive smell, faintly sweet, which made Skipper think of rice, and dried plums, and the kind of scent bar girls in Colombo wore. Beside Kittens' feet was an unidentifiable mass, which looked like the body of a seabird washed up on the shore. Skipper prodded it with his toe. It was possibly the sodden top of a leather helmet, with shreds of what could be bone and hair inside it. Skipper brought his heel down on it, with a squelch. There was a little disc, like a button, which Skipper automatically put in the pocket of his flying overalls.

'Don't touch anything!' Somebody was shouting from above.

'Oh, I won't, I *won't*…'

Skipper got to his feet. The ship was turning sharply again to starboard and the flight deck was heeling away from him so that he had a moment of vertigo, as though he were looking straight down at the sea from a height. He grasped the steel edge in front of him. There was no sign of the Sub-Lieutenant of the Bofors guns and his crew, which had been within a few feet of him only a few seconds before. Something had scraped them out of the mounting and flung them all into the sea, or across the flight deck, or high into the air, Skipper had no idea where. But they were definitely gone. The lack of that Bofors mounting, which he could remember so well and so clearly, momentarily disorientated Skipper, so that he could not recall where he was, or what he had been doing, or why he had been lying down in that walkway.

Skipper lifted one knee and then the other. He moved his head to the right, to the front, to the left and back to the front again. He let go one hand from the rail and flexed the fingers on it. Then he tried the other. He cleared his throat and started to speak. 'Testing, testing, testing...' and burst into a peal of idiotic laughter. There was no doubt about it. He was alive and well, all present and correct and absolutely unhurt, having survived a kamikaze suicide bomber near miss which had exploded in the sea under a hundred feet away. By ordering hard-a-starboard at the critical moment, the Captain had swung the ship's stern sharply to port, causing the kamikaze pilot to miss his aim and crash into the sea close alongside. The flight deck was still heeling to port, the ship still turning to starboard, and Skipper realised that the steering must have been jammed in that position by the explosion. It was the old trouble again. *Miss Britannia* was now turning complete circles, helplessly, in the middle of the task force. Soon, Skipper felt the deck trembling underfoot and knew the shafts were going astern. The Captain was taking the way off the ship, whilst the emergency parties repaired the steering gear.

Skipper's ears were still ringing and he could not make out what the flight-deck broadcast was saying. It sounded like some madman gargling underwater. The flight-deck was a scene of frenzied activity, through which Skipper walked unnoticed and in a daze. Men were dragging hoses about, and driving their small tractors, and the big crane was coming up. Skipper looked up at its great jib. It seemed to go on and on, up into the sky, like Jack's beanstalk. Skipper walked on in a kind of shocked ecstasy, as though disembodied, walking outside himself, numb from head to foot, seeing everything as though he were not in the ship at all but watching from somewhere outside. Everybody was busy. Skipper stopped to watch a man brushing away at fire-fighting foam in a puddle. He was brushing forward so the flight-deck wind was blowing the foam back as fast as he was brushing it. But he brushed ever faster and faster, and Skipper could well understand his anxiety to brush that foam forward. All at once, the man began to make progress and Skipper understood why. The ship, still turning circles, had turned out of the wind.

The doctor was waiting in the entrance door to the island. He seemed to Skipper to be studying hard the faces of everybody who passed him. Skipper hoped the doctor would not notice him, but he placed himself in Skipper's path so that he could not walk by. The doctor lightly but firmly grasped Skipper's chin and turned his head to one side.

'Where were you, Skipper?'

The ringing in Skipper's ears was still bad. The doctor's voice sounded remote, as though on a very bad long-distance telephone connection.

'Down on the starboard after walkway. There's another dead body down there, somewhere. I've just remembered.'

'So that went up just by you?' The doctor turned Skipper's head to look the other way, and then let go.

'Probably.'

Probably?' The doctor was incredulous. 'Didn't you notice it?'

'Oh, sure. Can't you see?' Skipper had noticed how wet he was. His hair, his overalls, his pants, his socks, were drenched. His shoes were full of water. People talked about being soaked to the skin. That very rarely happened, even in the heaviest rainstorm. But it had certainly happened now. Skipper was wet through, to the very skin.

'You'd better come in here to the sick bay for a moment.'

'I'm perfectly well.'

'I'm sure. But there's something, *somebody*, I want you to see.'

Skipper looked up as he went through the doorway. All the windows in the island he could see gaped empty, like eye sockets in a skull. The deck inside was littered with glass fragments. So much for the armoured glass. There were four long man-sized bundles, covered in blankets, lying on the deck outside the flight-deck sick bay door. The doctor caught Skipper's look.

'Flight-deck handlers. The blast of the first suicider. Come in here a moment.'

The flight-deck sick bay was a small compartment, one more that had been improvised from something else in the original ship design. There was room only for four bunks, in pairs, one above the other. They were all full. Skipper could not see who was in them, but he could hear a man groaning and hawking in agony, and he could smell the odour of sticky wounds and ether. The space between the bunks was almost entirely filled by a camp-bed, and lying on it, covered by a blanket, was Richard Fenton.

Fenton lay quite still. He did not move at Skipper's entrance, did not even appear to be breathing. His grey parchment-coloured face was looking at the deckhead above him.

'Is he alive?'

'Yes. Still. He was waiting to fly off when the suicider hit us. He was all strapped in, ready to go. Couldn't move a muscle to help himself.'

At the sound, Fenton's eyes moved and he looked at Skipper, in a glance of such rage, and pain, and frustration, and realisation of his fate, that Skipper felt a lump in his throat.

Skipper moved his lips, in a whisper. 'He's dying.'

'I'm afraid, almost certainly, yes.' The doctor, too, was whispering. 'There's always hope, but he's very badly burned and he's got something, a bullet perhaps, or a piece of metal, in his back. He's paralysed. Can't move a muscle.'

'Great God Almighty.' So much for the killing boy. So much for the lad who was going to outlive this day and come safe home. Badly burned and paralysed, not over enemy territory, not on a sortie, not in combat at all, but sitting strapped in his cockpit, waiting to go off.

'We'll take him down to the sick bay now. We'll set up the table and have a go. We've got one or two like him.'

'Thank you.'

'By the way, Hitler's dead.'

'Oh, good.'

'If I were you I'd get out of that wet gear.'

'Oh, sure…'

But outside the door, Wings was beckoning from the top of the ladder leading up to the Operations Room.

'Thank God you're here, Skipper. I was beginning to think you'd had it, like almost everybody today. You OK to lead a RAMROD now? Michael's up already, the Kiwis are flying CAPs, Douglas Mayhew's got a bullet in his wrist…' Wings gave an expressive shrug of theatrical dismay. 'So, are you on?'

Skipper knew that he was not really fit. He still felt shocked and dazed. But after all that had passed between him and Wings already, he could not stand himself down from flying. And, after all, the doctor had just seen him and had said nothing about not flying.

'Of course.'

'*Right*. Briefing, then. *Now*.'

Skipper could not prevent himself shivering as his damp clothes began to dry, but he listened to the briefing in a trancelike state of concentration. It was like watching somebody's lips moving endlessly, telling some extremely boring anecdote, in an extremely dull bar, at the end of a long, long and drunken, but unsuccessful run ashore. It was true, he did feel slightly drunk. Not nervous or afraid, but shocked into a state where he suspected that his speech, his reactions and his normal coordination were dislocated. But he managed to conceal it, and in the chaos of that day, his behaviour passed muster. In any case, it was Ishigaki again and he could have repeated the briefing from memory: the same airfield, with the same courses to fly, the same map coordinates, the same time to and over the target, the same height, distance and flak barrage.

It was the same take-off and form-up, although after a few minutes Skipper became aware that Stanley was addressing him.

'Drumbeat Leader, this is *Miss Britannia* ... you're high-stepping. Slow, slow, quick-quick-slow, swing it and swing it.'

'This is Drumbeat Leader ... roger.' Stanley was trying to tell him he was going too fast. Skipper frowned. Where *had* he heard him talking like that before? Skipper throttled back, and in a few moments his flight came swimming up gracefully to. join him. Skipper could not even think of their names. It was not Fenton anyway, so they would not be close enough. But good enough. Skipper felt supremely confident. He was not nervous, as he usually was. All that caution was crap. He would sail in and simply nail those buggers. Drumbeat was a good name for this flight. It felt like a drumbeat in one's temples, throbbing away, like a Zulu impi going to war. *Other nations go into battle, the Chatti go to war…*

As it happened, it was a perfect attack. They swept in over the town and there were two more Oscars on the end of the runway, their cockpits empty. Everybody left town when Drumbeat Flight came in. Very sensible of them. Parts flew off the Oscars, and yet they did not catch fire, which was disappointing. But as they pulled up and away, meaning to go home, Skipper heard a voice which sounded just like Fenton.

'Drumbeat Leader, this is Drumbeat Four.' It *did* sound unbelievably like Fenton. 'Neither of those is flaming. Shall we go down and finish them off? Drumbeat Four, out…'

'Drumbeat, Drumbeat, this is Drumbeat Leader, one more run … Keep close … Drumbeat, keep close … One more run … *Break…*'

As he said it, Skipper knew it was wrong. The rule of survival here was one run only, fast in and fast out. However, like a drunk who steps on a stair, knowing it is going to give way but goes on just the same, Skipper banked steeply, turned and came in for a second run, along the identical path of the first.

He could have set his watch by the flak. It came up on cue, making him curl his toes inside his canvas shoes. It seemed a little thicker than the first time, but they flashed through it and had actually reached the other end of the runway before Skipper's Corsair suffered the hit that he knew, once it had happened, had been coming all along. He felt the detonation through the soles of his feet as he began to climb up the inland hillside towards the crests. The rudder bar suddenly went stiff, so that he could barely move it. He thrust out with all his strength and the pedals, just as suddenly, swung loosely. He cleared the top of the nearest hill, knowing by the lack of noise in his ears that his radio was dead. He tried the pedals again.

They swung like a schoolgirl's pigtails. He could push at them all day and all he would get would be the exercise.

He could turn using the elevators only, but when he cautiously tried it the Corsair began to shake itself to pieces, just as the other one had tried to do the last time the flak hit him. He had to be careful now to avoid a spin, because it was rule one, line one, in the Corsair pilot's handling notes that a Corsair would not, repeat *not*, recover from a spin. He would have to turn, using the greatest care, even if it took several miles to get round. Out of the corner of his eye he saw Edward coming up on his port side and pointing aft to the tailplane. So it was that again. Curious how these gunners always caught the tail. The rear-view mirror was cracked and he could see nothing in it, but for all the response he was getting to the controls the whole tailplane might as well have been shot away. That was not meant to be a joke. He 'zobbed' a message to Edward with his bunched fist, hoping to get it across to him that he could not manoeuvre. He tried the radio again, but it was still dead. He started another careful turn, but the whole aircraft from wingtip to wingtip at once began to shake and shudder as though it were itself trying to peel the very fabric off its metal ribs.

The visibility around and below was perfect. Jolly jumping weather. He could see the north-western shore of Ishigaki just passing beneath him now, and the line of surf on the beach. It looked a good place to bathe. It was weeks since he had been over this side of the island. The surf line was directly below now, and the Corsair was still heading out to the north. The engine note was still regular and confident, so he did have a choice. In a Seafire you never, but never, ditched if you could avoid it, but a Corsair was at least a ditching proposition. The altimeter showed 3,000 feet, but looking over the side it seemed a lot less than that. He could see white horses on the water and a considerable swell running up from the south-east once he had passed out of the lee of the island.

There was nothing to be gained by going on much further. He was out of range of Japanese guns from shore, and the further north he went the further the air-sea rescue attempt would have to come to fetch him and the greater chance of them missing him. *If it were done when 'tis done, then 'twere well it were done quickly. If the assassination could trammel up the consequence* … Without making any conscious decision to do so, he pushed the joystick carefully forward and began the long, tender glide down towards the sea.

The nearer it came, the rougher the sea looked. Some of those white horses were really quite big. He shouted 'Mayday, Mayday' at the top of his voice into the dead mouthpiece and felt the tears running down his cheeks into the sides of his mouth. He ought to try and fly along the line of the swell but he dared not risk it. If anything happened at this time, there would not be enough height left to bale out. He jettisoned the canopy, lowered hook and flaps but not the undercarriage. He wanted the Corsair to stop rapidly, but not to turn on its nose.

The aircraft seemed to make up its own mind to go down. At over a hundred knots the first touch was surprisingly light, but that was what they always said. Wait for the second bounce. The second was certainly the real thing. The jar of it threw him helplessly forward against his straps, his nose only just missing a crippling smash against the instrument panel in front. The Corsair seemed to have stopped dead in the sea and he could already see water frothing towards him along the engine cowling. He punched the harness-release button on his midriff, whipped out the intercom jackpoint plug, smashed away the cockpit side panel, which was already lower than the sea, thrust both feet down against the deck of the cockpit and slid out sideways, taking the dinghy pack with him. It was just as they had done it in the swimming pool, only the swimming pool did not have this huge wave which swamped him and drove him downwards, two or three feet under water. Through the tip of his right toe, he felt the last touch of metal of his cockpit windscreen as the Corsair sank away, Heaven knew how deep. He pulled out the small tags on the carbon dioxide bottles and, to his amazement, his lifejacket inflated and the dinghy came flapping to the surface, thrashing about like a demented yellow seal, swelling and growing in front of his eyes as though the little bottle had contained some miraculous nutritious ingredient. He seized the foot of the dinghy and hauled himself up and into it. It was just as the training manual said. The manual also said it was unwise to vomit. It aggravated the shock to the body, removed valuable food content still in the stomach and, above all, lost priceless moisture from the body. That might be what the manual said and no doubt the manual was right, but he could not help it. The waves washed the vomit from his face and the rubber sides of the dinghy, but it was some time before he lay back again, dry-mouthed, panting, staring in front of him.

CHAPTER NINE

So there it was. Nothing to do now, except wait. Skipper's first thought was, inconsequentially, of Chief Air Rigger Petre. He had let himself down in Petre's eyes. Always in his relationship with the Chief, unspoken but understood, was the assumption that he, Skipper, was a cut above the rest, much too good a flyer ever to get himself shot down like the others. But here he was, one with the great majority, dunked like a ship's biscuit on a wet make-and-mend.

The waves looked much higher at this level than anyone would ever have suspected from the air. Every now and again, a larger one slopped over the rubber bulwarks and into the dinghy. On Skipper's twice-soaked clothes, the sea curiously felt much warmer than the air. But at this rate the dinghy would soon fill with the water and might well overturn. Skipper felt down his right side and tore away a retaining strip which covered the rubber sheet. He drew it across his body and secured it with the press-studs provided along the top of the dinghy's round sides. That would keep most of the water off. He wished he could remember more of the safety equipment lectures. He could plainly see in his mind's eye the actual scene, the grubby little hut at Yeovilton, the high sunlight streaming in and catching bright motes of dust, the high nasal tones of the petty officer instructor, the class standing around with their shoulders slumped in boredom. *It will never happen to me* ... Besides, the design of these dinghies was always changing in slight particulars. It would take a man all his time to keep up with the mods. They ought to have a standard design and stick to it.

Skipper remembered there was a baler somewhere, a tiny cup of rubber stretched on a frame. It was small but effective. He stripped back part of the rubber covering sheet and began to bale. In a few minutes most of the water was out, and the exercise had warmed him up. He searched around the dingy sides and found a small package, tied and sealed. This was like opening a Christmas stocking. A mirror heliograph for flashing. A whistle. Yellow dye stain marker. A can of water, sealed with a tear-off strip, which covered a nipple for drinking. Chocolate. Another small package of greased paper, and inside it a tiny hand-pistol, with a pack of six tiny flares. Everything was on such a midget scale. This was air-sea rescue for Lilliputians.

The roar of engines made Skipper look up. The rest of his flight had come down low over his dinghy. He waved, and their wings rocked in answer. They would have his position exactly. Soon the air-sea rescue organisation would grind into action. To his left, as the waves lifted his dinghy, Skipper caught a glimpse of land, hills and clouds. Those had not been there before. Maybe he was drifting closer inshore. The prevailing winds were south-easterly, but it was possible that here, to the north of the island, he was still in the lee of Ishigaki.

There was a light, thin aluminium mast in the survival kit. It was as flimsy and flexible to the touch as a birch twig. Skipper was reminded of his tiny rubber-band-driven Frog aircraft toy at home. There was a time just before the war when every boy had one for Christmas. There was a tiny red sail, too, made of cotton, with a sheet attached to it, no thicker than parcel string. The mast fitted in a hole in the bows of the dinghy, not much bigger than a cigarette-holder. All part of the Lilliputian navy. However, the red sail would take him out to sea and make him more easily visible on the surface. But even the whistle looked as if it had come out of a Christmas cracker.

There was no need to send up flares, or stain the sea yellow, or flash with the mirror. They knew where he was, and all those physical means of attracting attention could wait until some form of rescue was actually in sight. Meantime, as the lectures said, warmth and patience and optimism were the watchwords.

This, Skipper guessed, was a little beyond the range of the ASR Walrus, because it would have to skirt the northern end of the island. But the Americans had long-range Dumbo flying boats which could land even in this weather, or there might even be a lifeguard submarine.

Looking at the waves, their shapes and size, as they rose above his head, Skipper began to wonder whether in fact any aircraft could land or take off in this sea. It really was beginning to look most uncomfortable. The dinghy jerked and slid and rocked, as though a tremendous hand were determined to give the occupant no rest. *Where the remote Bermudas ride. In the Ocean's bosome unespyed. From a small boat that rowed along. The listening winds received this song.* One hoped that this small boat would not be unespied.

Settled in the dinghy, with the mast bucking and whipping and the sail drawing well, Skipper's mood changed to one of irritation. There was so much to be done on board. It was a bad time to leave the ship. Michael would have to lead the squadron for the rest of the day, for even if Skipper were picked up soon he doubted if he would be in time for anything much, except possibly the very last sortie of the day. Maybe the last two, if he were exceptionally lucky.

Then there was Fenton's family to write to, if he died. They deserved a letter, even if he did not die. Kittens' family certainly had to have a letter. And Geoffrey's. Skipper thought over the next of kin lists, but for the life of him he could not recall where Kittens came from. He could not remember where Fenton's home town was, come to that. He really ought to apologise to that Sub-Lieutenant and his Bofors crew. He had been very unfair to them, in the heat of the moment. When his own aircraft identification had been put to the test, he had been as wrong as anybody. For one split second he had thought that that suicider was actually Fenton, showing off. It had certainly looked risky, but friendly. With a shock which made him blush, Skipper remembered that the Sub-Lieutenant and all his crew were dead. No sign of any of them. That suicider's wing had scooped them out of life and into death, like a bloody great soup ladle.

Skipper broke off a piece of chocolate and swallowed it. His stomach heaved it up again almost at once. His vomit did not clear the side of the dinghy, and it mixed with the water lying in the bottom. The colour and stain of it remained, no matter how hard he tried to clean himself and the dinghy. It had a sweet smell which reminded Skipper of fungus on a wall. This was what squalor was really like, to lie in a mixture of sea water and chocolate and one's own vomit.

Skipper would have liked to be able to lie back and concentrate his thoughts, to think of his life on board and to plan what he would do when he returned. But the dinghy would not allow him any peace. The weather really was getting worse. The little sail was straining and pulling. It was as much as Skipper could do to hold on to the sheet. The tiny mast looked as if it might bend at any moment. Skipper leaned forward to try and unship it, but the dinghy at once gave a great uneasy lurch and almost turned over. He tried again and this time the dinghy tipped on one side, so that his right elbow was actually in the sea, and a wave poured in from that side. Without his covering sheet he would have been swamped. He decided to let the sail take its course. It might actually have a stabilising effect, dragging the dinghy after it. Otherwise, the little rudderless, guideless dinghy would be spinning round and round, slopping to and fro and up and down the sides of the waves, like one of those crazy machines in the fairground that came after every harvest. Skipper let the sheet go and at once the sail seemed to take off and streamed in front of the dinghy, as though pointing the way like a finger post.

The motion of the dinghy became ever more violent. It was clear that something would have to be done or the dinghy would finally capsize. He must try and retrieve that sail. Unconsciously choosing his moment as the dinghy swooped upwards and poised on the top of a wave, Skipper ripped back the rubber sheet and leaned forward, grasped the pole and pulled. It came out easily and he flung himself backwards, holding mast and sail to his chest as another wave crashed across his thighs. His fingers were almost too numb to be useful, but he looped the end of the sheet through a ring on the side of the dinghy. He needed some form of sea-anchor, anything that would serve to steady the dinghy and stop this mad pitching, which sooner or later was going to overturn everything.

Skipper remembered his canvas flying shoes. They had laces in them. To his surprise he could only feel a shoe on his right foot. He had not noticed the left one go. He prised the shoe off with the toes of his other foot, and feeling down as though in bed he grasped the shoe, pulled it up and pressed it to his chest. He could feel nothing through his fingertips and it took him several minutes, while the dinghy heeled and sideslipped as though about to dive under the surface. With a length of line, the mast, the sail and one shoe, he had something like an anchor. He wanted to use the baler, too, but he needed that on board. His trousers would have been ideal, but he dared not try to wriggle out of them with the dinghy tossing like a mad thing; he would be over the side long before he had them off. It was not much, but it might just be enough.

It was difficult to tell, at first, whether the slight anchor was having any effect. Perhaps, as he watched, the dinghy did check just a little as the wave-crests slid past. Perhaps, momentarily, the dinghy was behaving a little less like a demented rocking-horse. Maybe there was just a little improvement. Skipper lay back and rested his head on the great roll of rubber behind him, astonished to find himself panting, and sweating hard.

The sun was noticeably lower now in the west and clouds were coming up which would soon hide it. Skipper sat up and craned his head from side to side. There was no sign of the shore, no aircraft overhead, nothing but the waves and this little dinghy, and high above an irrelevant blue sky gradually changing to grey.

Half-past four. Tea time, and he had been down five hours. In the wardroom they would be having toast and that rather nice Australian jam, if there was any left. Obviously, rescue was not to be an immediate affair. Skipper wondered what the delay was. His flight had his position to the nearest hundred yards, but he had not seen or heard an aircraft since they went. Skipper pondered on whether he might have been too premature in hoisting his little sail. It might have been better to have landed and taken one's choice with the Japanese. But what a choice, what a *ridiculous* choice! To land on Japanese-held Ishigaki, or sail to China across the bay. *Where the dawn comes up like thunder, out of China, crorst the Bay.* Skipper cleared his throat, raised his voice, coughed and cleared his throat again. *Come you back to Mandalay ... Where the old Flotilla lay ... Can't you 'ear their paddles chunkin' from Rangoon to Mandalay?* Skipper broke off, laughing and coughing, as spray flew across and hit his forehead. *My Christ*, he thought, *I'm going off my bloody head. Thus sung they in the English boat. An holy and a cheerful note.*

Just possibly, he might have to spend a night in the dinghy. Surely not. There was a huge organisation for air-sea rescue and it was not as though they even had to look for him. They knew where he was. There was no doubt the makeshift sea-anchor was making the dinghy a little steadier. Such fine shadings could mean the difference between life and death. One extra mouthful of water, an extra inch of line, a bite of chocolate, one more ounce of hope, and one man lived while another died. That was what the survival man said. It was all in the mind in the end, he said. Survival is as much a matter of attitude as anything else. Make up your mind you are not, repeat *not*, going to die. Given the same conditions, the same food and water and shelter, one man died after a few hours in a boat, another lived for fifty days and died in his bed fifty years later, surrounded by his grandchildren and his great-grandchildren. It was the same in lifeboats, it was the same in the prison camps. The man who wanted to badly enough, lived.

Now came ... *how does it go? Now came still evening on and twilight grey.* Hope to God it didn't. He surely should be picked up by then. Skipper felt the same rime on his lips. He broke the seal on the water container. The nipple was vaguely sexy. He remembered what the survival man said. Wet the whole mouth and swill the water about first, before swallowing. Skipper took two careful mouthfuls. He had no idea how much the container held. It looked about half a pint.

As the sun went down, so too did the wind and sea. The sky cleared and the stars came out. Shortly after midnight, the moon rose. Skipper watched it carefully. It came at first like the loom of a strange lighthouse, then a spot of light like a ship, and then in bands of golden light against the sky, like somebody's barn on fire miles away. The waves, coming towards him and slapping against his dinghy's hull, gave Skipper the impression that he was moving at a rate of knots up the path of light towards the moon. Looking over the side, he fancied he saw huge silver fish swimming fathoms below, keeping pace with the dinghy. This was the same sea he had watched so many times from the flight deck at night, but now it was no longer remote, spread out like romantic scenery. It was here, at face level, its lights sparkling only a few feet away and its depths immediately below. The sea-anchor was still trailing behind the dinghy but it was lit in silver light now, looking like a fish, like a hand, like a festival banner, like a bunch of tree roots, as it moved in the sea.

Skipper dozed and awoke, and dozed again. Each time he woke he noticed that the moon had moved higher in the sky. Once he awoke with a cough and a splutter, as spray flung itself across his face. He was horrified by the thought that he must have been sleeping with his mouth wide open. Once, a great seabird flew a few feet overhead, with a sharp, dramatic flap of its wings as it suddenly caught sight of the dinghy and the man in it. Skipper was thirstier than ever, and though he tried to restrain himself he took several long gulps of his water, without swilling them around in his mouth. He took out the chocolate again, but again his stomach squirmed.

Skipper was no longer angry at not being picked up. Something had obviously gone wrong. Everybody had problems. *All God's chillun got problems.* But however long it took, Skipper was prepared to wait. If survival was all in the mind, as the man said, then Skipper was prepared to survive until doomsday. It might be a good idea to send up one of the flares at dawn. There might be searchers quite close in the night, who only needed a little guidance when the sun came up. Again, the man said don't waste your flares. Wait until you can see your rescuers. Don't waste anything. Even when you're sure you have been spotted, keep your food and your water. There's many a slip 'twixt a sighting and a rescue. Oh, they were full of good advice. Skipper wondered whether the man who wrote the survival book had ever been shot down into a dinghy all night.

Waiting for the dawn, Skipper missed it when it came. He awoke from another doze to find it already light. Sky and sea were dead grey and there were several patches of mist. Morning mist was a feature off the Sakishima Gunto, but Skipper knew it would clear and by noon the sun would be blazing in the sky. As the sun rose, its force seemed to beat the sea down. Everything became so calm, it was difficult to see whether the sea ended and the sky began. This mist and flat calm would make things more difficult for air-sea rescue. Skipper knew the flying boat boys never liked operating when it was Harry Flatters like this.

Skipper's fingers were now so numb he could feel nothing at all through them. But he banged the side of his dinghy with his fist, to test it. It still seemed hard and full. As the sun grew hotter the gas would expand, and he might even have to vent some of it, although whether he would have the energy left to blow it up again at sunset was an interesting question.

It was not too late for a dawn flare. His helpless fingers fumbled with the pistol. He was shocked to see how bleached-white and wrinkled his fingers had become, like those of an old, old man. He dropped the pistol on his chest, and felt for it under the rubber sheet. He had a disconcerting memory of prep school, in the dormitory, trying to read a book with a torch under the blankets. He had to lift himself awkwardly and feel around the bottom of the dinghy to find the pistol. Oddly, this effort seemed to bring some sensation back into his fingers. The more he tried, the better he became. He made up his mind he would exercise his fingers, exercise his whole body somehow, down to his toes.

The flare fitted in with a metallic snap. Skipper held the pistol up, pulled the little red tab. There was a brief fizzing sound and, wonder of wonders, the thing ignited and soared into the air, miles and miles high, so that Skipper had to lie back to watch it leaving a faint red trail, before it exploded in red smoke and a cluster of tiny red stars. It seemed miraculous.

But it was not miraculous enough to attract a rescuer. The big flying boat would come soon, but in the meantime it was important to survive. The sun dried Skipper's hair as it climbed. His skin seemed to contract, tightening his forehead and his eyebrows, until he imagined he was wearing a permanent expression of superciliousness. He fancied he could actually feel the salt lying in grains on his scalp and itching, as though with some skin disease.

Skipper was not hungry or thirsty, or uncomfortable. He did not mind the rocking of the dinghy any more. He tried to sing, but his cracked voice surprised and depressed him. That was no way to cheer oneself up. The only way was simply to be here, to carry on being here, until the flying boat came.

In the afternoon Skipper was roused by the smell of hot rubber. The sun beating on his rubber covering sheet had heated it to the point where it was almost painful to the touch of the palm of his hand. He stripped it back and away with his knuckles, and stared at his bare feet. They were white and gaunt, as though belonging to somebody else. They were like corpse feet he had seen as a child, when somebody from the village was killed in an accident with the steam thrashing machine. It had been a breathlessly hot day, like this, and he had stared down at those bare feet sticking out from beneath somebody's overcoat.

Skipper remembered his resolution to exercise. He curled his toes, raised his knees, and extended his legs straight. He rubbed his thighs with his hands, swung his arms across his chest, worked his shoulders in a circular movement, moved his head from side to side. *Mens sana in corpore sano.* He would have the most *sano corpore* any survivor ever had. *Mens sana*, too. But the exertion left him breathless and rocked the dinghy so alarmingly that he had to stop.

It struck Skipper that this was an extraordinarily *empty* sea. There were no birds, no signs of life. Towards the evening he thought he caught sight of an aircraft to the south, towards Ishigaki, where he would expect to see it. But nothing came overhead. He watched the evening sun with resignation. And the evening and the morning were the first day. He could see his father reading the lesson in Daughton church. And when the sun was going down, a deep sleep fell upon Abraham, and lo, a horror of great darkness fell upon him. Pray God it was not so.

That night the moon was hidden behind cloud, but Skipper knew when it rose, by the general lightening of the night sky. The moon was there, although he could not see it. Once again, he woke from a light sleep with a throat like a furnace. He had behaved very well towards his water during the day but now, again, he could not stop himself taking several long swallows. He shook the light can. There really did not seem a great deal left in it. The chocolate still sickened him. But in a way it was doing him a service, quelling again and again any longing for food.

When dawn came, Skipper almost forgot his flare. The rasping noise the back of his hand made against the stubble on his chin unaccountably reminded him of the grating, fizzing noise of the flare. This time he did not bother to follow its flight. He could tell it had ignited successfully and to tip his head back now made his shoulders and back ache unbearably.

But, this time, the miracle did happen. Skipper heard noises behind him. Paddling forward with his right arm and backing water with his left, he spun the dingy around. His heart almost stopped with shock. Only a few feet away were the light grey bows of a submarine. A long row of holes by the waterline looked exactly like the grinning of a great shark. But there were men up on the casing and, beyond them, more men watching from the conning tower. They were white men and they were waving, so it was not a Japanese but an American submarine.

Two men in swimming trunks, wearing lifejackets, with goggles over their eyes and lines round their waists, jumped into the water. Their goggled faces, to Skipper unreal and fantastic, like beings from one of those films about the war of the worlds, appeared one on either side of the dinghy.

A great brown hand landed on the rubber side of the dinghy. Skipper vaguely resented it. It was an invasion of his own space and, besides, it would not take much to upset his dinghy. He tried to brush the hand away.

'OK, Bud, you just take it easy now. Just take it easy.'

'All right. I'm … I'm very much obliged to you.'

He saw them exchange glances.

'Hey, a Limey! What's a *Limey* doing out here?'

'It's a … It's a … fairly longish story.'

'OK, well you just take it easy and we'll have you out of here.' Skipper raised his arms and knew at once that he was helpless. He would not be able to move a muscle to assist himself. Left to himself, he knew he would die.

'Now you lie still, Bud.'

Skipper felt the dinghy bumping against the side of the submarine. More lines were thrown, hands were reaching, more faces gathering. The dinghy left the water, hesitated, and then swiftly and surely rose through the air, with Skipper still in it. An American sailor with a puzzled expression on his face handed in the thin line, with the mast and the sail, and the sodden shoe still attached to it.

'Can you get up?'

'Of course, of course.' Once more Skipper sensed the rustle of amazement his accent caused amongst his listeners. But he could not get up. He seemed fixed in the dinghy. Several arms grasped him under the armpits and round the waist, and he found himself propped upright with a sailor on either side of him. Looking over the shoulder of one of them, Skipper saw something which made him break out into a hard sweat, while the skin prickled on his scalp. A huge black skull, with grey eye sockets, glared at him from the base of the submarine's conning tower.

'This is the USS *Skullfish*.'

'I'm really much obliged to you.' It was a fantastic sensation, to be rescued by these men from some other world. *Take me to your leader,* he should be saying. He laughed at his own thought.

'OK, yes, well, we know it's funny.' One of the men, Skipper could see, was an officer. 'We can see its funny side too. Can you walk OK?'

'Of course, of course!' But he could not. His legs simply would not move, one in front of the other. The officer nodded, the sailors hefted his weight and Skipper felt himself being lifted. He was carried towards the conning tower, while the skull swayed towards him, getting larger and larger. Skipper was astonished by the width of the submarine's casing. He had always imagined them as narrow slippery walkways. But this was a great broad-ribbed deck; one could have a dinner and dance out here.

While Skipper continued to insist that he could manage by himself, they carried him to a small door in the base of the conning tower and manhandled him through it and up a short set of brass steps, cold to the touch and smelling of salt and tidal rocks, to a large almost circular bridge, again much larger than Skipper would ever have dreamed. There was a Bofors gun at each end, both manned, and four lookouts, two on either side, with binoculars pressed to their eyes. Above, two radar aerials kept on turning.

A man, clearly the commanding officer, in a clean, pressed khaki uniform and a blue peaked baseball cap with gold lace around its rim, was waiting to shake hands.

'Sam Mellow, Captain of the *Skullfish*.'

'How do you do, sir?' Skipper shook hands. 'I'm much obliged to you for all this … for your very kind service to aviators in reduced circumstances.'

It was a weak joke, the weakest of jokes, and it fell entirely by the wayside. The faintest of frowns briefly crossed Commander Mellow's face. But his main reaction was astonishment.

'Goddamn it, a Limey! Since when have the Limeys been in this war?'

'Oh, since the third of September 1939, sir.'

Commander Mellow's smile cracked a little. 'I mean this war out here.' He did not actually say it, but his manner clearly said, *this* real *war*.

'Oh, well,' Skipper gestured vaguely at the horizon. 'Some time now.'

Commander Mellow seemed to realise that he was perhaps being less than wholly welcoming to a fellow mariner in distress. 'Well, glad to have you aboard. What's your name?'

Skipper gave it, then paused. This was obviously going to be difficult to explain. 'But everybody calls me Skipper.'

Once again, Commander Mellow frowned. '*I'm* the Skipper here. Though nobody calls me that to my face. Say, what made you shoot a flare right then?'

'I don't know, sir. It just said in the book that dawn was a good time, because there might be somebody quite close, looking for you overnight.'

'That must be a pretty good book. You're a good piece to the north-west of where you were reported. But that flare put us right on, lucky for you. But nobody told us we were looking for a *Limey* pilot!'

'You mean, if you caught one you might have to throw it back again?' But once more, the feeblest of jokes fell on stony ground. Commander Mellow was clearly baffled, unsure whether his new guest was mocking him or not. Skipper meanwhile was cursing his own bravado in hoisting that little red sail. A gesture like that, although it had given him encouragement at the time, might very nearly have cost him his life. He might even now be still floating out there in that dinghy.

'Now, I suggest you get below, Commander. Have a shower, take some coffee, rest up. You're just about bushed, I can see that. We'll signal your ship we've got you alive and well … well, moderately well … I guess they'll be glad to know that. So will your folks.'

The sailors from the casing had deflated the dinghy and were bringing it up the steps to the bridge. The two men on either side of Skipper helped him towards the oval hatchway in the centre of the bridge.

'Can you make it OK by yourself?'

'Of course, of course.'

'I'll go in front of you, sir. If you fall —' the man grinned — 'you won't fall far, sir.'

In the event, Skipper did not need the help, although it was a narrow shave. He could not feel the rungs of the ladder at all on his bare feet, and his numbed fingers could only just hang on. There was an interesting and not unpleasant smell, of oil and some form of cooking. There were massed banks of gauges, and shining dials, and curious faces. To the crew of the submarine, any pilot would have been exotic, but a Limey pilot, that was something altogether rich and strange. Skipper was very conscious of his hair, sticking up in salty spikes, two days' bristle on his chin, his stained flying overalls, battered lifejacket and bare feet. But the faces, some of them bearded, were all smiling. There was no doubt about their welcome. The words 'Glad to have you' echoed here and there, running amongst the watching sailors like some joyful password.

A sailor, bare-chested with a towel wound round his waist and sandals on his feet, led Skipper into a small, brightly lit compartment near the central control room. It had several doors leading off it, a table in the middle with a green baize cloth on it, and a picture of President Roosevelt sitting at an enormous desk, with the flags of the Stars and Stripes crossed and draped behind him. In one corner a large glass container with some dark liquid, almost certainly coffee, bubbling in it, sat on what looked like a large heating-ring. On the bulkhead above it was the ship's badge and its number, 448. The badge was an athletic-looking skeleton, with an overlarge skull, spearing a small warship with its trident. The warship had been drawn as plump and juicy, and somehow vulnerable, rather like a tender pork sausage. The skeleton, on the other hand, was brilliantly represented as vengeful, and menacing, and successful. Skipper wondered why it was that American ship's heraldry was so much crisper, more economical of design, and so much more eye-catching than the Royal Navy's. The compartment was quiet except for the soft but noticeable sound of ventilation fans. A dark, swarthy steward, probably a Filipino, was waiting with a cloth over one arm. This was clearly the submarine's wardroom.

'Coffee, sir?'

'Yes, please … I don't know your name?'

'Geronimo, sir, the wardroom mess boy, sir. You like it with sugar and cream?'

'Oh, yes, please.'

Another sailor came in. 'Pharmacist's Mate, sir. Can I just look you over, to see what shape you're in?'

'I'm fine.'

'Yeah, sure.'

There were many questions Skipper wanted to ask. What was the submarine's programme? Was there any chance of being transferred to *Miss Britannia* today? Tomorrow? If not, then when? Skipper knew from others' experience in the past that aircrew separated from their carriers were liable to lead a disjointed, unregarded existence, belonging nowhere, being nobody's responsibility and nobody's care. If a pilot was not careful and did not press hard, he could spend weeks getting back to his ship. But for the time being it was easier and simpler just to do what was asked of him. An overpowering weariness had sapped all Skipper's ability to make decisions for himself. Besides, he found himself in the care of the *Skullfish* team, who seemed to have practised their drill for picking up an aviator from his dinghy and looking after him, and were now overjoyed to have a chance to put it into effect.

They took off his clothes and put him in a shower stall, where they soaped and washed him. Then they showered him. Another sailor held out a towel, and two of them rubbed and dried him. Somebody had already sized up Skipper's physique and they had clean khaki uniform, underclothes and slippers ready for him. Skipper found their energy, their conversation, their questions, their sheer pleasure in their own efficiency, curiously reviving. Except for the tingling in his fingers and toes, as sensation returned fully to them, and a sore throat where the hot coffee seemed to have seared a broad, painful path right down to his stomach, Skipper returned to the wardroom feeling, for the time being, almost normal.

An officer sitting at the table got up to shake hands. He was a big bruiser of a man, with heavy shoulders, ginger hair and a fighter's jaw.

'I'm Red, the Exec. Glad to meet you. Skipper, is it?'

'How do you do? That's what everybody calls me.'

'Glad to have you aboard, Skipper. You're a lucky man.'

'I realise.'

'We did a search all night and we were just about to haul off to the south-east again when we saw your flare. We couldn't believe you'd got this far up. You trying to make China?'

Skipper felt his cheeks reddening. 'Not really. Just trying to stay alive.'

'OK, that reminds me, Geronimo's got some chicken for you. Like to try it?'

The slices of chicken were cooked in a sauce, and they looked delicious. But they seemed to turn to pith and wood in Skipper's mouth. He tried to swallow them but was physically unable.

Red shook his head. 'That's OK. It's understandable. Like some ice cream?'

The ice cream was better, and it counteracted the effects of the hot coffee earlier. But Skipper did not allow it to divert him from his main preoccupation. 'What chance is there of me getting back to my ship?'

'Don't know. But I do know there's a spare bunk in that stateroom and I suggest you hit it.'

'But what happens if somebody comes to pick me up?'

'Then we'll rouse you out of there, Skipper. But there's no word on that yet. We're on our way back to Guam. We stopped off to look for you, but we're back on schedule again now.'

'So you're not a regular lifeguard submarine?'

'Hell no, this is an *operational* boat. We were on a patrol.'

Once again, Skipper was aware that he had committed some solecism. Living with these people was going to be more difficult than he had supposed. They spoke English, they were on the same side in the war, but they were still foreigners. But Skipper's professional interest was aroused by the mention of a patrol.

'How did the patrol go?'

'OK. Landed a coupla agents on Formosa.' The information confirmed Skipper's suspicions that there was some form of

Allied organisation for intelligence on that island. Those photographs of the locomotives had been remarkably up to date.

'Then we went on into the East China Sea. Caught up with a convoy inshore off China. Sank two Marus. Then we got a chance at a big cruiser, on her way back to Japan. The Captain — our Skipper, that is — he missed. So he was as sore as a bear in a barrel about it. Still is. So don't you mention big Japanese cruisers to the Captain when you talk to him.'

'Oh, no, I won't, I won't, I promise.'

It was odd that in the silences between words, Skipper could still hear the water slapping against the sides of the dinghy, and although the deck was firm and solid beneath his feet his head still rocked to the dinghy's crazy motion.

Red led the way into a very small cabin, a stateroom as they called it, with three bunks. The middle and top bunks were occupied. The curtains were drawn across and Skipper sensed the presence of the men sleeping behind them. Skipper stripped, while Red and the Pharmacist's Mate, who stood in the doorway, watched him curiously. He felt they were expecting him to have feathers or scales instead of skin, or a concealed pair of wings or horns underneath his shirt. Skipper had never in his life, not even on his first night at boarding school, felt a more closely scrutinised outsider.

The noise and motion of a submarine were utterly different from those of an aircraft carrier. Skipper's body was in any case still bracing itself against the violent rocking of the dinghy, and mentally he was still preparing himself to resist, to endure. But on these memories were now imposed a whole range of other sensations, of water tearing past the thin skin of metal beside his head, of distant unknown machinery rumbling and clicking, of liquids racing and slamming through pipes quite close by, and the quick roll and sharp righting movement of the submarine's hull. Skipper was afraid the sheer oddness of his surroundings might keep him awake, but he had only had time to decide that he had probably been given some kind of sleeping pill in that coffee before he drifted off into dreams of horrifying turbulence, of struggling and drowning, in which images of perishing under a wide-open sky fought with fears of a lonely, confined death in a deep pit hidden from the light.

When he awoke, Skipper's watch showed one o'clock, but it had stopped, and Skipper knew by the weariness in his limbs that he must have slept for a very long time. Except for an ache in his back, a relic of his crouched posture in that dinghy, he felt fit and well, and very hungry. He pulled back the bunk curtain. The compartment was in darkness, but there was a strip of light down one side of the door leading back into the wardroom.

Geronimo had heard, or been waiting for, the sound of the curtain being drawn back, and came into the stateroom. Once again, Skipper enjoyed the sensation of being looked after. Clothes, shoes, shaving gear were all ready for him.

There were four officers sitting in the wardroom when Skipper went in, Red the Exec, and three others, who rose to shake hands, curiously introducing themselves with their names, and not their departments on board but their home towns.

'Bubba Reeves, from Passport, Idaho. Glad to have you aboard, Commander.'

'Jerry Guardiello, from New York. Glad to know you, Commander.'

'Jim Donovan, from Peacetown, Wisconsin. Glad to have you aboard, Commander.'

Red was grinning. 'I'm from Chicago. You can see we're from all over.'

Skipper shook everybody's hands. They were just finishing breakfast. Geronimo brought him coffee, iced fruit juice, some things like flapjacks or crumpets, and some substance on a plate which puzzled Skipper.

'What's this, do you mind my asking?'

'Them's grits, sir.'

'What's grits?'

Geronimo rolled his eyes and looked baffled by such ignorance. 'Grits is ... well, they's just grits, sir.'

'That's an all-American breakfast you got there, Commander.'

'It tastes fine.'

'One thing to settle, Commander, is your own things. What's gonna happen to them?'

What's gonna happen to them? Skipper could not imagine why they asked. His old clothes, salt-stained, battered, torn, could hardly be worth anything. He would be happy to see the back of them. Was something expected of him? But the dinghy and the equipment in it, perhaps they were all in some mysterious official way in his charge still, on his permanent loan list? That was impossible: he had just lost a whole Corsair with all its equipment, fittings and armament. The Pusser could hardly concern himself with a mere rubber dinghy after that.

But Skipper could see in their faces that he was expected to say something. They were all waiting for him to reach the right decision. What could it possibly be? He was as keen as they were, desperately keen, to say the right thing.

'Well, I suppose I should collect everything together ... I suppose...' He saw their faces fall. So that was wrong. 'It's very good of you to fit me up with new togs like this. I wonder, would you mind … could I ask somebody to dispose of all my old things for me? … if you wouldn't mind…'

That was it. He could see by their beaming faces he had hit on it, whatever it was.

'That's really good of you, Commander. We'll be happy to take care of your things. The guys were wondering about souvenirs. They're always hassling about who should have what. They're all crazy to have souvenirs to take home. By the way, we've got your private things here.'

Skipper was taken aback by the number of objects he had had in his pockets. He had always impressed on the squadron to empty their pockets of everything that might possibly be of use to enemy intelligence when they flew on a sortie. But here was his notebook, dried out now, with its pages soiled and curled; and his pocket handkerchief, now washed and ironed; his penknife and pocket compass, and a tin of cough pastilles Chief Air Rigger Petre had given him; a copy of *Miss Britannia*'s wardroom mess committee minutes, folded and crumpled; a stub of pencil and a few coins and a keyring, with the key of the squadron safe, his cabin door, his briefcase and his writing case, and the ignition keys of his motorbike at Daughton, which for some reason he had carried with him.

There was also a small, blackened button, which had clearly come from some uniform. Skipper picked it up. It was not a Royal Navy button. He could not recall anything about it.

'We tried to clean that up, Commander, but it's been burned pretty bad. It's got some kind of flower design on it.'

Skipper could remember seeing that kind of flower before, with its symmetrical shape and spreading petals in a wide fan. They had some of those at home, rows of them. Chrysanthemums. Floating chrysanthemums. Skipper remembered. It was the button he had picked up on the little walkway after the suicider had hit the ship.

'Do you know what this is? This is a button from a kamikaze pilot's uniform.'

Red drew in a hissing breath. They all looked at the button with longing eyes. This time Skipper was in no doubt what to do.

'That'll make a good souvenir, won't it? I'll give it to your captain, on behalf of the whole lot of you. If he'll accept it, with my compliments.'

'Accept it?' breathed Red, enviously. 'Gee, what a souvenir.'

A sailor wearing a white US Navy cap, the first Skipper had seen on board, drew back the wardroom door and looked at Skipper. 'Beg pardon, sir. Captain sends his compliments, sir, to you, sir, and he would be much obliged if you would step up to the bridge when you've finished your chow, sir.'

Like a squadron, Skipper guessed, a submarine had its grapevine. No doubt the Captain had known that Skipper was awake almost as soon as he had awoken.

'Hey, Shylock.' Red gave the button to the sailor at the door. 'Give this to the Skipper, compliments of our guest here. It's a kamikaze pilot's uniform button.'

'Say!' Shylock's eyes goggled as he gingerly turned the button over in his fingers as though it were red hot. 'Gee, what a souvenir!'

'You got it, so now get up there and give it to the Skipper.'

The scene on the bridge had not changed. The four lookouts were still there, binoculars pressed to their eyes. The radar aerials were still turning. Commander Mellow got up from a small chair bolted to the forward periscope standard.

'Morning, Commander. You sleep OK?'

'Fine, fine, sir. I'm very grateful for the way you're looking after me.'

'Forget it. We're grateful to you. This button here … Hell, that's really some souvenir.' While he was talking, Commander Mellow's eyes never rested but continued to roam along the horizon. In that, he was just like Skipper's own captain in *Miss Britannia*.

'It's the least I could do, sir.'

'Don't call me sir.'

'I always call captains of ships "sir", sir. It's a Limey idiosyncrasy, sir.'

'OK, OK.'

It was a beautiful morning, with sunshine, blue sky and a brisk wind, brisker indeed than Skipper had expected. It seemed they were travelling much faster than usual. Commander Mellow noticed Skipper looking over the side.

'We're going balls out, as you would say. Just got the word of another crew down. A B-29 crew on their way back to Saipan. Came down about fifty miles ahead, we think. We're way out now into the Philippine Sea, heading for Guam.'

'I was wondering about that, sir, about any chance of getting back to my ship?'

Commander Mellow shook his head. 'Not much chance now. I guess your ship was busy when we first reported you, and I expect we're too far out now. You've been asleep for twenty-four hours. We're way out. Your ships had a hard time from those kamikazes. Reports of three of your carriers damaged. We'll put you ashore in Guam and you can make your own way back. That's not my side of things. But we'll do our best for you, pull a few strings and get you a flight if we can. I got friends in Guam. Oh, I got a signal here, came in while you were below.'

It was dated the day before, which was two days after Skipper himself had been shot down. *Lieutenant Commander (A) Robert Weston RNVR. Missing over Ishigaki.* There was no other name. Nobody else had been lost.

So dear old Robert had kept his reputation to the end. He had never lost a wingman.

CHAPTER TEN

'Did you know him, Skipper?'

'Yes, I did, sir.' Somebody up in *Miss Britannia*'s island — Skipper had a sudden, aching longing to be back there — had remembered him out here in this submarine and, out of politeness, had told him about his friend.

'That's why they sent us this, I guess. We don't normally get signals about Limey aircrew. Not unless they want us to pick them *up*, of course.'

That would mean yet another letter. He really must get down to it and write them. He certainly had to write to Cicely. The toast of their training course. The Wren of all their dreams. Everybody was in love with her. Only Robert Weston had married her. It was an odd thought, but it was very probable that Cicely, sitting at her desk in the operations room at Lee, had seen this signal long before Skipper. That was the problem about marrying Wrens. They were too close to the war and knew too much about it. But that certainly meant another letter: that was one to Fenton's people, one to Geoffrey's, one to Kittens' wife and now one to Cicely Weston. He could always get a job as an obituary writer after the war.

'Know him well?'

'Very well, sir. This man was on my flying training course. Joined the Navy on the same day as me. I even knew him before the war.' Skipper involuntarily shuddered as he said it: that was like saying one had known somebody in the Middle Ages.

'I can see it's hit you. Don't think I'm not sympathetic, Skipper, because it's happened to me more than once, but you gotta just pick yourself up, dust yourself off, as they say, and start in all over.'

'Oh, I know that, sir.' It was the universal advice, but it was curious to hear it from a Yankee submarine captain, miles out here in the Philippine Sea.

'He could be picked up yet.'

'Maybe.' It was possible, in the same way that it was possible a 100-1 outsider might win the Derby. No British aircrew shot down over the Sakishima Gunto had yet been reported as a prisoner of war.

The broadcast loudspeaker mounted on the forward bridge bulkhead crackled, and a voice reported something which Skipper, because of the American accent and the quality of the sound, could not catch. But Commander Mellow immediately put his binoculars to his eyes and searched the sky ahead and to starboard.

'Can't see it yet. Radar reports an aircraft. It will be one of the Dumbos.'

Commander Mellow put his binoculars down. 'Skipper, you haven't met Henry Jordan, our Gunnery Officer and Officer of the Watch right now. Henry Jordan Three, to be exact.'

'Glad to meet you, Commander.' Henry Jordan III was like the others, with neat blond crew-cut hair, but unlike the others he had a small moustache. 'I'm from Paris.'

'Paris?'

'Not Paris, France. Paris, Missouri.'

'And this is our Vasco da Gama.' There was yet another officer standing beside the periscope standards. 'Navigator.'

'Glad to know you, Commander. I'm Joe Brewster.' He paused. 'From Bangor, Maine.'

'What's the word on these B-29 boys, Joe?'

'Well, sir.' Joe Brewster spread out a chart, folded in two halves, on a tiny shelf fitted for that purpose on the port side of the bridge. 'We're fifty miles from the datum position right now. With zigging, it should take us about two hours and forty minutes, sir. And we should see a coupla Dumbo aircraft up ahead before we get there. If we don't find 'em right away, why then, we start the usual square search out to twenty miles and then … well, sir, it's up to us what we do. With the aircraft up top there, and visibility and sea like they are, we got a good chance of getting them. Should be no problem, sir.'

'Don't say that, Joe. That's like painting the devil on the wall.'

'I guess I'm sorry, sir.'

'You should be. Don't let me ever hear you talk like that again. Hey, we got some time in hand, how would you like to see round our boat, Skipper?'

'I'd be glad to, sir. I've never been in a submarine before.'

'Never been in a … hey, pass the word for Frankie Rinaldo in the control room, on the double. He'll look after you.'

Frankie Rinaldo was waiting at the bottom of the ladder by the time Skipper reached it. He was a very young man indeed. He looked to Skipper about seventeen years old. He was wearing sandals, bathing trunks and an open-necked khaki shirt.

'Glad to know you, Commander. I'm Frank Rinaldo, from San Diego. Lieutenant jg. Very j. very g.'

'How do you do? What's your job on board, Frank?'

'Oh, a little bit of this, a little bit of that. I keep the books, I keep some watches, and most of all I keep out of the Exec's way. You heard of sucking on the hind tit? I'm the hind tit around here. In some boats they call it Laundry and Morale

Officer. In this boat they just say "send for Frank Rinaldo. OK, so shall we start right in?' Frank Rinaldo pulled back a door. 'This here is Buddy Leggett, our radio man, and this here is our radio shack. Buddy is from Des Moines, Iowa.'

Frank Rinaldo, as the eighth and most junior officer on board, seemed on excellent terms with the ship's company. He knew every man's name and his home town, and introduced every one with a neat précis of his job. Skipper met two men from Kentucky who looked after various pumps, and the Texan who did the cooking, and a huge Sioux Indian who maintained the water distiller. There were rows of gauges and machinery of various kinds, and storerooms, and a radar display compartment, and forward a large compartment for torpedo stowage. Everywhere, *Skullfish*'s men paused from their work, wiped their hands on the seats of their trousers and shook hands with Skipper, delighted and honoured by this unaccustomed social call, as though entertaining some high-ranking visitor from Mars. They listened with the utmost care to his unfamiliar accent, but once they had the gist of his questions they were only too glad to show him their part of the ship.

Skipper was struck by the space in the torpedo compartment. 'It's huge compared with the rest of the ship. Where are all the torpedoes?'

'Fired them. Pooped them off, Commander, this has been a busy patrol. We only got three left and they're up the tubes. Just in case we need 'em.'

'Is your patrol normally as busy?'

'This is my first, Commander, but from what I hear this Skipper is a hot-shot.'

That was what they all said. Everyone on board was respectful, but slightly frightened, of Sam Mellow. It seemed that he was a particularly successful submarine captain and an especially good torpedo shot. That had made the missed Japanese cruiser rankle all the more. Sam Mellow had in fact just been promoted to Commander as a result of his last patrol, Skipper learned from Frank Rinaldo. He had led a wolf-pack of four submarines into the Sea of Japan, where they had cut a wide swathe of destruction amongst Japanese shipping, unprepared for such an assault so close to home waters.

The whole submarine had a buoyant, alert atmosphere which both impressed and saddened Skipper. This, he knew, was the way he himself had felt two years earlier. Two years of operations later he was not so resilient, nor so optimistic. But here, on every side — in the slogan *Go Get 'Em!* pasted above a doorway, in the cartoon on the noticeboard showing a submarine scattering Japanese in disarray — were signs that the true offensive spirit still burned.

Skipper realised, talking to *Skullfish*'s men, listening to their conversation and observing their manner, that here was a whole war about which he knew almost nothing. The newspapers and the intelligence summaries gave only the palest idea of the ruthless, relentless offensive that was being conducted against Japanese shipping. The ugly side of this war lay just beneath a casual phrase. It could suddenly be conjured up in the most inconsequential way.

When Frank Rinaldo led Skipper back to the wardroom for coffee, the Exec was sitting reading the signal log and Jerry Guardiello, who had engineering duties on board, was adding up columns of figures in a large notebook. Geronimo brought them all fresh cups of coffee.

'Enjoy your tour, Commander?'

'Oh, very much. It's very good of you to make me so welcome.'

Guardiello looked up from his notebook. Skipper had already sensed a faint Anglophobic undercurrent in his attitude. Guardiello the New Yorker was certainly no friend of the English. 'Well, sir, I sure hope you have a better trip than our last passenger.'

The others looked at him. Skipper noticed Geronimo standing, paying close attention, beside the wardroom door. Guardiello's face showed that he was aware of some solecism, but was stubbornly resolved to brazen it out.

'Why, what happened?'

'Well...'

'Jerry, let it be.'

'No, no, no ... this Limey Commander here asks a question, we should give him an answer.'

'But I didn't ask any questions!' Skipper felt the protest was worth making.

'OK, Jerry, I'll tell it.' Red had moved smoothly into the centre of attention, relieving Guardiello of the responsibility. 'We took a prisoner from the last Maru we sank. He was out cold when we got him, so we laid him out forrard to sleep it off. But when he came to he was wild as a crazy man. You couldn't do nothing with him. Tried to hang himself, first thing off. Then when we stopped that, he broke a plate and tried to slit his own goddamned throat. He attacked everybody who came near him. Wouldn't touch no food nor water. Not a thing. So we collared him and tied him up and he just lay there, for twenty-four hours, just a-glaring and a-staring at us. When we came to let him loose, for mercy's sake, he jumped on poor Sparky the Pharmacist's Mate and damn near throttled him. It took three of us to get his goddamned fingers off of Sparky's windpipe. He never seemed to go to sleep, and he must have been starving. But he never touched a drop of water, never ate a mouthful of food for seven days. It seemed to us he was going clear out of his mind. Never touched nothing all the time he was on board. Geronimo there —' Red nodded towards the doorway — 'tried harder than anybody. The Japanese, they sure have kicked the shit out of the Filipinos this war, but Geronimo there, he did his best. But it was no dice.'

With foreboding, Skipper realised that they had been speaking of the Japanese prisoner in the past tense. 'What happened to him in the end?'

'So we gave him a lethal shot of morphine and dropped him over the side one dark night.'

'Ye gods!' Skipper had not meant to betray his shocked reaction so clearly, but he could not help himself. That was precious close to a war crime.

'I know what you're thinking, Commander.' Neither in voice nor manner did Red show that he was at all surprised or concerned by Skipper's reaction. 'But you wouldn't know what life is like in these boats. It's one for all and all for one in this neck of the woods. You get a Jap prisoner acting up like that, why he puts a man in mind of things he shouldn't. Maybe he don't concentrate so hard on his job because of that. Next thing is, he makes a mistake, or I make a mistake, or somebody somewhere makes a mistake because he ain't got his whole mind on the job. Maybe he don't do his job, maybe he don't give the captain the information, the service, the duty he wants and the next thing is, we get a Jap tin can dropping goodnight pills right on top of us and then it's all of us way down the Swanee river. Ain't that so, Geronimo?'

'Yes, sir, it sure is, sir.'

'So there you are, Commander. The Captain, none of us, we ain't got nothing to be ashamed of. The details are in our log and the Captain has written his report. ComSubPac will see it when we get in.'

'Of course.' Skipper knew that it was presumptuous of him to judge these men in their own conduct of their own war. 'It just means that I'll have to be very careful what I do and say if one of you guys comes and shakes me in the middle of the night. I don't want to be too sudden, do I?'

The others laughed as though it was the first joke they had heard during that war. For the first time Skipper felt himself closer to being accepted amongst them. They were interrupted by Red cocking his head for an announcement on the ship's broadcast. In his own ship, Skipper could understand every pipe perfectly well, but in *Skullfish* the unfamiliar terminology and the accent, blurred and muffled by the transmission through the speakers, combined to defeat him. It seemed they had found the B-29 dinghy.

It was, Skipper learned, the Captain who had first sighted the slight flaw on the horizon which grew into the dinghy. It was within a mile of the datum position, slightly downwind, as they might have expected. Standing in the control room, listening to the sounds of the rescue, Skipper had to stand aside for the two swimmers, lifejackets on, goggles slung round their necks, to climb up the ladder. He peered up after them, catching sight of a sliver of blue sky at the top of the tower. He hoped that Commander Mellow might remember him and ask him to come up.

It was, it seemed, a very large dinghy, big enough to hold the whole bomber's crew. But the whole crew were not there. There was, in fact, only one survivor and the control room soon learned he was badly burned. A minute later, the news came that the man was dead.

The control room was crowded. Red was there, and Frank Rinaldo, Guardiello, and a dozen or more sailors. Everyone, Skipper noticed as he looked round, had his eyes fixed on the deck, as though already in mourning. The submarine was stopped with no way on. The deck rolled gently from side to side. The helmsman, keeping his head strictly to his front, spun the steering wheel several turns to starboard and back to port again. He had been given a course to steer, but there was no steerage way.

In the silence, they could all hear sounds from the casing above: bumps and shouts, and a voice calling down the tower for another rope to be sent up.

The dinghy came down first. It was a great flabby shapeless red and yellow mass, like some huge flopping rubber shroud. Skipper wondered why they bothered to bring such a thing down into a submarine, where space was already at such a premium. Possibly, he thought, its designers wanted to examine it after operational use. And then there was always the *Skullfish* souvenirs industry.

It took some time to pull the dinghy down and stow it away, and the activity it aroused distracted attention from the tower. A call from above made Skipper look round. The sight there made sweat start into the palms of his hands and stand cold on his brow. Two naked feet, swinging to the slight motion of the submarine, had appeared in the lower hatchway. One foot was purple and blistered, and there was matted blood on the ankle. Involuntarily Skipper sprang forward to help, but voices from above made him stop. Looking up, he could see that the tower was lined all round with men, all looking down at him. It was a totally unexpected cortège, standing ready to help the corpse on its way down, and to prevent it touching any part of the submarine in its descent. There was a rope, doubled and looped and tied under the dead man's shoulders. They lowered him rapidly into the control room, where Sparky the Pharmacist's Mate and the chef from Texas were waiting with a light metal-framed stretcher.

Much of the dead man's body was naked, for much of his clothing had been burned away. Skipper fancied he could even smell the burned flesh. If he had not died of his burns the man would almost certainly have died of exposure. He had no lifejacket and only a few tattered rags around his waist. The skin Skipper could see was blackened and scorched, and one thigh was pink and raw and mottled. The right hand was badly burned, so that the fingers were glued together, almost as though their separate flesh had melted and fused in the heat. There were enormous blisters on his body, which were already encrusted with blood and pus. He must have survived long enough to climb into the dinghy, but the salt and the wind and the heat of the sun on those burns must have caused him pain which beggared the imagination. They had put a towel over his face but as he swung round when Sparky caught him, the towel slipped. His head was burned bald and seemed to have been charred a horrifyingly healthy-looking deep brown. By a trick of the harsh control-room lighting, his eyelids appeared to be gummed shut but he continued to stare directly at Skipper as though with great pale-red eyes. Skipper had to turn away to protect himself from that sight. That face had said, as clearly as though it had spoken out loud, *Look at me, this might have been you.* In that scorched bundle of flesh and tatters, hanging on the end of a rope, Skipper might have been looking at himself.

He caught a movement out of the corner of his eye, and saw one of the men he had met that morning in the diesel room crossing himself. A single sound, between a groan and a sigh, like a convulsive expression of disgust, horror and pity, rose from every man in the control room.

While Sparky and the Texan chef laid the corpse out on the stretcher and covered him wholly with a white blanket, the message came down from the bridge that the dead man had been the B-29's bomb-aimer. Apparently, the identification dog-tags around his neck, and some items of personal equipment, had survived the charring. Even then, when his mouth was still swimming with saliva and he was still half afraid he might be sick, Skipper could admire Sam Mellow's concern for his ship's company. He knew, as a good captain should, that at a time like this every scrap of information he could give them was priceless.

The clear bells of the engine-room telegraphs rang, like precious reminders of normality, and the submarine got under way again, heading out, as Sam Mellow explained over the bridge broadcast, in ever-widening patterns to search for any more survivors, who might be still floating alive in their lifejackets. The new direction, the fresh sense of purpose, seemed to hearten everyone on board.

Nevertheless, the dead bomb-aimer had inflicted a deep psychological blow on the ship's company. Skipper was astounded by the change in the atmosphere on board. The event had cast a gloom over the whole submarine. Orders were passed in much quieter tones, and men shuffled along the passageway as though anxious not to cause any affront with their usual noise. The dead man was a shocking reminder of their own mortality. Like Skipper, he had come from that other war which they knew little about. But Skipper had been so alive and so well he had reassured them that there was no actual danger. That burned face in the control had been a hard awakening.

Skipper had another moment of stress, and again had to control his feelings, when he returned to the wardroom and saw Red tipping the contents out of a large brown envelope. It contained the bomb-aimer's personal belongings: some scraps of charred paper, the tags, a couple of buttons, a fraternity ring with an indecipherable design on its flat face, and a pair of sunglasses, their smoked glass warped by the heat into two grotesque teardrops. Once again, Skipper felt his throat tightening, realising that these could have been his own effects laid out on the wardroom table there.

'Doesn't it make you feel a lucky man, Commander?'

'That isn't my chief feeling.' For some reason, Skipper felt he must now conceal his own selfish thoughts. 'I must admit, I *did* think that. But now all I want to say is, well, that poor man…'

'Well, let's not dwell on it.' Red briskly scooped the dead man's belongings back into the envelope. 'I guess there's a bit too much gloom going on around here. The sooner we get that funeral over the better. I'm gonna fix it with the Captain right now. We'll send these back to his squadron on Tinian when we get in.' Red looked up and caught Skipper's eye. '*No* souvenirs.'

For the rest of the day, until almost an hour before dusk, *Skullfish* traced out the careful pattern of search, as laid down in the air-sea rescue manual. From time to time a Dumbo aircraft came up on the air-sea rescue radio wavelength to report a possible survivor sighting. But they were all false. The rest of that crew had followed their B-29 down into the sea. Only the bomb-aimer, surmounting unimaginable obstacles of pain and fatigue and loneliness, had inflated the dinghy, climbed into it and set out. to be rescued, sometime, by somebody. The story of the bomber's last sortie had perished with him.

It was a funeral by proxy. The submarine's operational life carried on as usual. The watchkeepers were all closed up at their stations, and the usual number of lookouts were posted. But the Chief of the Boat, and three other men who had balloted for the privilege, made up a small funeral party, which was allowed on the casing to tip the body into the sea at the Captain's signal. Meanwhile, the rest of the ship's company, every officer and man who could, mustered below. Skipper was impressed by the turn-out. The control room was jammed full with men standing in ranks. More men stood in the passageways on either side. Every man, Skipper noticed, wore a cap, and the officers were in full khakis with medal ribbons.

One of the torpedomen he had met that morning — Skipper recognised the lurid dragon's tattoo on the man's forearm — nudged Skipper gently. 'The Captain, he reads good.' The funeral party had taken the body, which was sewn up in a sheet and wrapped in the Stars and Stripes, up the tower. In a few moments Sam Mellow began the funeral service, speaking to the men below over the usual bridge broadcast.

The Captain did, as the man had said, read well. Skipper listened to the words, which seemed absolutely right and familiar, although as he knew he rarely heard them read aloud. *'Man that is born of woman hath but a short time to live, and is full of misery. He cometh up and is cut down, like a flower. He fleeth as it were a shadow and never continueth in one stay...'*

In the quiet of the control room, the men below strained to hear the sounds from the casing above, but they could hear nothing. There was only the Captain's voice. *'We therefore commit his body to the deep, to be turned into corruption, looking for the resurrection of the body. When the sea shall give up her dead...'*

Skipper had an unexpected thought of the Japanese, the last man to be carried up that tower. The sea would give him up too. In spite of the bomb-aimer's injuries, and the fate of those aircrew shot down over Sumatra, it was hard at this moment to be gleeful over the death of one more Japanese. That man had died amongst strangers who were to him as barbarians from another world. To the physical disgrace of capture had been added a terrible spiritual isolation, with not a word of a common language, nor a reassuring face of his own people; food which must have seemed poisoned and water tainted. And he had spent his last hours trussed up like an animal in a submarine, which itself must have appeared to him an invention of infernal spirits. The drug must have come in the end as a merciful release.

When the ship's company replaced their caps and fell out, the gloom in the boat seemed to lift at once. The funeral had been an act of exorcism, a shrugging off of cares. *Let the dead bury its dead.* It was tough on that bomb-aimer, but that was the way the cookie crumbled. Skipper was once again surprised by his hosts' resilience.

They were always surprising him by making him more conscious of his own identity. The more American they were, the more English they made him feel. As submariners, they made him all the more conscious of being an aviator. He was always made aware of his accent, his background, his history. They thought that the war had only begun with the Japanese attack on Pearl Harbor. They believed that London was constantly shrouded in fogs generated by Charles Dickens. Their occupational diseases were constipation, from their diet and restricted exercise, and styes, from pressing their eyelids for long hours against the periscope eye-pieces. They came from a great democratic country, but they were much more punctilious in observing ranks and subtle divisions of status than any British ship's company. Their navy had a record unsurpassed for daring and initiative. But they were still careful to write everything down in full, with several copies, before and after.

The wardroom had none of the social life of a RN ship. The officers spent most of their time on watch or asleep in their staterooms. The wardroom was, as Red said, not much more than a 'watering hole'. Skipper adapted to their way of life very rapidly and the days began to pass indistinguishably from each other. The submarine dived twice a day, at dawn and dusk, to be safe, and also, as Red explained, to catch a trim in case she had to dive in an emergency. Stores were consumed, fuel was expended, the sea water's temperature and density were constantly changing by minute amounts, and the submarine's bodily weight had to be adjusted, by admitting or pumping out water, so that she could dive and achieve equilibrium and a state of neutral buoyancy within a few seconds of leaving the surface.

Diving, Skipper found, was a curious experience, almost a mirror image of the existence on the surface. Dived, there was silence where there had been sound, stillness where there had been movement. Positions were manned which were left empty on the surface. New duties were performed. Unsuspected lights glowed, familiar ones were extinguished. The whole ship's company wore a new air of ease and confidence. It was the surface, as Skipper came to realise, that made them nervous.

On the surface, Commander Mellow was the most nervous of them all. He never left the bridge, from the time the water drained off the tower to the moment the hooters sounded and the top hatch shut as the water rose up the casing sides again. 'I never leave this place on the surface,' he told Skipper. 'I eat up here, I wash up here, I sleep up here. And I know what you're thinking.'

'Yes, I was wondering about that, sir.'

'I go while we're dived every morning. Otherwise I use that pig's ear back aft. Or if I'm desperate, why, I just stick my ass out over the side. How are you getting on in that direction?'

'Oh, fine, sir. It isn't as difficult as I thought.' Throughout his time in the Navy, Skipper had heard vague rumours of the oddities and hazards of using the heads in submarines, of unpleasant happenings whilst blowing and flushing and running water.

'We got a sewage tank in this boat. Makes life a lot easier. In the old days, using the head was quite a task for a new boy. Liable to get your own back if you weren't careful.'

Commander Mellow seemed to welcome company on the bridge for limited periods, although his eyes never ceased to roam the horizon and his ears were always cocked for any sound, from inside or outside the boat. A lookout only had to stiffen, or shift his feet, or alter his stance the slightest amount, and Commander Mellow already had his binoculars up, looking out on that man's sector.

'D'you know why I always stay up here?'

'No, sir.'

'Well, it was something that happened to a great friend of mine. One of the best captains and the greatest fellow I ever served under. It was early on, spring of '42, I guess, and I was the Exec in an old S-boat off the Aleutians, or rather on our way up to the Aleutians. You ever been up to the Aleutians?'

'No, sir.'

'Don't. If anybody asks you, say you'll leave 'em to the Aleuts. Miserable weather, miserable scenery, miserable climate, miserable hell. You wouldn't wish it on a dog. It was early morning on a foul day, just getting light, and a Jap fighter-bomber came out of the fog and mist and gunned the bridge. Killed the Officer of the Watch and one of the lookouts, badly shot up another lookout's leg and put him in hospital for months, ruined the forrard periscope, and made one hell of a mess of the bridge up there. It was nothing but splinters and blood up there. Didn't have submarine radar in those days.'

Commander Mellow stopped, to watch and to hear Frank Rinaldo order a new course on the zigzag pattern.

'The Captain was below at the time, sleeping in his bunk. It was not his fault, Skipper. He hadn't had no more than two hours' sleep in the last forty-eight. He was bushed. Maybe he did sleep a little soundly. But nothing, you understand, nothing to worry about. But he did worry. It sort of preyed on his mind. He went all moody, as people sometimes do in boats. He hadn't been up there when his ship was attacked. He'd been down below, fast asleep, when his guys were getting gunned down on top. When we got back to Pearl nobody blamed him. But he took his own life just the same. He started his car, shut the garage door, put a hose from the exhaust through the window and just went to sleep. So, with that lesson in front of me, I got it. One: I get as much sleep as I can, even if it's only cat-napping up here. It *is* only cat-napping, but it keeps me going. Two: I never leave the bridge when we're on the surface.'

There was a strict protocol about access to *Skullfish*'s bridge. Normally, Commander Mellow allowed nobody up there except the lookouts, and officers on duty. But as the submarine came nearer to Guam and further from the operational area, two or three sailors at a time were permitted to sun themselves and take the air in the space by the after Bofors gun at the back of the bridge. Skipper, however, was allowed to come up whenever he asked. He recognised his own privileged position, and compared himself to the visiting knight on his quest, in the old troubadour's tales, to whom as a temporary guest all favours were granted and all things explained. As their conversations lengthened and their acquaintance deepened, Commander Mellow began to unbend to Skipper in a way he would never have dreamed of doing to anybody else in the submarine, or even to anyone else in his own Navy. Like the stranger in the railway compartment whom one would never meet again, Skipper had a special status.

Skipper went up to the bridge for the last time on the night before they were due to arrive at Guam. It was a glorious night, with brilliant stars, a warm balmy wind from the east, and a last-quarter moon low on the horizon. Skipper fancied he could actually smell the earth and spices of the islands just below the horizon. The bridge seemed to be rushing through the space between sea and sky. On either side, as the submarine rolled gently, Skipper could hear the sound of water tearing across the saddle tanks. It was homeward-bound night, with an atmosphere of tremendous anticipation on board. On such a night, the war seemed easily won. On such a night, one might hear at any moment the old seaman's cry of 'Land ho!'

Commander Mellow, however, was in sombre mood. 'You know I missed a Jap cruiser ten days ago?'

'I heard, sir. Frankly, I'm amazed anybody can hit anything looking through a periscope.' Skipper had tried it himself. At first he had been able to distinguish nothing at all. His eyes had simply refused to make sense of what they could see. Even when the wash of blue sky and opaque sea had orientated themselves in his vision, he still marvelled that anybody could unravel, from this strange fish-eyed view, enough data to carry out an attack.

'It's a knack. It comes to you. And I suppose you were told not to mention that cruiser to me, if you valued your life?'

'Yes, I was, sir.'

'Very wise. No, what got me mad was my own feelings. I was mad at myself for *not* getting mad. Two years ago I would have been as sore as hell, but for a different reason. Two years ago I wouldn't have missed though — I been at sea now nearly four years, except for leave and a commanding officer's course, and I reckon I'm getting numb. I was mad because I disappointed my team. You saw them all when that B-29 bomb-aimer was brought on board. Anybody'd think we lost the whole war. That's the problem about submarine people — they get depressed easy. They get up high, and they come down low again just as quick. It's all part of our life, I guess. After this trip, you know, I can go ashore. I been offered an assignment to duty training submariners back in the States. You think I should take it? What should I do?'

'Go back to the States, sir.'

'Go back to the reservation and let the younger braves come out and wear the war-paint?'

'If the powers that be think you're more use to the side training others, then that's what you should do. It shouldn't be a personal decision at all, in fact.'

'*Say.*' From the change in the voice, and the silhouette of his face against the sky, Skipper knew that Commander Mellow had turned to look directly at him. 'Say, that's a career Navy man's answer you just gave me. You're a reservist. You going to stay on? From what I know of you, I think you'd make it as a career man. You going to stay, if they ask you?'

'That I just don't know, sir.'

'They talked to you about it already?'

'Sort of.'

'Well I should *sort of* bear it in mind, Skipper,' Sam Mellow paused to listen to a routine report on the broadcast from the control room, which Red, who was on watch, acknowledged. Skipper was not sure whether Red had been listening to them or not. 'You ready to get back into the saddle again? You're not bothered by what happened back out there?'

'Hope not, sir. Time will tell. I reckon I was very lucky.'

'You sure were. You had a lot of guys gone?'

'Oh, yes, it's been pretty bad over the years. You see, we've been at it damned nearly six years. You don't notice it at first. I haven't been in touch with many of the blokes in my training class, the ones who started off with me, for some time now, but I wouldn't be at all surprised to find there are very few of us left now. I sometimes see their names in the lists, in the signals. At one time I used to see them quite a lot, a familiar name almost every time I looked. That hasn't happened recently. That may well be because most of them have gone already. You just get out of touch, and as the years go by I get less concerned by it all. It's like a kind of numbness.'

'Skipper, I know just what you mean. That's what I was saying. And it's not the guys you'd think who get it, either, is it?'

'It's not any particular guys who get it. That's the strange thing about it. It doesn't make any sense at all. You see it happen to Squadron COs, experienced aviators, and you see it happen to new boys. It happens to the get-up-and-go types who're all for it, and it happens to those you suspect are hanging back a bit. They get killed their first day, they get killed their last day, they get killed *after* their last day, on their way home. Brilliant, so-so, it doesn't make any difference. You see it happen to a really brave, kick-the-tyre, light-the-fire and smash-off type, so you put your money on a canny percentage player. And then it happens to him. We analyse every loss, we go over it with a fine toothcomb to see if we can learn from it, and we get reports from other squadrons and we go over them too. Of course, there are lessons you can learn, things you can do to put it right, whatever went wrong, but in the end it doesn't add up to anything logical, no overall pattern to it in the end. As we say, it's just like a bloody great game. Certainly a bloody game. It's like the cards falling, the dice rolling by and bouncing, the pieces on the board getting knocked off, any clichéd words you like to think of.'

'When you gotta go, you gotta go.'

'That's right. It shakes you. Because we all think we're immortal. We have to, or I don't think we could go on. We're all invulnerable. You have to convince yourself by taking thought you increase your chances of survival. But you can't. In the end, you have to admit to yourself that it is nothing to do with you at all. Being a better pilot, being a better *bloke*, has nothing to do with it. And that's really the most terrible feeling in the world. I think that's the beginning of what we call the twitch. Knowing that you're not the master of your own fate and feeling that fate is about to catch you up.'

'Skipper, I know just what you mean. Only I guess I never ever heard it put quite so well.' Sam Mellow stretched, picked up a waterproof jacket and huddled it round his shoulders. 'It's getting chilly. I should turn in now. We should raise Guam soon after dawn tomorrow. I'll pass the word for somebody to call you.'

'Thank you. Goodnight, sir.'

'Goodnight, Skipper. And look, if I don't get a chance to say it tomorrow, I really enjoyed having you aboard. Next time we hear of a Limey down in the water, the *Skullfish*'ll volunteer to pick him up!'

'Can't say fairer than that, sir.'

The islands showed up on the radar screens a few minutes before dawn. Skipper was already awake and heard the reports coming over the broadcast speaker in the wardroom as he shaved. He was almost dressed when there was a knock at the stateroom door and a voice said, 'Commander, sir, Cap'n says Guam's coming up.'

'OK, I got it.' Skipper wondered at his own ready use of American speech. He was sure he now spoke with a Yankee twang. As he knotted the khaki tie somebody had once lent him, he felt a submariner of several years' standing. He had been on board *Skullfish* for so long his previous existence now seemed unutterably remote.

On the bridge, Skipper noticed that Sam Mellow was also miraculously washed and shaved and wearing a clean and pressed uniform, his best cap and sunglasses, with a short duffel watch-coat over his shoulders. It seemed to Skipper nothing short of marvellous that Sam Mellow managed to keep himself so well turned out. He had always believed that submariners were, as the saying went, scruffy little men in scruffy little boats. But here was Sam Mellow, looking as though he were about to lunch with Admiral Chester Nimitz.

'Morning, Skipper. Last lap.'

'Morning, sir, last lap indeed.' Skipper saw that all four lookouts were still closed up and still searching as carefully as ever.

'OK, I know it's the last lap.' Sam Mellow seemed to have sensed Skipper's surprise. 'But we don't want to get thumped now. That would be a dumb thing to do. That's the time when somebody is likely to jump you, just when you thought you were home.'

Guam had been on the radar screens for some time before it actually appeared as a faint black irregularity on the horizon, difficult to pick out against the red glare of the sun rising in the east. The sun began to climb into layers of coral pink cloud, up into a sky of pale purple streaked with orange.

'Red sky in the morning. Shepherd's warning.'

'It could be. We got the typhoon season coming up.'

There were more clouds on the horizon to the north-east shrouding the peak of the next island in the archipelago, Rota. The Marianas were a line of volcanic islands, spread out for 400 miles roughly north-south in a great curving arc, as though they had been scattered out at random against the prevailing easterly wind. Guam, in silhouette, was now looking like a distant grey camel kneeling on the horizon. To take that island from the Japanese had cost the Marines and the US infantry some 7,000 dead, missing or wounded, with an unknown number of casualties amongst the Chamorro native population. Even those casualties had been less than on the neighbouring islands of Saipan and Tinian. As for the Japanese, Skipper had heard that 12,000 dead bodies had been counted on Guam alone. Over a thousand Japanese had surrendered and more of them, lone men or small parties, were being flushed out of hiding or surrendering every week.

As the island came nearer, and began to take on colour and contours, Skipper noticed that the buildings he could see through binoculars, built here and there in the deep green trees, were all new. Clearly, almost every existing building had been pounded to rubble during the fighting and everything had had to be rebuilt from the foundations.

Over to starboard, as they neared the entrance, great cliffs, between a hundred and two hundred feet high, rose up to the peninsula of Orote. There was an airstrip there because, as

Skipper watched, a single Hellcat appeared, folding its undercarriage as it glided out over the cliff edge.

Skipper had already forgotten the Hellcat when it suddenly roared overhead only about fifty feet up, its wings rocking in salute.

'Just checking up on us, I guess.'

To port the shoreline was much lower, with a breakwater and an anchorage for ammunition ships. The main harbour of Apra, which they were now approaching, was crammed with shipping and there were many more ships, visible over the line of the breakwater, anchored in Agana Bay to the north. There was a small, grey-painted vessel, looking like a tug or a salvage vessel but wearing the Stars and Stripes, waiting near the end of the breakwater to meet the submarine.

Sam Mellow insisted on correct protocol to the end. 'I'm afraid I'm going to have to ask you to go below while we get in, Skipper. I'm very sorry, but we gotta do it by the book now we're back in Guam. This is ComSubPac country hereabouts. Like Injun country, only worse. The book says no spectators on deck, entering or leaving. ComSubPac will have his great big goo-goo eyes on us right now. An' CincPac himself is right up there, in his fort there up on the left, in the hills there. He's got a sharp eye for submarines, as an old submariner himself. Sorry about that.'

Down below, the control room had an atmosphere of suppressed glee. The Chief of the Boat had silenced, with a great roar of reprimand, any audible signs of jubilation, so the sailors had to content themselves by punching their fists into the palms, opening and shutting their mouths in silent cheers, and shaking their clasped hands over their heads in a boxer's gesture of triumph, whenever bumps and clangs from above showed that the submarine was coming alongside.

When Skipper next reached the casing, through the unaccustomed access of the open forward torpedo hatch, he hardly recognised the submarine. The sunlight seemed so much brighter than at sea, splintering off the water in the harbour with an intensity which dazzled the eyes. The guns were at last hidden in covers. The radar aerials were stationary and had been lowered. *Skullfish* was at rest and, temporarily, at peace. But her casing seemed to be swarming with men, many of them strangers from the two submarines alongside her and the massive depot ship inboard of them all. The deck was strewn with bags of mail, boxes and containers of stores, and the gear of men going ashore, and criss-crossed with ropes and wires, and hoses of various sizes.

Sam Mellow, carrying a leather briefcase and wearing an unusually subdued expression, was waiting by the gangplank. 'I gotta go ashore now and report to all the top brass. Tell 'em how the cookie crumbled and how come we missed, when we missed. But Red here will take care of you. We fixed a jeep to take you up to Orote field and there'll be a flight sometime today, so you should be OK. In the meantime, now…' Sam Mellow held out his hand. 'Skipper, it's been a real pleasure having you aboard. Say, keep in touch, will you? Care of ComSubPac will always find me.'

They watched the Captain threading his way through men and stores on the casings of the adjacent submarines and climbing up the gangway ladder to the depot ship's upper deck. At the top he waved, and Skipper waved back.

Geronimo had come on deck with a small canvas bag marked USN, which Skipper recognised as the kind of Navy pattern handy hold-all in which Sparky the Pharmacist's Mate carried all his instruments, drugs and bandages.

'I put a towel in here and your shaving things and other things, sir. You'll need them on your trip.'

Skipper was surprised by the strength of his own gratitude. This was *luggage*, which gave a stateless, paper-less person like himself an identity. *Real* people always had luggage on their journeys. It proved he had really started out from somewhere, from people who knew who he was. He was surprised, too, by the size of his send-off committee. Most of the officers were there, and many of the sailors, lining up on the casing to shake hands. They nodded and smiled and clapped Skipper on the shoulder. 'Nice to know you,' they said, and 'Up the Limeys'. 'Sir, sir, Commander *sir*!' The Chief of the Boat's face registered consternation. 'Sir, I'm *really* sorry we rebelled that way back in '76!'

In the roar of laughter, Red led the way ashore. Skipper had an impression of rows of faces on the depot ship, more hoses crossing the deck, a large torpedo swinging on the end of a crane jib, and a ladder the other side leading down to the jetty, where a jeep was waiting.

Like the others, Red shook hands warmly. 'Like the Captain said, it's been a real pleasure. I guess we all learned a lot. If any of our guys ever hears a word against the Limeys, why, then — how do you say it? — we'll knock their blocks off!' Red thumped on the bonnet of the jeep and pointed his thumb at the driver. 'You take good care of this Limey, you hear me, boy?'

The driver beamed. 'Yes, sir. No sweat, sir.'

Skipper climbed up beside the driver, the jeep jerked violently and began to accelerate along the jetty. At the end it slowed and turned. Skipper looked back. Red was still standing at the salute and grinning.

CHAPTER ELEVEN

'Sir, you going back to Eng-a-land?' The driver shouted the word, in three separate syllables, over the roar of the engine. The jeep meanwhile turned violently to the left and Skipper had to hang on tightly, while still retaining his small bag from *Skullfish*.

'No such luck,' Skipper yelled back. He realised, for the first time, that in fact he had no idea of his destination. *Skullfish* had taken charge of his destiny and brought him to Guam. Now he was on his own again, with his own decisions to make. Leyte was probably the best solution, or failing that the larger fleet base at Manus, down in the Admiralty Islands, near the Equator. The ships, sooner or later, would pass through there.

The driver seemed to sense his indecision. 'Sir, you'd better get it together for those guys at Orote. They'll sure want to know.'

'Yes, they will.'

The jeep turned right, into what seemed to be the main street of the town, beside the dock area. The road surface was very good, made of crushed rock or possibly coral, which gave off thick clouds of fine dust. The whole of Guam seemed to be a scene of furious activity, imposed upon a smashed desolation. The island had been pounded into rubble first, and was now being built up again. They passed bulldozers, and lorries piled with rock, wide spaces stacked with wood spars, coils of wire, fencing posts and drums of assorted heights. Beside a large two-storeyed hut, a parade ground had been levelled, and a squad of men in overalls were marching up and down, calling out some form of monotonous chant as they marched.

The jeep crossed a bridge over a stream and Skipper caught sight of a notice, on a post. THIS BRIDGE WAS MADE BY THE 165TH MARINE CONSTRUCTION … Skipper could read no more as they rocketed past it. Americans seemed to need identification. Every jeep had its owner's name stencilled on the bonnet, every helmet wore its wearer's identity; even the numerous police had MP painted on their huge white steel helmets. Across the entrance to another large building, set back from the roar, was a gateway very similar to a Japanese shinto arch, with a great slogan blazoned above it: THROUGH THESE PORTALS, Skipper read, PASS THE FINEST GODDAMN FIGHTING TROOPS IN THE WORLD.

The jeep climbed a short hill, passed through a sentry post, with a barrier raised, and rolled out on to a smooth cemented runway. It stopped in front of yet another long row of huts. Skipper got out.

For the first time since he had come ashore, he felt again a cool breeze blowing off the sea. Dispersal bays for aircraft and pathways for taxiing, each as broad as Pall Mall, had been bulldozed through the scrub and low trees at the side of the main runway. Skipper could see several aircraft, half-hidden in the dark trees. Though the airfield, Skipper knew, ended in cliffs, there was still the sensation of the wide sea, stretching out infinitely beyond the limit of his sight but undoubtedly there.

'You need me any more, sir?'

Skipper hesitated. He should be getting a flight some time soon, and should not need a jeep any longer. But something made him pause.

'Can you hang on, whilst I get fixed up?'

'Sure. No sweat, sir.' The driver leaned back in his seat, tipped his hat over his eyes and folded his arms, his body a wonderfully loose-limbed design of relaxed ease.

Skipper had no papers, no authorisation or routing order. Nobody knew anything about him. His name was on no list, his face on no photograph. He had no cap, no badges of rank, no unit insignia, nothing except his accent even to indicate his nationality. His Limey accent, as Skipper soon discovered, had a certain novelty value but carried no priority whatsoever for aircraft seats. Inside the nearest long hut at Orote the first of several American officers that day, in a sweat-stained khaki shirt, shook Skipper by the hand, remarked on his accent, greeted him warmly, understood his predicament, assured him there would be no problem, picked up a telephone, spoke for a few moments and then gave Skipper wholly misleading information. In a minute or two, Skipper was outside the hut and driving through Guam again, to another airfield at Agana. An hour later he was again in the jeep driving to a third airfield, called the Depot Field, the most northerly in the island. There, somebody pointed out a Dakota, its propellers already spinning.

'That's one for Manus. If you get going, you can catch it.'

Skipper ran across the crushed coral to the open doorway. An aircrewman helped him. Something made Skipper ask the man, 'This is OK for Manus, isn't it?' He felt the absurdity of it. This was like checking trains at home.

The man shook his head. 'Eniwetok, through to Kwajalein and Pearl.'

The door was just shutting when Skipper launched himself through it and landed, stumbling on his knees, on the runway. The aircraft was turning, and the fierce wind from its propellers blew a stinging dust in Skipper's eyes. The aircraft had gone by the time he could open his eyes again.

'Hey, what the hell were you doing out there when that plane was taking off?' Two MPs with white helmets were sitting in a jeep. 'You got an ID card?'

It was Skipper's driver who once again saved him. 'It's OK, sergeant, this officer came ashore from the *Skullfish* this morning. He's a Limey, sergeant. Aircrew, shot down and picked up by our submarines.'

The policemen looked at Skipper as though at some fabulous sea monster.

'OK. So where are you going now?'

'Back to Orote Field, I guess.'

'Get going, then.'

This time, the officer at the desk had the grace to look abashed when Skipper appeared.

'I'm sorry, Commander. You best just wait now. We'll let you know.'

Skipper's driver nodded and grinned. 'OK, Commander, you don't have to say it. I'll wait. I'll be outside, or over at the M/T pool.'

The impetus given to Skipper's journey by *Skullfish*'s arrangements had now entirely ebbed away. He was now just one more anonymous figure in transit. It was Skipper's first experience for some time of life outside the immediate operational war zone. In his squadron, and in *Skullfish*, an operational urgency had governed everything they did. But here, a thousand ages in their sight were like an evening gone. This was a place for the displaced. There was a clock on the hut wall but the only significant division of time was a nod or call from the man at the nearest desk. The men there were a random collection, like people in a railway waiting room, but gathered together by the extra stress and chances of war. Four men, sitting stripped to the waist in the heat, were playing poker at the end of one of the tables. Another man in air force uniform was writing what was clearly some form of report. There were American newspapers and magazines piled on one bench. Military band music was coming from a speaker on a pillar in the centre of the hut. The floor was boards, laid on the same ubiquitous crushed rock. Further away, at the other end of the hut, behind a low partition, were tiers of wooden bunks. That space was dark, and some of the bunks were ominously occupied, suggesting a long-term wait for the very unfortunate. Between Skipper and the partition were kitbags and suitcases in heaps; six or seven steel helmets strung together by a cord through their chinstraps; what looked like a portable radio set in its canvas webbing; and other miscellaneous luggage, lying about like flotsam and jetsam, like the people, in fact, temporarily washed up high and dry in the transit hut.

'I should get yourself some chow now, Commander. There won't be anything for some time.'

They had lunch at a separate table by the door, of spam, dehydrated mashed potatoes, coffee and a great tin plate each of assorted ice creams. It was served by a black messman, who asked for a dollar as payment. When Skipper said he had no money, the man brought a pad of chits. Skipper signed the top one *Admiral Sir Andrew Cunningham, First Sea Lord*. The man looked at it and took it away.

The officer at the desk put down his telephone receiver. 'Hey, Commander! If you can get yourself over to Agana, there's a C-47 for Manus, getting out of here in forty minutes.'

'I don't believe it.' Nevertheless, Skipper ran outside, where his driver was already climbing into his seat. This time, miraculously, the Dakota was there, propellers turning. This time, the man nodded: 'Manus and Pelelieu.'

This time, there was a seat of canvas fitted in behind some stores. Around him Skipper could see the airframe, arcs of curved metal, festoons of wire and handles, and in front of him stencilled rows of figures in white paint, upon a stacked pile of wooden boxes. He fancied there was another passenger on the other side, but he could not see him and, once they had reached the end of the runway and the pilot opened his throttles, could not have heard him either. The cabin, unheated and unpressurised, grew steadily colder as they gained height. The seat began to feel as hard as granite. By some quirk of the aircraft's design, a blast of hot air blew steadily over Skipper's ankles. He had no space to move, nowhere to rest his feet out of the draught; he had to sit motionless but in torment, while the lower half of his body grew numb except for his ankles, which he could feel swelling out like balloons.

After hours of agony, the Dakota landed and when the door opened Skipper was surprised to see that it was still bright daylight. Five o'clock, tea time. Skipper had to be helped out of his cramped seat and he landed on the ground with a jar that sent shooting pains up his numbed legs.

'Where's this?'

'Pelelieu. In the Palaus.'

Skipper had vaguely heard of it as an island the United States Marines had assaulted and captured, with heavy casualties, some months before. There were still signs of some of that fighting on a low ridge to the north of the airstrip, where there was a tangle of smashed palm trunks, the foundations of buildings now razed to rubble and the traces of a line of entrenchments. The island was tiny, and the airstrip, running on an east-west axis, stretched almost from beach to beach. At the western end of the runway, there was a flagpole flying the Stars and Stripes set in a carefully gardened space, a wide lawn, like a neat green quarterdeck. The lawn was bordered with rows of small white crosses. It was a graveyard, of the Marines who had died taking the island. Skipper was surprised, and touched, and reassured to see it. He was grateful for the reminder that there was a war on, that there was a sharp end to existence beyond these great flabby ganglia of logistics.

A cloud of graceful white seabirds flew in on the brisk wind which was picking up from the east, but otherwise Peleliu had little to recommend it. Skipper hobbled on numbed feet across the runway, which was much rougher and more pock-marked than at Guam, to huts which were smaller and smellier. There was a stink of latrines, and the food was only just edible: Spam, curled at the edges, lukewarm beans, gritty coffee and almost melted ice cream.

The pilot came back from the traffic control hut, swinging his leather helmet by its strap. 'We stay here tonight.'

The crew got out small two-man tents and set them up under the aircraft's starboard wing. They had sleeping bags and mosquito nets, and the appearance of men well used to camping out. At sunset, a bugler sounded a call and a Marine lowered the flag. Skipper stood to attention at the salute, bareheaded. Once again, he was glad of the reassurance this unexpected ceremony gave him.

Lying, waiting for sleep, Skipper was perplexed by the absence of mosquitoes. The Americans had either wiped them out, or they had simply never arrived. Unless man brought them in his clothing or equipment, all insects on these remote oceanic islands would have to be windborne. Skipper watched the moon rise. The seabirds took off with a multitude of cries. From the western end, Skipper could hear the surf.

In the hurly-burly of ship and squadron life, Skipper naturally had little time for introspection. But now, understandably, the further and longer he was removed from what he still thought of as his everyday life, the greater his distance from normality, the better his ability to view himself. He wondered why he was in such haste to return to his ship, in the face of such difficulties. Why hurry back so to the battle? Nobody he had met since he landed from *Skullfish* had given that aspect a moment's thought. He was a skilled and experienced pilot, and a leader of other pilots, at a time when pilots were more precious than rubies, and one would have thought no effort would have been spared, no string left unpulled, to return him to his proper duty as soon as possible. On the contrary: he had met obstacles rather than encouragement. Left to himself, he could have stayed at Guam for weeks. He could have let matters drift, and ceased to press for a quicker passage back into danger. His anxiety to return had now brought him here to this sleeping bag, spending the night under the wing of a strange aircraft, next to strangers who had never enquired into his identity, on a strange island whose name he had scarcely heard of until that evening. As for himself, nobody within a thousand miles even knew his name. And yet this succession of seemingly unconnected sights, sounds and experiences, each with its own impact, had an almost literary relish. It was like Peregrine Pickle, peregrinating from one pickle to another. Roderick, literally, at random. *In his novels of the picaresque, Smollett transmutes most convincingly into art the random sequence of circumstance which makes up normal human existence. Discuss.*

They were up in the morning, when it was barely light, and washed in a lean-to space behind the fuelling dump. There was a GI in overalls there, getting up water with a hand-pump and filter. The man saw Skipper looking at the Japanese characters on the pump barrel.

'It's called an Ishii water filter. One of the only things we got from the Japs that works.'

The pilot had come back from the control tower, which stood on legs, rather like an important building in a native village. He had his leather cap on.

'OK, citizens, onwards to victory.'

This time, some of the stores had been removed and Skipper had a little more room. He also had a small box, which he put on the deck to lift his ankles out of the furnace draught. Somebody had given him a piece of thick sacking to place on his seat. He was almost comfortable. Again, he could see nothing of their passage, and had to guess from the notes of the engines, the vibrations and small shudders of the airframe against the small of his back. The flight seemed to last about as long as the previous one, before they landed again.

When the door was opened, the heat was so vicious it seemed to take Skipper by the throat. Sweat seemed to spring out at once from every pore on his body. He could feel sweat dripping down to his chin and flooding the palms of his hands, as he sat there without moving. The effort of climbing out on to the runway seemed to soak his clothes through and through, so that his body ran with perspiration, just as he stood. There was a foul stench of rank vegetation. The jungle came right to the perimeter of the airstrip and Skipper at once thought of the edges of a raw wound, forcibly but only temporarily pushed backwards. Given time, that jungle would flow out again and reoccupy it all. There were the same smashed palm trunks, as at the last airstrip, with the piled wings of shattered aircraft and the blackened remains of wrecked vehicles. Combat waste again, like that nice little island where they had tried to have a peaceful banyan.

'Wewak. New Guinea.'

Another stinking latrine smell, more spam and coffee and ice cream, and, one variation, small hard rolls of white bread. A short sharp rainstorm drummed on the corrugated roofs of the transit hut. Somebody gave Skipper another chit to sign. He wrote *Admiral Sir Thomas Handley VC, DSO, BBC* on it and gave it back. Once again, the man looked at it expressionlessly and took it away.

The jungle was so close that Skipper, sitting at the table, could very nearly stretch out his hand and touch the nearest growth. It seemed to have entrances in it, which made one shudder. Once in there, one would never come out. Skipper thought of the men who had to fight in that. He wondered how they kept sane. It would take ten minutes to hack yourself forward ten feet. Skipper suddenly had the terrifying thought that he could stay at Wewak if he wanted. If he vanished into that jungle, nobody would go after him or lift a finger to stop him. The Dakota would take off and he would simply have disappeared. The crew would assume that something had caused him to change his mind. And yet he knew that that would not be quite the end. The Admiralty mills sometimes ground slow, but they always ground small. In 1947 or 1948, or sometime when the war had ended, letters would be written, somebody would check up, to establish as far as possible what had happened to him.

Further along the airstrip was a compound for Japanese prisoners. Some of them, Skipper was told, had only just been brought in. Their hut was surrounded by a stout palisade of thick palm trunks. An armed Marine sentry sat in a jeep, parked facing the compound. He had a revolver at his hip and a rifle laid across the front ledge, behind the windscreen. He sat forward, his forearms resting on the steering wheel, his gaze fixed seemingly unblinkingly on the captives inside.

Skipper could only see two of them, in sandals, wearing only a triangular loin-cloth. They were standing outside, in the light rain. Skipper looked at them, and they looked back impassively. It was not the same as looking at animals in a zoo. These were men, and they were thinking about him. They were not menacing or ingratiating. They were just Japanese, the same height and appearance as he had always imagined them. They were actually the first Japanese he had ever seen, if he discounted the black shapes glimpsed in fighter cockpits as they flashed by. Skipper felt he should have experienced something, some reaction of dislike or repulsion, or even hatred. But when his mild curiosity had been satisfied on what they looked like, he felt nothing at all.

'OK, citizens, onwards to victory.'

On this last lap of his flight, Skipper actually had a cushion which the engineer gave him, and a blanket to put round his shoulders against the cold of altitude. The warm air which had hitherto played exclusively on Skipper's ankles was now directed to the cabin space at large. Best of all, enough stores had been removed to allow Skipper a view out of the nearest window. The flight from Wewak to Manus, the shortest leg of his journey, was only some two hours old when Skipper felt the Dakota banking steeply, and he saw far down below a line of white beach, green jungle and a native village, with wooden jetties and fishing vessels drawn up on the sand. Then there was a series of bumps, as though the aircraft were riding down a staircase of air, and a view of a great lagoon, with ships large and small. As they passed overhead, Skipper could see the colours of the water going from black to deep blue and to shining silver, as the angle of the sunlight striking upon it changed.

When the door opened, Skipper was surprised to see an American Red Cross girl, in a jeep, waiting to meet them. She had, more amazingly still, a plate of spam and a small can of some drink, which she offered to Skipper. Skipper refused the spam but accepted the drink — which was fruit syrup, thick and sugary — and a lift in the jeep. This, he felt, was almost civilised.

The jeep drove amongst more avenues, carved out of the jungle; there were wide bays on either side, one or two of them with aircraft parked. They crossed a space of blinding sunlight and drew up at another, but much larger, row of huts. Clearly, the longer the Americans occupied a place the more they did to it. In a year, or maybe even only a few months, there might be skyscrapers here, and drug stores with soda fountains. It was not until he had left the jeep and was standing once more in front of an American in a sweat-stained shirt, seated behind several telephones, that Skipper remembered he had not said goodbye or thanked the Dakota crew. For that matter, he had not even thanked his helpful jeep driver in Guam.

'Nice to have you, Commander.'

'Nice to be here, I can assure you. I've had quite a trip round the bazaars.'

At the sound of Skipper's voice, an officer in white shorts and shirt who was just going out stopped, turned and came back. He looked at Skipper wonderingly, as though not quite able to believe his own ears.

'Are you *British*?'

He had a commander's cap under his arm, with gold lace on the peak, and a commander's gold stripes on his shoulders. With a small shock, Skipper realised that he was once more looking, as though after an interval of several years, at an officer in RN uniform.

'Yes. Lieutenant Commander RNVR, sir. Aircrew. I'm in transit after being shot down. I've had quite a journey.'

The Commander seemed quite perturbed at this intelligence. 'But nobody told me you were coming here. I am Commander Leintwardine, British Base Press and Broadcasting Liaison Officer.' The man seemed to be muttering to himself, and Skipper could only just hear him. 'Why did you come here?'

'I don't know really, sir.' In his relief at once more being able to speak to one of his own countrymen, Skipper was still baffled by the strange commander's reaction to his arrival. 'It seemed a good idea to get out of Guam...'

'*Guam? Guam!* You've been to *Guam*?'

'Yes...'

'But why didn't the British Liaison Officer in Guam let us know you were coming?'

'I'm afraid I've never heard of the British Liaison Officer in Guam, sir.' Now that Skipper came to think of it, he knew there would have been such a personage, and it might well have smoothed his passage to have got in touch with him. With some official representation and backing, his journey might have been made much easier. On the other hand, if such an officer did exist he must have known of Skipper's presence in *Skullfish*, but had made no attempt to meet him when he arrived, or to enquire after his whereabouts. 'And I'm afraid he has never heard of me either.'

'Never heard of ... well, that really is most irregular. It's *your* duty to get in touch with him. This is going to mean more forms to fill in. *Endless* forms. More bumph. Where will it all end?'

'I'm very sorry to give so much trouble, sir,' said Skipper, without meaning it.

Commander Leintwardine turned a furious glare on him. 'Oh, *you* can't help it. You lot never can. Where's your gear, your baggage? Your tin trunk, with your number one uniform, your sword and all that?'

Skipper jerked back his head as though suddenly grasped by the throat. Tin trunk? Number one uniform? *Sword?*

'I'm afraid I only have this.' He held up Sparky's little bag, now creased and stained with the mud and sweat of Pelelieu and Wewak. 'And my only gear is what I've got on.'

Commander Leintwardine had bright blue eyes, a dark red beard streaked with grey, and was bald except for a fringe of red hair, like an enlarged tonsure, around the rim of his head. The beard and the baldness gave him a curious, inverted appearance, as though his face had been presented upside down. His conversation, too, had a disconcertingly surrealist note in it.

'How *very* odd, to travel without baggage.'

'But as I said, sir, I have no baggage. I was shot down. In an aircraft. A Corsair.'

Commander Leintwardine gave a blank stare. Clearly, the words had no lexical meaning for him.

Skipper tried again. 'I was shot down, sir. Into the sea. In just what I stood up in. Or rather, just what I floated about in.' Skipper thought that must have been as sensational an introduction as anybody had ever given himself.

At last, Commander Leintwardine seemed to realise that some reaction was expected of him, if only for courtesy's sake, and he bellowed with forced laughter. 'Well, never mind. You couldn't help it. RNVR, did you say? You'd better come with me, now you're here.'

Commander Leintwardine led the way outside to his jeep, which, Skipper noticed, was painted dark navy blue and gleamed, as though lovingly polished every day. A crisp, clean White Ensign flew from the bonnet, along the side of which was painted the legend COMMANDER JOHN STEPNEY LEINTWARDINE, ROYAL NAVY, ROYAL NAVY BASE MISCELLANEOUS WEAPONS DEVELOPMENT OFFICER, MANUS.

'It's very lucky I was here. I don't normally come here. But I just happened to be here trying to ward off a party of press correspondents. Trying to frighten them off from coming here. Get in.'

Trying to frighten off a party of press correspondents seemed an odd occupation for the British Base Press and Broadcasting Officer, but Skipper made no comment and climbed into the jeep.

'But it seems they're coming after all. Typical Yank inefficiency. Can't trust them to do anything. Like children, really.' This was not Skipper's experience of Americans at all, but again he said nothing. 'Come on, come on, hop in the boat. We'll get you your own jeep tomorrow.'

'Well, I hope I shan't be staying long enough to make that worthwhile?'

Commander Leintwardine grunted as the jeep moved off in a series of alarming jumps, as though the clutch were not properly engaged. In spite of his flamboyant physical appearance and his important-looking jeep, Commander Leintwardine drove with the utmost care. His only gesture of insouciance was his gear-changing, which he carried out by seizing the gear-lever knob, waving it about at random until it found a home where it would go in and then forcibly pushing it, against a howling and grinding of gear-teeth. Sometimes he remembered to jab his foot at the clutch pedal. Skipper was reminded of the vicar at home in Daughton.

Traffic drove on the right in the American fashion, all except Commander Leintwardine, who drove on the left in the British fashion. After a quarter of a mile, Skipper saw a huge grey lorry approaching them, with a star painted on its bonnet. When the lorry was close enough for Skipper to see the whites of the driver's eyes, the man seemed to realise that Commander Leintwardine was determined, wrenched his wheel aside and drove off the road, in a storm of indignant shouts and furious horn-hooting. Commander Leintwardine drove on, to a bend where there was a large advisory sign, HORN CURVE, indicating that oncoming traffic should sound their horns. Commander Leintwardine, needless to say, did not.

The roads, as on Guam, were very good, metalled with the same crushed rock and coral and laid out with the same lavish efficiency. On every side Skipper could see evidence of the Seabees' restless industry. Where there was a slope it was gouged flat, and where there was a hollow it was filled in. To the right, Skipper saw a sign to a hospital and on the other side a huge open-air cinema, with the screen hung between four large palm trees. The place was set with wooden benches and the bare ground had been trodden flat by thousands of feet. Skipper was reminded of the elephants' dancing ground in the Kipling story, or the campfire site for one of the pre-war Boy Scout jamborees.

The road passed along the top of a bluff and Skipper looked down at a small inlet, an arm of the sea, where the water was lying like green glass. To his amazement, Skipper saw a hut down there, painted garishly in blue and yellow stripes. There were tables outside it, each with its striped umbrella, and there were figures actually sunbathing on the rocks beside the water. A sign said OFFICERS' CLUB.

'This is quite a big island, isn't it? I had no idea Manus was so big.'

'This isn't Manus.' Commander Leintwardine deftly changed down a gear, although the jeep was increasing speed along a flat stretch of road. When he reached a slight hill at the end, he changed up a gear. 'This is Los Negros, next door to Manus. We've got about an hour's drive to go yet before we get to civilisation.'

They crossed from one island to the other, on a causeway built over floating pontoons. Again, Skipper marvelled at the expenditure of man-hours and materials. There were more signs — to another hospital, to a military camp, to an airfield — and much more traffic on the road. Skipper noticed that Commander Leintwardine became more circumspect about driving on the right-hand side of the road.

After about an hour's driving, as Commander Leintwardine had said, they came to the largest sign of all, whereupon the Commander reverted to driving on the left so suddenly that Skipper was nearly projected out on to the road. ROYAL NAVY BASE, MANUS, the sign said, with above it the Royal Coat of Arms and a Union Jack.

'Civilisation,' said Commander Leintwardine. 'Almost.'

A few yards further on was a second sign, even larger. DRIVE ON THE LEFT. A third sign said PROPERTY OF THE CROWN. KEEP OUT. TRESPASSERS WILL BE PROSECUTED.

'I had those put up,' said the Commander.

There were more signs beside a small hut: GENTLEMEN. LADIES. GENTLEMEN WILL PLEASE ADJUST THEIR DRESS BEFORE LEAVING. KEEP OFF THE GRASS.

Commander Leintwardine changed gear again and this time his empirical methods defeated even the jeep and the engine stalled.

'Bloody awful place, this.'

There was another jeep just off the road, with the front of its radiator stove in. Commander Leintwardine saw Skipper staring at it. 'Bloody Yank. Wouldn't drive on the left.' The jeep lay there, a mute casualty of Commander Leintwardine's power struggle with the Allies. The jeep jerked forward again.

The signs multiplied. NAVAL STORE OFFICE. SAFETY EQUIPMENT STORE. CAPTAIN'S OFFICE. PAY OFFICE. SHIP'S COMPANY DINING HALL. PHOTOGRAPHIC STORE. Where this last should have been, there was only a rough hole in the ground. Again, Commander Leintwardine followed Skipper's gaze.

'Not finished yet. We're still waiting for the mosquito-repellent ointment.'

Skipper made no comment.

'Are you in charge here, sir?'

'No I'm *not*.' Commander Leintwardine's voice was regretful. 'The Captain is away at the moment, with most of the staff. They're all down seeing the C-in-C in Sydney. Getting ready for the big operation in the autumn.'

'What big operation in the autumn is that?'

'Haven't you heard? The invasion of Japan.'

The invasion of Japan. The very syllables struck like the tolling of a bell. *God*, thought Skipper, *which of us will survive that?* He had known, everybody had known, that there was bound to be an invasion of Japan. Like the invasion of Europe, it had had to come sooner or later. But hearing it expressed openly like that made it seem all the more ominous.

'So I'm in the chair here until the Captain gets back. Did you say you were shot down?'

'Yes. Yes, I did.'

'You'd better have a make and mend then.'

'Would you send a signal to say I'm here? The ship will want to know and the sooner I can get fixed up to return the better.'

Commander Leintwardine seemed to ignore the comment. 'See you for dinner tonight. You didn't bring your mess undress with you, did you?'

This time it was Skipper who did not reply. It was as much as he could do to refrain from striking this stupid, unheeding, selfish, red-bearded snob off the seat of his jeep.

Commander Leintwardine stopped the jeep outside a two-storeyed hut, with the beginnings of a flower garden already dug outside it. It was, in the catchphrase which Skipper was already growing to associate with Manus, almost civilised. Commander Leintwardine looked at his watch.

'I'll leave you here, to sling your hammock. I must get off. Busy day today. Got to prepare all the orders for a Royal Visit.' Commander Leintwardine turned, to see Skipper staring at him. 'Yes, you can stare, you can stare, but somebody's got to do it. After all, I *am* Base Royal Visits Officer, amongst all the other hats that I wear. Tucker will look after you.'

Tucker was a Sub-Lieutenant RNVR of the Supply and Secretariat Branch. He popped suddenly into view from under the shade of a small veranda. Skipper was struck by his appearance. He looked well over fifty years of age, ancient for his junior rank. With his gold pince-nez, his wrinkled throat, his pipe-stem legs and his bare hermit's feet inside large sandals, he looked like somebody's solicitor uncle in tropical fancy dress.

While Commander Leintwardine drove grindingly away, Tucker looked Skipper up and down, but this time with concern at his clothes and his predicament. 'I'll get you some gear from slops this afternoon. Do until you catch up with your own gear.'

'Do you want to keep the clothes I've got on?'

Tucker's eyebrows soared up above his pince-nez. 'Whatever for?'

As soon as he said the word 'Souvenir?', Skipper knew he had erred.

'*Souvenir.* What a quaint idea. I should say those are only fit for the bonfire. Did he say anything about dressing for dinner?' Tucker had no need to say whom. 'Forget it. Wear a shirt and trousers, just like he does himself. Although I should wear long sleeves in the evenings. The Yanks say they've squashed the mosquito on these islands but that's not quite true. *Mess undress!*' Tucker snorted, so that the pince-nez leaped forward on his nose. 'He's mad, you know, mad as the proverbial hatter. The question is, will he shoot somebody before somebody shoots him?'

Tucker showed Skipper a cabin. With its bunk and sheets and mosquito net it was, as they said, almost civilised.

'I've got to go now. Must leave you. Got to go and type out his list of recommendations for the Victoria Cross.' Tucker's face was expressionless. 'Should have been in last month.'

There was even an electric fan set in the centre of the deckhead and when Skipper switched it on it actually began to turn, with a faint, soporific wheezing sound.

With the stirring of air from the fan on his face, Skipper went to sleep almost at once, as he had done in *Skullfish*, and slept the sleep of the utterly exhausted.

When he awoke, it was quite dark and, as in *Skullfish*, it was some moments before he could remember where he was. It was a very hot tropical night, with the slow creaking of the fan quite drowned in the roar of sound from outside. Skipper groped under the net and went to the window. There was no blackout on Manus. The roads and buildings nearby were brightly lit, and the harbour, seen through the fringe of trees, was a blaze of light. There were shrillings and clickings of nocturnal insects around the huts, and above all, and permeating the night, were the rumblings and hummings of engines, the clatter of riveting machines, the boom of distant explosions and the constant reverberation of faraway industry. At Manus, work went on night and day.

Tucker had left some clothes on the chair. Skipper washed and shaved. The skin on his fingertips, he noticed, was still rough and insensitive. He dressed in the clean khaki shirt and slacks, and knotted a black uniform tie.

The wardroom was some yards away, across a stretch of crushed rock. A line of lights hung on a wire led him to the doorway. Inside, there was a long table, with the portraits of the King and Queen above the head, a bar, an electric fan motor whirring in one corner, and, near the door, some wicker armchairs, one of them occupied by Tucker.

'Where *is* everybody?'

Tucker shrugged. 'Some down in Sydney. Some have gone off to have a meal in one of the ships. Some have gone down to cadge some food and see a film show with the Americans.' Nobody in their senses, Tucker's manner implied, stayed here if he could help it. 'I'm duty boy tonight.'

Commander Leintwardine, dressed as Skipper was, came in, nodded and sat down at the top of the table. A steward brought plates of soup, a large pink gin and a book for Commander Leintwardine.

'Grace,' said the Commander, standing up. 'I will say grace. No Padre. Thank God.' He sat down again and began to drink his soup. After a moment he held up his book. 'Ever heard of him? He's a genius. Percy F Westerman.'

Skipper recognised the name of an author from his schooldays, the writer of thrilling yarns for boys.

'He's a genius. He's a relative of my wife's. *Under Fire in Spain.* Marvellous book. All about the Spanish Civil War. Marvellous. I should get it out of the library if I were you, when you get back home.'

'I'll make a point of it, sir,' said Skipper.

There were a couple of other officers, who looked at Skipper incuriously, evidently placing him as transient Leintwardine-fodder, just passing through. There was also a man in a light grey tropical suit, oddly formal for the surroundings, who told Skipper he was a war correspondent. Skipper wondered how he had evaded Commander Leintwardine's ukase on the press and penetrated to the naval base. He had some pills, which he tipped out of a bottle and crunched noisily. He had been there a week, he told Skipper.

'I don't think I'll ever get away.' He looked up at the end of the table and called out to Commander Leintwardine, 'Any chance of a flight tomorrow, Commander?'

Commander Leintwardine ignored the interruption and began on his next course, which was a sort of fish-steak. Skipper found it unusually resistant to his knife and fork, but pleasant in a resilient way, like reinforced cod. There was also an unexpectedly fresh and pleasing green salad, which was served on individual side plates, in the American fashion. Again, it was almost civilised.

'What's this we're eating?'

'Barracuda,' said Tucker.

The meal continued, with Commander Leintwardine sipping his pink gin and reading out extracts from Percy F Westerman in a loud, hectoring voice.

'Rather like the old monasteries,' remarked Tucker. 'They used to have one of the brethren reading improving texts while they ate.'

After dinner, they all went outside to a space among the trees where some chairs had been set out and a cinema screen hung between two palms. Tucker carried out the projector and set it up, while Commander Leintwardine sat alone at the front, calling out 'Come on, come on, this will never do for the fleet.'

When Tucker eventually had the projector working, the film turned out to be called *Objective Burma*. *Skullfish* had had it on their previous patrol, and it had had a great effect upon them. They had believed it implicitly. It showed Errol Flynn, the film star, capturing Burma single-handed. It had, Skipper understood, caused something of a *furore* amongst the troops in South-East Asia Command who were actually still engaged in capturing Burma. It was a lively piece and Skipper enjoyed it, while recognising its inaccuracies. One could still enjoy a film even if it were patently nonsense. But Skipper could quite understand why it had aroused such protests.

Commander Leintwardine also seemed to enjoy it. Perhaps the film struck an agreeably familiar note of surrealism in his imagination, because he had a suitably improbable comment to make on it.

'Nice lad, Flynn. I once taught him Greek and Latin, you know.'

Skipper attempted some form of reply but discovered, not for the first time in Commander Leintwardine's company, that there was nothing he could say. There simply was no answer to that.

Sitting in the darkness, mulling over the Commander's latest scrap of biographical information, Skipper felt an alarming sense of being disconnected from his surroundings. This man, this base, those lights and sounds, was all this really connected with the war? *Miss Britannia* now seemed immeasurably far away, her realities and dangers lodged on another planet. He had once wondered whether the Japanese knew they had men like Richard Fenton against them. As he went to sleep for the second time, Skipper wondered whether the Japanese knew they were opposed by such as Commander Leintwardine.

In the morning, Skipper could not avoid noticing that there was an apparently brand-new jeep parked outside his window. He was looking at it in mild surprise, when he noticed, with a shock that made his back hair prickle, his own name painted along the bonnet and, underneath it, the legend: ASSISTANT BASE TRANSPORT OFFICER.

CHAPTER TWELVE

Commander Leintwardine was not in his office — which, Skipper noted, was marked POLITICAL AND STRATEGIC WARFARE ADVISER TO THE C-IN-C, BRITISH PACIFIC FLEET — but Tucker was. Tucker was apparently transferring sheafs of paper from one wire basket to another. He had the air of a hotel manager who had rather expected this visitor, and this complaint.

'He's out in the harbour this morning. Laying out danbuoys for a fleet regatta course, I believe.'

'Good God.' The answer quite threw Skipper out of his stride and made him forget his own preoccupations.

'Did you want to see him about the jeep?'

'Of course I do. How the hell did that...? I'm not *staying* here ... I've got to get back to my ship ... to my squadron. All this messing about. Do you know anything about it?'

'Of course I do. *I* had it painted with your name. Had to change it from the last bloke. Fleet Recreations and Recuperations Officer, I think he was called. He's still around somewhere, I do believe. Only he didn't seem to be using the jeep, so he thought you might as well have it. As you've been kind enough to drop in on us...'

'But I'm not going to be here...' The situation was so preposterous Skipper had to search for words to describe it. 'It's absolutely *ridiculous* ... I *insist* on sending a signal.'

'You can't insist. No signals can be sent without the authorisation of the senior officer in the base and that for the time being is Commander Leintwardine. Look,' Tucker adjusted his pince-nez and looked searchingly at Skipper, 'do you mind if I say something? You look to me badly in need of a rest. No ... no, let me finish, please. Looking at you, I'd say you'd been under a very great strain in the last few weeks, perhaps for months. It's showing in your face, believe me. Frankly, you ought to be sent on leave for a very long time, in my opinion. If you don't mind my saying so, why don't you just climb down and let it happen? You will get back to your ship, all too quickly. Of course you will. But in the meanwhile, why don't you just let things take their course? Unbend a little. Don't press so hard. Unharness yourself for the time being. When you do get back, you'll probably look back on this and wish you were here.'

Tucker looked as if he had heard Skipper's snort of derision before. 'Well, you may feel like that now. It's understandable.'

'Tell me, what exactly *is* your job here?'

'I don't know exactly what *is* my job here. Part of it certainly seems to be giving advice like that to people like you. My title seems to change every week. I was on my way to join a ship. But I got stuck here, for some unaccountable reason. So here I stick. It's really almost civilised, when you get used to it.'

Skipper found himself impressed and touched by this philosophical view of life. They also served who stood by and offered advice, like Tucker.

'What did you do before the war, if you don't mind my asking?'

'No, I don't mind your asking. I was a salesman, a traveller for a firm of veterinary suppliers, down in the West Country.'

'What firm?'

Skipper knew them. His father sometimes dealt with them. He did not remember Tucker but he could well have passed him or seen him without knowing, in Devizes or Marlborough.

The mere memory of those names made Skipper ache with yearning to be home again and see them.

'Since you *are* Assistant Base Transport Officer, chosen from thousands of applicants, I should use the transport.'

'I will. Is there a signal office here in the base?'

'Oh, yes.' Once more Tucker had that wary look, of having seen and heard it all before. 'Drive the same way the jeep is facing now to the end of the compound and it's a biggish hut, with the aerials above it.'

The Main Signal Office, Skipper guessed, was probably the largest building on the base. It had a form of air-conditioning, not for the comfort of the men but for the efficiency of the electronic equipment. Even with that help, the building was still uncomfortably hot, because it seemed to have many more men on watch than *Miss Britannia*'s signal office even at a busy time. Skipper estimated there were more than twenty watchkeepers there, and he wondered at the activity. Who were all these signals to and from? Why were they all so urgent, and classified secret? He had the appropriate thought that perhaps all this traffic, all this business, was generated by Commander Leintwardine himself. Maybe all these signals were going from Commander Leintwardine, Royal Naval Base Miscellaneous Weapons Development Officer, to Commander Leintwardine, Political and Strategic Warfare Adviser to the C-in-C, British Pacific Fleet, repeated for information to Commander Leintwardine, Base Royal Visits Officer, and Commander Leintwardine, Fleet Regatta Danbuoys Officer.

The Petty Officer Yeoman of the Watch was sitting at a kind of raised deck, wearing only a pair of swimming trunks, sandals and a gold cross on a chain round his neck. He was polite and genuinely sorry, but firm.

'Can't send any signals without the Commander's signature, sir. He'd play hell with me if I did, sir. I'm very sorry, sir. We've had other officers like you in here, sir, and the answer's always the same. I'm dead sorry, sir, I am.'

Commander Leintwardine did not appear for lunch. Evidently the regatta danbuoys were a trickier problem than had been planned for. Skipper went back to his cabin afterwards. The whole base worked a tropical routine, which meant an earlier morning start but a siesta time in the afternoons. It was a routine which suited Skipper well enough. He seemed to be able to fall asleep almost at once, even in this heat and humidity. It was as though he had great reservoirs for sleep which had been drained and were still to be refilled.

In the evening, when Skipper went across to the wardroom, Commander Leintwardine was there, clearly in a state of scarcely suppressed excitement. Skipper looked cautiously round the hut. Could it be that Royalty or the C-in-C had actually arrived?

The Commander was standing to attention but visibly quivering, with his pink gin raised aloft, addressing the portraits of the King and Queen. 'God save the King.'

'Hear hear,' said Skipper.

'Have you heard?'

'Have I heard what?'

'War's over.'

'What?'

'In Europe. Just come over the air. Complete and unconditional surrender of all Axis forces in the west. U-boats are surfacing all over the place, flying black flags.'

'Why *black* flags?'

'To show they're surrendering.'

'But I thought you showed a *white* flag when you surrendered?'

'Black flag,' said Commander Leintwardine sombrely. 'Black flag it is.'

The German surrender appeared to have put the Commander in reflective mood. Over the barracuda, he seemed to be pondering the past.

'My father was there when the German High Seas Fleet surrendered in 1918, you know,' he said conversationally, as though surrenders of enemy fleets ran in his family, like red hair. 'He used to tell us how he watched them, *Seydlitz, Moltke, Derflinger, Hindenburg, Von der Tann*, all the great names. He said he should have been pleased and excited about it, but he was so dead tired he hardly took any notice. Still, he said, it was a good job done.'

'Your father was in the Navy?'

'Oh, yes.' Commander Leintwardine spoke as though Skipper had hardly needed to ask. 'Never got very far, though. Like me. Grandfather, too.'

Skipper suddenly had a more sympathetic view of the Commander. Evidently his family had sent their sons into the Navy, for generation after generation, not in the hope of high advancement or of great reward but simply through their own conception of service to the Crown. There were such families, Skipper knew. Some of their members did well in the Services, others hated the life and did not prosper, but they all served. Commander Leintwardine was, in his own eccentric way, a true representative of them, and Skipper looked at him in a new light. '

'Well.' Commander Leintwardine stood up at the end of the meal in a dismissive way. 'Going now. We've got problems over getting proper wicker fenders for the boom defence vessels.'

So numbed had Skipper become by Commander Leintwardine's personality that it was some minutes before Skipper realised the fantasy, the sheer preposterous absurdity, of dealing with 'proper wicker fenders' for boom defence vessels on the night victory in Europe had been declared. Skipper was still reflecting on this when Tucker came in.

Tucker at once went round behind the bar to get himself a drink. There was, understandably, no steward that night.

'Here's to the end of the war.' Tucker held up his glass. He had tears in his eyes. 'Damn it.'

'Why, don't you want it to end?' asked Skipper, astonished.

'No bloody fear.' Tucker belched so forcefully his pince-nez bounced down to the end of his nose. He pushed them back carefully. Even in his cups, Tucker had a certain drunken precision. 'Have a little sense, my good friend. What the hell am I and people like me going to do when the war's over?'

'Can't you —?'

'Go back to what we were doing before? After living like this? All right, the climate's bloody, and one has to put up with raving lunatics like Commander Leintwardine, but to be an officer in His Majesty's Navy ... that's *something*. Go back to calling on cloddish farmers and being polite to their flabby wives and their louts of sons? How many farmers have joined the Colours in this war?'

Now that Skipper came to think of it, all their tenant farmers and their strong, strapping sons, and all the other farmers round about Daughton and their sons, were indeed still at home and had been throughout the whole war.

'So, here's to Tojo, I say. Good on yer, mate. Keep at it, old son. May yer shadow never grow less, old cobber.'

Skipper looked round. 'I must say, I wouldn't let Commander Leintwardine hear you say that.'

'Fuck Commander Leintwardine,' said Tucker convincingly.

Skipper had expected there would be some celebration of VE Day — Victory in Europe Day — as it was being called, but the base seemed unmoved. There was some shouting from the ship's company canteen and somebody started up a jeep and roared round the compound for a little while, but otherwise, like Commander Leintwardine's father's experience at the previous German surrender, it all seemed to fall a little flat. Skipper walked round the base for a space before going to bed. He came to a clearing high above the harbour. It had probably been designed as a gun-site, but the guns had long since been removed, or had never been positioned.

The harbour was as brightly lit and as busy as any other night. No fireworks, but the flicker of welding torches over on the floating dock; no saluting guns, but the throbbing of constant engines, crossing and recrossing the harbour still. War was over in Europe, but it made not the slightest difference here in the Pacific. But they would be celebrating at home. *Mafficking*, was the old word for it. There would be a bonfire at Daughton just as, so the story went, there was for the Spanish Armada, and for Waterloo, and for Queen Victoria's Diamond Jubilee, and for Mafeking. There would be crowds in Trafalgar Square and the lights would be on in Piccadilly. There was a song about that, 'I'm gonna get lit up when the lights go on in London'. Skipper wondered whether that singer was putting her promise into effect.

It would be ten days since they had had firm news of him at Daughton. It was disgraceful, it was scarcely believable, that he should be obstructed by somebody like Commander

Leintwardine. Skipper made up his mind he would try the signal office again in the morning.

But in the morning, Commander Leintwardine forestalled him. At breakfast he was frowning. Something, clearly, was bothering him.

'Here's a funny thing. Have you been to the Main Signal Office?'

'Yes.' Skipper realised, too late, that Commander Leintwardine had a finely tuned grapevine which told him of everything on the base. 'Yes, I tried to send a signal telling the world I'm here.'

'But I have drafted a signal. Like to see it?'

Commander Leintwardine pushed the signal log across the table. Skipper read the top signal with a feeling of shock, wonder and anger which sent tingles down to his toenails.

Request psychiatric advice … aftermath of air accident … facilities in Manus insufficient for proper restraint … patient security paramount…

Skipper read it again and again. It was supposed to be about himself.

Then he began to laugh, the first real, uncontrolled, uninhibited helpless laughter he had experienced for months and months. He laughed until his eyes smarted with tears. He laughed until he could hardly draw breath any longer. It was just as Tucker had said: Commander Leintwardine was mad. This place was mad. The whole world was mad. The best thing to do was to relax and let it take its course. Somehow, somewhere, sanity would come back, but until then — as Tucker said — let it happen.

'Yes,' he said soberly, at last. 'That seems to say it all. I should get that off right away.'

Commander Leintwardine took the signal log back across the table, with a puzzled grimace. For the very first time in their acquaintance, Skipper felt that he had gained some form of advantage over that curious mentality opposite him.

'What shall I do this morning, sir?'

'Do, do, *do*? You're the Base Cinema Officer, I should get on with that.'

'Aye, aye, sir.'

'I should get round the bazaars and see what films some of the ships want.'

With Commander Leintwardine, as Skipper had learned, a nod was as good as a violent kick in the backside. There was a new jetty at the end of the path down from the gun-site, with a hut to keep off the rain, and a quartermaster and a sentry who both saluted, and a boat routine, a typed sheet tacked to the trunk of a palm tree. Boats came and went, bearing the names of some of the store ships, tankers and other miscellaneous vessels out in the lagoon. One boat, Skipper saw, was a 'round the harbour' trip, very popular with ratings who could catch it and lose themselves from authority for a whole forenoon.

Skipper himself caught the boat. He found it pleasant to sit in the stern sheets in the hot sunshine, with a cooling breeze from the boat's own speed to refresh him. Ratings got on and off, gangways came and went. Would these boats still run after the war had ended? Like the rest of this base, so unobtrusively well organised, did the boat routine have a vitality, a life of its own, which would keep it running on after the need for it had gone?

At what seemed to be the last ship before the boat headed for the jetty again, Skipper got off. It was an Empire-class tanker and there was nobody at all at the top of the gangway when Skipper climbed it. When a sailor did appear and Skipper told him he was the Base Cinema Officer, he took him into the after superstructure. The officers there received Skipper without any curiosity, gave him a drink and followed it with lunch. They were, apparently, accustomed to officers from the naval base calling upon them. It was, so to speak, an occupational risk. Later, in the afternoon, full of gin and curry, Skipper caught another boat back to the jetty. At no time had anybody asked his name, or mentioned cinemas.

Commander Leintwardine's grapevine extended even to the ships in the harbour. At dinner that evening, he seemed to know all about Skipper's expedition.

'Strange life those tanker boys lead, you know. *I* couldn't bear it. I was at her launch, did you know that?'

Skipper had not known that, but he was growing used to the astounding range of acquaintanceship and experience which Commander Leintwardine claimed. It seemed he knew everybody, had been everywhere, seen everything. Just as his wife was related to Percy F Westerman, and he had taught Errol Flynn Latin and Greek, so he had been at Dunkirk, dined with the King, grown coffee, sold encyclopaedias. From biographical fragments Skipper managed to disentangle, it seemed that Commander Leintwardine had been in the Navy, left sometime between the wars, been a schoolmaster, a planter, a salesman, and generally knocked about the world, before rejoining at 'the outbreak of hostilities,' as he himself called them. Skipper suspected that for Commander Leintwardine, as for Tucker, the war had been welcome.

The Commander also claimed to have learned to fly. Here, Skipper felt, he could at last pin his adversary down. 'What squadron? What aircraft?'

'Fairey Flycatchers. Lovely aircraft. Before your time, my boy. A real gentleman's conveyance. I crashed and broke me neck, did you know that? I still have a joint in it or something slightly out of kilter. Listen.' Commander Leintwardine bent forward and twisted his neck in such a way that it gave out a shattering bone-cracking sound which made Skipper purse his lips in disgust and shock.

'Amusing, isn't it? Great trick for children's parties. Oh, yes, Uncle Jack's broken neck was much in demand at birthdays and Christmas time.'

To that there seemed nothing more to be said. Once again Commander Leintwardine had succeeded in developing a subject to a point where Skipper simply did not fancy following it any further. Yet his comments often had a kind of deranged logic, a random certainty. In all his ramblings he often revealed a perspective which struck Skipper as true. Listening to him was like wafting through cloud to strike suddenly on solid rock, as in his reaction to the news, which Skipper let slip one evening, that he might consider a permanent commission in the Royal Navy. Commander Leintwardine seemed quite perturbed at that prospect.

'But do you know what you are doing, what you're up against? You, an RNVR. Think you'll succeed?'

'I think I might.'

'I think you won't. You haven't been broken in. Dartmouth used to do that. Why do you think we all survive in the Navy whatever happens? Because nothing in later life could ever be as bad as Dartmouth was in the Twenties and Thirties. The war, prison camps, the depression, plagues, earthquakes, volcanoes, shipwreck, financial ruin, sickness and slump, they're all *pinpricks* compared with Dartmouth under the old system. You're not stupid enough, in a very special way, to be a regular naval officer. You'll always have your tongue half in your cheek. That would never do. I must say this had never occurred to me.' Commander Leintwardine looked gloomily up at the deckhead as though he could see in his mind's eye endless ranks of ex-RNVR officers, advancing towards him like a series of amateur Zulu impis.

But, nevertheless, as the days slipped by, Skipper sensed that the Commander's attitude towards himself had now changed in some subtle way, as though the possibility that Skipper might have a permanent commission had somehow given him a real identity, as though he had now become someone whose existence Commander Leintwardine might one day have actually to acknowledge. Meanwhile, Skipper drove his jeep where he pleased, sunbathed beside the water's edge, paid visits to the American transit camp and swam in their pool, watched a film outside the wardroom with Commander Leintwardine every evening, and every night went to sleep as though he had not slept for a week.

Some days he went fishing in the harbour. There was a skiff, left over from some unknown ship, which Skipper commandeered. Skipper adored fishing. He had fished their own beats at Daughton ever since he could walk. But at Manus there seemed only barracuda to catch. Skipper put scraps of an old cap-cover on a large hook and tossed it over the side. The first barracuda tore at it, rising like a guided torpedo, and took it with a force that wrenched the line from Skipper's hand. The violence of it sickened him. That was not fishing. That was more like war. Instead, he fashioned himself a glass-bottomed box, to drift along the reefs and study the sea bed. There were multi-coloured coral outcrops, and swathes of brilliant seaweed, and thousands and thousands of rainbow-coloured fish, which swam together and changed direction faultlessly and with lightning speed. There must, Skipper thought, be a master fish amongst them, on whom they all took station, and whom they all obeyed. Skipper wished he had wingmen who could fly as accurately as those fish could swim.

He took the chance, in the days of idleness, to write the letters he knew were still outstanding: to Fenton's people, to Cicely Weston, to Kittens' wife, and others. His letters were dutiful rather than compassionate. He could not recapture, in the long drowsy afternoons of Manus, the tense concern of being on board. Mail come in to the base, too, but there was never any for Skipper. Nobody knew he was there. He really was living an existence out of time and space, and, in a curious unexpected way, he was enjoying the holiday Tucker had advised him to take.

With the mail there were occasional newspapers. Skipper was always disappointed to see that it was just as the men in the fleet believed. They were hardly ever mentioned. SEAC had its own newspaper, which sometimes reached Manus a week or so late. There was news, and occasional interest, such as a long and splenetic letter from an American glider pilot complaining about *Objective Burma*. There was with one issue a special VE Day insert. AND NOW TO FINISH THE JAPS, the headline said. That was the genuine 1939 spirit. Much more to the point, in Skipper's experience, was the cartoon printed beside it of some soldiers working on a bridge somewhere in Burma. Their sergeant was saying to them, 'All right, chaps, Armistice in Europe has been declared — break for five minutes' smoke!' There were exhortatory messages, from the Supreme Allied Commander, from his American deputy, from the C-in-C Allied Land Forces, C-in-C East Indies Fleet and the C-in-C Air Command. 'The quickest way home is the longest way round — through Tokyo.'

That was certainly true, Skipper thought, as his attention was caught by a long poem on the same page. It was by Edmund

Blunden, a poet he had read and discussed at Oxford. He had served in the Great War and Skipper had read his verses, of somewhat stiff and self-conscious resemblance to Wilfred Owen's. But they had had some poetic feeling, which was more than could be said for his 'victory' here. This was at best dutiful doggerel. *Through dragon's country midnight-black we went ... A widening wonder glitters on our view ... Once more we have come through*. He was certainly right there. They had come through — in Europe. *Swept the broad sea till nothing showed there to pursue*. It rhymed, sometimes, but it frequently failed to scan. Skipper tossed the newspaper down, more depressed than angry. It seemed that six years of war had tired the poets along with everybody else.

Skipper himself had been long enough at Manus. He could see that in the faces of other officers passing through. They all looked at him as though he had the lotus-eater's caste mark on him, and asked him questions about the place in a tone which showed they believed he belonged there. Some of them were on their way to Guam and Leyte, or down to Sydney. Skipper told them his story and asked them to report his presence, rather as a shipwrecked sailor might put his tale in a bottle and throw it into the sea, hoping one day it would come to shore. But, like the majority of messages in bottles, Skipper's passed into oblivion.

The original war correspondent of Skipper's first night had disappeared, to some unknown destination, but others arrived occasionally. They were apprehensive about this strange war out here which was, annoyingly, still continuing when the war at home had ended. They were amazed by the number of ships the fleet had. One of them called Skipper a liar when he remarked that the task force at sea had had twenty-four ships when he left it.

But everybody who called, or arrived, or stayed at the Base, paled in Skipper's view before the spectacle of Commander Leintwardine. That great red spade-like beard seemed to fill the sky. His shout arrested the sun. Skipper seemed to meet him everywhere, driving his jeep in jerky leaps about the Base, supervising the erection of fresh and bigger noticeboards, pacing out a parade-ground for a Royal march-past, munching his evening barracuda, reading out Percy F Westerman and retailing his surrealist anecdotes.

Skipper had fully expected to be able to feel superior to this intellectual backswoodsman, this reserve fleet warrior who had clearly never heard a shot fired in anger. But Commander Leintwardine had about him an air of crazy certainty which made him invulnerable. Skipper simply could not challenge a man who was capable of stopping him in the middle of the day and telling him, at length, that if it were still peacetime, if he were back in the Channel Fleet and if he, Commander Leintwardine, were the First Lieutenant, he would by this date already have ordered the ship's company to change to white cap-covers. There simply was no debating with someone who wrote and rewrote his orders for a fleet review, who daily sent furious signals to Sydney demanding a year's supply of wicker fenders, and who seriously debated whether or not to recommend the Chief Yeoman of Signals for the Victoria Cross.

On Skipper's last night, Commander Leintwardine shot one of the war correspondents in the foot. There were still Japanese, an unknown number of them, at large in the central part of the main island, known as the Reservation. Occasionally, an energetic company commander would make a sortie into the interior to flush some of them out, but generally they were left alone, except when starvation drove them down to the base perimeter, like deer in a hard winter in search of food.

Skipper awoke to the noise of engines and the glow of headlights gliding across the bulkhead of his cabin. He got up and looked out. Three jeeps full of Marines, and a troop carrier with a machine gun, were driving, on the right-hand side of the road, through the naval base. There were several shots, angry shouts, and Commander Leintwardine's voice was clearly audible. For a mad moment, Skipper thought the Commander had shot somebody for driving on the wrong side of the road.

When Skipper went outside, there was quite a crowd standing in the road, and the sound of a man crying, and somebody lying on a stretcher. Skipper heard the word 'Japanese'.

'Is that a Jap?'

The great beard swung round in Skipper's direction. 'No, it bloody well isn't. It's one of those blasted war correspondents. I tried to stop them coming. These bloody Yanks. I thought it was the Japanese.'

The man on the stretcher began to howl loudly.

'Oh, for God's sake, *shut up*, will you? If you *will* run around the base at dead of night, no wonder somebody takes a pot-shot at you.'

'I wasn't running around,' said the man on the stretcher. 'I was lying in my *bunk*. It came through the wall.'

'*Rubbish,*' said Commander Leintwardine. 'Take him down to the sick bay. And *you*, think yourself lucky you weren't killed.'

Nevertheless, in the morning, several grim-faced Americans in white steel helmets arrived in front of Commander Leintwardine's office and, for the first time in their acquaintance, Skipper saw the Commander apparently disconcerted. He would have like to have stayed to see his discomfiture, but experience had taught him that Commander Leintwardine had a trick of spreading the impact of such catastrophes to include all bystanders. It was wiser to go fishing, out of the way.

Skipper was staring at fish through his glass when the wash of a passing boat rocked his skiff so violently it slopped water up in his face and nearly tipped him over the side. He looked up, to swear at the offender, and then paused.

It was the Captain's barge, planing in to the landing stage. Skipper recognised the Coxswain. He sat up and looked round. There, down at the far end of the anchorage, was an aircraft carrier. He recognised her funnel and the radar aerials, and the pattern of the faded camouflage paint. He could even see the familiar aircraft on her flight deck. How she had managed to arrive so unexpectedly, how he had managed to miss seeing her name in a signal, Skipper had no idea, but there was no doubt about it. There — large as life and twice as natural — was *Miss Britannia*.

The barge was coming back. Skipper waved with all his might and shouted at the top of his voice. The bow wave dropped, and the boat turned towards him.

'Any luck, sir?' said the Captain's Coxswain.

'*Luck?*'

'Fishing, sir.'

'God, don't mind about *that* — can you take me back on board?'

'Like that, sir?'

Skipper looked down at himself. He was wearing his oldest khaki shorts. His torso was bronzed by the sun. He must have looked like a beachcomber. But there was nothing he needed back in his cabin. He had everything he valued with him, and he dare not let Commander Leintwardine delay him.

'Yes, just as I am.'

'Of course, sir. What about the boat, sir?'

'Oh, let that go, it doesn't matter about that. Just get me back on board.'

But the Coxswain's seaman's instinct rebelled at such wastefulness. 'We'll take it back in tow, sir, if you don't mind. If you don't want it, maybe the side party can use it.'

'All right, all right, but let's get going.'

Skipper gathered together his towel and his shirt, and climbed across to the Captain's barge. He was leaving Manus just as he had arrived, with nothing much more than what he stood up in. He even had Sparky's little bag with him, with his fishing gear in it.

And so, once more, as though after a lapse of several years, Skipper came under the great dark overhang of *Miss Britannia*'s flight deck. With the same feelings of apprehension, anticipation and joy, he mounted the steps of the gangway again. The Officer of the Watch, who was the Mate of the Upper Deck, stood at the salute, and then stepped forward to shake hands.

'Robinson Crusoe, I presume?' he said.

CHAPTER THIRTEEN

'We simply couldn't get any hard news about you, no matter how hard we tried.'

'Yes, I'm sorry, sir.'

Skipper sat awkwardly, sipping the Captain's pink gin. Still wearing his bathing costume, just as he had come aboard, he was sitting in the Captain's day cabin under the quarterdeck, feeling the first peculiar sensations of accustoming himself to being back in his ship, back in civilised and familiar surroundings, back amongst well-known friends and superiors.

'We know you'd been picked up by a submarine and were heading for Guam and all points east, but nobody seemed to know what happened to you at Guam. You just seemed to take off into space. Our liaison team there were a bit slow off the mark and by the time they'd clued up to you you'd gone. All they could find out was that you had been last seen driving at top speed around the island with a black man.'

Skipper laughed, in sheer relief from nervous tension.

'Why on earth didn't you let us know where you'd got to?'

'I tried, sir, I did try, believe me. But I just couldn't get a signal off from Manus. But wasn't there one about me needing psychiatric treatment?'

'No?' The Captain looked baffled. 'What a curious idea. Ah, I've got it. Is old Leintwardine still there?'

'Yes, sir.'

'Ah that explains it. *He's* the one that needs psychiatric treatment. Is that old tiger *still* dashing about the bazaars? Did he tell you he was related to Nelson?'

'No, sir, that was one of the things he didn't tell me.'

'Well, he is. Most of the things he tells you are true, you know. I served with him once many years ago. Mad as a coot with a brainstorm. I would have thought the men in white coats would have come and taken him away long ago. And yet … and yet. With only the slightest turn the other way he could have been an admiral. Well, all's well that ends well. I must say, Skipper, you're looking extremely brown and fit and well. How are you, *in yourself*, as the old PMO in my first ship used to say?'

'I'm very fit, sir.' Skipper was conscious that the Captain was staring intently at him, conscious that he was being assessed coolly and unsentimentally.

The Captain was looking for future results. He would not let Auld Lang Syne sway him.

'Sure?'

'Oh, yes, sir.'

'We've got a tough programme ahead. You've done your fair share, in my opinion. I won't say I'm not glad to hear you're fit, but you could be relieved, you know. It's time.'

'I know, sir. But I'm fine.'

'Good. But what about Michael, your senior P? I think he should go.'

'Oh, no, sir!' Skipper was horrified by the thought. 'He's a very valuable man, absolutely vital.'

'He *is* a very valuable man. But he's not vital.'

'Oh, no, sir, I couldn't do it as well without Michael.'

The Captain looked at Skipper for some moments without speaking. 'Well,' he said at last, 'for once I'm going to go against my better judgment and let things stay. I hope you're right.' He looked at his watch. 'Now you'd better go and make your number with everybody and let them know Skipper's himself again. We're off in forty minutes.' The Captain noticed

Skipper's look of surprise. 'We only came in to drop some documents, pick up some mail, take up some passengers and some spare gear. We're on our way to Sydney for three weeks. New pilots, new aircraft, patch up all our damage, whoop it up if we can, where we can, and then back again.'

Skipper reflected that if he had overslept that morning, if he had chosen to go over to Los Negros or to the American base — even if he had merely failed to look out into the harbour — he would have missed the ship and would still be back there with Commander Leintwardine.

As the Captain had said, Skipper was himself again and it was surprising to him how easily and comfortably he slipped back into his old place on board. His key still fitted in his cabin door, his clothes were still in their places, his mail had piled up on his desk. The ship may not have known where he was, but they knew he was still alive. His presence, his memory, had been kept on board.

Skipper plunged back effortlessly into the daily minutiae of his squadron's life — the paperwork, the routine, the requestmen, the squadron watch and duty bill, the engine and the air-frame periodic examinations. Chief Air Rigger Petre and the other squadron ratings received Skipper back with few visible signs of relief or excitement.

'You'd like to come down to the chief's mess at tot time, sir? We'll give you a wet.' Petre's pebble-like eyes showed neither surprise nor curiosity at the Squadron CO's reappearance. 'You were lucky, sir, but I knew you would be. I knew you'd been picked up. I knew by the way we heard the news.'

That, Skipper thought, was a most curious remark, which could only have been made by a man with long experience in the Fleet Air Arm. It had never occurred to Skipper before that there could be significance in the way, the *pace*, at which news was received on board. There was, it seemed, something to be learned from the very intervals between the facts as they arrived. According to Chief Air Rigger Petre, he had heard nothing of Skipper for just long enough to reassure him that Skipper was still alive.

'It's a funny thing, Chief, but I thought of you when I was floating in my little dinghy. Somehow I felt I had almost let the squadron down, if you know what I mean?'

'Oh, yes, sir.' Petre nodded. 'I know exactly what you mean. But you didn't let anybody down. The pace you were going then, something was going to happen. Sure to. It's from now on you'll have to watch out. That's if you're staying, sir?'

'Of course I am.'

'That's good, sir. It's just that the Senior Pilot seemed to think you'd be moving on.'

'Good God, no.'

To Skipper's surprise and faint unease, Wings also seemed to have the same thought. 'You staying on with us, then, Skipper?'

'Of course.'

'Good. Tell me, now you *are* back, what made you take a second pass at that airstrip that day? You know the rules. One run only.'

'Yes, that's the rule all right.' Skipper stroked the bridge of his nose with a finger and thumb. It all seemed so very far away and long ago. He had to pause for some time while he collected his memories and marshalled his thoughts. 'I don't know ... it just seemed good to do. It seems such a hell of a long time ago now that it's difficult to bring it all back.' Skipper felt his resentment rising against Wings for reopening this subject. Surely there was nothing to be gained, nothing to be learned, now, after this interval? If it had been a mistake, then surely he had paid for it?

'I think it was the day of the kamikaze, as I remember. I suppose I was a bit shaken up by that, without properly realising it…'

'The first kamikaze, I suppose you mean. There were several, you know — in this ship and in all the other carriers.' Skipper could not help noticing Wings' sardonic tone of voice, and his faintly stressed implication that Skipper had been absent while the ship had been in great danger.

'Yes, it was the first one. It was a mistake, that attack. I've learned from it, believe me.' Guiltily, Skipper remembered Fenton. He should have enquired about him long ago. 'Tell me, what about Richard Fenton? Did he get away?'

'Oh, he died. They got him as far as the hospital ship and did their best, but it was those burns. They were too much. But it took a week before he died.'

Skipper could well imagine it. A character like that would never give up without a titanic struggle for life. Skipper knew he would never again get a wingman like Richard Fenton. He wondered who he would get.

Wings seemed to have read his thoughts. 'We've got some new faces. You won't recognise the place.'

'Good. We mustn't allow ourselves to get in a rut, must we?' Skipper felt he must hit back, no matter how feebly. He must not allow Wings to get the better of him, especially not now. But there was one thing he had to ask.

'What about Robert Weston? What happened there?'

'Oh, yes, I'd forgotten you were away and missed that, too. He got *your* disease. One pass too many over Ishigaki.'

'That's easy to say, from someone who never leaves the island.'

Wings was silent for so long that Skipper had time to begin to think about other things, so long in fact that — as Skipper realised with eventual respect — Wings had waited until his temper was under control.

'You'll want a flight as soon as possible, won't you? Get back in the saddle?'

'Yes, please.'

'We'll lay on a special performance this afternoon.'

It was a special performance. The ship went to flying stations, specially for Skipper, and a Corsair was ranged on deck and fuelled, specially for Skipper. The whole task force turned into the south-easterly wind, specially for Skipper. Skipper himself was delighted that the feel, the touch, the *rapport* with the aircraft all came back to him as if he had never been away. The rough texture of the joystick ring, the way the gauge-needles swung, the snap of the switches, the familiar knobs and protuberances, right where his fingers felt for them, the same smell of dope and oil, the same thundering engine note — and, as he released the brakes and began to roll, the same certainty of control, the same thrill as he felt the Corsair become airborne.

He had the only aircraft in the sky at the time and he knew that the eyes of the whole task force were on him, from the Admiral in the flagship to the palest off-watch stoker sunning himself in the goofers. He made up his mind to give them a show.

He began with the most simple of turns, the steadiest of rolls, concentrating on making each one as true in its curve, as pure in shape, as smooth and sustained and perfect as possible, as though he were engraving lines in the sky, like a skater's marks on ice, for the judges to examine. Then he tightened the curves and steepened the climbs, and flew so low over the water that he felt again that delicious, apprehensive prickling of his skin as the propeller seemed to fan the very wave-tops, and he climbed so high that he hung in the air, falling into his straps, and dragged the canopy back so that he could actually stare straight down at the sea and the ships. At the top of a climb he put the stick down and the Corsair tipped over, creating a feeling of airy weightlessness in his body. At the bottom of the dive he pulled the stick back and felt the blood draining from his neck and cheeks. His limbs went leaden, and he gritted his teeth, grinning, grimacing against gravity. Here was a freedom he had not felt for weeks. It was as far from travelling in that Dakota to Manus as leading a carthorse was from riding the winner of the Derby. That was mere aerial transportation. This was flying. He spun and jinked and rolled again and again, exulting in that marvellous harmony of hand and foot and eye which had never failed him. Absence had only made him fresher. Like a dancer moving from one improvised routine to another, he shifted his position about the sky, now by banking, now by diving, now by climbing, making each successive manoeuvre just as it occurred to him.

He heard Stanley's old voice crackling in his ears again. 'Prodigal, Prodigal.' *Prodigal*, that was a nicely chosen code-word. 'This is *Miss Britannia*. Fun?'

'This is Prodigal Son. The greatest fun in all the world...'

'OK, well, we've got the fatted calf ready now.'

Far below, the wakes of the task force were curling into the wind. Again, every ship was moving in unison, just for his benefit.

Once more he did his cockpit checks, picked up the line of the landing circuit and swung round to land on. There was Tiny with his bats. He knew the landing would be good, just by the angle of the deck and sea, and so it was.

When Skipper reached the bridge, the Captain already had a signal from the flagship in his hand, evidence that Skipper's performance had been approved by others outside *Miss Britannia*'s own packed galleries of goofers. How did that song go? Skipper thought. *But I forgot all the masts that stick up from Formid., and a seat in the goofers was worthy forty quid. Cracking show, I'm alive...*

'Here you are, Skipper,' the Captain called. 'This one's for you. From flag, what are you going to do for an encore?' The Captain's grin had faded to a faint frown. Witty signals from the Admiral always had to be handled with care. One must frame a suitably witty reply without being noticeably wittier than Father.

'I should make back, sir. My next trick is impossible.'

The whole bridge laughed, and Skipper joined in, laughing more than perhaps his joke was worth. But he laughed from relief, from thankfulness, from a sense of homecoming. The accident over Ishigaki, the ordeal in the dinghy, the passage in *Skullfish*, the air voyage, Manus, all were rapidly receding into the past now that he was here, back where he really belonged.

'So be it,' said the Captain. 'You seemed to be enjoying yourself up there, Skipper. Better now?'

'Oh, yes, sir.'

Michael was standing in a group of officers in the nearest of the goofing galleries, where he had obviously been watching Skipper's air display and deck landing. Skipper was pleased and triumphant, relaxed yet excited, like a batsman who has just come in after making a hundred. But at the sight of the expression on Michael's face, Skipper's delight was inexplicably dimmed. He could not tell what Michael was thinking, but he was clearly not wholeheartedly pleased by Skipper's success. There was a hint of jealousy there, a touch of resentment. For the first time, Skipper had the thought that Michael was not completely loyal. Maybe it would have been wiser to have taken the Captain's advice. But, Skipper decided, there was no point in jobbing backwards and thinking of what might have been. The time to get rid of Michael was when the Captain suggested it. That time was now past, and he must make the best of it. Perhaps, after all, he had misjudged his old friend and all would still be well.

But in the days of the passage down to Sydney, Skipper realised that his first suspicions had been correct. The old relationship between them, of Squadron CO and senior pilot, of first and second fliers, of friend and comrade, had vanished totally. Michael had enjoyed acting as CO and he retained a proprietary attitude towards the squadron, which he betrayed in his guarded conversation, in his reluctance to tell Skipper the full facts of what had happened while he had been away, and, above all, in his attitude towards Richard Trumble. The lad was only one of the pilots, and one of the most recently joined and inexperienced. But Michael treated him as though he were the senior pilot, as though he were the crown prince and heir to Michael's own throne. Several times Skipper made up his mind to challenge Michael and assert his own position. But each time he drew back. He admitted to himself he was afraid of publicly putting to the sword a friendship which had sustained and delighted him for nearly two years.

Young though Trumble was, he was old compared with some of the newcomers Skipper tried out in the few hours' flying they had on passage. All aircrew were absurdly young; that was one of the war's great clichés. But these were merely children, looking as though they were not just fresh from college or public school but from prep school. That, as Henry Darling remarked of his own squadron, was a sign of age:

when not only the policemen but the replacement aircrews began to look younger. He was, he said, surprised to hear that some of their voices had broken. Nevertheless, most of them could certainly fly. By report, they had acquitted themselves well in the operations after Skipper's departure, and they were perhaps the only men on board who actually looked forward to the coming operations off Japan, which were now beginning to loom at the back of everybody's consciousness.

As the task force steamed south and east towards Australia the weather grew pleasantly cooler. The Coral Sea was as calm as a postcard. No typhoons crossed its surface and the weather was seldom other than perfect. The south-east trade wind blew steadily and refreshingly over the port bow. Even when cloud crossed the sun, it was only like a temporary shade drawn over its normal brilliance. On the starboard beam were the great mountain ranges and primeval jungles of New Guinea and Papua in which the Australians had inflicted upon the Japanese their first land defeat of the war, and far off, below the horizon on the port quarter, was the island of Guadalcanal, that ominous name. But it was difficult to imagine the furious battles fought in this paradisial scenery, almost impossible to visualise a vicious struggle by sea and air happening off islands named the Louisiades.

Skipper was walking the flight deck one evening, when the great white wash of the Barrier Reef and the orange and slate-coloured lands of Australia were to starboard, when he passed Tucker walking the other way. He stopped in amazement. Tucker must have come on board at Manus. But he had not met him in the mess, nor seen his name on any list, or cabin, or daily orders.

'Hey!' Tucker's whites were just as trim, his pince-nez still gleaming.

'I'd no idea *you* were on board!' Skipper remembered that Tucker had gone out of his way to help him at Manus. 'Why didn't you say ... are you fixed up all right, cabin and everything?'

'Yes, thanks. Got everything. Saw you flying the other day.'

Skipper knew it was unworthy of him, but he could not help feeling pleased that Tucker had watched. It might have seemed like showing off, but it had restored his confidence. Because now, of course, their relationship had been completely reversed. Now it was Skipper on his own ground, a ship's personality, known to all, who had publicly demonstrated his celebrity status. Now Tucker was the displaced person, the passenger, with no recognised place on board.

'You taking passage with us down to Sydney, I suppose?'

Tucker pushed his pince-nez precisely into place. 'Yes, I'm going down to collect my Victoria Cross.'

Skipper grinned and nodded. It was an exquisitely accurate reply, seeming to sum up at once his own experience at Manus, and his own and Tucker's dealings with Commander Leintwardine. That, he had to admit, said it all. It was only some time later, when the ship was about to enter Sydney, that Skipper remembered that Tucker must have known *Miss Britannia* was due to arrive at Manus, so as to fix his own passage, but had forborne to mention it to Skipper.

The ship's company were prepared in advance for the impact of Australia as carefully and thoroughly as though they were about to land upon some alien planet, whose flora and fauna, and botany and geology, and very climate and atmospheric parameters were totally foreign to them. The ship's noticeboards were covered with lists of figures prepared by the Schoolie and the Padre of the population and land areas of the Australian states, the average daily sunshine, differing zone times of, and distances between, major Australian cities. There were minatory warnings about over-indulgence in Australian 'plonk', the dangers of unwholesome contacts amongst the local population, and the necessity of acknowledging hospitality in the proper manner. There was even a glossary of local patois. *You beaut,* they were informed, could mean good or bad according to circumstances, as could *bonza, bobby dazzler,* and *humdinger. Ain't it a fair cow*: 'the worst has happened'. *Wouldn't it?*: shortened form of 'wouldn't it give you a pain?' or 'Wouldn't it tear you to ribbons?' *Dinkum*: all right, honest, reliable. *Dinkum oil*: straight from the horse's mouth.

'There's obviously something called Australian English,' said Skipper, as he studied the lists.

'Too right, cobber. You ignorant Pom,' somebody called from the bar.

'Look at this. They even have a special coinage. A pound is a fiddly, short for "fiddly did". Five shillings is a dollar, or an Oxford scholar, or a Caser. A bob is a deaner, sixpence is a zac, and a threepenny bit is a *trey*.'

'Stop complaining, you ruddy Pom. Be like the Sheilas: lie back and enjoy it.'

In the early morning, before they reached Sydney, the task force flew off all the aircraft that were still operational or defined as 'flyable duds'. Henry Darling led his Avengers down the coast south of Sydney to the Mobile Naval Air Base at Jervis Bay. Douglas Mayhew and Michael took the remaining Corsairs, only a dozen of them still flyable between both squadrons, to another airfield at Nowra, a few miles inland of Jervis Bay.

On board, it was odd to see so much space in the hangar, which had a kind of holiday emptiness, like a gigantic classroom after everybody had gone home. Skipper had debated whether to lead the two Corsair flights ashore himself but had decided to let Michael do it. If Michael considered himself the squadron king, then he might as well wear the secondary crown. Besides, Skipper had had more than enough of Nowra on the ship's last visit. He had been so busy working up the squadron and practising for the new tests ahead of them that he had hardly seen Sydney. He had not seen the harbour at all, having flown ashore before the ship arrived and having flown out to her after she had left.

Skipper watched from the flag-bridge, as he had done so often in the past. Like the others, he felt strange and vaguely uncomfortable in his blue uniform. The reefer jackets sat heavily on shoulders more used to shirts, and collars and ties were awkwardly restricting around unaccustomed necks. Entering and leaving harbour was beginning to afflict Skipper with a new sense of melancholy. So much had happened between visits, so many faces had gone, so many others had arrived whom he had neither the time nor any longer the interest to get to know. Over the weeks and months, the wardroom was slowly filling with strangers, who knew not Joseph. He had seen it happening without taking much notice. It was only since he had returned to the ship from Manus that he had realised how many people on board were now unfamiliar to him. But at least the guard and band had paraded on the flight deck for entering harbour, and the sailors were lining the sides in the usual way. The 'non-flyable duds' had all been ranged on deck, in short but warlike lines. As somebody on the flag-bridge said, 'We *look* fierce, anyway.'

There was an Australian lieutenant commander up there, with a disconcertingly obtrusive accent, who had taken it upon himself to act as guide and mentor.

'Y'see those cliffs over to port there? That's the Gap. There's a monument right there, with a plaque and an anchor.' He pronounced it 'pleck' and 'encher'. 'Marks the place where the troopship *Dunbar* went down in a storm in August 1857. August is the end of winter here in Australia, y'know. Every man jack on board was drowned except one. A hundred and fifty-three Poms went down there.'

Skipper gazed across at the Gap. The rocks did look mildly bleak, and even on a fine calm day such as this there was surf breaking against their feet, but otherwise it seemed a pleasant enough headland, with its red-roofed houses, green bushes and trees, and striped candy-box lighthouse. Simon Peter went up and drew the net to land full of great fishes, one hundred and fifty-three. And for all there were so many, yet was not the net broken. Skipper wondered about the one survivor.

'...his name was James Johnson. Now we're coming up to famous Sydney 'Eads. *Sydney 'Arbour.* Justly famous.'

'Eads?' said somebody on the flag-bridge.

''Eads! With a capital H. Cap'n Cook called this a small inlet. It was Cap'n Phillips who rightly discovered Sydney 'Arbour, eighteen years later.'

The cliffs on the Heads were impressive, but otherwise Skipper found himself agreeing with Captain Phillips. It certainly was a small entrance for such a magnificent interior. And, as the scenery of the harbour unfolded, it certainly was magnificent, with a kind of postcard splendour, an almost theatrical gloss. Like the Alps, like the Norfolk Broads or the better-known parts of the Lake District, it had been visited too often, photographed and stared and described by too many. Inside, there were hundreds of houses with their red roofs, more headlands of green trees and bush, tiny jetties, and scores of tiny boats, all steering out for the main channel. The task force's arrival had of course been an operational secret, but the appearance of the first grey ship off the Heads had been the signal for every small-boat owner in Sydney to put to sea.

'Watson's Bay, Parsley Bay, Vaucluse Bay, Shark Bay.' Their guide was still reeling off the names of the bays as they passed. He was quite helpful, in a grating way. Here and there, there was some variety. Some graceful white seaplanes at their moorings, a large building with a rich Victorian mulberry-coloured roof.

'Royal Sydney Golf Club,' said their tireless commentator.

To starboard a headland came suddenly, almost alarmingly, very close to the ship, so that Skipper was amazed to hear, above the noise of the ship's fans and broadcasts, the strident shrilling of millions of cicadas. It was an oddly earthy, agricultural sound to hear in a ship still under way.

'Fine example of flooded river topography. Small rivers eroded the fjord-like inlets that became inundated by a rise in the sea level caused by melting of snow and ice from the polar ice caps...'

'God, I wish somebody would bloody well come and inundate him,' said a voice from behind Skipper. 'Do we have to have this all the way in ... *wye* in, I should say.'

The ship turned to starboard and there ahead was the bridge, a great iron leap in the sky, a man-made double rainbow, as dramatic and as satisfying as it appeared in all its photographs.

'Sydney Bridge. City of Three Ours, that's us. Our Bridge, our 'Arbour, our Bradman, as we always say.'

'Bradman?' said another voice, *sotto voce*. 'D'y'know, I don't think I've ever heard of him.'

'Just ahead now, we've got Fort Denison.' It was a grim-looking little island in the middle of the harbour, with concrete banks, resembling a miniature version of Corregidor.

'Pinchgut, it was called. It was fortified during the Crimean War, when we thought the Russkis were going to invade us.'

That, Skipper thought, was an interesting revelation. So the Great War was not the first global war. As long ago as the 1850s there had been a fear of Russian attack, even down here in Sydney.

'Used to be for the solitary confinement of criminals…'

'But I thought you were *all* criminals in those days, old boy?'

The further they went up the harbour, the taller became the houses and the closer they grew together, until a true city had established itself on the southern shore, with a skyline of skyscrapers as incredible as New York. When the bridge was so close that its girders seemed actually to hang above the watchers, the ship saluted Admiralty House to starboard and almost at once turned to port, lining up for her berth alongside Garden Island. Several ships were already there and beyond the first roofs was the fighting top of a battleship, in the great graving dock. Skipper remembered one of the lectures he had attended at Greenwich. How much better might it have been, as the worthy professor had argued, to have made the main naval base in the Far East here in Sydney, instead of Singapore?

'Woolloomooloo,' said the Australian voice.

Skipper stayed up on the flag-bridge for some time after the ship had been secured alongside, so long in fact that he was the last to leave by some twenty minutes. By then, the bridge and sea watches had fallen out, the lights on all the instruments had been extinguished and all the pointers had sunk back to zero. The action broadcast was silent, but that had been replaced by an almost incessant babbling from the ship's main broadcast. The bosun's mate was announcing the names and titles of unfamiliar personages who must already have come aboard.

Skipper stared down the sheer starboard side of the island, at the corresponding activity on the jetty. Already, four wide gangways had been lifted into place and an unbroken procession of figures was passing up and down them. Already, the ship was tied to the shore by a score of wires and hawsers, criss-crossing forward and aft. As Skipper watched, further fuelling pipes and electrical power cables were being hauled on board. A large crane, travelling on rails, had just lifted out the first of the non-flyable duds and deposited it upon the back of a long motor-driven trailer. Large official cars with flags flying from their bonnets came and went, their passings marked by bugle calls and bursts of band music from the loudspeakers, sounding like a giant wireless set tuned at random to some faraway station. An Australian voice had taken over the broadcast, to explain some apparently knotty points of procedure about the British Centre, the shore rest and recreation facility for the ship's company. The Australians, and especially the Australian girls, it seemed, were all prepared to engage the fleet. *You beauts*, thought Skipper.

A sound-powered telephone on the far bulkhead gave a faint phantom wail and, as the only person present, Skipper answered it.

'That you, Skipper? You still up there?' It was Wings. 'Mustn't get moody, you know. Look, we've got a lady reporter on board, from an Australian women's magazine. Wants to interview a fighter pilot from the fleet. You've been chosen from thousands of applicants. Can you get down to the wardroom?'

'I don't think that's much in my style…'

'She's all agog, Skipper. Quite good-looking too, like a kind of cuddly kangaroo … We'll expect you in five minutes. Don't let the Old Country down, you ruddy *Pom*.'

The wardroom bar had just opened for the pre-lunch session, and the anteroom was already beginning to fill up. Skipper saw her sitting at the far end, beside the fireplace, with the Commander and Wings. It was curiously incongruous, like having a cocktail party in a gun-turret, to see females in the wardroom after it had been such a purely masculine, functional compartment for so long. She was wearing a crisp green-and-white striped dress, and she had red hair, with some freckles over the bridge of her nose. She was, as they said, quite good-looking in an unalarming way.

'Here we are. Evadne, meet Skipper, our most intrepid birdman. Skipper, this is Evadne Marshall.'

Evadne, Skipper thought. *That* is *a fine old Australian name.*

'Hi, and how do you do, Skipper?' She had a noticeable but not jarring Australian accent. When she shook hands, Skipper was surprised by the strength of her grip, like a chief stoker's. She had a glass of orange squash or juice of some kind.

'Is that stuff strong enough for you?' he said, as he sat down.

'Quite strong enough, when I'm working.'

'What newspaper is this?'

'Magazine. *New Australian Woman?*' She had a way of ending the occasional statement with an interrogative upturn in the tone of her voice, making it into a question.

Skipper blinked. 'Is there a new Australian woman?'

''Deedy, yes. Features, articles, fashion of course, radio programmes, bit of sport. Agony column?'

'Golly, do I come under the agony column?'

'Not unless you want to.'

Wings had come back from the bar with a glass of gin and bitters for Skipper. 'Nothing confidential, Skipper,' he said. 'This is unclassified, so nothing secret or confidential. This is a family magazine, isn't it, Evadne?'

''Deedy, yes.'

'I'll leave you to it.'

'Cheers,' said Skipper. 'Down with the Poms.'

'Hear, hear. Is this the first time you've ever been interviewed?'

Skipper was about to say yes when he remembered the newspaper in the United States, after Joe had killed himself. The squadron's first loss, during the very early days of type-training on Corsairs. 'Not quite the first time.'

But she had already noticed the hesitation. 'Was there something about that newspaper interview? I see you hesitated just a little?'

This, as Skipper now saw, was going to be much more of a contest than he had expected. It was already obvious that she was professionally quick to notice a hesitation or a change in the tone of voice, to go on with a supplementary question prompted by the injudiciously added word. It struck him that she would make a good debriefer. Women's magazines might, in his previous opinion, be the lowest form of mental life, but this one's representative clearly deserved respect.

'What do you think of Australia?'

'Oh, marvellous.'

'I'll write that down. *Skipper thinks Australia is marvellous.*'

'I'm sorry. I should be trying harder with this.'

'No, no, no, *don't* try harder. That would be fatal.'

'I say marvellous, I've hardly ever seen any of it. I was working up a new squadron…'

'Was that hard work?'

'Bloody hard work.'

'Tell me how you do it.'

'Well, I can't really, it would take too long.'

'I've got lots of time?'

'Yes, but it comes a little too close to being confidential stuff...'

'I've got it. What did you do before you joined the Navy, Skipper?'

He told her about Daughton, about his home, about Oxford. Slowly, and much against his will, he found himself beginning to relax and enjoy such close questioning about himself. There was a seductive appeal, impossible to resist, in such intense professional interest in his background and family history. Father always made a point of having his hand read in the fortune-teller's tent at the Daughton annual church fete down in the village. Although everybody said it was a waste of time and everybody knew it was only Miss Dunnage, Father always said it was worth a bob of anybody's money 'just to have somebody talk about me for five minutes'. Father was quite right, and this was like having one's palm read by an expert who knew her business.

'Are you married, Skipper? Girl at home?'

He shook his head. Of course there had been girls at home, of an experimental kind, and there were the Wrens one met. But they always clamoured too hard after aircrew, as though competing for a limited number of parts in some glorious long-running musical. There had been Wrens in Ceylon, although he had never managed to have any particular success himself. He had heard of a fabulous all-female compound, somewhere outside Kandy, with no less than 500 FANYs. Edward, who was always the squadron's womaniser, claimed to have been there.

'Would you say you were a public-school type?'

He recognised that there might be an edge to the question. 'I suppose I must be. I certainly went to one, if that's what you mean.'

'How much land does your father own?'

Skipper blinked again. There was nothing like being direct. 'About 2,000 acres.'

He expected some reaction, but, when it came, it was totally unexpected. 'My father owns 200,000. Down south, between here and the Snowy.'

'Good God. So you don't come from Sydney?'

'Oh, yes. 'Deedy, yes. I was born here. This is my town. By the way, it's not good etiquette here in Australia to ask a man how much land he's got. It's like asking him how much money he's got in the bank.'

'Well, then, why did you ask me?'

'Because I wanted to know how much money you had in the bank.' She had taken out a large notebook from a bag slung over her shoulder. 'What's it like?'

'What's what like?' he said, although he knew very well what she was leading up to.

'Over there. Over Japanese territory. The enemy.'

'*Well…*' Nothing confidential, they said. But it was *all* confidential. It was all secret, so secret one dare not tell anybody, although it was always there like the dark space above the top of the stairs, on the landing, where one would never go alone as a child after nanny had gone. It was hard enough to explain it at debriefing, where they at least spoke the same language and were professionally concerned to find the truth. But, as he had already decided, maybe this girl would make a good debriefer.

'It's difficult to put words to it, to a woman, if you'll excuse my saying so…'

'Try me?'

Did she get her kicks from this sort of thing, he wondered. There were women who loved the smell of blood on the clothing. *Give me the daggers.*

'Well ... actually you forget what it's like between sorties, but once you get back, it all comes back to you...'

'Like having a baby. Or so I've been told, I should say.'

'Just as though you'd never been away. It's terrifying, and yet it's exciting. In some ways it's very scary indeed, and yet it's all so quick. We're talking about matters of seconds only. A few feet up or down, a few seconds early or late. One attack, one run only, and then maybe nothing more at that place for two days.'

She was writing in her notebook now, the shorthand hieroglyphics flowing swiftly and apparently fluently across the pages, which she flipped over, one by one as they were filled, with a practised thumb.

'Are you a good shot?'

'Yes ... I can say that. I am a good shot.'

'Have you ever shot anybody down? A Japanese?'

'Yes.'

'What did that feel like?'

'Again, exciting. Yet somehow predictable. It was one of the few things in life that was exactly as you expected it to be.'

'You mean some things did *not* live up to expectations?'

'Well ... Yes, I suppose...' He paused. Was there a hint of sexual appeal there?

'It's my impression, Skipper, that you're bloody good at it.'

'Why? Why do you think that?' Even from a casual remark from a woman journalist, something professionally valuable might be gleaned. She might artlessly point out some way a man could survive.

'I don't know really.' She was clearly abashed by his sudden riposte. 'You just seem to me to be the type?'

'What type? How many of us have you known?'

'None. None at all, before now. I just think … you just seem a little sad, when you talk about it?'

'I *am* sad. It *is* sad.'

The roar of voices from the crowded bar was now obtrusive. There were many strange faces in the crowd. Some of them were Australian officers, some Australian Wrens. All looked curiously down at Evadne, where she sat with her notebook underneath the portraits of the King and Queen either side of the fireplace. One particular Australian pushed himself through the crush. He was wearing a checked suit, like a bookmaker, and he had leather straps across his chest, raw cheekbones and the rawest Australian accent Skipper had ever heard. The man jutted his chin out at Evadne.

'Beneath the Southern Cross we stand!' he bellowed. 'United in our Mother Land! Austryelia! *Whacko!*'

'Ah, it's Kimbo, my photographer. I was wondering where he'd got to.'

Kimbo thrust a great hand forward. 'G'day, sport.'

For some reason, Skipper suddenly felt protective towards Evadne. 'Look, shall we go up to the flight deck or somewhere? Much more space and light there for pictures.'

'Good on yer, sport. We'll follow you.'

At the top of the first ladder, Skipper had to turn and wait. He was surprised to find how far behind the others had already fallen. He realised he was used to these ladders and passageways, being up and down them many times a day. But strangers found them steep going. Kimbo was already complaining. 'Hold on, sport. You trying to win the Melbourne Cup? Cor, this is like a bloody Pommy obstacle race.'

As they walked along, Skipper looked over the port outboard side automatically, from force of habit. He had grown used to noticing what was happening to the ship, who was alongside, who was passing to and fro. It was all part of what his squadron called his 'regular RN syndrome'. Skipper saw that there was a gash-barge of some sort alongside, and just astern of it a sailor was sculling the little skiff he had picked up in Manus. It had SKIPPER painted on its pert little counter. The Chief Bosun's Mate had welcomed the skiff for his side party. Their usual copper punt had been melted down in one of the suicide bombers' attacks.

When they reached the flight deck, Skipper himself was taken aback by the change which had come over it in the short interval since he left the island. Already there were stores, and piles of packing cases, stacked in rows. Aircraft were being manhandled towards the big crane. Dockyard workmen with pneumatic drills were attacking the temporary cement which had repaired the flight deck after the impact of the kamikazes. The arrestor wires had been coiled away. There was the flash and glare of acetylene burners at the base of one safety barrier stanchion, which had been damaged in a flight-deck mishap early on in the operations. The island passageway outside the ACR was crowded with men, and a mess of tangled electric cables. In a few minutes the flight deck had been changed from a smooth, polished war platform into a mixture of a builder's and a ship-breaking yard, where roadworks and gas-main repairs had simultaneously begun.

But Kimbo was thrilled by the flight deck, and ecstatic when Skipper fetched a leather flying helmet from the ready room and posed in the cockpit of a Corsair. The aircraft was a non-flyable dud, with no engine and a tailplane badly damaged by flak. It had been cannibalised for spare parts for other aircraft and was just about to go over the side. But Kimbo was entranced by it and gleefully capered about to find the best photographic angle.

'Pommy pilot ready to take off on a strike against the Nips!' he yelled delightedly, scribbling the information in a grubby little notebook. 'What a caption! Poms against the Rising Sun!'

Skipper looked resignedly at Evadne. In war the first casualty was always the truth.

'Can we have one or two more?'

Kimbo took Skipper seated and standing, bare-headed and leather-helmeted, grinning and serious, standing against the sky, standing against the island, standing against Sydney Bridge. He patted his camera with satisfaction.

'That's just fine. I'll get on now. G'day, sport.'

'Just one thing. You'll have to show your film to the censor on the C-in-C's press staff.'

'Yep, I know them. G'day, sport.'

Kimbo leaped down off the flight deck on to a sponson which had no exit, or any ladder downwards. They could hear him scrambling about and swearing down there. 'Bloody Pommy bastard Pommy bastard bloody Pommy *ship...*'

Skipper stopped one of his own squadron ratings who was passing by. 'Here, Willoughby, can you show the photographer down to the gangway?'

Kimbo reappeared on the flight deck, all smiles. 'Lead on, MacPom!' He went off with all his equipment dangling and clinking and clanking behind him.

Evadne had been looking around the flight deck while Kimbo was putting on his performance.

'What about all these things, Skipper?'

Skipper showed her round, explaining the purpose of the fittings and the platforms and the machinery and the places the men stood. There were workmen all over the place, but still he tried to communicate to her something of the flight deck's dangers, its urgency, its atmosphere, its occasional embarrassments and its rituals and its pantomime. It was like trying to describe a stage to someone who had never seen a play, but Evadne made a good audience.

'You're really interested in all this, aren't you, Skipper?'

'Of course I am. I have to be. It's my best way of surviving.'

'I meant something more than that. You're interested in it as a way of life, aren't you?'

'I suppose I could be.' He could now begin to follow the pattern of her questions. She had, it seemed, built up a rapid mental image of him on first meeting and all her questions had been intended to flesh out, to justify, that first conception. Certainly it was one way of conducting an interview, and certainly there might be some truth in it.

'Tell me — you're used to meeting people and summing them up. You know I'm only in this as long as the war lasts. From what you've seen, do you think I should stay on afterwards?'

He had expected her to prevaricate, but her reply was startingly certain. 'Yes, I do. I think, as I said, you'll be very good at it.'

'Well, I must say, that's definite enough.'

'You'll find us very definite in Australia.' She looked at her watch. 'Look, you say you haven't seen much of Sydney. I'll show you something. This is my town. Perhaps we can continue the interview then.'

'Oh, dear.' Skipper found that prospect unexpectedly depressing. Even the pleasure of taking a girl out for the evening was darkened by his profession. The war was going to follow him ashore. But still, there was an old and true naval rule that gift horses should never be looked in the mouth when visiting foreign ports.

'What do you have in mind?'

'I've to go back to the office now. There's an office car I can borrow. Say I come back and pick you up here and show you some of Sydney. What time?'

'Bar opens on board here at six.'

CHAPTER FOURTEEN

'You're a jammy bastard, Skipper, d'you know that?'

'I am, aren't I, sir? But so are we all, all jammy bastards. We've got it made. All lying before us. Sydney, goddamn.'

Skipper loved to see the wardroom in such good form as it was that evening. Over the months of the last year, at sea and in harbour, on hectic days and on slack, he had come to enjoy wardroom life more and more. He had grown more and more sensitive to the shades of its humours, to the balance and individual flavour of its personalities. The wardroom's moods could swing violently, from a stag party to a funeral wake, and indeed it had staged both more than once. Its individuals, too, had their moods and officers could often tell at a glance who was up and who was down. Tonight, it seemed, everybody was up.

Skipper particularly admired the skilful way in which the Commander, as President of the Mess, led his temperamental flock. He had the wisdom of Solomon, the presence of Jove and the humour of Puck. He handled the aircrews with an especially delicate touch. Skipper well remembered the first mess dinner of the commission, a rare event in wartime, and liable at any time to become a trial of strength, a direct clash of wills, between the President and the wilder members of the mess. At one point, one pilot had let off a thunder-flash. When the deafening noise had died away, and end of the table was once more visible in the clearing smoke, the whole wardroom had fallen silent at the sound of the Commander's gavel. Breathlessly, they all waited for his reaction. 'Gentlemen,' he said, pausing for the full theatrical effect, 'you may now smoke.' The great shout of relief and laughter and admiration which went up confirmed once and for all the Commander's grip on the wardroom mess. Skipper had watched and listened, and noted the psychological sleight of hand for possible future reference. Now, he could see, the Commander himself was revelling in the atmosphere of anticipation in the wardroom.

'Have you ever noticed, Skipper, how the first night into a place generally sets the tone for the whole visit?'

'I hadn't actually, sir, but if that's true, then this one should be a cracker!'

'Look at those noticeboards. Hanging with invitations already. Digger hospitality. There's nobody like them when it comes to pushing the boat out. I think everybody on board deserves a bit of a holiday. Nice to see some wenches on board, too, for a change. When's yours supposed to be turning up, Skipper?'

Skipper looked at his wristwatch. 'She's adrift now, as a matter of fact, sir. I've asked the quarterdeck to let me know when she arrives.'

She was nearly an hour late, but she made no apology and Skipper was left to assume that her work had delayed her. She was, he noticed, still wearing the same dress but she had added some fresh, bright and rather garish lipstick which clashed somewhat with her hair. She also asked for orange squash again. So, Skipper thought, she was still working.

He was amused by the way a circle of unattached officers soon closed in on them, and they became the centre of a crowd. He was less amused when he noticed she was still studying him closely as he talked to others and introduced people to her. It annoyed him to know that she was observing him in his natural habitat, as though he were some rare specimen of animal, moving, feeding, resting and, if possible, mating. Was she, he wondered, also a sexual *voyeur*? *Voyeuse*, should it be?

'What shall we do this evening?' The crowd at the bar was thinning, as some went ashore and others went in to eat supper.

'Will you put yourself in my hands?'

'Love to. What are your hands like?'

'*Now*, then. We'll go to one or two places I know? See a bit of Sydney? As I said, it's my town. Meet some people, have a few drinks and a few laughs?'

'Sounds OK.'

When they reached the quarterdeck, it was dark outside. Looking up, Skipper could see the bright red tracery, glowing against the indigo sky, of the warning lights on the giant radio aerials above the city. From where he stood, he could hear the hum of city traffic and pick out the bulk of its mysterious skyline. It was odd to stand for a moment on the quarterdeck where he had stood so many times alone at sea, and hear and see a great city now only a stone's throw away.

It was one of the best feelings in the Navy, to step ashore on a fine cool evening, dressed in your best, with fresh foreign notes in your pocket, and a strange, foreign, exciting city, a new world, all before you. Better still, to have a girl *and* a car. As the Commander had said, a jammy bastard indeed.

She had an old battered Ford saloon, with books and papers all over the back seats. 'It's the office car. Everybody drives it. Would you like to drive?'

'Do you know, I can't? I haven't got a licence.' He was ashamed to admit it. Somehow it seemed absurd, to be able to drive a fighter aeroplane but not a car. 'I was just learning before I joined up. I never really had the need for a car in those days.'

'Didn't you have tractors on your place?'

'One. One only. Brand new. My father just got it a few days before I joined the Navy. We're still based on the horse on our farms, you know.'

'Oh, well. Hop in, then.'

She drove off boldly and confidently, turned up the hill towards the British Centre, and then right for the main city. Skipper was impressed by the size and prosperity of the buildings. Here was a city hanging on the edge of the world, where the sun was in the *north* at midday. Even Herodotus said he did not believe the Phoenicians when they said they saw the sun on the wrong hand. Here in the Antipodes, literally poles apart, they had winter in mid-summer. But here he was, driving along with a girl at his side.

They crossed a square with large olive-black trees in its centre. There were trams in the middle of the street. A row of bushy palms stood at regular intervals along one side. At the corner, Skipper saw a statue of an imposing-looking gentleman with his hand on his hip, nonchalantly posed, and then a very large foul anchor and a cannon.

'What's that there? That anchor?'

'That,' she said, without looking, 'probably came from some ship that wrecked itself on Australia. The people who've run into Australia, you wouldn't believe. It's not as if it isn't big enough. Why don't they look where they're going?'

That, Skipper thought, was certainly an original comment on the ancient art of haven-finding. He made up his mind to remember to put it to the Navigating Officer.

'All those trees on the right there, that's Hyde Park. That's the ANZAC Memorial, only you can't see it because it's too dark. It's got a dome on top of it and inside the dome there are 120,000 gold stars, one for each member of the forces from New South Wales who enlisted in the Great War.'

'You'll need another one when this is all over.'

'Too right.'

Skipper watched the names of the shops gliding by, and the occasional hoardings advertising war savings, or beer, or hair lotion. To his eyes, after so long at sea, the processions of colour and letters slid by incomprehensibly, like part of the scenery of a dream.

Evadne suddenly braked, so sharply the brakes squealed and she cursed. 'Bloody Poms! Some of your sailors, Skipper.'

They were indeed sailors, lurching across in the middle of the traffic. They had clearly been looking upon the native Australian beer when it was a very gory colour indeed.

'Oh, dear. Oh, dear.'

'I wonder if the Japs know what's coming to them?'

Skipper had been growing aware of Sydney Bridge as they approached it. He saw it first as a dramatic backdrop, like a gigantic spider's web, at the end of one canyon-like street. At the end of the next street it was much nearer, so that he could see the lights of traffic streaming across it. Then, before Skipper was properly aware of how close they were, Evadne was driving down a broad dual carriageway road and out on to the bridge. He tried to look down to see the ships below Woolloomooloo, but the bridge was too broad. It really was a monster creation, with its great girders swinging past overhead one by one, like the strides of a metal ogre in his seven-league boots. They drove on the left-hand side of the road, Skipper noticed, with a thought for Commander Leintwardine.

'It's got six lanes of traffic,' said Evadne. 'Two tramlines and two railway tracks. And two footpaths for those who want to hike it.'

'Quite impressive.'

'*Quite impressive?* You supercilious Pom.' Her Australian accent had deepened and thickened. 'It's the biggest bloody bridge and the best in the whole world, mate.'

'Sorry. Tell me, where are we going?'

'A place I know on Manly Beach.'

'Is that near Bondi beach?'

'You've heard of Bondi?'

'I've heard of the girls that are supposed to be there.'

'You won't need to go to Bondi, I can guarantee that, my little cookie.'

'Oh, I say, jolly good,' said Skipper in his most determinedly English accent.

They were speeding down broad roads, with little traffic, lined on either side with large prosperous-looking houses. But for the exotic shapes of the palm trees in the gardens, and the same trilling of a million cicadas whenever the car slowed down enough for Skipper to hear them, they might have been driving through the posher parts of Bournemouth or Dulwich.

'I must say, I'm beginning to be impressed by Sydney.'

'Ah, it's a great city. The best.'

Evadne stopped the car in a space beside the sea, and when Skipper got out he saw they were under a row of huge trees whose branches, like a gloomy ceiling, stretched to right and left as far as Skipper could see in the darkness.

'They come from Norfolk Island,' Evadne said. 'Norfolk Island pines. Some nutter planted them to keep the sun off.'

Skipper stood looking at the great clear sweep of the beach. So powerful were his memories of the beaches at home in

England, with their barbed-wire barricades, pill-boxes and rows of concrete anti-landing-craft obstacles, that this free beach — like those he had seen in South Africa and Ceylon — still came as a surprise. He watched the dim shape of a long wave, curling and breaking successively all along its crest, and heard the sound of its collapse and the following sucking and hissing as the waters withdrew. These were sounds one never heard at sea. This was a landsman's, a holidaymaker's, view of the sea, here where it ended and merged with the land.

'There are sharks around these beaches, aren't there?'

'They put up nets at certain times. You do have to be careful, but it's generally shark-proof.'

'Yes, but do the *sharks* know it's shark-proof?'

'Probably they do, but being Australian sharks they take no notice.'

Evadne's tone of voice had suggested that the place they were going to was something out of the ordinary, to be anticipated, but the club was only a beach hut set under the trees, or rather four or five huts put together to make a long, low building split into sections, with a bar at the end nearest the door and compartments linked by a central passageway. Evadne had crossed the sand towards it with a confident air, but at the threshold she stopped, as though someone had just flung cold water in her face.

'Here,' she said, 'this isn't the Mugsy's we used to know and love. This has changed hands since I was here last. Why didn't I know about that?'

Even to Skipper, a stranger to Australia, it was obvious what kind of bar Evadne had taken him to. There was not another woman in sight. Most of the men there were carefully and neatly dressed in dark sober suits, but the rest all had a touch of the exotic: the flash of an ostentatious signet ring, a pearl tie-pin thrust between the points of a gaudily coloured shirt, tasselled laces in yellow leather moccasin shoes.

'Whatever happened to Mugsy?' Evadne asked the flaxen-haired barman.

'Gone back to the big city, Miss.'

'Don't call me *Miss*.' She turned to Skipper. 'We might as well have one while we're here.'

There was only wine to drink, Australian white wine, served chilled in half bottles. As Evadne said, the licensing laws in Australia were '*très* crook' and one had to drink what one could where and when one could. Skipper found it very palatable. Evadne herself still drank juice, as she was still, evidently, working.

The atmosphere was not hostile to women, but it certainly was not welcoming. 'I'll be honest,' said Evadne. 'I don't like this place. They make me feel anxious.'

Skipper himself was as keen to go, but for another reason. Glancing through the space in the partition to the next-door compartment, he had seen Michael sitting with Richard Trumble. They were talking to another fair-haired man and a much smaller man with a wizened, simian face. Skipper wondered about Richard Trumble. The beaches might or might not be shark-proof, but the bars were not. Michael must have got transport back from Nowra and had not reported back on board, or if he had, he had not bothered to find Skipper. That was behaviour unlike Michael. To antagonise one's Squadron CO was the act of a lunatic or a very brave man. A fighter pilot needed all the friends, all the assistance, he could get. Maybe Michael had grown, as the Captain had hinted, past caring. Possibly his splendid technique, his impeccable attention to detail, his compleat professional approach, were all crumbling.

'I was watching you there, back on board.' Evadne never strayed far from her main theme.

'I know you were.'

'Yes, well, it is my job, you understand. You love it, don't you, all the business of being a Fleet Air Arm pilot, the whole thing — you adore it, don't you? I always believe in first impressions, and the moment I laid eyes on you I knew you didn't look like a part-timer.'

'Good God, we're none of us part-timers...'

'I know. You didn't look like the reservist type, I meant. You looked the part. You looked like one of them.'

'How can you tell? You say you've never seen any of us before?'

'I don't know how I know. All I know is I know the real thing when I see it. What is it you like about them?'

'I think it's ... I suppose it's their confidence. The way they all seem to know each other from years back. They always have a proper Navy way of doing things which they all know about from experience, *long* experience, hundreds of years of experience, and it's always the best way. They all seem to wake every morning knowing all about it. They're much quicker to learn than anybody ever gives them credit for. Not Colonel Blimp types at all. They didn't know much about aircraft, for instance, when the war broke out, but by God, they do now!'

Skipper thought of the Captain's advice about Michael. Undoubtedly he should have got rid of him, for Michael's own good if nothing else.

'What's the matter?'

'Nothing's the matter.'

'You've gone all sad again.'

'Have I?' Skipper carefully leaned back on his stool, afraid that at any moment Michael might see him. The encounter would be more ammunition for Evadne.

'Let's try somewhere else. Do you like Chinese food?'

'Anything. I'm in your hands.'

Outside, Evadne jerked her head at the door they had just left.

'I doubt if that place'll be there long. Our police are pretty hot on that. It must be new because I'd never even heard of it.'

Skipper thought it even more remarkable that Michael had managed to find himself such sympathetic surroundings so quickly, literally within hours of landing upon a strange continent. He was more than ever glad that there had no sign of recognition.

So, once again, they went bowling back down the roads they had come, until they reached the bridge again.

'Can you drive in the left-hand lane, please? I want to see if I can pick out the ship.'

After a pause to find his bearings and to realise which ships he was looking at he saw her, tiny at that distance but surprisingly solid and three-dimensional, the flight deck a greyish sandstone colour in that light.

'See her?'

'Yes, I've got her. It's rather like the view of her you get when you're circling around overhead waiting to come on.'

She took up the point at once, just as he had feared she would, to ask him what his sensations were while approaching the flight deck. Skipper was vexed by his own inability apparently to talk normally to a woman. He seemed to have slipped out of the way of it, being alternately at a baffled loss or irritated by her persistence. It annoyed him that she kept on returning to the subject of his work and his life on board in such a clinical manner. He was a specimen still, rather than a male personality in his own right. He suspected she might not even bother to keep him company if it were not for her magazine story. It was insulting to be reminded that she was on business, still drinking squash.

'Are you going to go on drinking that? Wouldn't you like some of the hard stuff?'

'I don't think you can get anything except this or tea here.'

They were sitting opposite each other, looking across a small table which was crowded with plates and bowls and cups and receptacles, all the panoply of a Chinese meal in full plenary session. It was curious, Skipper reflected, that everywhere east of Suez all the western-style cooking tasted oriental and all the Chinese cooking tasted as it did in England.

'Tell me, Evadne, do you have a boyfriend?'

'That's getting personal.'

'Well, blow me, you've been getting pretty personal with me!'

'Fair enough. Naaah…' She wrinkled her nose. 'I don't have anybody right now. It's very difficult in my job anyway. You keep on having to stand people up. There used to be a chap. He was in the army.'

'Was?'

'Probably still is. I haven't heard from him for months. *Years.* He went to Papua. The Kokoda Trail. The Golden Staircase over the mountain. You ever heard of it?'

Skipper shook his head, knowing very well he was about to provoke a violent reaction.

'Cor.' She sucked her teeth disgustedly. 'Ruddy *Poms.* Anything that happens outside the North Sea, you don't want to know about it.'

'Oh, of course, I remember now. The name just didn't mean anything at first.'

Skipper was now coming to have a clearer idea of what was bothering him about Evadne. In his pride, he was not used to such offhand treatment. At home, a Fleet Air Arm pilot had a certain glamour. For any English girl, a pilot from the fleet would have an interest heightened by sexual attraction. His dangerous profession, his uniform, his acknowledged short expectancy of life, contrasted with the age-old traditions of his Service, all combined to give aircrew a status only remotely connected with their own physical appearance or native intelligence. But Evadne clearly took a different and typically antipodean stance, in which a respect for the Mother Country, as they called it, was very much tempered by disrespect for its citizens. In other words, Evadne had a peculiarly Australian capacity for venerating England whilst at the same time deriding Poms.

In an effort to impress her somehow, Skipper found himself telling her the story of a particularly harrowing deck-landing crash from the early days. It was hardly dinner-party conversation, he acknowledged, but desperate measures were needed. A young pilot from another squadron was doing his first series of deck landings. Skipper, himself newly joined, was goofing from the round gallery at the after end of the island. The lad made a good landing and took the first wire correctly. Then, by a thousand to once chance, the arrester hook as it flailed the flight deck picked up a second wire. Subjected to twice the retarding force, the hook was strained beyond its designed limits and either straightened or broke out. The Corsair still had considerable speed and momentum and careered out of control across the flight deck, where it crashed into an eight-barrelled pompom mounting just below Skipper and blew up. The blast and flames scorched Skipper's eyebrows and the front lock of his hair, and singed his nose and cheekbones. Down below, the pilot died. The guns' crew, an ordnance artificer who happened to be there, and two aircraft handlers standing nearby, all died.

At times, Skipper could still see and hear that accident, and feel the soreness of his face, as though it had just happened. It was by far the worst he had ever seen or read or heard about. The memory lay in the back of his mind always,, with the knowledge that he or any of his colleagues might also end like that. That possibility lurked on a flight deck every time he flew towards one. He might forget it for weeks and then, one day, as he taxied past that part of the island, the sensation of it would come back. He knew that Michael had also seen it and the memory haunted him, too, in his black moments. Skipper made up his mind that, officially, he had not seen Michael ashore that evening.

Skipper despised himself for telling the story. It was a cheap way of trying to impress a woman, the kind of ploy a greenhorn pilot with freshly shipped wings would use. Surely he at his time of life did not need such tactics? However, it did have one desired effect.

'That's really terrible,' said Evadne. 'I can see that in your face. I think we've talked enough about flying and flight decks for a bit, don't you? Let's get on.'

As Evadne said, Sydney was her town, but even so she moved in it with what seemed to Skipper an extraordinary surefootedness, which would have been surprising in England and was astounding in Australia. Sydney night life in wartime reminded Skipper very much of the West End of London, but he had seen enough of Australian society to know that it was rigidly and unashamedly a man's world. Australian men, he could see, did not regard conversation with women as conversation at all in the true sense but merely chatter, like the crackling of thorns under a pot. An Australian talked to his mates, his *male* mates. In a society where a woman on her own was not only surpassingly brave but almost unique, Evadne seemed to have acquaintances in every club and to recognise familiar faces at every bar. Americans in uniform, with names like 'Scottie' and 'Marvin' and 'Junior', embraced her whilst casting an appraising look over Skipper. One of them actually remarked 'You making time with Limeys now, 'Vadne?'

In one club, one of those who embraced Evadne was Tucker. He had a friend with him, whom he introduced. Skipper did not catch the name and did not bother to have it repeated. It sounded like Bolger, and Bolger was unmistakably what Father would have called a base-wallah, one of those who also served wherever it was safest to do so. Bolger had the base-wallah's self-justifying aggressiveness towards those recently returned from active service.

'One of the death-or-glory boys, eh?' he said to Skipper.

'Hardly,' said Skipper, forcing a smile. 'In fact neither, actually.'

'So you're one of those we keep reading about who's winning the war for us…'

'Yes, and I'm doing it singlehandedly, too,' said Skipper, determined to keep it light.

'Just like Errol Flynn.'

'Yes, I sometimes give him a hand. Just as you do here in Sydney.'

It was the ancient tension between those who fought in the line and those who stayed behind. Every now and again those who stayed felt the urge to prove themselves and the best way was to measure themselves against a returned fighting man. But Skipper was resolved not to be drawn into the argument he knew the base-wallah was aching to have. As Mrs

Fleetwood used to say to her sister about Daughton village gossip, 'Rise above it, dear, rise above it.'

All the same, Skipper was very tempted. Some day, some time, somebody was going to have to put Bolger in his place.

'But for these vile guns,' Skipper murmured, *'he would himself have been a soldier.'*

To his astonishment, Tucker recognised the line. '*And twixt his finger and his thumb he held a pouncet-box, which ever and anon he gave his nose and took it away again.* That's very good, Skipper. You'd better look out 'Vadne, this man's not just a bone-headed flyer. I expect he's just as good in bed, too.'

Evadne turned sharply, with a bright wary glance, as though waiting for some further movement. Skipper knew that expression exactly, that unblinking beady eye: it was that of a hen pheasant when the keeper came into her pen, calculating whether to run or stand. Even the line of her forearm reminded Skipper of a pheasant's poised leg stopped in mid-stride.

'Have you decided to switch to the hard stuff yet, Evadne?' It was not in fact hard spirits but Australian beer, drunk ice-cold out of tiny pony glasses.

'No, not yet. Let's go see if we can find Mugsy's.'

They found Mugsy's on the third floor of an old warehouse on the road back to Woolloomooloo. There was a bar and tables, a piano and a space which might be a dance floor. Behind the bar was — Skipper presumed — Mugsy himself, a grossly fat man with black sweat marks under his armpits, who looked like an Italian and spoke like an American. There was the same cold beer to drink, but Evadne was still working.

'The pianist's name is Mike,' she said. 'He says he's an abo.'

'What's an abo?'

'Aborigine. The original Aussies. The old native people of Australia who still live out in the bush, most of them.'

At the nearest table, Skipper suddenly recognised Chief Air Rigger Petre.

'Like to join us, sir?'

Skipper hesitated, but Evadne accepted the offer at once. Petre was with four other senior air chief petty officers, one from Douglas Mayhew's squadron, one from the Avengers, and two more from the ship's air department. They were, as Skipper realised, five of the most important men in the ship. If this table were blown up, a most serious blow would have been dealt to the ship's war potential. The five of them had the easy, companionable air of men who had known each other for a very long time, as Skipper knew they had. They had also, he could see, been drinking together that night for a very long time.

'Good evening, Miss.'

'Don't call me *Miss*.'

'Ah, but you're with one of the pigs now. That makes you Miss.'

'What a snobby lot you Poms are!'

'That's the way our world goes. We're a democratic navy. Half the ship for the pigs, half for the lads. That's democracy.'

'Doesn't sound it to me. What do you boys think of Sydney?'

'Hasn't changed much, except the prices have gone up.'

'You been here before, then?'

They had all been to Sydney before, in various ships during the Thirties. All five of them had served a commission in the Far East in the old carrier *Eagle*. It was, by their account, a romantic period, of hunts for Chinese pirates, and chases after drug smugglers, and ordinary seamen consumed by sharks, and ships driven ashore by typhoons, and runs ashore in Hong Kong and Yokohama and Singapore and the Fiji Islands.

As he listened to them, Skipper became aware that Evadne was paying professional attention to him again. She had observed him talking to other officers. Now she was watching him talking to the ship's company. She was also, he found, talking to Chief Air Rigger Petre about him.

'Oh, yes, he's one of them all right, Miss.' Petre grinned at Skipper, without malice. 'He's a pig all right. Through and through. Talks like it, acts like it, thinks like it. Never you mind, sir. I'm actually paying you a compliment, after a fashion.'

'But it's still not a very complimentary name for people, is it — *pigs*?' Evadne said.

'Suits 'em. Mind you, we don't object. Officers, *pigs*, in their place, us in ours. That's the way the world goes best. With some of these RNVR officers you don't know whether you're coming or going. The pre-war way was best. That was the best system.'

Pre-war. It was like the proclamation of a vintage. Even so, Skipper thought privately, it was very unlikely indeed that the Navy would return to its old ways after the war. The old deference, the old divide, would never come back, whatever Chief Air Rigger Petre might think.

'You remember —' they were back on the trail of their reminiscences again — 'you remember that time when the *Furious* and the *Courageous* and the *Glorious* was all together in Grand Harbour all at the same time? All the ship's air departments went on a run ashore...'

'Yes, down the Gut...'

'The Gyppo Queen!'

'The Galvanized Donkey, better known as the Silver Horse!'

'Blue label beer!'

Each one contributed to the painting of the picture of memory, drawing from his own store with delighted grins.

'You remember, there was you, Charlie, and Lofty Holroyd, and Aggie Weston and Taffy ... Taffy Soames ... He was still on the *Glorious* with you, Charlie, when she went down...'

'Yes, by God, I can see him now, with his banjo and his daft recitations.'

It was difficult for Skipper to think of Chief Air Rigger Petre as having the name Charlie. Obviously he must have a Christian name, but, like a headmaster or the chief constable of the county, one never considered him in Christian-name terms.

'You were in *Glorious* that day, weren't you, Chief? What exactly happened? I've always wanted to ask you.'

Petre frowned. He grimaced, as though with the effort of bringing back the past. 'Well, sir, to be quite honest, I don't *know* exactly what happened, even to this day. It all seems like a horrible dream now, really. I was up on the flight deck. I didn't even know we'd sighted any German ships, or that there were any around, when they put a shell into the island. I think it must have killed everybody up there, straight off. The whole lot just seemed to cave in. Everything vanished in a great cloud of smoke and flame and shit. Blokes were running about all over the place and shouting, but you couldn't hear what they were saying. You couldn't make yourself think straight, the noise, it just went right through you and took all the spunk out of you.

'Then I heard somebody say we were abandoning ship and I looked over the side, the starboard side that was, and it seemed as if the sea was coming right up to meet you. We had a hell of a list to starboard on. Blokes were just jumping into the sea as they got to the rail, but we were still going at a rate of knots, and they were just whisked away astern and you couldn't see them any longer. I don't suppose any of them survived. There was a very big sea running, a very long swell with waves breaking all along the crests every now and again, and it didn't look at all pleasant, I can tell you. I followed a lot of blokes who were jumping and trying to swim out to some Carley floats. It was in the Arctic and even though it was June it was bitterly cold. That water, it felt as though somebody had grasped my whole body and squeezed it. I couldn't hardly breathe. But I got to one of the floats and somebody pulled me in. There were a lot of RAF types in that one, they had only just flown on board that morning. They didn't know nothing about boat work, and some of them didn't even seem to want to stay alive, they were so shocked.

'You had to want to stay alive. We were very crowded at first, with fellows hanging on to the sides, treading water. But in no time at all there seemed to be much more room. The main thing was to keep awake. Because you could see that anybody who had a kip, even for a moment, was gone. I don't know to this day why nobody came to pick us up, but we were in those floats for hours, *days*. Three days, it was. Not a drop of water to drink. Not a bite to eat. Freezing to death the whole time. I made up my mind from the start that if anybody was going to die it wasn't going to be me. Although it was bloody hard to keep holding on to that idea, when blokes were going off their heads all around you. They used to wave and claim that people in other rafts were waving back. Blokes kept on reporting imaginary ships and aircraft and couldn't understand why they never came any nearer. One chap said he saw a Swordfish, gave us the number and all. The number was right. It was one of the Swordfish in our squadron. But it never came. And when they never came, the blokes just gave up and went over the side. One bloke said to me, "Hold on," he said, "just keep my place for me, will you, I'm just going down to collect my tot," and with that he just rolled over the side. There were only three of us left alive, out of eighty who started off on that float, when a Norwegian trawler suddenly appeared and picked us up. We were so numb we were just slung on board like sacks of spuds. Couldn't move a muscle.

'And then what happened next was almost worse than anything else, when the circulation came back to our bodies. It was the worst agony I've ever had. Somebody was shouting with pain, and one of the Norwegians came up to him where he was lying in a bunk and said, "Don't cry," he said, "there are plenty more who will never cry again. Think yourself lucky," he said. That was on the afternoon of the third day. It was up in the Arctic, you see, during the Norwegian business. I lost some toes through frostbite finally, but I lost some good friends, too. Lot of good blokes went down in that ship ... I can still feel that ship giving a bloody great shudder, right through the soles of my feet, which must have been more shells hitting us...'

'Turn it up, Charlie, you're enough to turn all the milk sour!'

'Cor, play the violins again, Charlie! You won't have a dry eye in the house at this rate!'

Petre grinned. 'Yes, maybe I did ham it up a bit. But it's true, every word.'

Evadne let a long breath. 'I think it's a bloody *marvellous* story.'

'Cor blimey, cheer up, Charlie, we're supposed to be on a run ashore, *enjoying* ourselves, not hearing your life and hard times. You're in Aussie land now, not the Arctic. What was that dance we used to do, down the Gut, when we'd had a few basinfuls? That old dance Aggie Weston used to do as his party piece...'

'The Priest of Paris...'

'*Aye, zig a zumba zumba zumba ... Hold him down, ye Swazee warrior...*'

'No, no, no, that's a pig's tune. The pigs sing that in the wardroom.'

The five of them got up, clumsily, so that they knocked over a couple of chairs, thus attracting Mugsy's attention to themselves. Mike the pianist, who was just finishing a glass of beer, looked at them questioningly as they solemnly joined hands and began to dance in a circle. At this incredible sight, the conversation in the rest of the club began to falter, and as the noise level dropped, the voices of the five senior air department chiefs could be heard in song as they shuffled round.

'*We're dockyard maties' children...*'

'*Sitting on the dockyard wall...*' Mike picked up the tune, *Just Like the Ivy*, and improvised an accompaniment.

'*Just like our fathers...*'

'*Doing fuck all...*'

The five chiefs hopped and skipped in unison as they sang, and at the same time removed their jackets and ties, dropping them on the floor.

'*We're dockyard maties' children...*'

'Are there any other words to this?' Evadne asked.

'I'm afraid not,' said Skipper.

As they circled, the chiefs began to discard more and more of their clothing, dropping each piece neatly on their own individual piles.

Evadne put her hands up to her face and stared through her fingers. 'I don't think I want to watch this. I don't think I *should.*'

Mugsy left the bar and came out on the dance floor. 'Hey, tone it down, you crazy Poms, you wanna get me shut down?'

The rest of the room roared at him, while the chiefs, now naked except for shoes and socks, which they apparently wished to retain, ignored him. They stood in a circle while Petre, with a knotted tie in his hand, pointed an accusatory finger.

'Who is the Priest of Paris? You, sir?'

'Me, sir? No, sir, please sir…'

'Please sir, me sir, no sir…'

'Wrong. *Salute*!' The erring chief presented his backside, which Petre whacked with the knotted tie. 'Who *now* is the Priest of Paris? You, sir, *you*, sir?'

While the extraordinary ritual went on, Mugsy placed himself with his back to the door, arms outstretched, as though to prevent the entry of the constabulary. The rest of the room kept on staring, hushed and fascinated, at this absurd prancing. It was entirely ridiculous, without even the sustaining logic of a children's game, but, being in the best of bad taste, it had a peculiarly hypnotic grip on its audience.

'Who sir you sir me sir no sir please sir … Wrong … *Salute*!'

'You won't listen to me, will ya?' wailed Mugsy. 'You're gonna have me out of business.'

Chief Air Rigger Petre now held up a newspaper. 'Ladies and gentlemen … by special request … as performed … since time immemorial … before the Crowned 'Eads of Europe … before your very eyes … the Grand Dance of the Flaming … *Arseholes*.'

'Keep it clean, will ya, you crazy Poms…' Mugsy had flattened himself desperately against the door.

Swiftly, Petre tore the paper into strips, one of which each member of his *corps de ballet* placed between his thighs. Petre struck a match, the five torches flared, Mike began to play, the dance began again, while the whole club began to clap hands in time to the shuffling dancers. One by one the torches burned down. One by one the dancers gave a shout of pain as the flames reached their skin.

Chief Air Rigger Petre pointed at the author of the longest, loudest and last yell. '*You* are the Priest of Paris, until our next regular meeting, of which every raw curate will be informed.'

The five chiefs picked up their clothes and returned to their table, settling down to drink beer with renewed vigour.

'I wonder,' Evadne said, as she drove away from Mugsy's, 'I wonder if the Japs know what's in store for them?'

'Doubt it, or they'd give up. Wish to God they would.'

'You're a bit frightened, aren't you, of the next round of things, up there in Japan?'

'Yes, I am, I admit it.'

'Still, you're not alone, are you? You've got some good cobbers in your ship, like those comedians back there. I've never seen anything like that in all my life. They like you, you know, those men back in there.'

'I don't care whether they like me or not.'

'Yes, you do. You wouldn't be normal if you didn't?'

'The last thing any naval officer must do is to try and be popular with the lads. It's fatal. The sailors twig on to it right away. Popularity Jacks, they call officers like that.'

'Now you *are* talking like a pig, aren't you? I didn't say you should *try*. I just said you do care. Besides, you must be able to do your job better, be a better officer if they like you — if they're with you, and not against you all the time?'

'That's certainly true.' He looked out at the rows of houses passing. He was still haunted by images from Petre's story of

Glorious. So much of it agreed exactly with his own experience in the dinghy, but in Petre's story every detail was enlarged to a horrific extent, every feeling raised to a much higher power, so that it approached the limits of a genuine tragedy.

'Where are we going now?'

'My house. If that suits you.'

'That should be nice.'

'Yes, it will be nice.'

Was this, he wondered, more research for her article, or a just reward for a returning hero, or sampling a rare Pom, or curiosity, or what? His not to wonder why, his just to lie back and enjoy it. Lie back and think of Australia. He had not, until now, felt the slightest sexual attraction towards her. Still, as Jolly Jack always said, after a few beers they all begin to look like Betty Grable.

Her house was one of a row in a neat terrace, each with the most beautifully delicate wrought-iron balcony on its first floor. The street sloped so that Skipper could see the water of the harbour shining beyond the roof of the houses at the lower end. The moon was shining, so that one half of the street was bright silver and the other half in blackness. Hers was on the moonlit side. He looked around him as she got out her key. This really could have been in an English fishing village or small holiday seaside town.

Inside, the furniture seemed oddly ill-assorted and too large, as though it had come from a much larger house. 'We used to have a huge house in Sydney in the old days.'

He had expected and prepared for some foreplay, some decent preliminaries, an overture of some kind. But time seemed to have been telescoped.

'How would you like me?'

'Aren't you going to have a drink or anything?'

'No.'

'Still working?'

'I should slap your face for that, shouldn't I? How would you like me?'

'With nothing on, preferably.'

It seemed a hundred years since he had last seen a woman naked. Incredibly, he had forgotten how arousing the sight was. All the magazine pictures, all the girls posted up on mess deck locker doors, had not a thousandth part of the impact of the reality.

'I would prefer you to kneel on the bed…'

'You mean you mean you don't even want to look me in the face? You just want a sexy thing to look at?'

'Yes, please. A sexy thing to look at is just what I want. That's right.' And no nonsense about love. There was no time for that.

'You despise women, don't you? And you despise Australians, don't you?'

'No, I don't despise women and I don't despise Australians. Just hold it like that, please.'

'Did you know, this is the way the abos do it? We call this the aborigine position. As opposed to the white missionary position.'

'Do they? Well, the abos know a thing or two. Can you put your shoulders down, can you relax a bit, so that your shoulders are resting on the bed? The angle of your back is very important. It's got to be right.'

'You're not flying one of your bloody aircraft now, you know!'

'Yes, I know that. Just keep like that. That's very nice. What a very beatable bottom.'

'Don't you dare bring all your Pommy tricks over here!'

'No, I'm not. I'm just remarking on what a beautiful shape you are. I was just admiring you.'

'Because don't you mock me! Don't you mock Australia!'

'I'm not mocking you, and I'm not mocking Australia.' He looked up. There was a small pink glass chandelier hanging in the centre of the bedroom. Mrs Fleetwood had one just like it in her parlour at Daughton.

'Lovely.'

It was a supremely satisfying physical moment, a purging, a slaking of a long thirst, an exquisite explosion, as necessary as a great sneeze.

'You *beaut*!'

'You *bastard*!'

CHAPTER FIFTEEN

From the air, the first sign of the task force was the wake of the last destroyer in the screen. The weather was sunny but there was a haze down on the water and the destroyer was in sight for some time before any other ships could be seen. The white, creamy trail of broken water pointed to the whereabouts of the fleet like a signpost, saying *Here am I, follow me.* Skipper remembered reading in an intelligence report of Midway that the American dive-bombers had followed just such a Tail-End Charlie destroyer, which had led them direct to the main Japanese fleet. He made up his mind to mention it when he landed on board, although it was difficult to see what could be done about it; the fleet had to have a destroyer screen and there had to be a rear marker in it.

Meanwhile in his earphones Skipper could hear the murmurings and squabblings of half a dozen radio conversations. Some of the fleet's new fighters had been delivered by road or lighter and hoisted on board by crane, but most of them had been taken over at Nowra, down the coast, and were now airborne, on their way to join the fleet. It would be asking a great deal of the flight-deck crews, after nearly four weeks in Sydney, to take on board almost the whole fighter air group at once, but, as, Wings said, they would have to do it sometime and they might as well do it sooner rather than later.

Sydney had been, as it had always promised, a hectic time. The Australians, and especially the Australian girls, had exerted themselves to be hospitable. The first turn of the screw, it was said, mended all broken hearts. But if only half the tales in wardroom and squadron were to be believed, nothing could mend all those broken maidenheads. No doubt in due course there would be a small village population of hybrid Poms.

The British Centre, up the hill from the ships in Woolloomooloo, with its curious stone beasts outside the entrance and its air of bracing hospitality, had been literally as well as in name the centre of hospitality for the British. Thousands of volunteers had helped to man and run it. Hundreds of girls had presented themselves nightly as partners in the dances. Scores of weddings were planned, and there were not a few deserters already. Skipper was glad that his squadron and the others were all present and correct on sailing, but he had heard there were quite serious losses due to absentees in the engine-room departments of this and other ships. Who could blame them? The living conditions of some of those machinery spaces in the tropics were not fit for a dog, especially when there were so many attractions ashore.

The men of the fleet, Skipper knew, would remember Australia all their lives. They had gone skiing on Mount Kosciusko, in the Snowy Mountains to the south, or visited sheep stations, or gaped at the giant multi-coloured stalactites and stalagmites in the Jenolan Caves. They had visited the Botanical Gardens and caught trams to Botany Bay, and swum at Bondi and a dozen other beaches. They had bathed in torrents of Australian beer, Australian wine and Australian sun. As somebody said, they would all remember Australia as a large busty blonde with open arms and open legs. As for Skipper, he had not seen Evadne again after the day and the night of their interview. He had rung her office, always to find her out, and she had never rung back. It did not matter.

In the last two weeks, in fact, pleasure had turned to business. Skipper could not recall another fortnight's more intensive flying training. They had gone to Nowra, a depressing place, of scrub, low bush, insects, a dry hot wind blowing from the centre of the continent, a shortage of beer, and a sun that hit the head like a sledgehammer every day. There they flew their new Corsairs, Mark IV's, with improved performance, range, endurance and weapon load. They were armed with bombs, 'blaze bombs', which were Corsair drop-tanks filled with explosives, or 500-lb semi-armour-piercing bombs. Over Japan, they were told, all Corsair sorties would start with bombs. They would be used less as CAPs and more on offensive fighter-bomber sweeps. There were rockets, sixty-pound projectiles slung four a side, for use against kamikazes. The Sakishima Gunto had demonstrated that it was no use peppering a suicider or trying to make him turn away. He had to be blown to matchwood.

Skipper took his squadron low-flying, along the sand dunes or out to sea. He was pleased with their progress. Michael was still there, with Richard Trumble, Edward and Rodney. The Kiwis were still there, in their own flight. But there were six new boys, all impressed to be flying operationally at last, and itching to do well. Skipper wondered how long that eagerness would last in the face of the new flying techniques. The days of sorties of flight or even squadron strength were over. Off Japan, the trick would be to launch as many aircraft on a sortie as possible and swamp the defence. 'Balbo' was the new codename, meaning an unseemly flood of aircraft climbing into the sky, every man shouting to everyone else to take formation upon him. As Michael said, some of the Balbos sounded like an aerial farmyard. Old MacDonald's Navy, he called them.

The fleet was now at sea, on its way to Manus and then onwards to the waters off the east coast of Japan, to operate for the first time in close company with the task groups of the

American Third Fleet under Admiral Halsey. There were still diplomatic and political squabbles in London, Washington and Guam over the exact role the fleet would play. Much would depend upon what the men on the spot, the Vice-Admiral and his staff, managed to agree with Halsey and his staff. But it was well known in the fleet that whatever the Americans might say at home, the Americans out in the Pacific, those who were actually fighting the war, welcomed all the assistance they could possibly get, from the British or anyone else.

Everybody now knew how fiercely the Japanese had resisted down to their last man on tiny islands which could have had no racial or cultural meaning or value for the Japanese nation. At Saipan, when the island was clearly lost, Japanese soldiers and surviving civilian families had gathered at the top of some cliffs at the most northerly point of the island. Whole families — men, women and children — had jumped to their deaths together. Any who hesitated were clubbed down by soldiers who threw the bodies over the cliffs and followed them themselves. Babies had their brains dashed out on stones and were tossed after their mothers. Officers knelt in rows along the cliff edge and assisted each other in slicing open their stomachs in an act of mass *seppuku*, or ceremonial suicide. Amongst those who committed suicide was Admiral Nagumo, the man who had led the carriers which attacked Pearl Harbor. The man who had taken Japanese arms from Hawaii across a third of the world's surface to the very shores of India had died by his own hand, kneeling in a cave overlooking the sea.

If this was how the Japanese had behaved on outlying territory, thousands of miles from home, what would they do when an invader first set foot on the sacred soil of Japan? One day Skipper had returned to the ship from Nowra for a staff briefing. He had found the passageways and flats full of human chains of sailors handing down stores. There were more stores piled on the flight deck and in every available space below. In the briefing room there were sheaves of signals to be read and operational orders by the massive bound volume. Amongst all this turmoil, the meeting had attempted to assess the prospects before them. Sooner or later, unless there was some form of divine intervention, the Japanese would have to be grappled with on their own ground. Every imagination boggled at the possibilities. The C-in-C's staff officers had quoted General MacArthur's staff projections that the Allies would incur a million casualties, just to take Kyushu, the southernmost island of the Japanese archipelago. The assault on Honshu and the Tokyo plain, which would follow, would cost at least another million and a half. These, the meeting was told, were conservative estimates.

Douglas Mayhew's squadron had gone — disbanded, broken up, the pilots and ratings dispersed — some home, some to other squadrons. They were replaced by a brand-new squadron fresh from home, keen but with no operational experience. Skipper had discovered with a profound shock that their CO, an RNVR called Duncan Brightmore, had only joined the Navy some months after Skipper had qualified as a pilot. Henry Darling was still there, with an even younger squadron of striplings, so that he more than ever seemed to tower over his squadron like some great shaggy father figure standing amongst his cub pack.

Madame Fifi had gone home, her war over, and had been replaced by a new and much larger carrier, known on the R/T circuits as *Little Billee*. Listening now to *Little Billee*'s fighter direction officers on the fighter net, Skipper could tell they were nervous like everybody else, anxious to start off on the right foot and not make fools of themselves. Their phrases were just a little too correct, their voice procedures just a little too close to the textbook.

'Brassband Leader, Brassband Leader, this is *Miss Britannia*, are you reading me this fine morning?' (Nobody could accuse Stanley's robust tones of being too academic.)

Skipper cleared his throat. 'This is Brassband Leader, reading you loud and clear, how me?'

'Loud and clear also. Wait one, wait one. Deck is not clear.'

Skipper raised his eyebrows. The delay meant somebody must be in trouble already. For a moment Skipper felt that deadly weariness which had begun to afflict him, as though he were poised at the foot of yet another great hillside which had to be climbed. He had a momentary vision of all the landings and crashes and sorties and accidents and losses there were bound to be in the next few weeks. He wished he could be as fresh and ignorant of it all as he had once been. He knew too much now.

He was pleased to see how neatly his squadron deployed into order for landing on, in a satisfactory line ahead, decently and prudently spaced to come on at intervals. They had of course practised this scores of times at Nowra — taking off, forming up, breaking for landing, taking off again, coming in one behind the other at shorter and shorter intervals. They had all done dozens of aerodrome dummy deck landings, ADDLs as they were always called. But it was one thing to practise on a steady level airfield, quite another to pitch down on a heaving deck, a disconcerting sixty feet above sea level and as narrow as the path to righteousness.

Duncan Brightmore's squadron had gone in first and Skipper followed. As he neared *Miss Britannia* he could only think how smart and clean she looked. The flight deck was freshly painted, with bright, clear stripes and numerals. There was a clean Flag Fox flying close up, and a newly laundered White Ensign. Even Tiny had new, brilliantly visible bats.

But as Skipper cut his engine and his Corsair glided heavily down on to the deck, he saw out to port an ugly ragged score mark scraped on the clean flight deck, looking like the track of some great metal lizard which had crawled off the deck and into the sea. He taxied up behind the nearest Corsair, switched off his engine and climbed out, to watch the rest of his Squadron COme on. Chief Air Rigger Petre was already there.

'What's that mark, Chief?'

'One of the new boys, sir. Missed all the wires, landed like a brick, one leg collapsed, went over the side. Took somebody with him, too.'

'Oh, my *God.*' Skipper turned away. 'It's starting already. What about the bod inside?'

Petre shook his head. 'No sign of him, sir.'

Skipper watched his men come on. Only one, a pleasant little lad, a cockney called 'Ginge' (not Ginger, he insisted), bounced badly and had to go round again. But the second time he came on like a good Christian should.

When Skipper reached the bridge, Duncan Brightmore was explaining to the Captain, Wings and the rest, what had gone wrong. Skipper felt for him. This was always a tense task for any Squadron CO and Duncan was almost a stranger to the ship's officers. He had spent most of his time since he joined down at Nowra and had hardly had a chance to make his number on board. He was trying, after this early disaster, to express appropriate gloom and contrition, and at the same time optimism and confidence in the future. It was a difficult task for anybody, and it seemed to be beyond Duncan Brightmore. He was a slight, brown-haired, pale-cheeked young man, with sharp features, a high voice and a nervous mannerism of slapping his flying helmet against his leg. He looked as young as any of his pilots. When the Captain nodded and Duncan Brightmore turned away to go, Skipper could sense the man's relief at being dismissed.

The Captain, too, to Skipper's eyes, was looking a little more lined, just a little more tired. He had had a heavy programme in Sydney, ashore and on board, and had had only two days' leave, which everybody knew was not enough. For the first time Skipper had an inkling that maybe even the Captain, who had always been such a giant tower of strength, such an unfailing source of confidence and reassurance, might be coming near the end of his stamina.

'How did it go for you, Skipper? Nice to have you back.'

'Nice to be back, sir. No problems, sir, at least nothing serious. Bit of rustiness, bit of greenness. All very well doing Addis at Nowra. Different when you come on board. It's good for us to be brought down to earth with a bump.'

'Literally, in *Little Billee*'s case. Did you hear, they lost five Seafires straight off the reel? We nearly had to take some of her Seafires whilst she got herself sorted out.'

'How about the blokes, sir?'

'All well, as far as I know.'

'Poor *Little Billee*.' Skipper grinned. 'They're a cocky lot over there, sir. Do *them* good to be brought down a peg or two.'

Down in the Ready Room, Skipper found his squadron waiting for him. He knew that praise was required of him. They were delighted with themselves, and they needed him to confirm their delight. He did so, always conscious of Michael's sardonic gaze in the background. But nothing could diminish the newcomers' euphoria, after their first successful real deck landings. It was almost a test of manhood, certainly a sign of coming of age as a fleet pilot. Skipper was not too old to have forgotten his own feelings at such a time, and he shared his squadron's pleasure.

'But don't go getting the idea you're any *good*,' he told them. 'We've got a long, *long* way to get yet.'

The Rear-Admiral (Aircraft Carriers) had visited Nowra and Jervis Bay to watch the progress of training, and he had, of course, studied the air groups' performances that day. His staff had conferred with their American counterparts, watched their combat films, read their reports and weighed up the significance of their flying techniques. They had decided, and most of the carrier Captains and Commanders (Air) agreed, that the fleet's air groups were nowhere near the standard of flying required to operate on an equal footing with the American task force. On leaving Sydney, the fleet embarked upon an intensive flying training programme. Every day, and several times a day, the carriers swung out of line and churned southward and eastward at high speeds to launch aircraft into light winds, doubling back to the north and west to regain their position before landing on aircraft again. The manoeuvres slowed the task force's progress northwards and eventually began to threaten the rendezvous date with the American task force, but, as the Admiral was reported to have said, there was no point in joining the Americans unless they could keep up with them.

The new training programme seemed to Skipper to bring a larger, broader dimension to their art. The normal combat unit was no longer a flight or even a squadron, but a carrier's whole fighter group. On most flying days there were regularly more than 200 aircraft in the air at once. The carriers no longer thought of themselves as single ships in a task group, but as a fourth share of a single force. On one day one carrier would open out to a distance of fifty miles and then launch her entire strike force against the other three, who combined their CAPs in a common defence. The next day, all four carriers' strike forces joined in an attack upon the battleship and the rest of the fleet.

For the Corsairs, flying had never been so varied. In the course of one day they would carry out a high-level CAP interception exercise, followed by a rocket shoot on a towed target, a low-level strafe on the destroyer screen and a bombing run over the nearest island. Aircrew, like orchestras, needed constant practice, and Skipper was gratified to see that his squadron were getting all the practice they required. Apart from Ginge, who was still erratic, the squadron were knitting together extremely well. Duncan Brightmore was not having the same success and Skipper knew, by Wings' attitude towards himself, that his was now the favourite, preferred Corsair squadron of the two.

Skipper watched Michael especially closely, looking for any sign of fading in that marvellous skill. But Michael seemed to have found a new certainty, as sure and seemingly as carefree and technically impeccable as when he had first come on board eighteen months earlier. His relationship with Skipper, however, was not the same. There were awkwardnesses, silences and absences, which were like tiny jagged flaws in an otherwise smooth surface. But as Skipper had told himself again and again, he could not concern himself with personal likes and dislikes. His job was to lead men against the Japanese.

The fleet did not reach the war zone until they crossed the Equator. Until then, the carriers could relax every day after flying. There was a deck hockey league, and a tug-of-war tournament, and a band concert on the flight deck. The ship was still darkened every evening, and there were still dawn and dusk action stations, but otherwise there was an atmosphere on board, as some of the old-timers said, almost like peacetime.

The war seemed to come back at Manus, with the sight of the harbour full of grey ships, with the blackened suicider damage on a cruiser's superstructure, and the ceaseless activity in the floating dock. It was in every way a grim place, where everybody's minds were still very much on the war. Skipper stared out over the quarterdeck rail at the hated shoreline, now barely visible in a heavy rainstorm. He wondered about Commander Leintwardine and when, at lunchtime, he recognised one of the naval base staff officers at the bar, he was curious enough to ask after him.

'Haven't you heard? Old Leintwardine had an accident.'

'What sort of accident?'

'He thought he heard something in the naval base one night and he went out in his jeep to look. Unfortunately for him he drove too near an American sentry, who challenged him. Of course old Leintwardine didn't take any notice of *that* and just drove on. But he was driving on the wrong side of the road. The sentry obviously thought, *Americans drive on the right. This man's driving on the left. He can't be an American. Therefore, he must be a Jap.* So he shot him.'

'Good *God*! Did he hurt him?'

'Killed him. Not right away. He lasted about a day. They took the bullet out of his back but he died. Pity really. He was a good bloke in a daft sort of way.'

'Leintwardine *dead*. I don't believe it.'

'Please yourself.'

So Commander John Stepney Leintwardine was dead. Idiosyncratic, nonconformist, individual to the end, the manner of his death suited him. Ironic that that was probably the only shot he had ever heard in anger out here.

There was more mail waiting at Manus, and Skipper had a letter from his mother describing the VE Day celebrations at Daughton. They had, it seemed, been fairly subdued. Daughton had taken the downfall of the Third Reich unemotionally.

Your father opened some pre-war champagne, but it was all flat somehow, without you. They lit a bonfire, saying that was what they did after Waterloo. But your father says they never had a bonfire after Waterloo. They did for Mafeking, but not for Waterloo. Then they had a sort of sing-song down in the Armistice Hall. There was a party of Land Army girls there, the same ones I have mentioned to you before, and one of them kept singing a song with a chorus about 'You'll be far better off in a home. You'll be far better off, far better, far better off, in a home'. Somehow I shall always associate that song with VE Day now. Another one had quite a good voice and she sang a song, 'Cherry cherry bing', I think that's how you spell it. It was good the first time but after that whenever there was a pause, and there were quite a lot of long pauses, she got up and started to sing 'Cherry cherry bing'. Still, everybody seemed to enjoy themselves and it does mean the end of a long war. It does seem such a very long time since it began. And it's hard to make people realise that your war is still going on. The papers still don't have much about you, nor does the BBC news.

Skipper also received a copy of *New Australian Woman*, with Evadne's article in it. Skipper thought it very flat and uninteresting: a very dutiful, carefully patriotic article. It hardly seemed worth all the trouble she had taken, all the time she had spent, all the questions she had asked. There was nothing of herself, and very little of Skipper, in it. Kimbo's pictures, the ones taken on the flight deck, were much better. Skipper could still hear Kimbo's ecstatic chucklings as he looked at his pictures. He wrapped up the magazine again, to send home to his mother.

Evadne had also written him a letter. Apparently, she now regretted not having rung him back, and was longing for him to come back to Sydney. It was, in her own stiff, self-conscious way, almost a love letter. *Ah, gather ye rosebuds while ye may, because the fleet's away, away, away. Never come back no more.* Skipper thought that maybe he ought to be more sympathetic, but he found he had no emotion towards her at all. She should have taken her chance while she had it. Now there was no time. He wondered whether he should write to her all the same, pretending a response he did not feel. But any letter would be worse than none at all. They were leaving Manus that evening and it was too late for letters.

The last ship in the task force had cleared the harbour entrance by dusk. Skipper watched them form up — a battleship, four carriers, six cruisers and fifteen destroyers. These were the Navy's present finest, the latest ships, and the fastest and the best. Gone were the days of makeshift formations, assembled in haste from whatever ships were available. This was a balanced, powerful fleet of a kind which would have altered the course of the war in the Far East had it been there three years earlier.

A destroyer was crossing *Miss Britannia*'s wake, to take up her station astern. She was a black smudge against the dark, lowering sky, but for a moment her forward gun, her bridge and foremast and her funnel, were all silhouetted against the glare of Manus harbour behind her. A blue light began to blink softly from her bridge. Skipper thought her one of the most romantic and thrilling sights he had ever seen, a vision of such power and purpose and beauty it made his heart ache to see her. To command such a ship would make everything else worthwhile.

Skipper noticed that the ship was steaming faster than her normal passage speed. The fleet was already thirty-six hours late in the original programme. Somewhere to the north the fleet train was waiting in the fuelling rendezvous position. If the time was to be made up, the fuelling would have to be faultless. Skipper did not envy the Vice-Admiral his task. He had to present his fleet to the Americans on time, with the squadrons worked up and the ships refuelled, regardless of the weather and the shortage of tankers.

The first night at sea, on the way to the operational area, was always a deadly nervous time. After the freedoms of Sydney and its cool climate, the heat and humidity of the darkened ship seemed even more oppressive. On that first night from Manus, the lights out, the ladders removed, the doors clipped shut, the passageways obscured by extra stores and gear, all added to the helpless claustrophobic sensation below decks, of being battened down in darkness and uncertainty while being carried towards a dangerous future.

The first night out was normally Michael's bad time, and Skipper was walking along the passageway to visit him when he passed the same bathroom and heard again the same whistling. He had hardly given Ronnie Bell a thought in the past few months, but somebody was there, singing and whistling, just as he used to do. Skipper walked into the bathroom, as he had done on that other night. One of the shower stalls was still steaming, its deck still wet with recent water. But there was nobody there. Skipper felt the hairs on his scalp prickle, as though he were standing in a cold wind. It was another omen, and it suited that night of darkness and stifling heat.

Skipper knocked on Michael's cabin door, heard his voice and pulled back the curtain. Michael and Richard Trumble were lying together, naked, on the bunk. They had made no attempt at concealment. They had not locked the cabin door. They had not even drawn it shut. Richard Trumble's expression was unrepentant and triumphant, like a little minx. But Michael's eyes held a look of such hopelessness and resignation that Skipper knew at once that his old friend ought not to be allowed to fly again, for his own good. Different men had different ways of indicating that they had passed their private limits, and Michael was signalling that he was past caring. But it would be impossible to take him off operational flying now. It would be like stopping a violinist in the middle of his cadenza. Yet Skipper knew now that Michael's performance was false. He was like a player playing superbly, but from memory.

'I am sorry.' Skipper stepped outside into the passageway and drew the curtain across. He thought of a remark the Commander had once made. He said that one always heard about this sort of thing, but in all his years in the Navy he had never actually come across a genuine incidence of it, except once, and even that was probably an unjust accusation to frame an unpopular Chief Petty Officer.

Skipper did not mention the incident again and the matter lay between them, unspoken, until two nights later, when Skipper was walking up and down the quarterdeck. A destroyer had been alongside to transfer documents by light jackstay and was just sheering away, her long hull crashing across the line of the waves. Skipper was absorbed in the spectacle of her manoeuvres when he heard Michael's voice behind him.

'Thank you for not making a scene in that bar, Skipper.'

'Bar, what bar?'

'In Sydney, first night in.'

'Good God, you mean you saw me?'

'Oh, yes. I saw you come in. I wondered whether you had noticed us. As you never seemed to look once in our direction, I knew you had. I could see by the way you looked back as you left.'

'Well, why should I make a scene, just because you were sitting in a bar?'

'You know what I mean. What are you going to do about the other night?'

'Nothing. Same as I did in the bar. There's nothing I can do and nothing I want to do, except ground you, and not for *that* reason, I should say. I need you as my Senior Pilot and provided you go on doing that, that's all that counts.'

'What about young Dickon?'

'What about him?'

'Aren't I guilty of corrupting him?'

'I doubt it. Whether you are or not, I need him too.'

'You're a very cool fish, aren't you, Skipper? I feel I know you very well now. You're a bloody good leader of men and yet you're not really interested in men. I don't know whether to be grateful to you or not, for not doing anything. I'm not even sure you're doing me a favour.'

'When we get back to Sydney —'

'*If* we get back to Sydney…'

'All right, if and when we get back to Sydney, I might take some action. That's unless you go and do something silly in the meantime.'

'We shan't. We're very discreet.'

Judging by the open door, Skipper did not think so, and they certainly were not discreet enough to deceive Chief Air Rigger Petre. Petre had been talking about them for some little time before Skipper actually realised who he was talking about. 'Funnily enough, sir, I've only really come across this once or twice in all me time in the Andrew. You hear a lot but it's a lot more talking and very little doing.' It was curious how Petre was almost echoing the Commander's words. 'I always says, sir, as long as they don't frighten the horses, they can do what they like.'

'You know about this, Chief?' Skipper said cautiously, conscious that he might be committing some serious naval solecism in discussing officers' behaviour with a rating, even such a senior rating as Petre.

'Of course I do, sir. You can't serve in ships for twenty years without knowing every time anybody on board so much as farts out of tune.'

If that was so, then the Captain almost certainly knew. The Captain had an almost telepathic sympathy with the ship and seemed to know at once when anything happened anywhere in her. He also had an intuitive knowledge of what the sailors were thinking, because he used what the Commander called his 'Stanley Baldwin stationmaster technique'. Envious fellow politicians always wondered how Mr Baldwin knew what the ordinary man was thinking. Somebody concluded that he must chat with the stationmaster when he went home to Worcestershire for the weekends. The Captain had not one but a stream of stationmasters who generally called on him on the bridge in the evenings. Skipper was one of them. He would have liked to have discussed his problem over Michael with the Captain. He decided he could not. The Captain would be bound to take an old-fashioned disciplinarian's view, and Skipper needed Michael in the squadron. And yet, if his suspicions about Michael's fighting capacity were justified, then should he not cut his losses now? It was insoluble.

'You thought any more about the future, Skipper?'

'I have, sir. It's the oddest thing, but several people have brought up the subject with me, quite unasked.'

'I don't know why I recommend the Navy. They're a bloody unforgiving sort of mob. One never gets the rewards, the notice, one is sure one deserves. I suppose it's all part of the process, stopping one getting too big for one's boots, but I must say they're an ungrateful lot. You dig out as hard as you can. All that happens is that somebody says to you, why didn't you do so and so? Not a word of praise. Ever read 'The Laws of the Navy'? No? I'll get it out for you. It's a poem by some versifying admiral. Sort of Kiplingesque pastiche, all the same Laws of the Jungle but there is some hard, solid, good sense in it. One verse has something about, *If you labour from morn until even ... And meet with reproof for your toil ...* I forget how it goes, but it ends something about *the gun must be humbled, the compressor must check the recoil.* I must say, the Navy does a lot of humbling and checking the recoil. Sometimes I think it's the most bloody-minded, ungrateful, infuriating service the world has ever seen. I suppose that's why we all love it so.'

Skipper looked through the bridge window. Although it was quite dark, he could see the shape of the nearest carrier to starboard and slightly abaft the beam. The great edge of her flight deck was rising to the swell. Now that he looked carefully and studied it, Skipper fancied that the weather was actually rougher than any he could remember. There were pale wisps of foam streaking the sides of the waves as they were blown off the crests. The ship herself was rising and falling heavily, occasionally seeming to slip rapidly sideways, as though trying to accommodate herself to a sea that was rather larger than she was used to. The wind was shrieking round the eaves of the bridge structure, and banging the glass panes of the windows so that they actually gave out a thudding sound.

Schoolie, the Met Officer, appeared with a sheaf of signals and a weather chart. 'Looks a bit funny tonight, sir. We're getting reports of high winds from most of the American weather stations. Guam, Pulo Anna, Pelelieu, Ulithi and Saipan are all a bit restive. They haven't actually said the word yet, sir, but I fancy there's a typhoon brewing. Our glass is dropping slightly. Wind and sea from the north. Both from the same direction. Both getting up a lot. Beginning to fall into the classical pattern of it, sir.'

'We've all got to fuel tomorrow.' The Captain stroked his chin thoughtfully. 'Hope we get through that all right.'

'Well, sir, I don't want to appear too much of a wet blanket, but it's force five, gusting to six or seven now, sir, and the sea is well up to it.'

'We *must* fuel. We're late as it is, and I know the Admiral is desperately keen that we join the Americans on the dot. Is this the typhoon season, Schoolie?'

'Smack in it, sir. Well, they come at any time in these parts, but this is the season all right, sir.'

'Look, just refresh my memory about this, will you?'

'Well, sir, they normally start in a fairly small way, but generally get up steam very rapidly, on or about latitude Ten North. Actually, anywhere between Seven and Fifteen North. The eye of the storm moves roughly west north-west at about twenty knots or so. The wind goes anti-clockwise round the centre, so that the wind keeps on backing as you approach the centre, or rather as it approaches you. Often when it gets up to about latitude Twenty North, it swings round in a sort of dog-leg and heads off in an east-north-east direction again. Where we are now, sir, I'd say we were in a potentially dangerous situation. If we press on at this speed, we may find the storm centre coming on our starboard bow or starboard quarter. If we miss it ahead or astern, it may swing round and catch us from the port side. On a northerly course as we are, I would say we are running a risk, sir.'

'You think a typhoon's on its way?'

'Well, sir, I've never actually experienced one, but I just have a funny feeling in my water. There's something about all those weather reports. When you plot them all, they all add up to a menacing sort of situation. I don't want to be too alarmist, but it's just a feeling I have, sir.'

'I know your feelings of old, Schoolie, and I agree with you we ought to alter course or slow down. I have a funny feeling about it too. But I also know we've got to meet the fuelling group tomorrow, that's for sure. What's the glass doing?'

There really was no need to look, but somebody did. 'Still dropping, sir.'

'How much?'

'Just over five millibars in the last hour, sir.'

The Captain grimaced. That, too, was another typical symptom of a typhoon's approach, although they had yet to experience the terrifying drop in barometric pressure which would mean the storm was almost upon them. The 'Talk Between Ships' low-frequency short-range broadcast speaker was murmuring in the corner, giving the Admiral's night intentions signal.

'Queen zero-one-one, Roger zero-eight...'

In the TBS argot, that meant the task-force course for the night would be eleven degrees and the mean speed eight knots. So the Admiral had already had to make some concession to the storm. Looking out of the bridge window at the blackness, until he could see once again the spacing of the waves, Skipper thought that the destroyers would be hard pressed even to make eight knots into the sea.

Skipper went below to his cabin by way of the hangar, 'that cavern measureless to man', as he called it. It was choc-a-bloc with aircraft, parked wing-stub to wing-stub and tail to tail, and there were three extra Corsairs on outriggers on the flight deck, just forward of the island. Parking this number of aircraft demanded the skills of a stage manager, a choreographer and a solver of jigsaw puzzles on a Napoleonic scale. The lighting threw deep shadows around the waiting aircraft. They were all secured to the deck by wire strops, doubled and redoubled. But even so, they all lurched alarmingly to leeward as the ship rolled. The deck was slippery with oil, and two or three ratings checking the lashings had to hold on while the deck tilted away from them.

Lying in his bunk, Skipper could hear and feel that the Schoolie's premonitions were being fully borne out. It was the roughest night he had ever experienced. The ship was labouring against a steep sea, with an unusually long period of roll and pitch, like a model toy rocked in a bath too large for her. Now and again the ship lurched far over and lay on her side for minutes at a time, while the cabin flat resounded with the noises of gear crashing to the deck, doors banging, desk-tops slamming, and the cries of cabin occupants who had literally rolled out of their bunks. Skipper himself was tipped out and noticed, with surprise, that he hit the side of the cabin bulkhead before he hit the deck.

When Skipper went out on to the quarterdeck the next morning, the fuelling group was in sight, but it seemed to him that it was quite impossible to begin fuelling. The nearest tanker was two miles away, level with *Miss Britannia*'s stern. Her black hull was from time to time hidden in great green waves which were washing her down from stem to stern. Her funnel smoke was being whipped away astern in a long straight stream. There was a gigantic swell running. Skipper estimated the distance between wave crests was some three or four hundred feet, and the height of the waves must be at least twenty feet. A destroyer was approaching the tanker from astern. She reared up so that the whole of her forefoot and part of her red keel were visible, before plunging half her length into a giant wave which sent a tower of spray mast-high over her bridge and funnels. The destroyer momentarily disappeared in the body of the wave, before rising up again with tons of water falling off her fo'c'sle.

Skipper heard the lifebuoy sentry shout and turned to see a wave level with his head. The crest broke inboard with a thundering, heaving weight of water. He leaped for the top of a hatch while the wave subsided alongside, leaving its remaining water sluicing and scouring into every corner of the quarterdeck. Choosing his moment, he ran for the after screen, slipped through the door and clipped it behind him.

'Just as well, sir,' said the sentry. 'I don't think they could turn and pick you up if you went overboard into *that*.'

'No, indeed.'

When he reached the bridge and took up an inconspicuous place at the back, Skipper could see that in spite of the weather they were indeed going to try and fuel. *Miss Britannia* herself was only four cables astern of a tanker and coming up on her port side. The fleet had long since given up the old, slow way of fuelling astern of a tanker — hauling the hoses in over the fo'c'sle — in favour of the newer, faster method, pioneered by the United States Navy, of fuelling abeam, with the fuelled ship steaming alongside the tanker. It was all done, as the Commander once told Skipper, on the 'Maid Marian principle':

Maid Marian was rescued from her tower, where the Sheriff of Nottingham had imprisoned her, by Robin Hood who shot an arrow trailing a fine thread through her window. Maid Marian pulled in the thread on which was tied a thicker string and on that in turn a rope capable of bearing the girl's weight.

Looking at the sea running, Skipper doubted whether even Robin Hood could have got a line across. The first four Coston gun lines were simply snatched away, long before they reached the tanker's desk. The fifth, fortunately fired in a comparative lull, snagged on the nearer rail. Two of the tanker's crew flung themselves upon it. Soon the heavier line was on its way and then, to Skipper's amazement, the thick black hose itself. It dipped into the water, rose again almost bar taut, dropped down into the body of wave, tautened again. Each violent movement appeared to be the end, but slowly, the hose was hauled across and, miraculously quickly it seemed to Skipper, the tanker's green flag waved to signal that she was actually pumping.

The Captain was standing out on the starboard bridge wing, his eyes flicking from the compass repeater in front of him to the hose, to the water in between the ships, to the beflagged line indicating the distance the ships were apart, and back to the compass again. He was ordering minute alterations of course, to stay with the tanker, and changes of engine revolutions, one or two revolutions at a time at most, to keep exactly level with her. This, Skipper realised, was one of the greatest tests of seamanship, and the Captain was going to have to keep it up for hours.

A larger wave swept down between the ships. The men on the tanker's fuelling deck, though they were almost thirty feet from the normal waterline, were standing waist-deep, clutching to winches, derricks, anything to support themselves. One man was hidden under the water and Skipper thought he was gone. But he was still there when the wave passed, saved by his lifeline, which was clipped to the deck rail.

'Ask the Commander (E) how long he thinks fuelling is going to take.'

'Aye aye, sir.'

Looking round, Skipper noticed with a genuine alarm and shock that every other ship except the tanker had disappeared. Visibility had dropped to less than half a mile, and it was becoming difficult to distinguish between sea and air. The spray being whipped off the water was now almost continuous.

'Commander (E) says the pumping rate is very slow, sir. At this rate we'll need another three hours.'

The Navigating Officer was plotting the dispositions of the task force and screen on his plot, using the radar echoes. 'At this rate it's going to be a very long three hours,' he said to Skipper.

The Navigating Officer was a small, dark man with a prominent nose, known to the Wardroom as Pilot, or by his nickname of Boney. He was a pleasant, unassuming man, who ran the ship's cricket team and had — Skipper remembered from parties back in the United Kingdom — an outstandingly beautiful wife.

'We need the fuel for two reasons now. First, we need it, of course, but secondly, empty tanks are not desirable in this sort of weather. If this goes on we might have to fill them with sea water, and nobody likes doing that very much.'

'Is this really a typhoon?'

'Oh, yes, I don't think there's any doubt now. We're still on the edges of it.'

'Good God, what must the centre be like?'

'True. But we seem to be steering more to the north-east all the time, heading into the wind as it very slowly veers. That's probably a good sign. Look…' Boney drew a rough circle on the edge of his plotting chart. 'Imagine this circle is the typhoon. You can split it, either side of its mean line of advance, into a starboard side and a port side. Anything to starboard of its line of advance is the dangerous sector, and we seem to be in that sector. But we must finish this fuelling. And we've got to catch up with the Yanks. If the bottom suddenly falls out of the barometer, that's a sure sign you're allowing yourself to get too close to the centre.'

'How can you tell where the centre is?'

'You can't really be certain, but I suspect we shall be able to see it on radar before very long. But there is an old rule of thumb, going back to the days of sailing ships. You face the wind, that's the true wind not the relative wind, and the storm centre is about ten points, that's about 110 degrees, on your right-hand side.' Boney looked at the anenometer gauge. 'It's about three-five-five, three-five-six now, just to the west of north. That makes the centre about due south-east or so from us, and it's heading west. If the Admiral's done his sums right we should be ahead of it, leaving it to pass astern of us.'

The TBS speaker crackled and spoke. 'Task Force three-seven, this is CTF three-seven. Formation Shrapnel, execute. Point option Queenie zero-one-one, Roger five knots.'

Boney lifted his head. 'Somebody acknowledge that. That's the order to scatter,' he said to Skipper.

'Blimey, that sounds ominous!'

'Not really, it's very sensible. Leave everybody to find their own way, but trying to follow point option. So we must all try to make good five knots on a course of zero-one-one. Though you can't fight a typhoon. We'll have to see how we get on.'

There was a cry from outside and Skipper dashed to the window in time to see a monster wave sweeping down between the tanker and *Miss Britannia*. All the lines and the hose sprang rigidly bar taut and then snapped. A gout of black fuel spread on the water, visible for a few moments before it was swept away. The tanker heeled off to starboard, while *Miss Britannia* swung to port. The two ships had lost contact. There was clearly not the slightest chance of picking up the fuelling hose again.

The Captain came back into the bridge, the water streaming off his oilskins. 'Well, it was inevitable, I suppose. Pass the word to the Commander: "Secure all fuelling gear and fuelling parties." Ask Commander (E) how much fuel he's got and tell him that's his lot!' The Captain grinned at Skipper. 'I would have liked to have gone on, but I think we've rather outstayed our welcome.'

'Commander (E) says 80 per cent, sir.'

'Well, that's not bad.' The Captain took off his oilskin hat and shook away the water. He studied the chart, the anenometer gauge, the revolution counters and the radar screens. He watched the rudder indicator for a little while.

'What do you think, Pilot?'

'I think we should steer north and then east, sir. I feel we are just about outstripping the storm centre. I've a feeling it's passing astern of us.'

'I hope you're right. It doesn't feel like it, I must say.'

It certainly did not. Every wave seemed higher than the last and the ship was no longer rising to them but trying to bullock her way through them. The Captain reduced speed to a crawl, barely enough to keep steerage way. This seemed to give the oncoming waves time to rear up to their full stature. They broke inboard upon the flight deck in great green cataracts, each one seeming to stun the ship to a temporary standstill before she wearily got under way again. The forward edge of the flight was only just visible in the spray. There was nothing else in sight. The whole task force and the fuelling group, all had vanished into the howling wastes on either side.

The sheer force of the wind created surrealist sights on the flight deck. One wave broke up forward and was at once flattened by the storm so that it passed the island in a streaming mass, six feet above the deck level, like a watery awning. The next was smoothed by the wind into the shape of a tidal bore. The biggest wave Skipper had ever seen, seeming to tower above *Miss Britannia*'s bridge, struck the starboard side forward, with a blow that Skipper could feel through the soles of his feet as it roared along the boat and crane decks, tearing and wrenching and ripping at anything not actually part of the ship herself.

Hardly believing what he saw, Skipper watched the two halves of his skiff from Manus land on the flight deck just below him and slide slowly aft, the two pieces exactly a foot apart, until they both disappeared over the side. They were followed by a rain of potato sacks from the spud locker. The sacks broke and were whisked away. Hundreds of pale-yellow potatoes lay quiet for an instant and then began to dance aft, pouring over the side in a hilarious, bobbing, suicidal torrent.

'Destroyer to port, sir.'

She was heeling away from *Miss Britannia*, forced so far over they could see her bottom and her starboard screw revolving in the air. She seemed to right herself, to a list of only about twenty degrees, and then fell over again. Skipper was sure she was sinking.

'Good Christ, she's going!'

'No, no, she's coming up again.'

Boney had been taking bearings of the wildly rolling mast. 'I think she's going to hit us, sir.'

'No, it's us that's going to hit her. We're making much more leeway than she is and drifting down on her. We'll go ahead a little bit faster.'

As they watched, the destroyer slowly drew aft and passed under *Miss Britannia*'s stern. Crossing over, Skipper saw her, still rolling wildly, come out again on the starboard quarter. He could look down on her bridge as though he were standing directly above it. He fancied he could see the men on it, hanging on to the windward rail, with their feet dangling out behind them in space. Her funnels were so far over they pointed sideways like the barrels of a great black shotgun.

'Whooweee! There goes our deck park!'

The forward Corsair on deck was adrift and in spinning away it caught its neighbour. Both aircraft whirled across the flight deck. There was a flash and an explosion, and one Corsair caught fire. There was no question of fighting the fire. No man could have stood upright on the flight deck. The third Corsair broke loose and drifted straight into the burning sides of the first, its impetus carrying them both over the side. The flaming wrecks appeared aft, embedded in the grey side of a wave, as they rose into sight and then vanished. The last Corsair stayed snagged in a gun sponson for a few moments, and then it too disappeared.

On the bridge, a sound-powered telephone was wailing.

'Message from hangar control, sir. Two aircraft broken loose up forrard, sir. Emergency in the hangar, sir!'

The Captain swung round in his chair and his gaze fell on Skipper. 'Your part of ship, Skipper. Off you go. See if you can sort it out. Let me know.'

'Aye aye, sir!'

CHAPTER SIXTEEN

The way to the nearest hangar access door was through Henry Darling's squadron's mess deck. Skipper knew it well, having passed through it, going in and out of the hangar, many times. But now he hardly recognised it. The hammocks were all slung. Henry Darling's men, like the rest of the ship's company, had all turned in until the weather moderated. One man was sitting at the mess table, with a bucket wedged between his knees. From his heaving shoulders and his pale face when he looked up, Skipper could see that he was obviously in the last throes of seasickness, having long since emptied his stomach of all its contents, but still continuing to retch.

Around the man's feet and right across the deck, water flowed to and fro as the ship rolled, taking with it sodden clothes, books, mess utensils and scraps of paper in a great dirty tide of debris, slopping from one side of the compartment to the other. The mess deck was dark, and smelled of oil and vomit. The water made a horrid slippery sound as it sluiced from side to side.

There was more water in the small hangar access compartment. As Skipper shut the outboard airlock door, the ship heaved and flung him across into the inboard door, where he lay on his back, pressed down against the door's surface, until the ship's next roll released him again. He turned and peered through the glass sight-hole. He could see very little in the faint light. One aircraft seemed to be adrift, and as he watched it seemed to swing round and charge its neighbour. Skipper could actually hear it, like a great ripping, tearing crackle, as of a metal fist striking stiff canvas. The aircraft rolled back and slid up against the far bulkhead, with another thudding impact. From inside the hangar access the collisions sounded like a giant wrestling match.

Choosing his moment, as the ship paused between rolls, Skipper opened the inner door and stepped inside the hangar. He was astonished to hear a voice from almost under his feet.

'Mind how you go, it's bloody slippery in here!'

An aircraft handler was lying on the hangar deck, holding on to a pipe low down on the bulkhead. As the ship moved again, his body swung out until his legs were pointing to the centre of the hangar, like a man doing exercises in a gymnasium.

The advice was too late for Skipper. He put one foot on the deck, which was glassy-smooth with oil or water, slipped and fell. His feet shot from under him, and he tobogganed on his bottom at terrifying speed towards the other side of the hangar. When he was sure he was about to dash himself against the far bulkhead, his flight was suddenly stopped by a shattering blow in his left side. Winded, Skipper flailed about, looking for the obstruction. It was an aircraft wheel. Looking up, he saw the shadowy wingspan of a Corsair.

The aircraft was already beginning to roll with the tilt of the deck. Skipper flung himself around the wheel, hoping to stop it turning, but the aircraft carried him, legs trailing behind him, across to the far side. There seemed to be more light on that side, and Skipper saw more aircraft handlers hanging on to the bulkhead pipes. But there seemed to be nobody in charge. The men were just watching the Corsair as it plunged towards them and repeated again.

Skipper could now see that there were indeed two Corsairs adrift, sliding out of control across the forward end of the hangar, savaging each other and the nearest three aircraft, which were still secured to the deck, as they went. It was only a matter of time before those three, too, broke adrift.

'Got any chocks there?'

The men shook their heads.

'Well, bloody hell…' Skipper could feel the Corsair beginning to slide back again, and he let go. It was as well: this time the Corsair slid clear across to the starboard side and hit the bulkhead with a force which would have broken Skipper's neck.

'I've got some here, sir.' It was Chief Air Rigger Petre, appearing as always just when he was most needed. 'I've got some here, sir.'

'Well done.'

'Look out, sir!'

Skipper looked over his shoulder in time to see the Corsair lunging at him, its round cowling rim protruding like the spreading ruff of a prehistoric monster, and its nearer wing-root air intake gaping like a mouth. He ducked and the great snout rammed into the bulkhead above him. For a moment it paused and, with amazing agility for such a big man, Petre ran round the oleo leg nearest him and placed a chock against the back of the wheel. He flung himself down behind it to act as a human barrier. The untethered leg and the tail wheel slithered round, as though trying to escape. It was, Skipper thought, just like trying to tether a mad bull.

As the angle of the deck steepened, the wheel rode up the chock, until it seemed it would carry over and even mount Chief Air Rigger Petre's body. But in time the deck slanted back again and the wheel slid down.

'Can you get a wire strop round this leg, sir?'

One of the men along the hangar bulkhead, at last activated by Petre's presence of mind, spun a strop round the leg and turned it up on a valve handwheel. This time, when the aircraft tried to escape, it was held steady at two points.

'Now another one…'

The Corsair obligingly swung its other leg in towards the bulkhead and an aircraft handler secured it with a second strop.

Still lying behind the first wheel, Chief Air Rigger Petre was giving out a stream of orders. 'One of you get another chock in. Two of you see if you can get on that tailwheel. I think we've been lucky, sir. The prop jammed behind that fire-fighting hose reel up there and just held it steady long enough.'

'Long enough for you, Chief. Well done.'

'This happened before, sir, when I was on the *Glorious*. There's still the other one cut loose, sir.'

As Petre was speaking, the second Corsair rolled forward until one wheel fell down into the lift-well and the aircraft subsided on to its belly, ripping open the fuel tank slung between the wheels. Gallons of petrol flowed out on to the hangar deck and into the lift-well. Skipper could smell it from where he stood. The metal of the aircraft grated against the deck, there was a spark and a flash, and the Corsair blew up, filling the whole of the forward part of the hangar with flame.

Before Skipper could open his mouth to give an order, or react in any way at all, he heard the jangling of the lift-bell as the forward lift started to come down. At once, as part of the ship's normal blackout precautions, all the hangar lights went out, but he could still see clearly in the glare of the flames one of the aircraft handlers with his hand on the lift control. The man was panic-stricken and had only one thought — to escape by the lift.

'You bloody fool! Put it up again, you're letting air down on the fire, you stupid fucking idiot!'

As he spoke, Skipper felt another great wave jar the ship's forefoot and, as he waited, he knew what was going to happen. He crouched, as though counting off the seconds to go, and then it came. A rushing, pouring torrent of water came in through the opened lift and smashed down into the hangar below. Normally, only a lunatic would use water against a petrol fire, but the sheer quantity of water made this the best fire extinguisher of all. It was like using one elemental force against another.

'Get that lift up again, at once, do you hear!'

In the hissing and clouds of steam, and the smell of charred cloth, the lift rose again and the lights came on. The Corsair down in the lift-well could only be raised by crane. Unintentionally, it had secured itself. Skipper realised that, incredibly, the crisis in the hangar had been averted, or rather that Chief Air Rigger Petre had brought it under control. The hangar parties, and Skipper noticed that there seemed to be many more of them, now that the situation was calmer, were securing the aircraft fully with more strops and chocks. The two runaway aircraft would probably have to be written off. The next row of Corsairs were still secured to the deck, but they had been badly damaged. Their propeller blades were bent or broken off, and their engine cowlings badly ripped and gored. One of them on the port side had a wing canted at the wrong angle. These might also have to be scrapped, or cannibalised for spares.

But as Skipper realised, it could have been much worse. In a few more minutes these three aircraft would also have broken adrift and they would have been followed by others. The whole hangar, of some forty aircraft, all of them fuelled and some of them armed, would have been wracked by fire and explosion from end to end. The ship herself might have been gutted or blown in two.

Going up to the bridge Skipper felt pleased with himself, and with Petre. The Chief, he decided, certainly deserved a medal, and he himself would put his name forward with the strongest recommendation.

Skipper was surprised that Wings did not share his jubilation.

'Two aircraft written off for certain?' Wings frowned. 'Another three damaged badly? One of them in the lift-well? That's not a very good place to leave it. How did that happen?'

'Well, the motion of the ship took it there, you see, sir.' Skipper felt his temper rising. He had, after all, been sent down to the hangar after a dangerous situation had already arisen. It had been none of his making and the hangar was not even his particular responsibility but the Hangar Control Officer's, whom, Skipper now remembered, he had not seen at any time. Skipper felt that he had managed to avert a serious crisis. Now Wings seemed to be holding him responsible.

'I didn't actually *put* the aircraft in the lift-well, sir, nor did I order it. It just slid in there and I must say I do feel it's safer in there for the moment, until things calm down a bit.' Skipper had to force himself to make a civil reply. Bloody hell, to keep it down to two write-offs was not just good, it was a bloody miracle, and here was Wings cavilling and complaining.

'All right.' Wings was scratching his nose. 'I suppose it *could* have been worse.'

'*Aye aye*, sir,' Skipper said loudly. He was turning away when he caught the Captain's eye. To his astonishment, the Captain gave one slow, gorgeous wink.

'Yes, I suppose it does have its funny side, sir.'

'Oh, I didn't mean that. I meant, do you remember what I was saying about the compressor and the recoil? Perfect example. I couldn't have asked for a better.'

'Yes, I suppose so, sir.'

'It was well done down there. Well done, Skipper. I knew you would sort it out.'

'It was not so much me, sir, but Chief Air Rigger Petre. This, with all the other thing's he's done, for the squadron and the ship, I think he deserves a gong, sir.'

'He'll get it. I'll see to it.' The Captain half-raised himself on one arm, to raise his sight level from his chair, and to stare around the horizon. 'Is it my wishful thinking, or is the weather getting just that bit better?'

'Barometer's given a great bounce upwards, sir.'

'Very good.'

With the rise in barometric pressure, the other storm phenomena began to subside. The wind, though still stronger than anything Skipper had experienced before, had not quite the same ferocious force, and the waves, though still enormous, were not hitting the ship with quite the same crushing impact.

The gloomy wrack of spray and low cloud had lifted slightly and other ships were in sight again. *Little Billee* was visible over on the port beam, digging her massive anvil-shaped bows into the waves, which were washing down her flight deck from forward to aft like a half-tide rock. Her signalling lamp was blinking from her flag-bridge.

'From *Little Billee*, sir: "Good evening."'

'Make to *Little Billee*: "Good God, so it is."' It was a weak joke, as the Captain would have been the first to admit, but as he said, 'You've got to say something,' and it did raise smiles all round the bridge. Everybody really did feel their spirits lifting.

It was a nice thought on the part of *Little Billee*'s captain to say anything at all.

The TBS repeater at the back of the bridge, which had been muttering indistinctly for some time, suddenly assumed a more peremptory tone as a new voice took over the speaker. The weather improvement had not escaped the Admiral. His Fleet Navigating Officer was gathering up the flock again, urging them onwards, giving a course to steer to the north-east once more and orders for working up to a proper passage speed. *You've got to hand it to that man*, Skipper thought. *He is absolutely determined to catch up with the Americans on time, and hell and high water will not stop him.*

In the event, they were late, but only by a few hours. The three American carrier task groups, which had begun air strikes against a range of targets on the Japanese mainland a few days earlier, had retired to refuel and they were spread out over a vast arc of the sea, some 200 miles from end to end. The ships came up in silhouette, not in ones or twos but in groups of twenty or thirty at a time, and the radar screens showed twice as many more out of sight over the western horizon. The watchers in *Miss Britannia* and in every other British ship could witness with their own eyes that this was the largest, fastest, most powerful and far-ranging fleet the world had ever seen. There seemed no end to the ships. It took most of the day for the British task force to reach their allotted station, in the place of honour, on the right or northern flank of the line. This the Admiral had arranged with Halsey that afternoon, when a destroyer took him and his staff over to the American flagship to confer with the Fleet Commander. Everyone was glad and relieved to be working fully in company with the American ships although, as the Captain said, 'We're going to have to put on our running shoes to keep up with this little lot.'

Skipper was one of the bunch of miscellaneous officers standing at the back of *Miss Britannia*'s bridge that evening when the combined fleets moved off in company to the west, heading for the coast of Japan. They all felt the historic significance of that moment. For the first time, they were granted a fresh perspective on the events of the war, as though they were able to stand outside their ships and look in at themselves. Up to this moment, it had been a war for individual navies. But now, it was demonstrably an allied effort. The Admiral, with his infallible sense of occasion, made a general signal to the fleet: 'This evening is yet another milestone in the long history of our two countries and our two navies. May we all be worthy of the trust and hope put in us. Good luck to us and may God be with us all.' Halsey's signal, to all task groups, commanders and units, was more succinct: 'Let's go get 'em.'

Like many long-awaited and anticipated events, the first day's attacks on Japan were a disappointment, at least for Skipper and his squadron, who were not tasked for any sorties over the mainland. Instead, through some operational quirk of briefing, they flew CAPs the whole day long. Droning high above the fleet, Skipper heard the snatches of conversation and reports of the sorties over Japan. They attacked a selection of airfields some 200 miles north of Tokyo. One lucky sortie had flown across the body of Japan to strafe shipping in the Sea of Japan, the first time British aircraft had penetrated so far over enemy mainland territory. Some dozen or so enemy aircraft were claimed destroyed, but three Corsairs were lost to flak. Skipper listened carefully to the details. All three pilots had been picked up by destroyers, but it seemed that the Japanese flak gunners were still ominously alert.

The Japanese were to be allowed no rest. In the evening, when the carriers disengaged, the battleship and a destroyer escort peeled off to join an American bombardment group, which spent some hours that night bombarding factories and oil refineries along the coast.

Skipper was called at three o'clock the next morning, and after early breakfast in the wardroom walked along the flight deck towards the island. It was an overcast night, with no stars, and a warm muggy wind was blowing from the direction of Japan. Every piece of metal was clammy with dew. Skipper threaded through the black bulks of the parked aircraft as much by instinct as by sight. By long practice he knew just when to turn, when to duck, when to step aside.

In the hard bright glare of the briefing room, Ops was ready with his blackboard, and his chalk, and his pointer, and his maps. 'This, gentlemen, is going to be a full muster, an all-out effort.'

Skipper closed his eyes and inwardly groaned. God, how many times had he heard that tired old battle cry?

'Today is the beginning of Judgment Day for what is left of the Imperial Japanese Navy. There's a battleship called *Nagato*, secured alongside in Yokosuka, but I'm afraid there's no use your eyes lighting up…'

My eyes weren't lighting up, thought Skipper. A ship like that would be bound to be defended by all the flak and shit in Honshu. He looked around at the faces of his squadron. Michael showed no signs of feeling or reaction, but the others were rapt and attentive. There was obviously something to be said for having very young, very green pilots. They simply didn't know. Ignorance was combat bliss. If you told them their next target was the Emperor's sitting room and lounge they would simply say 'Whoopee!'

'The Americans are determined to keep her for themselves...'

They're welcome.

'I understand there's been a bit of argy-bargy about it, about this and other matters, but the long and short of it is that they ... mind you, they haven't admitted this, of course ... but it seems they feel the Japanese Navy is their pigeon, after what happened at Pearl Harbor. They don't want anybody else sharing the credit. Ungenerous, maybe, but there we are. Our targets are therefore a clutch of airfields between Tokyo and the coast, and all around Tokyo on the Tokyo plain. There's a lot of scope there nevertheless, I can promise you. They're all reported to be stuffed with aircraft, ready to act as kamikazes when the day of invasion comes.

'Now, the routine is the same as ever. Quickly in and quickly out. Don't mess about. One run only. You won't be carrying bombs because this is your first run downtown and we want you to have as many knots behind you as possible. So this is cannons only, all same as Sakishima Gunto. Skipper, yours is here, place called Chosi, right by the coast. There's a barracks there, there's a bit of a harbour, a railway station and quite a big M/T depot. So after you've done your pass over the airfield you will have to decide by the intensity of flak or the lack of it whether you've outstayed your welcome or not. If you feel like it, you can make a couple of runs over the town and see what transpires. Anything to do with transport, or oil, or fuel of any kind, or shipping, they're all legitimate targets. If you see troops — *if* you see them — well, give them a couple of bursts up the kimono too.'

My God, Skipper thought, *how can he go on in this flippant manner?*

'Now. Air opposition. It's a puzzle, I'll be frank with you. There are several fighter groups in the area you're going to, but nobody has yet seen them. What standard they are we don't know, because they haven't come up yet. There's only been a handful of bogies over the whole combined fleet since we've been here. It seems clear the Japs are husbanding their resources against the day we actually land on the sacred soil of Japan.

'Flak. All these airfields are very strongly defended, although they don't seem to be as free with their ammo as they were over the Sakishima Gunto. Maybe they're getting a bit short, or maybe they're even keeping that too against the evil day.

'Weather. Not very good here, as you've probably seen, but better inland. In fact that seems to be the rather irritating pattern that's set itself up already. When it is clear here, it's all clagged in over there, and when it's all clag here, it's as clear as a bell there, *und so weiter.* Anyway, there it is.'

Skipper listened mechanically while Ops went on with the routine briefing, on call-signs, recognition signals, wavelengths, heights and dispositions of CAPs, distances and bearings of the fleet's radar picket destroyers.

'Escape and evasion. You won't be surprised when I tell you there isn't any, not on Japanese soil. So if you get hit, I hardly need to stress that your best, your *only* hope, is to get back over water. We've got a big lifeguard rescue organisation, with destroyers and Dumbos right into the Japanese shore. They picked up a Yankee Avenger pilot and his crew the other day, just before a Japanese rowboat got to them, in a lake *twenty miles* from the sea. On land, there's nothing as yet. At sea, everything. It's as stark and as brutal as that.'

It was drizzling when they took off just after dawn. Visibility was down to two miles, and to 500 yards in rain squalls. Forming up was an anxious time. In spite of all the intensive fleet practices the carriers were throwing up aircraft at all angles and heights and courses. Formations of aircraft glided across each other in the murk. At one point Skipper saw some strange section of Corsairs formatting off his starboard wing. He rolled violently and shook his fist at them, and they sheered off into the overcast. He was pleased to see his own two sections of four aircraft taking station correctly on him. Michael and his flight of four would fly on the next sortie.

They took departure at fifty feet above sea level, one of a long sequence of groups of aircraft, steadily sorting themselves out into squadrons as they closed the Japanese coastline. There was, in fact, plenty of time. The poor visibility was a defence as well as a hindrance, and all squadrons crossed the coastline in tight, neat, cohesive formation. In the circumstances, Skipper thought, it was a most creditable piece of fleet group flying.

When they reached Japan, the weather cleared and the sun came out, just as the Met forecast had said. Japan was as enchantingly beautiful as Skipper had always read and expected it to be. There were the intriguing inlets in the coastline, the small humped islands, the little green hills, the vegetation, the carefully cultivated crops following the contour lines, the early morning smoke, the little houses with their curved eaves, a temple with its terraced row of ornamental roofs, and the boat out in the bay, leaving its herringbone track behind it like a water boatman insect on one of the ponds back at Daughton. There, ahead and to port, miles away to the west, was Fujiyama, as breathtaking as Skipper could ever have wished it. Its slopes were as exquisitely curved, its height as impressive, its snow-cap as white and clean, as the Hokusai prints hanging in the back passages at Daughton; there was one, a famous picture, 'Great Wave off Kanagawa', of Japanese fishermen rowing furiously to escape a monstrous clutching wave curling over their boat with Fujiyama in the background. There was the mountain of the picture, there could be no mistaking it.

There was no flak at Chosi airfield; indeed, there was no reaction or any sign of life at all. Skipper suspected that it had been abandoned. It was, after all, far too close to the coast, and would be one of the first and easiest targets for an enemy to attack. They made one pass down the central runway and then climbed over the town.

Something clearly had happened here. Almost a third of the houses were reduced to rubble. The buildings, the streets, looked as though a giant flame-thrower had been sprayed to and fro, to and fro, many times across them. That, Skipper reflected, was almost precisely what had happened. Chosi had been subjected to a B-29 fire raid only the previous night, as part of a sustained campaign which was steadily burning the heart out of major Japanese cities and towns. Night after night, when the weather was suitable, the bombers flying from Saipan, escorted by fighters from Iwo, showered Japan with a deluge of flame. Thousands upon thousands of incendiaries aroused fierce firestorms which, in one major attack on Tokyo, had actually changed the weather for several hours. Skipper felt a twinge of pity, mixed with exasperation, for the Japanese. They had sown the wind and reaped the whirlwind. By all rational comparisons, by any normal criteria of war, they were hopelessly beaten. They *must* be. So why the bloody hell didn't they give in? As it is, there was still that shadow of the landing planned for the autumn.

They flew two more sorties that day. It really was, they discovered, the most exhilarating flying. There was a different target every time, a different stretch of countryside to fly over, a refreshingly different atmosphere after the long, weary battering at the same old features of the Sakishima Gunto. The flak was not quite as negligible as Ops had suggested; indeed, at some airfields it was as fierce as any they had ever experienced anywhere, but provided a sortie stuck to the principle of one fast pass and out; the guns were invariably too late.

Over Japan, Ginge, as he insisted on being called, demonstrated that he was a first-class combat pilot. His formation flying was, to put it charitably, empirical. He approached the ship to land on in a manner which brought every watcher's heart into his mouth and he put his Corsair down on deck every time as though he had no further use for it. As Skipper's starboard wingman, he wavered in and out of station so that Skipper never knew whether he was properly covered or not, but he had long since stopped trying to chivvy Ginge into place, because he knew that at the critical point, when the strafing run actually began, Ginge would always be there or thereabouts, at or in front of his shoulder. The lad had very little of Richard Fenton's technique, but all of his aggressiveness. He was so brave and so steadfast, so unshrinking from whatever was asked of him, that Skipper began secretly to fear for him. This was the sort of pilot who was lost. But Ginge seemed to bear a charmed life, for which Skipper was grateful.

As Ginge's stock in the squadron rose, so Michael's fell. Skipper could not put his finger on the precise point, the exact moment, when the rumours started. All he knew was that the squadron had decided one day, as one man, that Michael was over the hill. It was the subtlest of group expressions, the finest of nuances, but Skipper detected it. He had experienced it before. He knew, though nobody had breathed a word of it, that the squadron as a whole now expected Michael to be killed or injured, or to be sent home, or to give up of his own accord. It was not that they disliked him, or wished him ill, indeed it was precisely because they so liked and respected him that they feared for his future. Skipper took his squadron's feelings seriously because, in his experience, they were very rarely wrong on these occasions.

Skipper had had no recent opportunity to witness Michael's flying because the Senior Pilot normally led sorties of his own, separately from the Squadron CO. But one evening, at the end of two days' refuelling and replenishing, Skipper took the chance to wait on the island beside the ACR door to watch Michael land on a replacement Corsair which he had flown across from one of the ferry escort carriers in the Fleet Train.

There was not a trace of nervousness or hesitation in the approach, which was tight and controlled. The Corsair was flown at just the right angle for the pilot, as Skipper knew, to best hold the batsman in view. The Corsair rolled out, straightened and took the second wire. That was one for the scrapbook. As always, green pilots could learn from Michael's technique. Yet, as Skipper conceded, squadrons had instincts in these matters.

Michael saw Skipper waiting and his face showed that he knew why he was there.

'Well, Skipper?'

'Very well. Good landing.'

'Is that all?'

'Of course.'

'Oh, come off it, Skipper, don't treat me like a complete bloody idiot! Do you think I don't know what everybody's whispering and sniggering and signalling to each other about?'

Skipper could not remember ever seeing Michael so angry and contemptuous. 'They think I'm going to go spearing in one day, don't they? Well, they're wrong. I'm still going to be here, still flying sorties, and still coming back, long after most of them are pushing up the daisies.'

'Well, that's very brave talk.'

'Well. Now if you'll let me by, I'll go and see if I can find somebody to sign for that Corsair.'

'Mike...' Skipper was touched and shamed by the anger and misery on Michael's face. This man had, after all, been one of his greatest friends in the Service, his Senior Pilot, and his responsibility. It was on the tip of his tongue to say, *Come on, let bygones be bygones, let's get back to the old days. Let's start again?* But he could not do so, and the moment passed. It was as much Michael's fault. He must have known that the business with Richard Trumble would make matters impossibly hard to solve. The Navy simply would not abide that.

'Yes? What?'

But Skipper had nothing to say, and Michael could see he had nothing to say.

As the strike days began to mount up, so too did the task force's losses. The first nervousness, and the slight sense of awe at actually flying over the Japanese mainland, had made the pilots circumspect, but the sheer variety of the targets and the total lack of any airborne opposition soon removed their inhibitions. The brighter spirits began to gamble with the guns, despite repeated cautions from their Ops Rooms, and the casualties began. The losses were never dramatic. A pilot from one ship one day, two more the next, a break of two clear days, and then three pilots during a long day's flying. Duncan Brightmore lost his Senior Pilot and, by all accounts, was lucky to survive himself. Next day, Skipper lost one of his Kiwis, who was shot down whilst escorting an Avenger bomber raid on an airfield down in Shikoku. He ditched in the sea, with part of an explosive bullet in his thigh. The American destroyer who picked him up did all they could for him, but he died from loss of blood before he could be transferred to a bigger ship.

The other three Kiwis, who had flown with the dead man for more than eighteen months, were emotionally prostrated by the loss. Skipper could see they were unfit for further RAMROD fighter sweeps, so he put them on CAPs for the rest of the day, and he led them himself.

For Skipper, it was an eerie experience. He found himself the interloper. The other three had flown together for so long that, as the saying went, they 'flew like glue', as though with a single thought. Although they were supposed to formate on him, such was the suggestive power of the Kiwis' station-keeping that he had to restrain himself from surreptitiously sliding in beside them. Skipper was relieved when, on his second sortie with them, they were given a bogey. They tracked out to the unusually great range of fifty-three miles from the fleet where, on the edge of cloud, at a height of 26,000 feet, they caught and surprised a Dinah bomber, lurking above the destroyer radar pickets. They each gave it a burst, saw smoke and possible pieces of debris, before the Dinah vanished in the cloud. It could only be a possible, but the Kiwis returned to the ship as men refreshed. For the next RAMROD, Skipper gave them Ginge, and they all came back saying they had sunk two coasters and wrecked two trains.

But the Kiwis' success stories, and indeed all the British task force's successes that day, were eclipsed by the feats of the American task groups to the southward. They had, it seemed, had another red-letter day against the remnants of the Japanese Navy at the great naval base on the Inland Sea at Kure. The signal ran to two paragraphs of battleships, cruisers, an aircraft carrier and dozens of lesser warships, sunk or finally incapacitated. They had all been immobilised in any case, and had been little more than floating gun batteries for months. Nevertheless, the Japanese fleet had a symbolic and political significance far greater than its actual fighting capacity, which was nearly nil. Once again, the British aircrews had been prevented from taking part, but they did not feel deprived, any more than they had been on the first occasion. In their opinion, the Japanese ships were more heavily defended than they deserved. As Skipper said, 'We're not proud. If the Yanks want to go in after those ships, let them.' Only Ginge looked rueful at that.

It was during the next fuelling period that the news arrived of a sweeping Labour victory in the general election at home. From some of the results on the notice on the wardroom board, it seemed to have been a landslide, with a Labour majority of some 200 seats. Skipper saw that even their own Member for Daughton, who would have needed nothing less than a Marxist-Leninist revolution in Wiltshire to lose his seat, nevertheless had his majority drastically reduced. Skipper himself had only been dimly aware that a general election was in the offing. He had never bothered to complete and send home his proxy form. But others, according to Chief Air Rigger Petre, certainly had.

'I saw a lot of them, sir. They were all Labour to a man, sir. They think Labour'll get the lads home quicker after the war's over than the Conservatives would.'

'There might be something in that.'

'I doubt it, sir. All governments are the same when it comes to dealing with Jolly Jack. I've just been down to our mess and along the squadron mess decks, sir, and I'll tell you one thing. There's not one in ten of them who had any idea at all that voting Labour would mean Winston Churchill had to go…'

'Good God!' It had not occurred to Skipper either. 'So it does! I never thought of that.'

So Winston Churchill was no longer Prime Minister. It was difficult to get used to the idea. He had been there for so long, ever since those dark days when the war seemed lost. Now, when the war looked won, or almost won, he was dismissed. It seemed the most base ingratitude of any people in history.

That night, talking over the news of the election, was the only occasion when Skipper could ever remember the Captain discussing politics.

The Captain was sitting in his tall chair, smoking his evening cheroot. The last tanker had been slipped three-quarters of an hour before and the remnants of the Captain's supper had just been taken away on their tray. The ship's tanks were full, and his belly was full. The Captain was content, and at peace with the world.

'Did you vote, Skipper?'

'No, sir.'

'Ah, you should have done. You should always vote, even if you're the other side of the world. I get my wife to send me both candidates' literature and then I vote for the one that seems the least bloody one.'

'This landslide is probably a bit of a disaster for the Navy, isn't it, sir?'

'Could be. The Labour governments we had before the war were never much good for the Navy, but then nor were the Conservatives all that amazing either. No government will ever do much for the armed services unless the electorate wants it to. If there's votes in it, they'll do it. If not, not. It was Churchill, after all, who agreed to all manner of limiting treaties on the Navy. No, I think this is much more important than that. I genuinely think it was time for a change and I think every sailor on board thought that, if he ever stopped to think about it all, that is. We haven't had an election for ten years. It's time.' The Captain carefully knocked off some ash into the giant brass spittoon his steward brought on to the bridge whenever he had his cheroot alight. 'My wife's got a sister who lives in North Wales. Spinster, JP, pillar of the community — you know the sort. Had some evacuees from Liverpool at the beginning in the early days. She said she was horrified by the state they were in. She blamed the parents, but of course it wasn't them, it was *life*. She had no idea, she said. None of us did.

'One thing, I do think the Navy might be a bit more politically conscious. We've always suffered in silence or almost in silence. I think we should learn how to sing out loud and clear whenever we want something. Otherwise we're going to get nothing. The moment this war's over, there's going to be a mad rush with everybody trying to establish their own claims. If we're not careful, the Navy's going to get shut out.'

Skipper went down to the wardroom to look at the news noticeboard. He was surprised to find how often, and with how much greater attention, he was now studying the news. News from home or from other war fronts had naturally always been received and read on board with the greatest interest, but it seemed to Skipper there was now a new dimension of urgency, as though events were hurrying towards a climax, pressing in their import upon the ship. There was the victory in Burma, the Potsdam Declaration, the possibility of

Russia entering the war against Japan, the staff rumours of a landing to seize Singapore in the autumn. Once again, the news looked forward and back: the new Parliament had assembled for the first time, and the Eighth Army, which had fought from El Alamein to the Austrian Alps, had just been disbanded. Skipper braced himself against another long slow roll of the ship. The fleet had entered another giant typhoon swell, as though the sea itself were reflecting the tumultuous and unstable pattern of world events.

Fuelling and ammunition replenishment were completed in spite of the swell, and the fleets were due to strike again, when, at the last moment, with the first serials of aircraft actually warming up on deck, all strikes were cancelled and the fleets were ordered to withdraw 200 miles to the east because of a 'Special Operation'.

Now there could be no restraining the rumours and counter-rumours on board: the war was almost over; the Japanese were about to surrender; the Emperor was dead; the Japanese had launched a new secret weapon; there was about to be an Allied landing in Japan; the Allies were about to launch a secret weapon.

They knew the next morning, with the bald signal. Skipper was in the Briefing Room when Ops came in and clipped it into the log.

'"Little Boy Compels Sugar Mike How Able."'

'Sounds like a map reference.'

'It is. The town of Hiroshima down on the Inland Sea.'

'I remember it. We flew over it a fortnight or so ago. Or near it, anyway. Quite a bit of flak around the outskirts. What's Little Boy? Come on, Ops, you're looking all mysterious.'

'I don't really know, to be honest. It's something special anyway. The Captain is going to address the ship's company any moment now — that I *do* know.'

Skipper knew in his bones this was the announcement they had all been waiting for. He went down to his cabin, to lie on his bunk and listen, in quiet and privacy.

'D'you hear there? This is the Captain speaking … President Truman, speaking from on board the American cruiser *Augusta*, has just announced that at about eight o'clock this morning an American aircraft dropped an atomic bomb on the Japanese city of Hiroshima, in western Honshu. This bomb is many more times more powerful than any other bomb used by the RAF or any of the Allied air forces during the war. It is equivalent to about 20,000 tons of TNT and it was developed as a result of prolonged research by British and American scientists.

'The United Nations have again called on the Japanese government to accept the terms of the Potsdam Declaration, but they have not yet done so. Until they do, our offensive goes on. The programme has not yet been decided. We don't know when our next flying will be. But as soon as I have any information, I shall let you know. That's all.'

Skipper lay back and stared at the deckhead. *Please God, make them surrender.* Skipper knew nothing of atomic power but instinctively he realised that this new weapon had an element of the supernatural in it. Surely even the Japanese could recognise there was no loss of face in yielding to a force of nature. They would never bow to ordinary weapons, but this one showed that Japan's own deities had forsaken her. *Please God, make them surrender,* now.

But they did not surrender. Russia declared war, and the next day the fleets were back again in the striking area, for a full day's programme of RAMRODS and bombing. Skipper and his section began the day with an uneventful dawn CAP. It was, as ever, Skipper's favourite kind of sortie. He loved to rise up from darkness into light, and savour the sun before anybody else. He loved to watch the light arrive over the fleet below, capturing and illuminating ship after ship as it spread from the east. In his ears he could hear the murmurings, the reports and grumbles and comments of a great fleet waking up and preparing for another day. The signals were like the morning newspapers, the voices like the first callers. Even so, the R/T was silent for long minutes at a time as the CAP crept across the purple woolly sky, their heads ducking and craning, weaving and changing course and height constantly, from long ingrained habit. A man could fly CAPs safely for a year and still get himself chopped by flying steady for thirty seconds too long.

They landed on after two hours. Skipper sensed his section crowding close behind him, keen to land on with the briefest intervals and make a show of their expertise. Even Ginge brought off a passable landing, taking a wire neatly, without trying to make a flailing reef knot out of it as usual. The omens, Skipper thought, were good.

There was powdered egg for breakfast, for the first time since Sydney. The marvellous Australian food was beginning to run out, and the fleet were falling back on their old standbys. Skipper was stirring his coffee when he felt a gigantic clap on the back. It was the Commander.

'*And lo, Ben Adhem's name led all the rest!* Congratulations, Skipper, oh most honoured and decorated one!'

The signal was a long one, and in it Skipper recognised the fine Greek hand of the Captain. He and his secretary must have burned the midnight oil to make sure that everybody in

Miss Britannia got their due. There was a DSO for Wings, DSCs for himself, Henry Darling, the Commander and Little F, with more awards and mentions in despatches for a long list of ship and squadron personalities. Michael had a mention, and Skipper was especially delighted to see that Petre had a Conspicuous Gallantry Medal. *That,* he thought, would need some wetting when the Priest of Paris and his team got back to Sydney. The Captain himself, Skipper saw, had a CB.

'Sir, sir!' There was a face at the wardroom door. 'Your Senior Pilot, sir, message from Flyco, sir, he's just had a very bad prang, sir!'

Skipper reached the island in time to follow the stretcher into the flight-deck sick bay. He could see through the open island door the tangled wreck of a Corsair in the first safety barrier. By the look of it, it must have entered the wires at tremendous speed. The aircraft was almost unrecognisable.

Michael turned his head. His gaze was bright and clear and undimmed. 'I'm sorry, Skipper. I just forgot. It was amazing. I just forgot all about it.'

Skipper looked at Richard Trumble, who was walking beside the stretcher. '*What* did he forget?'

'I think he means cut, sir.'

'Yes.' Somebody's voice came from the ACR. 'Never cut when Bats told him to. Took the crash barrier at about a hundred knots. He should be dead, according to the book of words.'

But Michael was, miraculously, not even seriously injured. Even the doctor sounded surprised. 'It must be that he was well strapped in. He's got some pain in his side. Maybe a rib cracked or two. Possibly he's twisted his back in some way. Maybe not even that. I'll give him a good look over and let you know.'

'I'll be OK, Skipper,' Michael called up from the stretcher. 'Sure.'

Outside, Skipper took Richard Trumble's arm. 'Now what the hell happened out there?'

'It's as they all say, Skipper. For some unknown reason Michael just didn't cut. He came on after me, so I couldn't actually see clearly. When I climbed out of my cab and looked back, there he was driving full tilt into the barrier. I'm sure he'll be fine in a day or so.'

But when Skipper took that news up to the bridge, he found that the Captain had already made up his mind about Michael. 'He's not flying from this ship again. He's had his time.'

'Oh, I don't think it's anything very serious, sir, in fact I'm sure it's not. Given a few days —'

'That's not what I meant, Skipper. And I think you know what I *do* mean. I know why you did it. I know you needed your Senior Pilot. But enough's enough. It's time to get rid of him. I'm going to have him transferred to the hospital ship the very next chance we get. Funnily enough, I'm not particularly bothered personally by people with his propensities. I'm one of those who says that every man should be able to look after himself. But it is one matter on which the Navy is ninety-nine times out of a hundred right. It *is* bad for a ship, to have this sort of thing. I'm very disappointed you didn't come and consult me about it.'

'I'm very sorry, sir. I should have done. But I did need him in the squadron.'

'Yes, that was the easy decision, wasn't it? The hard decision always has to be made in the end, and it doesn't get any less hard for being put off. Now *I've* had to make it.'

'I see that now, sir.' Oddly, Skipper was flattered by the reproof. Would the Captain have taken this attitude if he were not already preparing to welcome Skipper into the ranks of the regulars? Would he talk like this to an outsider?

All the same, Skipper knew he must be wary of the constant psychological pressure the Captain was exerting on him. He knew he must not allow it to be assumed that he was going to accept a regular commission. Matters were by no means so cut and dried. There was still his father and Daughton. His father would be waiting, eager to account to him for his stewardship. His father, who lived and breathed Daughton, would not be able to comprehend a son who willingly turned his back on it. It was a very difficult decision, and Skipper knew that he was still a long, long way from making up his mind.

'I'll talk to you about all this after flying tonight. No time at the moment — you've got a sortie now, haven't you?'

'Yes, sir.'

'We'll leave it till you get back. By the way, congratulations on your gong!'

'Thank you, sir, and thank you very much, sir. Congratulations to you too, sir.'

'Thank *you*, Skipper.'

'At *last*,' said Ops, 'a proper target. Three times running the Yanks have shut us out of attacks on the Japanese Navy. We thought it was all over now bar the shouting. Not quite. There's still one carrier left. Not a big one, an escort carrier in fact. They gave her a going-over down in the Inland Sea, at a place called Beppu on the twenty-fourth of July, and then she seemed to disappear. They thought they'd sunk her, but she's turned up again, up here, in a small bay along the coast of Honshu and she's well within our sector today. How she got there, nobody seems to know, but anyway there she is in the photograph, large as life and twice as ugly, and it's our job today to finish her off. In the last six months she's been used to train kamikaze pilots, so we have a special interest in her.

'She's in what looks like a specially prepared berth, specially laid out for her, close into a bit of a cliff, so we are going to have to somehow winkle her out. You'll all be carrying bombs today, so you're going to start off with that, then the Fireflies with rockets, and then everybody with everything they've got left. These splodges here are gun batteries. Nobody knows how effective they are, but we think not very, not at this stage. She is supposed to be camouflaged, but as you can see she sticks out like a sore thumb, and you should have no difficulty in picking her up. She may even have her great big red meatball still painted on her flight deck. The Japs always seem reluctant to paint those out.

'I think the best way in is simply to smother the defences. The Seafires will go in first and keep the guns' crews heads down, while the bombs and rockets are wheeled into place. This is an all-out effort again. Every ship is putting a maximum effort up. So we stand a good chance of getting her.'

Wings was standing in the Briefing Room doorway. 'Just got another signal. Another bomb. On Nagasaki. As big as the last one.'

Skipper joined in the spontaneous cheer, but when it died down he was left with a feeling of unease. He mistrusted this new atmosphere of levity in the briefing room. This was not the way to prepare for a sortie over enemy territory. If people believed the war was as good as over, they might relax and make a mistake. Skipper thought it worthwhile getting his squadron together afterwards to make his point.

'Look, I don't know what the outcome will be of all this news we've been getting. But I do know that the war isn't over — not by a long chalk. Believe me, this is a very dangerous state of mind to get into. Those Japs out there haven't got the message yet and they'll be only too glad to hack you down. Until the thing is definite, we're just as much at war as we ever were. Otherwise you're going to be dead meat. Now, this is a real target we've got today, something we've all hoped and trained for. Let's not make a mess of it by thinking we're all home and dry already. Because we're *not*.'

Skipper was glad and relieved to see the smiles fading from their faces, and the solemn, serious expressions returning. It was hard to check their high spirits, but it was his job to lead them against the Japanese. 'Now let's see what we can do with this carrier. If the photographs are any good, it should be a piece of cake.'

As it turned out, the photographs were very good indeed. The carrier lay beside her protective cliff, just as they had expected to find her. The 'meatball' stood out plainly, and the first Seafires were gliding in over the sea towards the gun batteries. The guns had already opened fire and the sky ahead was black and stormy with bursting flak. Skipper shook his head. They were never going to surrender. They were going to go on and on, until the last man was dead, on both sides. They were going to have to be killed, every last man of them.

Skipper saw a wing appear at the edge of his peripheral vision to starboard. Ginge was already trying to jump the gun.

'Clockwork Four, this is Clockwork Leader, hold it, hold it. Must give the Seafires their chance.'

But the Seafires seemed to be having very little effect. The gunners were putting up a very respectable barrage, more than respectable; indeed, as Skipper realised, it was heavier than anything he had seen before. The Japanese must value this last carrier. His flight seemed to be flying into a banked mass of flak, as though at a predicted height, with lines and clusters and ripples of exploding clouds forming a daunting obstacle. These Japanese had clearly not heard that the war was nearly over. The turbulent ridge of black smoke was much closer now.

'Clockwork Flight, this is Clockwork Leader, steady now…'

The shell hit his starboard mainplane with a shattering impact which threw Skipper sharply back against his seat.

Recovering himself, he looked out to starboard and saw incredulously that most of the wing had vanished. The Corsair was already in a tight spin. Through the glass of his cockpit canopy he could see the red meatball on the carrier's flight deck crossing apparently overhead, like some weird speeded-up sun. It was time to go, time to leave. This would be his first bale-out. He put up one hand to the retaining knob of his canopy and pulled.

The knob would not budge. He tried again, bracing his feet against the rudder pedals to give himself more leverage. Still it stuck. The centrifugal force of the aircraft spinning had jammed the canopy on its runners. He tried again and again, but it was as firm as though it were locked. That water must be much nearer now. There was not a great deal of height to play with. A sheet of flame spread out between his legs, arousing a pain which he could scarcely credit. He bit his lip to control himself. That scream would have gone out all over the fighter R/T network. They would have heard that back in *Miss Britannia*.

The cockpit was filling with flame and smoke. There really could not be much time or height left now. He was conscious of the Corsair falling vertically, although he could see nothing. He was drowning, drowning behind smoked glass. His body knew what lay ahead before he did, and he felt his bowels evacuate fully. He was sitting in a warm, sticky mess. It was back to the nursery. That was where all good pilots ended up, back in the nursery. The sweat was running down the side of his face and into his mouth. He could not believe that *that* was his hand, with the leather of the glove smoking and peeling back to reveal flesh of that peculiar colour. The bottom half of his body was swathed in fire. He *must* get out soon. The pain was so great he could hardly feel it. Good Christ, he must get out or there would be nothing left of him. *It's just a game of blood, Skipper.* Many voices had said that. He made one more effort to open the canopy.

'*Miss Britannia*, this is Skipper. I can't … please … I can't seem to get the…'

A NOTE TO THE READER

If you have enjoyed this novel enough to leave a review on **Amazon** and **Goodreads**, then we would be truly grateful.

Sapere Books

Sapere Books is an exciting new publisher of brilliant fiction and popular history.

To find out more about our latest releases and our monthly bargain books visit our website: **saperebooks.com**

65614401R00225